Protecting Her

By Allie Everhart

Protecting Her
By Allie Everhart

Copyright © 2015 Allie Everhart
All rights reserved.
Published by Waltham Publishing, LLC
Cover design by Okay Creations
ISBN: 978-1-942781-04-2

CHAPTER ONE

PEARCE

I've been waiting all day to see her and the nurse finally gave me the okay. I walk in her room and see Rachel lying there resting, her eyes closed. She's hooked up to an IV and monitors.

I hate seeing her this way. They said she'll be okay, but still. I feel guilty, thinking maybe I should've told her no. I knew the risks involved with her having a child, and yet I let her do it anyway. And then she almost died giving birth. If she had, I would've blamed myself. I'd always blame myself if anything ever happened to her.

I sit on the side of her bed and gently take her hand in mine.

"Pearce." Her eyes open and she looks at me.

"I'm here, sweetheart." I lean down and kiss her forehead. "How are you feeling?"

"Tired," she says, struggling to keep her eyes open.

"Go ahead and rest. I'll be right here."

"I'm okay. I'll sleep later." She smiles weakly. "Did you hold him yet?"

"Yes." I smile, which seems to happen every time I think of him. "I've held him several times now."

Her face lights up, like she got a sudden burst of energy. "Tell me about him."

"He has your eyes. Beautiful blue eyes."

"Maybe they're *your* eyes. You have blue eyes too."

"Yes, but mine are a silvery blue. His are bright blue, like yours. Like a bright blue sky on a sunny day."

She smiles even wider. "When can I see him?"

"Whenever you're ready. The nurse was just waiting for you to wake up. I'll go tell her you're awake."

Just then, the door swings open and the nurse wheels the baby in. "Are you ready to meet your son?"

"Yes," Rachel says, smiling as she watches the nurse pick him up.

Rachel sits up straighter and the nurse hands her the baby.

"I'll give you some time with him," the nurse says.

When she's gone, I look over at Rachel and see tears running down her cheeks.

I lightly rub her arm. "Rachel, what's wrong?"

"Nothing's wrong," she says, gazing down at the baby. "Everything's perfect. Absolutely perfect. We have a baby, Pearce. A beautiful baby boy." She lifts him up and kisses him. "I love you so much," she says to him. "I loved you before you were even born."

She skims her finger over his cheek. His eyes are open, watching her. "Garret Evans Kensington," she says to him. "That's your name. Did your daddy already tell you that?"

I smile at him. "Yes. We went over that. We've already had several father-son talks while you were resting."

Garret's eyes moved over to me as I spoke, and are still on me now.

"Look at how he responds to you," Rachel says. "He knows your voice, Pearce. He knows you're his father."

"Yes. I noticed that earlier. He responds to you as well."

She speaks to the baby again. "You are so precious. And so sweet. And handsome like your daddy."

She talks to him some more, and kisses him, and looks at him. I just watch them interact. Rachel's so happy. Happier than I've ever seen her.

After a while, she looks up at me, "Would you like to hold him?"

"*You* should. You haven't had any time with him. I'll have plenty of time with him when I take him home."

"Will you be okay? Taking him home by yourself?"

"Yes. Of course." It's a lie. I'm terrified of taking him home. I don't know how to care for an infant. I was counting on Rachel to do that, and I'd just be there to help. But they're keeping her in the hospital for a few more days and sending the baby home with me sometime tomorrow.

"Pearce, it's a lot of work. He'll be up all night. You have to feed him, change him, get him to sleep."

"I know. I can handle it."

"Maybe one of the neighbors could help. Mrs. Landow had three children."

Rachel's referring to the woman who lives next door to us. She's a very nice woman, but she's elderly and has numerous health problems.

"Mrs. Landow can barely care for herself. And I don't like asking our neighbors for assistance. I can take care of him. It's just for a few days."

"Still, I think you might need some help. What about Martha?"

"Martha and Jack are still in Europe on vacation."

"That's right. I forgot." She pauses. "What about your mother?"

"No," I answer quickly. "That's not an option. Besides, she hired a nanny to care for me. She wouldn't know what to do with a baby."

"Pearce, I'm sure she took care of you at least some of the time. You should call her."

"My parents aren't even aware that we *had* the baby. And given that they haven't spoken to us in almost two years, I doubt my mother would even answer my call."

Rachel's eyes are on Garret. "Maybe it's time to end this. Maybe it's time to reach out to them and try to be a family again. I'm sure they'd like to meet their grandson."

"Let's not talk about this right now. Let's just enjoy the baby before the nurse comes back." As I say it, she walks in and takes Garret back to the nursery.

Rachel falls asleep. I remain there, waiting until she wakes up again, then spend a few more hours with her before heading home.

The next morning, I arrive at the hospital at eight. Rachel looks better; more rested and her skin has more color. I spend the day with her, and every time the nurse brings the baby in, Rachel's whole face lights up. I think mine does too.

Around four, the nurse brings him in again. I'm wondering if I could have them keep the baby here another night. Just one more, so I could get better prepared. Last night I stayed up reading all the baby books we have, but I still feel unprepared.

"Did the nurse say when they're sending him home?" Rachel asks, like she was reading my mind.

"She said sometime today. I'll ask when she comes to get him."

Rachel leans down and kisses him. "I don't want her to take him. I just want to hold him until you bring him home."

"I'll bring him back tomorrow." I put my hand on his head, which is covered in a little blue hat. "What time should we come visit your mother, Garret?"

His eyes open, but just slightly.

"Here." She offers him to me. "I like seeing you with him."

I take him in my arms, feeling that warmth that fills my chest every time I hold him.

"How does it feel?" Rachel asks. "To be a dad?" I hear the concern in her tone and see it on her face.

She knows how much I feared being a father. And now that I am, that fear has grown. I have this perfect little human being, a son, who depends on me, and I feel as though I'll never be a good enough father to him. But Rachel doesn't need to know that.

"It feels good," I say as I look at Garret, who's now sound asleep. "I wasn't sure how I would feel, but as soon as I saw him, I felt nothing but love."

She puts her hand on my arm. "You're going to be such a good father, Pearce. He already loves you. I can tell."

I smile at her. "And how can you tell? He just met me."

"Because when I was pregnant with him, he always kicked and moved around when he heard your voice. And just now, when he heard your voice, his eyes opened."

"Perhaps I just have a distinct voice."

"No." Her hand is still on my arm and she gently squeezes it. "It's you. He knows you're his father and he's trying to connect with you."

I know she's trying to assuage my fears, but her comment only makes me more anxious. What if I can't be what he needs? What if he expects more from me than I can give him? Will he grow up hating me?

I can't screw this up. I have to be a good father. The best father I can possibly be. I only have one chance to get this right. Garret is our only child. We won't be having another, at least I hope we won't. That's something Rachel and I need to discuss.

The doctor spoke with me earlier and told me that Rachel shouldn't be having more children. It's too dangerous. Her pregnancy, although difficult, went better than planned, but then she nearly died during the delivery. The doctor said it's ultimately up to Rachel and me, but that the best decision would be for Rachel to not get pregnant again.

"You should hold him now." I give the baby back to Rachel just as the nurse comes in.

"We're going to get him ready to take home," she says.

A tight knot forms in my stomach. I don't think I can do this. I can't take care of an infant by myself.

Rachel lifts the baby up to her face and kisses his cheek. "I guess you have to go. Mommy will be home soon. Your daddy will take good care of you. I love you, sweetie." She kisses him again, leaving her lips on his forehead as she closes her eyes and breathes him in. She always tells me she loves the smell of a baby's head. I don't get it. It doesn't smell like anything to me.

Rachel opens her eyes and hands him to the nurse. She puts him in his bassinet and wheels him out of the room.

"Did you talk to the doctor?" Rachel asks, a serious look on her face.

"Yes. She said you should be able to go home in a couple days."

"Not about that." She glances down at the bed. "About us having more children."

I hesitate, not ready to have this conversation. It's not the right time. We're both happy after just being with our baby and I don't want to bring the mood down by talking about this. I'm concerned that Rachel will want more children despite the risks, and I don't want to fight about it. Because it's going to be a fight. I'm not going to risk losing her again.

"Pearce, I'm going to have my tubes tied."

I hold her hand. "When did you decide this?"

"After the doctor told me what happened in the delivery room. Then she told me the risks of having another child, and I can't do it. I'm a mother and a wife. I can't risk something happening to me. I need to be here for you and Garret."

I pull her into my arms. "I'm sorry, Rachel. I know this isn't what you want. But it's too dangerous for you to do this again. When I almost lost you, I—" My voice cracks and I take a breath. "I can't lose you."

"I know." She gently pushes me back and puts her hand on my cheek, her eyes on mine. "I won't do that to you. Or to me. I don't need to. I have you and I have Garret and that's more than enough. I love you both so much."

"I love you too, sweetheart." I kiss her forehead, then sit back. "I don't want you going through more surgery. I'll get a vasectomy."

"No. I don't want..." She holds my hand and looks down at it.

"What is it, Rachel?"

"I don't want you getting a vasectomy, in case..." She looks up at me. "In case something ever happens to me."

6

Panic surges inside me, coursing through my veins. Why would she say that? Why would she even think it? Nothing is going to happen to her. I tell myself that every day so I can get through the guilt I feel for bringing her into my life. Into the darkness that is Dunamis. Despite my involvement with them, Rachel will be safe. She'll always be safe. Nothing bad will happen to her. I have to believe that and I need her to believe it as well.

Rachel's referring to something else that would take her away from me. A car accident. An illness. But I still don't want to hear it. Nothing bad will happen to her. That's all I choose to believe.

"Do not talk that way," I say firmly. "I would never let anything happen to you."

"I'm just being realistic," she says, softly rubbing my hand. "I never thought my parents would die so suddenly, but then they did. Accidents happen."

I keep my head down, my eyes on our hands. "Yes, well, they're not happening to you."

She lifts my chin up, forcing our gazes to meet. "But if something *did* happen, I would want you to find love again. And be able to have more children."

"No." I quickly back away and get up off the bed, angry that she would even suggest that. "Absolutely not. I would not marry someone else and I would not have more children. Stop talking about this. We're not having this conversation."

"Pearce." She reaches for me. "Come sit down."

"Rachel, we're done. I don't want to talk about this."

"Fine. But please come over here."

I sigh and sit back down beside her.

She takes my hand again. "So could you bring the baby by tomorrow morning?"

"Yes. Of course."

She smiles. "You're going to be such a great dad. You can take him to baseball games and teach him how to throw a football and give him advice about girls."

"He'll have to get advice about women from someone else. I'm definitely not an expert in that."

"You obviously are, or you wouldn't have convinced me to marry you just a few months after meeting you."

"Perhaps I caught you at a weak moment."

"Or perhaps you're a gentleman who knows how to treat a woman. Things you will someday teach our son so that he finds love just like you did."

"If he's able to find the kind of love that I feel for you, then he will be a very lucky man." I kiss her forehead, then bring her into my arms and hold her.

I'm so relieved she made the decision to not get pregnant again. If she'd decided otherwise, I would've had to convince her not to do it, then risk her resenting me for taking away her chance to have another child. But she already knew how I felt about this. Before she even got pregnant, I made it clear that if her health was ever put in jeopardy by having a child, I would not agree to having another one.

"I love you," she whispers by my ear.

"I love you too." I give her a kiss, then stand up. "I should get going. The nurse said she has things she needs to go over with me before I bring the baby home."

"Okay." She's smiling. "Good luck."

I smile back. "Are you saying I can't do this?"

She's laughing now. "No. I'm just wondering how bad the house is going to look when I get home. Dirty diapers everywhere. Spilled bottles all over the house. Who knows what else I'll find?"

I shake my head, still smiling. "I am perfectly capable of doing this. I head a division at a major corporation. I have degrees from Harvard and Yale. I think I can figure this out."

"Okay," she says, biting her lip so she doesn't laugh. But then she does.

"Rachel, he is an eight and a half pound baby who sleeps all the time. How much trouble could he be?"

"No trouble at all," she says trying to be serious. "I'm sure you two will be just fine together."

I kiss her goodbye. "I'm leaving before you destroy my confidence."

Truthfully, my confidence was destroyed before she even said those things. I have zero confidence I can do this. But I have to try, because as soon as I leave her room, the nurse approaches me and tells me Garret is ready to go home.

Shit. How the hell am I going to do this?

CHAPTER TWO

PEARCE

I managed to make it home with the baby and get him into the house. It's August, so it's hot and humid outside but the house is cool from the air conditioning. Maybe it's too cool for a baby. But I don't want him being too hot. There was nothing in the books about the proper room temperature for an infant, so how is one supposed to know? He can't tell me if he's hot or cold.

He's not crying so that's a good sign. I bring him upstairs, carefully taking each step so I don't drop him. I go in the nursery, which Rachel decorated during the few months she wasn't on bed rest. The walls are light green because we weren't sure if we were having a boy or a girl. There's a white rocking chair in the corner next to the crib and across from that is a white dresser and changing table. Rachel stocked the room with baby supplies, so at least I have what I need, although I'm not sure how to use them all.

"Garret, would you like to try out your crib?" I lower him into it, but as soon as I let go of him, he starts crying.

Now what do I do? Why is he crying? They just fed him and changed him at the hospital.

I pick him up again. He stops crying. So I guess he just wants to be held.

I go over and sit in the rocking chair. As I hold him and rock him, he watches me. He keeps doing this. Looking at me. Watching me. I hope he only sees the good in me and not the bad. I hope he never sees the bad. I will shield him from that, just like I shield Rachel from that side of my life. But someday, I may not be able to. If I can't find a way to get Garret out of the organization, I will be forced to tell him about it. And once he learns the truth and knows what the members do, he'll know what a horrible person his father is. I don't want him to know that. I need to get him out of his obligation. Or Jack does. We need to find a way to keep my son from ever having to join.

He fusses a little and I notice I stopped rocking him. I start up again and the fussing ends. Just looking at him, I feel a huge smile cross over my face. It happens automatically, just like it did when I met his mother. I couldn't wipe that big smile off my face.

After a half hour, I get up and try placing him in his crib again. This time he doesn't protest. He's sound asleep. I turn on the baby monitor, then go down to the kitchen because I'm starving. I didn't want the hospital food, so I haven't eaten all day. I take some deli meat from the fridge and quickly make a sandwich.

If my parents knew I was eating a cold sandwich, they'd be horrified. They'd feel that way about a lot of the things I eat now. Pizza. Grilled cheese sandwiches. Spaghetti and meatballs. Hamburgers. Rachel is the one who introduced me to those foods. I never had them when I was growing up. My parents forbid them, saying that's what trashy, unrefined people ate.

My son will eat all those foods, along with all the other foods his mother makes. Rachel is an excellent cook and can make most anything. But the past few months, since she couldn't be on her feet much during her pregnancy, I was in charge of dinner. I'd either get takeout or grill something. I've become quite good with the grill, which is another thing my parents would disapprove of. They would be very upset that I'm preparing my own food. They've always had a cook and they expect me to have one as well. A Kensington does not prepare food, or do other tasks my parents consider to be menial and beneath them, such as laundry or cleaning. But Rachel didn't want a cook or a maid, so we don't have either.

I've barely finished my sandwich when the baby monitor goes off. He was only asleep for twenty minutes, if that, and now he's crying again. I go upstairs and see his red, teary eyes. I feel bad for him, stuck here with me, his clueless father, when his mother would be doing a much better job.

"What's wrong, Garret?" I pick him up but he's still crying. The nurse said I wouldn't need to feed him for at least another hour. Maybe he needs a diaper change. I can change a diaper. I did it on a doll several times at those baby care classes.

I set him on the changing table and grab a diaper. Now he's crying even more. He does not like being on this table. I quickly get to work on his diaper, putting the new one on him as fast as possible because now he's screaming to the point that his whole face is red.

"We're almost done," I tell him, fastening the diaper in place. But I must've done it wrong because it's not a very tight fit.

Garret is still crying and I don't know what to do. The nurses told me infants find it soothing to be wrapped in a tightly bundled blanket, but I have no idea how to do that. I watched the nurse do it and it looked like she was doing origami. I take Garret's blanket and attempt to bundle him up the way the nurses did, but I can't figure it out. I give up and just wrap the blanket around him, then pick him up, and finally, the crying slows and eventually stops.

I haven't even been home for an hour and I'm already exhausted. Rachel's right. I need help. I can't do this alone. But I have no one to call.

Royce and Victoria had a baby in July, but they wouldn't be of any help. They've had a nanny taking care of their daughter since the day she came home from the hospital.

Maybe I should call my mother. As Rachel said, I'm sure my mother took care of me at least some of the time. She must know something about babies. I have no one else to call so I decide to just call her and tell her the news. Maybe I'll ask for her help, or maybe I won't. It'll depend on how the call goes.

I bring Garret downstairs and go in the family room and sit on the couch. He's quieted down now and is watching me again, probably realizing how incompetent I am and wishing he was back at the hospital.

The phone is next to me on the table. I pick it up and call my parents' number, but then remember that they have the hired help screen their calls. The help has been instructed not to put my calls through. That's why I haven't even bothered trying to call my parents for over a year, not even on Christmas.

"Kensington residence," someone answers. Probably the maid.

"I need to speak with Eleanor, please."

"Who may I ask is calling?"

I consider lying, but then change my mind. "Pearce. Eleanor's son."

There's silence and then, "One moment, please."

At least she didn't hang up. Perhaps she's new and doesn't know the rules. I wait for her to return and tell me that my mother is busy, or out somewhere, or whatever other excuse my mother gave her.

"Pearce." It's my mother's voice. "Are you there?"

"Yes. Hello, Mother. How have you been?"

"Fine." That's always her answer. She's always fine. "And how have you been?"

"Good. Very good."

"Work is going well?"

"Yes. It's going very well."

The phone is silent. She doesn't know what to say. I'm surprised she's not asking me about the pregnancy. I know her gossiping friends told her about it. Victoria knew Rachel was pregnant and she's the queen of gossip.

"I was calling, Mother, to tell you that Rachel and I had a baby."

"Oh. Well, congratulations." She sounds odd. I can't tell if she's happy for me or not. "What did you have?"

"A boy. We named him Garret." As I say his name, I look down at him in my arms. He's watching me again and I smile.

"That's a nice name," she says.

Was that a compliment? If so, it would be the first one I've heard from her in years.

Garret fusses and I rock him a little in my arms.

"Is that the baby?" my mother asks.

"Yes. I'm holding him."

"Are you at the hospital?"

"No. I'm at home."

"Why doesn't your wife have him?"

My mother is someone who finds it odd for men to be involved in childcare, so I'm not surprised by her question. I'm sure my father never held me when I was a baby.

"Rachel is still in the hospital," I say. "There were complications during the delivery. She lost a lot of blood so they're keeping her there for a few days."

"But you have a nanny, of course."

"No. We chose not to hire one. We'd rather care for Garret ourselves."

"You can't care for a baby, Pearce. Not by yourself. Babies are a lot of work."

"Yes. I know. I've only been home with him for an hour and I'm already feeling overwhelmed."

"I'll come right over. Where do you live?"

I almost drop the phone. She's actually coming over? Without my having to ask?

"Thank you, Mother. I would appreciate the help." I give her the address and she says she'll leave right away.

I can't believe this. Is she not angry with me anymore? Or does she just want to see her grandson?

Garret's now asleep in my arms. I'm afraid if I move, he'll start crying again. I turn on the TV, lowering the volume so he doesn't wake up. I flip through the channels, stopping on a cartoon.

When I was a child, I never watched cartoons. I wasn't allowed to. We only had one TV in the house and my father used it mainly to watch financial news. I'm going to let Garret watch cartoons. I'm not going to rob him of his childhood the way my parents took mine.

I flip to a sports channel. There's a baseball game on. That's another thing I'm going to do. Take Garret to baseball games. My father never took me to one, but I still went to games with people I knew from school.

I attended a private prep school with other very wealthy students. Some of them had fathers who were members. My friends were chosen for me by my parents. I didn't particularly like these friends, but having them in my life allowed me to do activities my parents had no interest in, such as going to ball games in New York. Or sometimes we'd meet up and play football. I played football in high school and my father never even asked me how I learned to play. He doesn't like sports so I was surprised he even let me be on the team. But he said it made me appear to be well-rounded, which would be good for my image. Of course, he never went to a game and neither did my mother.

There were no father-son activities when I was growing up. I had to teach myself how to do things. There was a time during my teen years that my father became so busy with work that he basically forgot I existed. I used that time to my advantage, doing things he'd never allow me to do if he were paying attention. That's when I discovered girls and alcohol. The alcohol came first, which gave me the courage to talk to girls. It didn't take long before I was drinking way too much, and by 15, I was having sex. I hid all of this from my father until one of the members caught me passed out drunk in my car with a half-naked girl.

When my father found out, he beat me. He took me outside and hit me repeatedly in a fit of rage. I wanted to fight back but

15

he had his gun on him, so I just waited for him to finish. His anger wasn't because I was drinking or with a girl. It was because I was caught by a fellow member, and that member told the other members, which embarrassed my father. My behavior made it look as though he didn't have control over me, and he couldn't stand the idea that people were saying he'd lost control of his son.

I was 16 at the time. After that incident, he kept a much closer eye on me. I didn't drink again until I was in college. And the girls I dated in high school were all picked by my father. I didn't actually date them. I escorted them to the events I was forced to go to with my parents. Sixteen was also the age my father told me about Dunamis, thus ending my childhood.

"I will never treat you that way," I say quietly to Garret. "I will never be like him." I lean down and kiss his forehead. "I love you. And I promise you, I will never be like him."

CHAPTER THREE

PEARCE

The doorbell rings. I notice the clock says it's a half hour later. I must've dozed off. I get up, with Garret in my arms, and go answer the door.

When I open it, my mother is standing there. She's wearing a white cotton blouse and black dress pants. That's casual for her. Usually she's in a dress or a suit.

"Hello, Mother."

She stares at my face like she hasn't seen me in years. The last time I saw her was at a party, before Rachel was pregnant, so it's been a while. And we didn't speak at that party. She and my father ignored me.

"Hello, Pearce." She says it slowly and quietly, which is different than her usual short, forceful speech pattern. She looks somewhat sad and regretful. It's almost as though she feels bad for disowning me, which is odd because if she *did* feel that way, she'd usually try to hide it.

"Come inside." I step aside to let her in, and as I do, she notices Garret in my arms.

She instantly smiles, her eyes on him. "Can I see him?"

"Of course." I turn him toward her. "This is Garret. Your grandson."

She moves the blanket that's around his head and just looks at him.

"Would you like to hold him?" I ask.

She glances up at me. "Yes."

I hand him to her and she smiles at him. "He looks just like you."

It's true. At first I didn't see it, but the more I look at him, the more I see the resemblance. But he definitely has Rachel's eyes.

"Why don't you sit down?" I motion her to the couch.

She nods and goes over to it. Once she's seated, she glances around the room. "So how do you like the house?"

"I like it very much." I hope she doesn't start telling me what a mistake I made buying it. We've had that fight and I'm not going to relive it. But I don't think she's here to fight. I think she really wants to help. I wonder what my father said about this. I'm sure he wasn't happy about it.

"You're wearing denim pants." I notice her eyeing them with disapproval. My parents never allowed me to wear jeans. What my parents consider to be casual pants are what most people would consider to be dress pants. This is the first time my mother has seen me in jeans.

"I wear jeans sometimes when I'm around the house." I also sometimes wear them when I go out, but I can't tell her that. She'd be horrified.

The baby squirms and fusses.

"Would you like me to take him?" I ask.

"He'll be fine." She bounces him a little. "Have you fed him yet?"

"No, but it *is* time for his feeding."

"Where's the kitchen?" She slowly stands up.

"Right this way." I take her in there. I have empty bottles lined up on the counter, next to the container of formula.

"You take him." She hands him to me. "I'll get the bottle."

I watch as she prepares it.

"Have you given him a bottle yet?" she asks, screwing the top on it.

"No. The nurses did, but I didn't."

She notices the family room off to the side and says, "Go sit with him over there."

I do as she says, taking a seat on the couch. I turn the TV off. Garret is crying now, his face getting red.

My mother comes over, a kitchen towel in her hand, which she sets on my shoulder. "You'll need this in case he spits up. Now lift him up slightly."

She hands me the bottle and continues to give me instruction, including how to burp him. I learned all of this in the classes but it's good to have someone actually here, making sure I'm doing it right. And I'm shocked that that person is my mother. Completely, utterly shocked. The woman is not the nurturing type at all. I certainly don't remember her that way. I guess that's not entirely true. There were moments where she expressed care or concern, but they were fleeting moments. I'm not saying she was a bad mother. She just wasn't someone who gave hugs or tucked you into bed at night. She kept her distance. As long as I was healthy and growing, she felt she was doing her job as a mother. And she always protected me from my father, standing up to him if he ever even considered hitting me. Unfortunately, she wasn't home that day he took me outside and beat me, but when she found out about it later, she made sure it never happened again.

After Garret's feeding, we go upstairs and I put him in his crib. He's knocked out after eating. I give my mother a brief tour of the upstairs, then the downstairs, and then we sit in the family room again.

"Do you need to be getting home?" I ask her. It's now seven, and she usually doesn't stay out this late without my father.

"I brought my things." She smooths her short blond hair. "In case you needed me to stay in the guest room."

"Oh, yes, that would be good." I'm shocked once again. She's willing to stay here overnight? In this house, which she doesn't approve of? "I'm glad that you're staying, Mother, but won't Father be upset?"

"I left him a note. I'm sure he's found it by now."

"A note. Why didn't you just tell him?"

She straightens up. "Your father and I are not speaking right now."

"How long has that been going on?"

"A month, perhaps? I've lost track of how long it's been."

A month? They haven't spoken for a month? They've never gone that long without talking.

"Perhaps I shouldn't ask, but…what is the cause of your argument?"

"You," she says simply. "I want my son back and your father is too stubborn to accept you back into our lives."

"It's because of Rachel, isn't it? He'll never accept her. You don't either, do you, Mother?"

She sighs. "I have nothing against the woman. She seems intelligent and I'm sure she treats you well. But she doesn't fit in our family, and you knew that and married her anyway. Obviously, I wish you had married someone else, but it's too late now and I feel the need to move on from this and move forward with our lives."

"I agree, but Father doesn't feel the same way."

"He'll have to get over it. This has gone on long enough and I will not allow it to continue. You're our only son and we haven't spoken to you for a year and a half. I had to find out about Rachel's pregnancy from Victoria. Do you know how humiliating that was? Victoria Sinclair knows before I do?"

"I would've called you, but you wouldn't accept my calls."

"I wanted to, but your father wouldn't allow it." She quickly shakes her head, like she's shaking him from her mind. "But now we have this beautiful grandchild and I am not going to miss out on his childhood. I don't care what your father says. I am not listening to him when it comes to this."

I don't think I've ever heard her this angry. She usually doesn't show emotion, especially negative emotion.

"Have you tried talking to him about this?"

"Of course. We've had numerous arguments, but they never go anywhere. You know how stubborn he is."

"So what are you going to do?"

20

"That is not your concern, Pearce. I will deal with your father. We are going to be part of your life again, whether he wants to or not."

"I don't want him to be part of my life if he's not going to treat Rachel well. She's my wife and I will not allow him to treat her poorly and put her down."

"I can only do so much when it comes to him. I can't control the words that come out of his mouth. But I will do my best to make him be civil to her." She pauses. "Speaking of your wife, what happened to her? You said there was a problem during the delivery?"

"Yes. She, uh…" I choke up just saying it. "She lost a lot of blood and her blood pressure dropped rapidly. The doctor said she could have died."

"I'm sorry to hear that," my mother says softly. "But she's doing better?"

"Yes. They gave her some blood and now they're monitoring her." I check my watch. "I need to call her. Would you excuse me?"

"Of course. Go ahead."

I get up to go to my office to call her, but then the baby monitor goes off.

"I'll check on him," my mother says.

I nod and continue to my office. I call Rachel's hospital room, and after several rings, she answers.

"Rachel, did I wake you?"

"Yes, but it's fine. I was waiting for your call and I just dozed off."

"Sweetheart, if you want to talk to me, just call."

"I didn't want to wake the baby. How is he?"

"He's good. He's sleeping. He doesn't seem to care for his crib though. He prefers to be held."

"He gets that from me. You know how much I like to be hugged."

I smile. "I hadn't considered that to be a genetic trait, but it makes sense now. He *is* like you that way."

"I already miss him. I miss both of you. Are you doing okay with him? I'm worried about you there alone without any help."

"I have some help. I called my mother."

"You did?"

"Yes. She's here now."

"Pearce, what happened? What did she say?"

"I called and told her we had a child, and before I could ask her for help, she volunteered. She was here within the hour. And she's staying the night. She's actually been quite helpful. She knows more about babies than I thought she did."

"What about your father?"

"My mother is no longer speaking to him. Apparently, they've been arguing for months about his refusal to allow me back into the family. My mother claims she's going to convince him to end this feud, and if he doesn't, I don't know what will happen."

"Do you think they'd divorce?"

"No. She wouldn't divorce him."

I can't tell Rachel this, but the truth is my mother is not allowed to divorce my father. It's against the rules of the organization. Only in rare cases does Dunamis allow divorces. I'm still surprised they allowed me to divorce Kristina, my first wife.

"Well, I'm glad that she's there for you. And spending time with her grandson. Maybe the baby will help bring us all back together as a family. It would be nice if Garret could have his grandparents in his life, or at least his grandmother."

It surprises me that Rachel would want my parents to be in Garret's life. My mother and father have either ignored Rachel or treated her horribly, and yet she chooses to forgive them and welcome them back into our lives.

"I don't know if my father will ever come around," I tell her, "but my mother seems committed to being part of our lives again."

"I'm happy to hear that, Pearce. I think it's good."

"Are you okay there? Do you need anything?"

"No. I'm fine. The nurses are taking good care of me."

"Maybe I should come by and see you before you go to sleep."

"You need to be home with the baby. I'll see you both tomorrow."

"That's not soon enough. I'm not used to being apart from you. I didn't sleep at all last night without you here, and I'm sure I won't sleep tonight either."

She laughs a little. "Our son will make sure of that. He'll probably be up every hour or two."

"Yes, I suppose you're right."

"Oh, I keep forgetting to ask, did you call Shelby?"

"No. Sorry. With everything going on, I haven't had time."

"That's okay. I'll call her. Maybe she could stop by when you're here with the baby tomorrow."

"Isn't she out of town?" I ask.

Shelby's mother won a trip to Las Vegas, so the two of them have been there all week.

"She should be back now. I think she got back last night."

Rachel is still friends with Shelby, despite my constant reminders to Shelby that she cannot be friends with my wife. They don't see each other as much as they used to, but they still talk on the phone.

At least Shelby finally broke up with Logan, but she dated him for over a year before she did it. They broke up last January, but they still talk to each other. Logan isn't giving up on her. I had lunch with him just a few weeks ago and asked him if he was dating anyone. He said he hasn't because he can't get over Shelby.

Rachel keeps trying to get Shelby to date Logan again. I keep telling Rachel to stop getting in the middle of it, but she won't. She thinks those two belong together, and I hate to admit it, but she's right. It doesn't make sense because Shelby and Logan are complete opposites. He's quiet, calm, and serious, and she's always joking around and talking and full of energy. I guess opposites really do attract sometimes.

Shelby and Logan love each other and I wish they could be together, but they can't, which is why Shelby finally ended things with him.

I hate the way the organization controls these girls. The way they don't allow them to have a life. Their contracts should be limited to just a few years, but instead, it's as long as the organization wants it to be. There is no end date, and even when our members decide they no longer want them, the women are still tracked and threatened so they don't tell our secrets. So they're never really free and can never have a normal life.

"Pearce, are you still there?"

"Yes, I'm sorry. I'm just tired."

"Go get some rest. Maybe your mom could watch the baby while you take a nap, then you can take the night shift."

"I suppose we could try that. Are you sure you don't need anything? Because I'll get you whatever you need."

"I know you would, but I'm fine. I'll see you tomorrow. I love you."

"I love you too. Goodnight."

I leave my office and go upstairs to the nursery. I stop before I go in because I hear my mother talking to Garret.

"You are a very handsome little boy," she says. "Your father was handsome too. When he was born, he had dark brown hair just like you. And blue eyes, a little darker than yours. And much like you, he did not enjoy being in his crib. He fussed and cried until I picked him up. But after a month or so, he became accustomed to the crib, and you will too. It just takes time." I hear the baby fussing. Then I hear my mother softly singing. It sounds like a lullaby.

Since when does my mother sing? I've never heard her sing. She finishes the song and the room becomes quiet.

I make some noise like I'm just now coming down the hall. I go in the nursery and see my mother in the rocking chair, holding the baby and smiling at him.

"How is everything going in here?" I whisper, noticing Garret's asleep.

She slowly gets up and gently places him in the crib. Then we both quietly leave and go back downstairs to the living room.

"Mother, if you don't mind, I was thinking I would take a quick nap. I'm sure I'll be up with him all night, so if you wouldn't mind just watching him for an hour or so."

"I don't mind," she says.

She's staring at me like she did earlier. Did she forget what I look like after all those months of not seeing me? I don't think I've changed that much.

"Okay, well, I'll be up in my room. Thank you again for your help." I turn to go up the stairs.

"Pearce."

"Yes?" I turn back to her.

She comes over and puts her arms around me. "I'm sorry."

She's giving me a real hug, not her normal shoulders-only hug. I hug her back. I can't remember the last time we hugged like this, but I'm sure it was when I was a child, so it's been a long time.

As for her apology, I don't ask her to elaborate. I know she's sorry for letting this silent treatment go on for so long. I also know how hard it was for her to tell me she's sorry, so I just keep quiet.

She holds onto me for longer than I expected, and when she finally lets me go, she says, "Go ahead and rest. I have no need to go to bed early, so sleep as long as you like. I'll watch the baby for you."

"Thank you, Mother." I go upstairs, stopping at the nursery to check on Garret. He's sleeping soundly. I enjoy watching him sleep. It makes me feel at peace.

He's so tiny, and just two days old, but he's already had a huge impact on our lives. He's bringing this family back together.

CHAPTER FOUR

RACHEL

It seems like I've been in this hospital forever. I'm hoping they'll let me out tomorrow. I'm so tired, but I find it hard to sleep with the nurses coming in and out of my room throughout the night. I also can't sleep because I miss Pearce and our home. And now that the baby isn't here, I miss him too.

Garret is the most adorable baby I've ever seen. He has the sweetest little face with his tiny nose and little pink lips and those big blue eyes. And when he's awake, he's so alert, always looking around, already curious about the world around him.

He looks just like Pearce. I immediately saw the resemblance. I wonder if he'll grow up to be just like his father. I hope he does. It would make me very proud for my son to be like his father. Strong. Kind. A gentleman.

When Pearce held him, he couldn't stop smiling. I knew he'd warm up to being a father when he saw the baby. He's going to make a great dad. He's still nervous about it, but he'll get over that the more time he spends with Garret.

I felt so bad watching Pearce leave yesterday. He looked scared to death when the nurse said they were sending Garret home with him. He assured me he'd be fine, but as soon as he left I started to worry. There's so much to know about caring for an infant, and he didn't really pay attention in the classes we went to. Luckily, his mother is helping him. She's not my favorite person but I'm grateful she offered to help. I'm hoping it's not a one-time thing. I hope she continues to come over. I'd like Pearce to have a relationship with his family again.

"You have some visitors." I hear Pearce's voice and look over and see him at the door, holding the baby.

"Pearce." My heart leaps at the sight of them. I love them both so much.

"Good morning, sweetheart." He hands me the baby, then kisses me.

"Good morning." I look down at Garret. "And how's my baby boy this morning? Did you let your daddy get some sleep?"

Garret's up and alert, his eyes darting around. I bring him closer and smell him and kiss him.

"He slept on and off all night," Pearce says. "My mother stayed up until midnight so I could sleep, then I took over after that."

"That was nice of her. Is she here?"

"No. I told her to stay home and rest since she was up so late."

"Is she staying again tonight?"

"Yes. She said she'd stay as long as we needed her to." He pauses. "She apologized last night."

"So does that mean this is over? Are they no longer disowning you?"

"I don't know yet. She hasn't talked to my father about it, but I think we'll be seeing my mother a lot more, even if my father disapproves."

"I'm happy she wants to be involved in his life." I gaze down at Garret. "He needs at least one grandparent to spoil him." Just saying the word 'grandparent' makes me tear up, because it reminds me that my parents are no longer here. "I wish they could've met him," I say softly to myself.

Pearce sits next to me on the bed and puts his arm around me. "They would've loved him. And he would've loved them."

I nod, as more tears fall. "They would've been the greatest grandparents ever. My dad would've taken him fishing and to baseball games and played catch with him on the farm. And my mom would've made him more cookies than he could ever eat." I smile through the tears. "I miss them, Pearce. I miss them so much."

"I know you do, sweetheart." He hugs me tighter and kisses my head. "I miss them too."

I lean down to kiss the baby. "They love you even though they're no longer here. Your grandparents. Your aunt. They're all in heaven but they love you."

Pearce picks up the box of tissues from the side table and hands it to me. I take a tissue and dab my eyes as he leans back on the bed.

"I'm sorry, Rachel," he says, gently rubbing my arm. "What can I do? Anything?"

"You already did." I smile at Garret. "You gave me *him.*"

It's true. Finding out I was pregnant was the greatest gift I've ever been given, and it came at the time I needed it the most. I was devastated when my parents died. I was consumed with grief. Those first few weeks after the accident were horrible. But Pearce was there for me through it all. Listening to me. Holding me. Sitting quietly with me. He was wonderful. The best husband I could ever ask for. And the best friend. My love for him grew exponentially during that time, and it continued to grow as he took care of me throughout my difficult pregnancy. And now, seeing him care for our son, I love him even more.

"Pearce."

"Yes?"

"I hope you know how much I love you. I know I tell you that every day, but I hope you know that I love you more than I can even say."

He cups my cheek and kisses me, then looks into my eyes. "I love you too. With all my heart." He pulls me into his side and we look at our baby.

Someone taps on the door.

"Come in," Pearce says, getting up off the bed.

Logan walks in. "Hello, Pearce. Rachel. Sorry to interrupt."

"Logan." Pearce goes up to him. "I didn't know you were coming. I've been so busy I didn't have a chance to call you about the baby. How'd you find out?"

"A friend I went to med school with works here and told me he saw you here yesterday. I assumed that meant Rachel had the baby." He smiles at me. "Congratulations."

"Thank you."

He holds his hand out to Pearce. "Congratulations, Pearce."

They shake hands. "Thank you."

I check the time. Shelby's going to be here any minute. That's probably not good. She broke up with Logan months ago, but she's still not over him. She broke up with him because he wanted to get more serious and she didn't. He was ready to propose so she ended their relationship before he could. But she still talks to him and she won't date anyone else, so I keep wondering if they'll get back together. She's miserable without him.

Logan has left her alone but he isn't giving up on her. He told Pearce that Shelby just needs more time. Pearce has become good friends with Logan the past year, now that he lives closer to us. They go golfing or meet for lunch. I keep telling Pearce to tell Logan that Shelby is still interested in him, but Pearce won't do it. He says he's not getting involved, which is frustrating because Shelby and Logan clearly belong together.

Logan comes over to me. "How are you feeling?"

"I'm a little tired. There were some complications during the delivery so they're making me stay here a few days. Hey, since you're a doctor, maybe you could pull some strings and get me out of here faster. I really want to go home."

He laughs. "Sorry, but it doesn't work that way. You're stuck here until they decide you're ready to leave." He takes a peek at the baby. "He's adorable. What's his name?"

"Garret."

"He looks just like you, Pearce."

Pearce stands next to Logan. "That's what everyone says."

"So did they send him home already?" Logan asks.

"Yes," Pearce answers. "I felt sorry for him, being sent home with his father, who can barely change a diaper."

"Pearce," I say, smiling. "You did fine."

"I'd love to see you change a diaper," Logan says kiddingly to Pearce.

He laughs. "Yes, I'm sure you would. Someday you'll be doing it yourself and you'll see it's not as easy as it looks."

The door opens and I see long legs topped with a bunch of giant helium balloons. "Congratulations!"

It's Shelby, but I can't see her through the balloons. She hurries in, then stops abruptly when she sees Logan. She stares at him, the balloons still in her hand, now held off to the side. The look on her face is one I've seen before, on her, and other girls I've known. It's that look that says you love the guy and want to be with him but aren't sure that you should. It's also the look that says you're hot for him and want to be alone with him as soon as possible.

Logan does look very handsome today in a suit and tie, his dark hair slicked back. Shelby's in a white sundress that's short and shows off her legs. She has a golden brown tan from hanging out at the pool in Las Vegas all week.

"Hello, Shelby," Logan says.

"Hi. I didn't know you'd be here."

"I heard Rachel had the baby and I wanted to stop by."

"Yeah. Me, too." She's breathless. She definitely wants him.

"I'll take these," Pearce says, taking the balloons from her. He ties them on the chair next to the bed.

"His name is Garret," Logan says to Shelby.

"What?" She's completely flustered. "Who?"

"The baby." He points to him. "His name is Garret."

"Oh. Yeah." She comes over and stands by my bed. "Can I see him?"

I hold him up for her and she smiles. "Oh my God, Rachel. He's so cute."

"Do you want to hold him?"

"No." She backs away, holding her hands up. "I can't hold a baby. I'd drop him, for sure."

"Do you need to be heading out?" Pearce asks Logan. I swear, Pearce is actively trying to keep Logan and Shelby apart. I have no idea why. "I can walk with you back to your car. We should schedule a golf game before the weather gets cool."

"I think I'll stay a few more minutes," Logan says, eyeing Shelby in that dress.

It's a cute white cotton dress that has thin straps and is fitted at the top, then flows out at the waist, ending about mid-thigh. And she's wearing strappy sandals that have a small heel.

"Rachel, how are you feeling?" she asks. "I was so worried about you after you told me what happened."

"I'm fine. They said I might be able to go home tomorrow."

She leans in to see the baby again. "You are so adorable." As she touches his face I notice light red marks circling both her wrists. "Shelby, what happened to your wrists?"

Pearce was saying something to Logan but he stops suddenly and looks at Shelby and me.

"It's nothing." Shelby backs away and stands up straight. "Actually, it's a funny story. I always keep rubber bands handy so I can put my hair up, and last week in Vegas, when I was at the pool, I put a rubber band on each wrist and then fell asleep on one of the lounge chairs, and when I woke up I had these big marks on my wrists."

Logan comes over and picks up her arm, looking at her wrist. "That doesn't look like a mark from a rubber band."

She yanks her arm back. "Well, it is. I was dumb and I forgot to take them off when I got to the pool."

He takes her hand, turning it palm-side up and running his finger over the mark. "You need to put something on that or it'll scar."

"I have stuff at home I can put on it." She's breathless again as his finger moves lightly over her wrist.

"I have a first-aid kit in my car." He lowers her hand but keeps hold of it. "Come on. Let's go. I'll get you fixed up." He gazes at her as he says it. A deep, intense, I-want-you gaze.

"Um, okay," she says, not taking her eyes off him. "Rachel, sorry I can't stay longer but I have to go into work later. I need to go home and get ready. But I'll call you tonight."

"Okay. Bye, Shelby. Bye, Logan."

"I hope they release you tomorrow." Logan smiles at me but motions to Pearce. "I don't think this guy can handle another night alone with the baby."

"I'm managing just fine, thank you," Pearce says, smiling. "Give me a call and we'll set up a time to golf."

He nods and leads Shelby to the door. As she's leaving, she glances back at Pearce and I realize they didn't say goodbye to each other.

When they're gone, I say, "Do you think they're going to get back together?"

"No. But I think they're going to do it in Logan's car."

I laugh. "I think so too. They couldn't take their eyes off each other. Maybe they'll make their own baby and we'll be here visiting *them* in nine months. They should just get married. They're perfect together."

Pearce doesn't respond.

"Pearce, don't you think they'd be good together?"

"I don't know. But Shelby obviously doesn't want that so Logan needs to give up on her."

"He's not giving up on her. That was some serious flirting going on just now. The way he touched her wrist like that? She practically melted into his arms."

"I didn't notice."

"Did you see her wrists? I agree with Logan. It didn't look like marks from a rubber band."

Garret cries a little and I look down and see his face scrunching up like he's getting ready to wail. Sure enough, he does.

"I'll get his bottle." Pearce takes it from the diaper bag. "My mother packed the bag for me before I left."

"Maybe he just needs a diaper change," I say, taking the bottle.

"No, that's his hungry face. And his hungry cry. I figured this out last night."

I give Garret the bottle and he immediately sucks down the liquid.

"You were right." I smile. "So does he have a way to tell us when he needs a diaper change?"

"Yes. It's more a fussy cry, not a full out wail like he just did. And his face looks more annoyed than angry. When he's hungry, he looks angry. He likes to eat and he doesn't like to wait."

I laugh. "Just like his father."

The nurse walks in. "Rachel, the doctor will be here in a few minutes. Your husband and son will need to go."

I nod. "Okay."

As she leaves, Pearce says, "We'll come back this afternoon."

When I'm finished feeding him, Pearce takes him and they leave, but I didn't want them to go. I missed them the second they left. I have to get out of this hospital. I can't take being away from the baby. He needs his mom. I need to be home.

And the next day, I am. The hospital released me at nine this morning and we just arrived at the house. As I'm walking in, I smile when I see that the entire living room is filled with flowers and balloons.

"Welcome home," Pearce says, kissing me.

"Thank you." I hug him. "When did you have time to do all this?"

He shrugs. "I've given up sleeping. I don't need it. You can get a lot done when you don't sleep."

I reach up and kiss him. "When did you really do it?"

"Garret and I went shopping yesterday after we left the hospital."

I smile. "You took him shopping?"

"It was short trip. He slept through most of it." He picks Garret up from the baby carrier and holds him. "Although while we were shopping for you, he found a few things for himself."

"Oh, really?" I kiss Garret's cheek. "What did your daddy buy you?"

Pearce points to a basket on the floor, which holds a mini football, baseball, and basketball. "He apparently likes sports."

I laugh. "Yes, I'm sure his father had nothing to do with that." I sit on the couch and take my shoes off. I'm still so tired. The doctor said it's from the loss of blood. She said it will take a while before I have energy again.

Pearce sits next to me. "That box on the table is for you."

It's a small box wrapped in silver paper. I pick it up. "You got me a gift?"

"It's from both of us," he says, meaning him and the baby. "Go ahead and open it."

I unwrap it and open the box. Inside is a gold necklace. It has two gold hearts hanging from it; a big one and a little one.

"The big heart is from me and the little one is from Garret," Pearce says. "They're lockets so you can put photos in them."

"Pearce, that's so sweet." I hug him. "Thank you. I love it. I'll wear it all the time."

"I'm glad you like it." He gives me a kiss. "I'm also glad you're home. I missed you."

"I missed you too."

Garret fusses and squirms a little in Pearce's arms.

"That's his diaper change look," he says as he stands up.

I stand up too. "I'll do it."

"No, you just got home. Just rest. I'll do it and bring him back down."

Pearce goes upstairs. He's already much more comfortable taking care of the baby. Maybe it was good for him to have these past couple days alone with Garret. If I'd been here, I would've taken over and Pearce would've just watched. But now, he's had a chance to practice caring for the baby and he's getting good at it.

"Hello, Rachel." Eleanor appears. She must've been in the kitchen. She's wearing navy pants and a short-sleeve white blouse, which is a more casual look than her usual suits and dresses.

"Hello, Eleanor." I smile, but it's not a big smile. I admit I'm still angry at her for disowning her son. I've forgiven her for being rude to me. She doesn't know me, and it's easy to be rude to someone you don't know. But treating your own son the way she did is inexcusable.

"How are you feeling?" she asks.

"Tired. But I'll be fine."

"I was very sorry to hear about your parents."

That was almost a year ago, so it's odd she'd say this now, but at least she said it.

"Yes, it came as quite a shock." I see her eyeing my outfit. I'm wearing one of my maternity dresses; a short sleeve, blue cotton dress. No matter what I wear, I always feel frumpy around Eleanor, because of the way she looks at me.

"Well, now that you're home, I'll go up and pack my things." She starts for the stairs, but I stop her.

"Eleanor, you don't have to leave. You're welcome to stay."

"I don't need to. Pearce has become quite adept at caring for the baby, and now that you're here, you two will manage just fine."

I don't argue with her. I *would* like to have time alone with just Pearce and Garret.

"Will you at least come over again? We'd love to see you more. And I know Garret would love to see his grandmother."

She smiles, and I think it's the first real smile I've ever seen on her. "Of course I will. Call and let me know when you would like me to come over." She pauses. "He's a beautiful baby. You two will make very good parents."

Did she just give me a compliment? Or two?

"Thank you," I say, smiling back. "And thank you for helping Pearce out the past couple days."

She nods and goes up the stairs as Pearce is coming down them.

"Where's Garret?" I ask him.

"Sleeping. I held him after the diaper change and he fell right to sleep."

"You're getting really good at this."

"Yes," he says confidently. "I think I actually am getting good at it."

"Oh, your mother is leaving. She's packing her things."

"Why?" Concern crosses his face. "Did something happen?"

"No, she just decided it was time to go. But I told her to come back whenever she'd like."

"I'll go up and help her with her bag."

He does, and a few minutes later, they come back down the stairs. We say goodbye and Eleanor leaves.

And at last, Pearce and I are alone with our son. Just the three of us. At our home. I've never been happier.

CHAPTER FIVE

PEARCE

It's been a week since Rachel had the baby and things are starting to settle down. We're getting into a routine. Feedings, diaper changes, and naps are forming somewhat of a schedule and we're taking shifts so we can both get some sleep.

Tomorrow I have to go back to work so I won't be able to help out as much, but I'll take over in the evenings and give Rachel a break. She says she doesn't need one but I know she does. I can see how tired she is. I'm tired too, but I'm used to it. Before meeting Rachel, I only slept three or four hours a night so this is like going back to my old sleep schedule.

I've been so busy with the baby that I haven't had time to deal with Shelby. Last week when she came by the hospital I saw the marks on her wrists, but couldn't get her alone to ask her who did it. I'm assuming it's Royce, but I need to confirm that with Shelby.

I'm calling her now while Rachel's asleep upstairs. I went in my office and shut the door.

"Hi, Rachel," Shelby answers.

"It's not Rachel. It's Pearce."

"Why are you calling? Did something happen to Rachel? Or the baby?"

"No. I'm calling to talk to you."

"About what?"

"You know why I'm calling. Now tell me who did it."

She's quiet, and then says, "I can't tell you. I'll get in trouble."

"You won't get in trouble. I'll take care of it myself. Was it Royce?"

She doesn't answer.

"Shelby, I know it was Royce. You don't have to cover for him."

"Don't do anything, Pearce. Please. Royce isn't stable. He's violent, and I'm afraid of what he'll do to me if you tell him I told you this."

"He left marks on you. I'll just tell him I saw the marks."

"No. Just leave it alone. Besides, I probably won't be seeing him much anymore. He doesn't have time now that he has a kid."

"He doesn't take care of the baby. He has a nanny. And the baby was born in July. Those marks on your wrists are newer than that. When did this happen?"

"Pearce, I mean it. Don't say anything. He'll come after me."

"He will not come after you. I will make sure of it."

"Why are getting involved in this?"

"Because what he's doing is wrong. He can't treat you that way. Do you know if he's done this to any of the others?"

"No, but I don't talk to the other girls. We're not allowed to."

I hear Rachel coming down the stairs. "I have to go. I'll take care of Royce. He won't bother you again."

I leave my office and Rachel is standing there. I give her a kiss. "Why aren't you resting?"

"Garret needs to be fed. I'm just getting his bottle."

"I can do it."

"That's okay. I want to do it. I like feeding him. And holding him." She smiles. "I just like spending time with him."

I smile back. "I know you do." Rachel's so happy being a mother. I've never seen her this happy. "Since you're up, would you mind if I go out for a while? I want to stop by the office for a couple hours and see what I'll be walking into tomorrow after being gone for so long."

"Sure, go ahead."

I give her a kiss, then go around her. "I'll see you soon."

It's seven at night so Royce should be home. I call him as I'm going to the car. "Royce, it's Pearce. Are you doing anything? I wanted to stop over."

"Stop over? You live forty-five minutes away."

"I'm heading out your way, so will you be around?"

"Yes. Victoria's at some charity event. I'm supposed to be spending quality time with the baby, whatever the hell that means. Anyway, I've got the nanny watching her, so come on over."

"I'll see you soon." As I'm driving there, my other phone rings. My Dunamis phone. My chest tightens, as it always does when they call.

"Hello?" I hear the recording and punch in my member number.

The recording continues. "You will soon be receiving an assignment. It will be given sometime within the next four to eight weeks. You must not travel until you have received and completed your assignment."

The phone clicks off and I toss it on the seat. I just had an assignment a month ago. I had to get rid of a police report involving one of our freelancers. He completed a kill job for one of the other members and left some evidence behind. It ended up being a complicated, time-consuming assignment, but it could've been worse. I'm hoping this next one will be forging documents or something else simple like that.

I drive through the entrance of Royce's estate. Royce now lives in a mansion, which he moved into after he married Victoria. It's 18,000 square feet, and Victoria decorated it in a style that I don't care for, but is common for wealthy people; white furniture, glass tables, crystal chandeliers, expensive paintings on the walls. It's very cold and sterile.

The maid greets me at the door and shows me to Royce's office. He doesn't work, so I don't know why he needs an office.

"Good evening, Pearce." He gets up from his desk to greet me. "I hear you have a child."

"Yes. A son. His name is Garret."

"Congratulations." Royce sits back down behind his desk. "I wish I'd had a son."

I sit across from him. "Royce, don't say that. You have a beautiful daughter."

"What the hell am I going to do with a daughter? I told Victoria she can take Sadie and I'll take the next one, which better be a boy."

It's no wonder Royce treats the associates so poorly. He has zero respect for women, even his own daughter.

"What was your son's name? Garret?" He chuckles. "Maybe Garret and Sadie will grow up and marry each other. We should just arrange it now. They could get married right after college, once your son is a full-fledged member."

"I think it's a little too soon to be marrying them off," I say, trying not to react to his comment. But inside I'm panicking. I have to get Garret out of his obligation. He cannot be in Dunamis.

"The other kid's probably a boy," he says under his breath.

"What other kid?"

"What?" He looks up from his desk.

"You just said something about some other kid."

He straightens up and clears his throat. "It was nothing. Never mind."

He's hiding something. And I know what it is. His risky behavior finally caught up with him.

"You got a woman pregnant," I say. "Was it one of the associates?"

The associates are all on birth control, but that's not always a hundred percent.

He hasn't answered me. He's looking at me like he wants to tell me, but can't.

"Who is it, Royce?"

He leans forward, his arms planted on his desk, his eyes narrowed. "If I tell you this, you cannot tell anyone. Ever! If you do, I swear I'll kill you."

"Do not threaten me," I say, glaring at him. "If you don't want to tell me, then fine. It was simply a question."

He sighs and sits back, rubbing his hand over his jaw. "I can't take this. I have to tell someone." He looks at me again. "You're right. I got a girl pregnant. But it wasn't an associate. It was a girl I met when I was on the road last year. On that campaign tour. We went out, had dinner, had some drinks, and ended up at her place."

"How old is this girl?"

He shrugs. "I don't know. Maybe 21? 22?"

"Did you see her again after that night?"

He hesitates, then says, "Yes. We had a brief affair."

"When did it end?"

"When I found out she was pregnant." He looks down at his desk, his jaw clenched. "The bitch should've been on birth control." His tone is suddenly very hostile. Aggressive. "I told her to get rid of it. I sent her more than enough money to have it done."

"But she didn't," I say.

"No!" He bursts up from his chair. "She said she would, but she didn't! Fucking bitch!" He slams his fist down on the desk. "How could she do this to me?" He storms off to the side of the room and starts pacing the floor.

I've never seen him like his. Within an instant he switched from being normal to acting almost deranged. Shelby's right. He's not stable. I haven't been around him for months. Like he said, he's been on the campaign trail for most of last year, following around one of our presidential candidates. The organization is grooming Royce to be president someday, and part of his training is to watch another candidate in action.

"Royce, just calm down."

He whips around, and storms back to me, slamming his fist on the desk again. "I will NOT calm down! That bitch is going to ruin my life! I'm going to be the fucking President of the United States! A president cannot have some bastard child running around!"

"What are you saying?"

"I'm saying the bitch is dead. I just haven't arranged for it yet because I just found out about this. All these months, I thought she got the abortion, so I was going to leave her alone. Then last week, I hired one of our freelancers to check on her to see what she was up to. Make sure she wasn't telling anyone about me. And yesterday he reported back to me and said he found her, living in some small town, and pregnant! She told me she'd take care of it!" He's screaming and his face is red, his eyes dark. "But she fucking lied to me!"

He collapses into his chair.

I wait a moment for him to calm down, then say, "When is she due?"

"I don't know. Maybe late September, early October. Who the fuck cares? She'll be dead by then. And so will her bastard child."

"Royce, no. Leave her alone."

He picks a letter opener off his desk and points it at me. "You're telling me you wouldn't do it? Some woman threatens your marriage? Your future? You'd just let her do it?"

"This woman hasn't threatened to do anything. She's left you alone. She probably just wants to have the baby and have nothing to do with you."

"How fucking naive are you, Pearce? The bitch knows I'm a billionaire. As soon as that kid's born, she'll sell her story to every tabloid, then come after me for money."

"She could've already done that. She has no reason to wait until the child's born."

"You can't talk me out of this. She's a liability. I can't risk having her around."

"You are not killing her. She's carrying your child. Are you seriously going to kill your own child?"

"It's not a child. It's a mistake."

I can't believe he said that. I want to reach over and beat him unconscious. I'm probably extra sensitive right now because I've just spent a week at home with my own child, who I love more than anything and would do anything to protect. But even if I didn't have Garret, I'd still feel this way.

"If you didn't want a child, then you should've used a goddamn condom. You're a grown man, Royce. Stop acting like a teenager and take some fucking responsibility for your actions."

"I AM taking responsibility. I'm cleaning up my mess. Getting rid of her."

"I will not allow you to do this. It's wrong, and you know it. You're a father. Just down the hall you have a baby girl. You would never harm Sadie, so why would you even think of killing your other child?"

"It's not the same," he says quietly.

"It IS the same! It's still your child! Please, Royce, just let her have the baby. It's just a few weeks from now. Let her have it and see what happens. I bet you anything she'll leave you alone."

"I can't risk it." His voice is calmer now, but the rest of him is still tense, his body rigid, his back straight. "Perhaps if I didn't have the presidency in my future, it would be a different story. But I can't put my future at risk. I'm going to be president. And no one is going to stand in my way."

"Do something else. Have someone keep watch on this woman to make sure she never tells anyone. Give her enough money to keep quiet. Anything. Just don't kill her."

"I'm done wasting my time on her. I'm putting the order in tomorrow. It should be done within the week."

How could he do this? The woman is nine months pregnant. With his child! How could he not think this is wrong?

I hesitate, because I know I shouldn't be doing this but I'm desperate. "Jack has shit on you."

"Yeah? So? He has shit on everyone."

"He'll use it against you. I'll tell him what you're planning to do and he'll stop you."

"Why the hell would Jack care?"

"Because he doesn't believe in killing pregnant women."

Royce laughs. "Most people don't, until they're backed in a corner with no way out."

"I'm serious, Royce. I'll tell Jack, and I'll get him to stop you unless you agree to call this off."

There's a knock on the door. "Who is it?" Royce yells.

The door opens and a woman, who I assume is the nanny, walks in with the baby. "Your wife wanted you to say goodnight to your daughter."

He nods. "Fine."

She brings the baby over, wrapped up in a pink blanket, and hands her to Royce.

"Could you give us a minute?" I say to the nanny.

She nods and walks away, shutting the door behind her.

"Look at her, Royce. Look at your daughter."

Sadie is awake and watching Royce like Garret watches me, so intently, searching his face like she's memorizing his features. She's a very cute baby. She's a month older than Garret, but she's only slightly bigger than him. She's very petite, with wispy strands of light brown hair and big brown eyes.

"It's not the same," he says quietly as he looks at her.

"They're both babies. They're both yours. They just have different mothers."

"Which is why I have to do it."

"You don't have to do anything. Just let her have the baby and see what happens. If this woman hasn't come after you by now, I doubt she will when the baby arrives. Just leave her alone, Royce."

Sadie gurgles and smiles at him. He shuts his eyes, like he doesn't want to see it. But she keeps gurgling and smiling and he opens his eyes again. And when he sees her, his body relaxes and his expression softens.

"You're a father, Royce. I know you don't want to hurt an innocent child and his or her mother."

"Fuck," he says under his breath as he looks down at Sadie. He sighs. "Fine. You win. I'll wait until she gives birth and see what happens. But if she tells anyone, she's dead, and the child will be an orphan. I'm not taking it in. And you have to promise not to tell Victoria. Or anyone."

I nod. "I won't tell anyone." I stand up. "I'll leave you two alone. I need to get home."

He doesn't say goodbye as I leave. When I get out to my car I realize I forgot to ask him about Shelby. But this wasn't the time to bring that up. After Royce told me about that woman, my priority was to save her and her child. I'll have to find another way to save Shelby.

I don't know what's happened to Royce, but it's starting to frighten me. He's becoming someone else. Someone dangerous. He's never been a caring or compassionate person, but tonight he was evil. Acting as though taking a life had no effect on him. It's like he's losing his humanity. And it's all because of his thirst for power. His insatiable need to be president.

When I get home, Rachel and the baby are both asleep. I go in the nursery and look at Garret in his crib. He's so small. So innocent. So helpless. I would kill anyone who even attempted to harm him.

I wonder if this woman Royce had the affair with is worried for her safety. I wonder if she knows what Royce is really like. Maybe that's why she moved to that small town. Maybe she was hiding out. Maybe she fears for her life and her child's life.

Royce better keep his word. I think he will. I saw the look on his face when he held his daughter. It's the look all us fathers get. The look that says how much you love your child. As long as he keeps remembering that feeling, he'll leave that woman and her child alone. At least I hope he does.

The next day at work, Jack stops by my office. He and Martha have been vacationing in Europe so I haven't seen him for a couple weeks. I've missed him. He's become somewhat of a father to me and I missed having him around.

He drops a box of cigars on my desk. "Welcome to fatherhood!" I stand up and go around my desk and he gives me a shoulder hug. "Congratulations."

"Thank you. We had a boy. His name is Garret."

"Yes, I heard. Martha called Rachel as soon as we got home last night."

"Oh, I didn't know. She was asleep when I got home."

"She said you came into the office last night. Why the hell were you in the office? You need to be home with your kid. These years go by fast, Pearce. You don't want to miss them."

"I wasn't here. I was with Royce."

"Royce? Why were you with Royce?"

I promised Royce I wouldn't tell anyone about that woman, and I have to keep my word or he might do something to her. But I can at least tell Jack about Shelby.

"Do you have a minute?" I go past him and close the door, then come back around to face him.

He checks his watch. "I have a meeting in five, but go ahead."

"Royce is abusing the associates again. One in particular."

"Your wife's friend?"

"Yes. You know her as Sophia but her name is Shelby."

"And you're sure it was Royce?"

"Yes. I asked Shelby if it was him and she wouldn't answer but she didn't deny it."

He shakes his head. "Leave it alone. Don't get involved in this, Pearce."

"And just let him continue to abuse these women?"

"Is he doing it to all of them? Or just this one?"

"I don't know. At the last Dunamis party, I looked at the other girls and I didn't see any bruisings or scars on them so maybe it's just Shelby. I saw her last week. She had marks along her wrists where he tied her up against her will. What can I do to stop him?"

"Nothing. Just let it go."

"I'm not letting it go. Jack, you said you have things you could use to blackmail Royce. So do it. Make him stop."

Jack sighs. "I can't. And neither can you. He's protected, Pearce. He's their presidential pick, and even though he's still a ways off from that, he shows more potential than any of the candidates we've had in the past. They need him, and Royce knows that. He can basically do whatever the hell he wants and they're not going to punish him. And as for abusing an associate? The organization wouldn't punish any of the members for that. They might be scolded and told not to do it, but nothing serious would happen. Those girls are on their own."

"That's just wrong," I say, shaking my head.

"I'm sorry, but that's just how it is. You can't help this girl."

"What if I made some kind of deal with the organization? A deal to get her out?"

"No. Stay the hell out of it. You're already in trouble for marrying Rachel. Don't go stirring up even more trouble by trying to save this girl. You're a husband and a father, Pearce. Think about your family. You can't put yourself at risk."

He's right, but I still want to do something to help Shelby. She's a nice girl who was just trying to help pay her father's medical bills, and now she's trapped in this life forever.

"So when do I get to see this baby of yours?" Jack's tone lightens and he smiles. "Martha's already buying out the stores. Baby clothes. Toys. Stuffed animals. She's considering your kid her grandkid, by the way, until we get our own."

I laugh. "She doesn't need to buy him anything. He's only a week old. He's too young for toys."

"Doesn't matter. She can't help herself. So when can we come over?"

"I don't know. Just have Martha call Rachel. The two of them can figure it out."

"Will do. I need to get to that meeting." He turns to leave, but then stops and turns back. "I'm happy for you, Pearce. You look good. Tired, but good. And happy."

"I am." I smile as I think of Garret. "You were right, Jack. He brings light to my darkness. Just like Rachel does. And now I'm more determined than ever to get him out of his obligation."

He nods. "You will. But don't worry about that right now. Just enjoy being a father. By the way, do your parents know about the baby?"

"Yes. My mother actually came over and helped. My father still isn't speaking to me."

"He'll come around." Jack opens the door. "I'll see you later. Get out of here early today and go spend time with your family."

After he leaves, I get back to work, but I keep getting sidetracked thinking about how to help Shelby. But there's nothing I can do. Even if there was, I couldn't do it, because like Jack said, it could get me in trouble and I can't risk it. I'm a husband. A father. I have a family. And I can't put them, or myself, at risk.

CHAPTER SIX
Six Weeks Later

RACHEL

"Martha, we're running out of room," I say, laughing, as she hauls in more toys for Garret. Stuffed bears, stuffed footballs, stuffed basketballs. She comes over a couple times a week and every time she comes, she brings more stuff.

"Would you just let me spoil him?" she asks as she drops a kiss on his cheek. I'm holding him and standing by the door, watching as she sets down yet another shopping bag. She comes back and smiles at him. "Look at you. You're getting so big. Tell your mommy that Granny Martha can buy you whatever she wants."

I reach over and hug her. "Thank you, Martha. It's very sweet of you to do all this. I'm sure when he's older, he will love all these toys."

Garret is now seven weeks old, and those weeks flew by. Everyone told me this time would go fast and they're completely right. Before I know it, Garret will no longer be a baby. I wish I could slow down time, but it just keeps going and my little boy just keeps getting bigger.

"I don't know how you do it, Rachel," she says, looking me up and down.

"Do what?"

"How do you manage to look so good just seven weeks after giving birth? You lost all the weight and you don't even look tired."

"Pearce helps out a lot at night so I can sleep, and as for the weight, just taking care of Garret is a workout. Plus, I've been swimming every day. Garret sits in his swing and watches. He loves being outside. We'll be sad when the weather gets cold. But Pearce bought me a membership for the gym in the next town over, so Garret and I will be going there all winter to use the pool."

"Are you going to teach him how to swim?" She sets her purse down on the couch.

"Definitely. I've already had him in the water a few times and he loved it. Who knows? Maybe he'll be on a swim team someday, like his mom." I kiss him. "Would you like that, Garret? To be a swimmer?"

The phone rings from the kitchen. "Martha, do you want to hold him while I get the phone?"

"Like you have to ask." She races over and takes him from me. She really does treat him like he's her grandson. She spoils him rotten.

I pick up the phone. "Hello?"

"Rachel, this is Eleanor."

"Hi, Eleanor. Are you coming over tomorrow?"

Eleanor comes over once a week now, usually on Fridays. I keep telling her she can come over more than that, but so far, she's kept her visits to once a week, which is fine. It's better than nothing. She's much nicer to me now. That's relative, of course. Most people would think she's rude with some of the comments she makes, but compared to how she used to be, I consider her to be nice.

Holton still won't talk to us or come see us. I don't know if Holton and Eleanor are still fighting. They keep going to social functions together so it's hard to say.

"I won't be able to make it tomorrow," she says, "but I was hoping the three of you could come here to the house for dinner on Sunday."

"Oh. Okay," I say, but then wonder if I should've agreed to it. I probably should've talked to Pearce first. He may not want to see his father.

"Cocktails will be at seven-thirty and dinner at eight."

"Could it maybe be a little earlier? I don't like to have the baby out that late."

Actually, we've never taken Garret out at night at all. We've hardly taken him anywhere. We spend most of our time at home. He's been to the grocery store and the park and around the neighborhood, but that's about it.

"What time would work better for you?" She sounds annoyed.

"Could cocktails be at six-thirty and dinner at seven?"

"Holton and I generally don't like to have dinner that early, but I'm sure it'll be fine. We'll plan on six-thirty."

"Okay. We'll see you then."

"Oh, and please dress appropriately. No denim pants. And no shorts."

I almost laugh. Did she really think I'd wear jeans or shorts? I know better than that. I've never been to their house, but knowing how formal they are, I would never show up in casual clothes.

"Goodbye, Rachel."

"Goodbye, Eleanor." I hang up just as Martha walks into the kitchen. She doesn't have Garret and I panic. "Where's the baby?"

"With his father," she says.

"Pearce is home? It's only four o'clock."

"Jack sent him home early." She hugs me. "I have to go. According to your husband, I have to meet Jack at some restaurant for drinks with a client and his wife." She rolls her eyes. "Of course he doesn't bother to give me any notice. That man. He drives me crazy."

I laugh. "I'll walk you to the door."

When we get to the living room, Pearce is there, holding Garret and talking to him. It's so cute. I love watching them together. Pearce never uses baby-talk. He uses his formal, serious tone, like he's talking to a business colleague. It's very funny.

"Hello, sweetheart." He kisses me on my way to the door.

"Hi." I give him a flirtatious smile. He's in his suit and tie and looks super hot, like he always does.

We say goodbye to Martha and I close the door. "So you got off work early again?"

"Yes." He nods, smiling. "Jack doesn't seem to believe in a full work day."

"I'm glad you're home," I hug his side, then turn to face him. "Oh, um, I hope you're not mad, but I kind of agreed to have dinner at your parents' house on Sunday night."

He looks surprised. "My parents invited us for dinner?"

"Well, your mother did."

"Will my father be there?"

"Yes," I say, biting my lip. "Is that bad? Should I not have agreed to it? I don't want you two fighting at dinner."

"We won't fight. What time do we need to be there?"

"Six-thirty. Dinner is at seven."

His brows rise. "Seven? That's early for dinner. My parents usually eat at eight or eight-thirty."

"That was the original plan, but I didn't want Garret out too late so I asked her if it could be earlier and she agreed to it."

"That just shows how much my mother likes you. If she didn't, she'd never agree to have dinner that early."

I look down at Garret. His eyes are shut and his little head is tucked in the crook of Pearce's elbow. "He fell asleep in your arms," I say to Pearce.

"He always does that. I must have comfortable arms."

"Why don't you go put him in his crib?" I reach up and give Pearce a kiss as I slip my hand under his suit jacket and along his abs. "Then maybe you and I could meet in the bedroom."

He smiles. "I thought you weren't able to do it yet."

"It's been seven weeks. And I saw the doctor today and got the okay."

He smiles even wider. "I'm glad I came home early. Get upstairs. I'll put the baby down. He better take a long nap."

I laugh as I run up the stairs. I've been dying to be with Pearce again. We didn't do it the last month of my pregnancy so it's been a long time.

When Pearce comes in the bedroom, I'm waiting for him at the door in a black lace bra and matching panties. He looks me up and down, his eyes filled with desire.

"You're killing me, Rachel." He shoves his jacket off and rips off his tie. "We may not even make it to the bed."

His hand moves to the side of my face as his mouth covers mine, giving me those slow sensual kisses of his that I love so much. He hasn't given me those for a while because we both know they always lead to sex, and since we weren't able to do it, they'd just get us worked up for nothing. But now, we can finally do it and I'm realizing how much I missed these kisses. His tongue sweeps over mine as his hand lowers to my breast, causing my whole body to come alive, an aching need building inside me.

We finish undressing each other as we kiss, and then he asks, "Where do you want it?" His head dips down to kiss my shoulder. "The bed?" I close my eyes as I feel his warm breath by my ear. "The shower?" He kisses his way down my neck. "Against the wall?"

I'm so turned on I can't even remember the options. "They all sound good," I whisper. "Just pick one."

He lifts me up and takes me to the bed. Normally he'd spend time caressing me, teasing me. But right now, there's no time for that. It's been too long. We're both desperate for each other.

He pushes inside me, breathing out at the feel of it while I softly moan. He moves slowly, worried he might hurt me. It's sweet and caring and I love him for it, but he won't hurt me. I'm fine. I lift my hips up, coaxing him to go faster. And when he does, I feel the build, the tension spiraling deep within my core, getting stronger as I anticipate the release. He thrusts harder and faster, and then it comes, unraveling inside me, over and over.

Pearce comes at nearly the same time, his body shuddering from the release.

We stay there, catching our breath.

"We have gone way too long without doing that," I say, breathing hard.

"Believe me," he says, hovering over me. "I have been counting the days since we could do this again."

"You have?" I smile.

"You know I have." He kisses me. "We're doing it again later tonight."

"I can't. The doctor said only once a week for the next month." I try to act serious.

"Really?" I feel his body sigh. "If I'd known that I would've made it last longer."

I laugh. "I'm kidding. We can do it as much as we want."

"That is not funny, Rachel." He kisses my neck fast and quick, tickling me and making me laugh even more.

The baby monitor goes off. Pearce sighs and rolls off me. "I guess we're done."

I scoot off the bed. "I'll get him." I grab my robe and head to the door.

As I'm leaving, I hear Pearce say, "Tell him he needs to take longer naps."

On Sunday night, as we're on our way to Pearce's parents' house, I say, "Do I need to know anything before we get there? Any rules I should be aware of?"

I'm joking, but he answers seriously. "Make sure you don't have any dirt on your shoes that might show on the white tile. Never do anything yourself. Let the hired help do it. Don't go looking for the bathroom, or any other room, by yourself. Always ask first. Don't touch any of the artwork or sculptures or the glass tables. Don't—"

"Pearce, I was kidding. Are you telling me they really have that many rules?"

"I was just getting started." He turns down a street lined with big iron gates and tall green bushes.

"Did you have to follow all those rules as a child?"

"Of course. There were so many rules, my parents wrote them out so I'd remember them. One time my father even made me memorize them and recite them back to him."

"Nobody should have to follow that many rules, especially children, who naturally touch things. When Garret is older, he is not going to be forced to follow all those rules when he goes to his grandparents' house."

"Then he probably won't be going there. They'll have to come to our house if they want to see him." Pearce pulls up to a tall iron gate. "This is it."

He puts his window down and a voice comes out of the speaker box next to the gate. "Good evening, Mr. Kensington."

"Good evening."

The gate slowly opens and we drive down the long entrance road to the stone-covered mansion. The place is huge and sprawling.

"Did you used to get lost living here?" I ask.

He nods. "Yes. That happened several times when I was a young child. In fact two of my nannies were fired for it. They were supposed to keep track of me and ended up losing me in the house. My mother found me both times."

Pearce had such a different childhood than mine, or anyone's, really. It's amazing he turned out normal.

"Let the man get your door," he says as a man in a black suit comes up to the car. I wait for him to open it.

"Welcome," he says, taking my hand to help me out. Is this really necessary? Do Eleanor and Holton really need people on staff to help them get out of their car?

There's another man on Pearce's side, holding the car door while Pearce gets Garret out of the back seat. He meets me on the other side and we walk to the door as one of the men drives our car around to the back of the house.

Pearce rings the doorbell and a woman in a maid's uniform answers. "Hello, sir." She bows slightly to Pearce. "Madam," she says to me.

She shows us to the living room, and as we're walking I realize I forgot to check my shoes for dirt. I check the white tiles behind me. They look clean and shiny. I glance up and almost run right into a statue. It's just a tall marble rectangle but it probably cost a fortune. There are big statues everywhere I look and large paintings on the walls.

"Pearce. Rachel." Eleanor comes up to us. "I'm pleased you could make it."

"Thank you for inviting us," Pearce says as she gives him a shoulder hug. Eleanor doesn't give full hugs. It's shoulders only and it's always quick. She gives me the same type of hug, and as she's doing so, I see Holton coming up behind her.

"Pearce," he says, holding his hand out.

"Father." Pearce shakes his hand.

I do not understand this odd relationship they have. They act as though they just talked last week, when in fact they haven't talked in over a year.

"Hello, Holton," I say, since he didn't acknowledge me.

He just nods. He has the same scowl on his face that he had the last time I saw him. I guess it's permanent.

"Holton, meet your grandson," Eleanor says, nudging Holton to the baby carrier that Pearce is holding.

He steps up, glances at the baby, then steps back again, next to Eleanor. That's it? This is the first time he's seeing his grandson and he just takes a quick glance at him? It infuriates me.

I pick Garret up and hold him. Now I regret coming here. I thought this would be a fresh start. I thought Holton might accept us now that Pearce and I have a child together, but he's just as cold and awful as always. And this house is cold and uncomfortable. I just want to leave.

Garret seems to agree. He starts fussing and then he cries. Holton glares at him, as if babies shouldn't cry. It angers me even more.

"It's okay," I say to Garret, bouncing him a little.

"Let's take him upstairs," Eleanor says, sensing Holton's temper rising the more the baby cries.

"What's upstairs?" I ask.

She smiles as she leads me to the stairs. "I set up a nursery for when he comes over."

A nursery? Here? I don't think I like that. Garret is not going to be over here enough to need a nursery.

I look back at Pearce and he nods at me to go along with it. I go up the long winding staircase to the upper level. It's huge. There must be at least ten rooms up here. Eleanor shows me to one that's halfway down the hall. The room has cream-colored walls and a dark wood crib and matching changing table. There's a light-blue upholstered rocking chair off to the side.

"You could add your own personal touches if you'd like," she says. "I simple bought the furniture. We weren't using this room, so I converted it to a nursery so that Garret would have a place to sleep if you and Pearce ever stay here overnight, or want us to babysit."

She smiles, and I see that she's just being nice. At first, I thought she was being controlling, assuming I'd let her keep Garret overnight, or longer than that. I'm so used to both her and Holton trying to control everything. But I think she's just trying to be helpful.

"If you need to change him, there are diapers and other supplies on the changing table."

"Thank you, but he's fine." I hold him against my chest. He stopped crying as soon as we got away from Holton.

"Go ahead and put him down," she says. "We'll join the men for cocktails."

"Oh, um, I don't want to leave him up here. I'll just take him downstairs."

"This evening is for adults. The baby can stay up here. He'll be fine. I'll have the maid check on him."

"No." I hold Garret even closer. "I'm sorry, but he needs to be with me. I'm not leaving him up here."

She rests her hand on my arm. "Rachel, I know as a new mother it's hard to detach yourself from your child, but it's just for a few hours. Certainly you can be apart from him for a few hours. He'll be right here. You can check on him whenever you'd like."

Why is she pushing me to do this? I don't want him up here all alone in this cold, stark room. He'll be scared and lonely. And I don't want the maid checking on him. I don't even know the maid.

"Eleanor, I appreciate you setting up the nursery, but I need to keep him with me. If it ruins your dinner, then maybe we should leave."

"No. Of course not. We'll try to make it work."

Make *what* work? Dinner? Why wouldn't it work?

We go back down the stairs. Pearce and his father are no longer in the foyer.

"Right this way." Eleanor takes me down a long hallway to a very large dining room. There's a bar in the back, complete with a bartender. Pearce and Holton are there, having a drink.

Holton eyes the baby. "I thought we were having cocktails, Eleanor."

She fakes a smile. "We are. I'll have a gin and tonic."

"And *you?*" Holton asks, refusing once again to use my name.

"Nothing for me."

Pearce wraps his arm around me. "Are you sure? There's sparkling water, soda, anything you'd like."

"No, thank you. I'm fine."

Holton coughs and takes a drink. Then he coughs again, repeatedly.

"Do you have a cold?" I ask him, not wanting him around Garret if he's sick.

"He's not sick," Eleanor says. "Something's just been irritating his throat lately."

"Have you seen a doctor?" Pearce asks him.

"I'm going this week," he says.

Eleanor smiles. "I'm sure it's nothing. Shall we go sit down?"

She leads us to the formal living room that's just off the dining room. Pearce and I seat ourselves on the beige sofa and his parents sit across from us in high-backed upholstered chairs, then everyone, except me, has their drinks. Holton keeps giving me annoyed looks for having the baby here, but I don't care. This is a huge house and I feel like Garret would be miles away up in that nursery.

At seven, a man in a white shirt, black vest, and black pants, who I'm guessing is our server, comes in and announces that dinner is ready.

"Could you go get the baby carrier?" I ask Pearce.

"Mother said there's a crib upstairs. He can be up there while we have dinner."

"I don't want him up there," I say quietly, but Holton hears, and I swear he almost rolls his eyes. "I'd rather have him here with us."

Pearce senses my anxiousness and says, "I'll go get it."

During dinner, Garret sleeps quietly in his baby carrier, which I put on the chair next to me. Holton and Eleanor are at the ends of the table and can't even see the baby from there so they have no reason to complain.

"How is your job, Pearce?" Holton asks.

So far, the dinner conversation has been mostly about Kensington Chemical. Holton has monopolized the conversation, mainly just talking to Pearce. I tried to ask Holton a question, pretending to act interested in what he was saying, but he interrupted me, acting like he didn't hear me.

"The job keeps me busy," Pearce says, purposely being vague. He doesn't want to talk about his job with his father because he knows Holton will just find fault with it. Pearce said his father hates Jack.

When dessert is served, Pearce tries to include me in the conversation. "Rachel, tell my parents how you're teaching Garret to swim."

"He's not really swimming," I say. "I'm just getting him used to the water."

"Rachel used to swim in college. She's very good. She has several medals and trophies."

There's a loud ringing noise and Pearce quickly gets up and takes out his phone. It's the cell phone he uses for work.

"I'll be right back," he says, racing out of the room.

Why is he answering his phone during dinner? Surely his parents don't approve of that. But they don't seem angry. They're calmly eating their dessert as if the phone call didn't happen.

"Did you enjoy the meal?" Eleanor asks me.

"Yes. It was very good." I'm just being polite. It wasn't very good. I'm not even sure what I ate. The main course was some type of meat but it wasn't beef, chicken, or pork. At least the dessert is good. It's a chocolate torte with raspberry filling.

We finish our dessert in silence, and when we're done, Pearce finally comes back. He's walking really fast and looks stressed.

"Is something wrong at work?" I ask him.

His father chuckles. "Yes, Pearce, tell us. Did the boss give you a difficult assignment?"

Pearce clears his throat. "It's nothing, but we do need to go. It's late and we need to get Garret to bed."

I point to his plate. "What about your dessert?"

"He doesn't eat dessert," Eleanor says. "But we always serve it to him anyway."

"You didn't know your husband doesn't eat dessert?" Holton smirks. "I wonder what else you don't know about him." He chuckles again.

The man never laughs or smiles, so he's obviously trying to tell me something, or he's just being rude. Either way, I'm ready to leave. This has been a long evening.

"Will you be coming for dinner next Sunday as well?" Eleanor asks. She looks desperate for me to say yes. She clearly wants to reunite the family and I feel like I should make an effort to help her, even though I dislike Holton.

"I don't think we'll be able to make it," Pearce says, since I didn't answer.

"Maybe you could come to *our* house next week," I offer. "I'm happy to make dinner. Maybe on Friday night?"

"Fine." Eleanor glances at Holton, who's mumbling something under his breath. "Holton and I will be there next week for dinner. What time should we arrive?"

"Let's say seven. That's usually when Garret goes to sleep so it'll be a good time to have dinner."

"Eleanor," Holton barks, his eyes on her.

She ignores him. "Seven it is."

"We can see ourselves out," Pearce says as he takes the baby carrier.

"No. I'll walk you out," his mother says, following us to the door.

We say goodbye as we wait for the car to be brought around to the front.

When we're in the car, driving away, Pearce takes my hand. "Thank you for inviting them to dinner. You didn't have to do that."

"I wanted to. Your mother and I are both trying to get this family back together." I check the back seat and see Garret soundly sleeping. "So what did you think of our evening?"

"I thought it went quite well. I know my father ignored you, which would be rude behavior for anyone else, but for him it's actually a good thing. It means he tolerates you, and that's far better than the alternative. At least he wasn't tossing insults at you all night."

"That's true. I guess it could've been worse. I was surprised by the nursery. Pearce, I don't want Garret staying over there without us. It doesn't feel right."

"He won't be staying there. My mother has so many rooms she doesn't know what to do with them all. This gave her an excuse to convert one of them into something useful. But if she never uses it, that's fine. She won't be upset by it."

"I can't believe your parents didn't even react when your phone went off at dinner. I thought for sure they'd yell at you, but they didn't. Didn't you find that odd?"

"No. They understand that work doesn't end at five. If it were my personal phone, they wouldn't have allowed it."

"Was Jack calling you?"

"No. It was someone else. There was an issue with the new product line."

"And they had to call you at night about that?"

"Rachel, I'd rather not talk about work. I'm very tired, and thinking about work just makes me more tired."

The car is silent for a moment, then I ask, "So do you really not like dessert?"

"I don't care for sweets. I never have."

I laugh. "And I'm just finding this out now? Pearce, I make you desserts all the time. Why didn't you tell me you don't like them?"

"Because I like the ones *you* make. But I don't like other desserts, like that torte they were serving. It's too sweet."

"I make you chocolate cake. That's not that different than a chocolate torte."

"I don't know what to tell you, Rachel." He lifts my hand up and kisses it. "I like your desserts but nobody else's. I can't explain it."

I can't explain it either. I can't explain a lot of things that happened tonight, especially that call Pearce got and the fact that his parents didn't get mad about it. Pearce almost never gets calls on that phone. I think that's only the third time I've heard it ring. Yet he takes it with him everywhere he goes. And I don't know why he needs two phones. He could just use his personal phone for work. But he insists on keeping the other one. I don't understand it.

CHAPTER SEVEN

PEARCE

I received a call from Dunamis last night during dinner at my parents' house. It was horrible timing. Rachel was questioning me about the call and then my father was making jokes about it, causing Rachel to question it even more. To make matters worse, the call was about my assignment, which is a kill assignment. I took the phone to my parents' study and listened carefully to the instructions. When I returned to the dining room, I felt tense and anxious, but I did my best to act natural and pretend it was just a call from the office.

When we got home, I couldn't sleep because I kept thinking about the assignment. So I told Rachel to go to sleep and that I'd get up with the baby during the night. Holding Garret calmed me, and by morning I felt a little better. But then I got to work and starting feeling stressed again. The person on the phone last night told me I have to take care of this today. I have to arrange for a murder. Today.

A folder with details regarding the assignment was delivered to me this morning and I've been going through it so I can figure out which freelancer would be best for the job. The man being killed is another freelancer. I wasn't told what he did wrong. Maybe he told someone about us, or botched a job. Whatever it was, the outcome is the same. He has to be killed.

The information I was given says he's the father of two young children. Their mother has custody of them and he never sees them. He was in prison before he became a freelancer. He killed two people during a robbery, so he's a bad guy but he's still a person. And a father. And now I have to kill him.

I can't think about it. I just need to get it over with. I look through my contact list and find a freelancer I know can get the job done quickly. I call him and explain what to do and tell him to get it done today. Then I hang up, realizing that by the end of today, I will have killed a man. Even though I'm not actually the one doing it, I still arranged for it, so I feel responsible for his death.

There's a knock on the door and Jack comes in. "There's a meeting in ten minutes. Are you coming?"

"Yes, I'll be there."

He walks into my office. "What's wrong with *you*? You look like hell today. Were you up with the kid all night?"

"Yes, but that's not why I look this way." I rub my hand over my jaw. "I just gave an order."

He closes the door. "When's it happening?"

"Today. I got the assignment last night while I was at my parents' house having dinner."

"You went to your parents' house? Was Holton there?"

"Yes. My mother forced him to have dinner with us. She's trying to reunite the family now that she has a grandchild."

"How did the dinner go?"

"It was a typical Kensington dinner. My father talked nonstop about work, monopolizing the conversation. He ignored Rachel all night."

"That's good."

I nod. "Yes. I told her that and she looked at me like I was crazy. She doesn't understand how being ignored in my family is a good thing. Maybe my father is finally accepting her now that Rachel and I have a child together."

"So he's no longer disowning you?"

"He didn't say those exact words, but yes, it sounds like I'm allowed back in their lives. Truthfully, I'd rather not be, at least as far as my father's concerned, but for Garret's sake, it would probably be good to try to be a family again. My father even

64

invited me to go golfing next week. I'm sure it was my mother's idea."

"You and I should go golfing before the weather turns cold. It's already the second week of October. We can't wait much longer. I went golfing with Arlin and Royce last—"

"Shit!" I jump up from my chair, grabbing my keys. "Can I miss this meeting?"

"Maybe. What's this about?"

"I need to go talk to Royce about something."

"Right now?"

"Yes. I need to know something and it can't wait."

"Why don't you just call him?"

"This needs to be discussed in person." I go to the door. "I'm sorry, Jack. I'll have to miss the meeting. I'll work late tonight to make up for missing it."

He waves me on. "Forget it. Just go."

I hurry to my car and drive to Royce's house. I need to know if he killed that woman. He's been on the campaign trail the past few weeks and he wouldn't answer my calls. He got back last night.

I need to know if he killed her, or if he listened to me and left her alone. I have to know if I was able to save two innocent lives. I know it doesn't make up for the fact that I'm having a man killed today, but still. If I can save someone, I will.

When I get to the gate outside Royce's mansion, I have to wait for the guard to ask Royce if I can enter. Royce must've agreed to it because the gate slowly opens.

The maid answers the door, but Victoria pushes past her. "Pearce, you cannot just show up here unannounced," she says, scolding me.

She's wearing a white pantsuit, and her dark hair hangs down over her shoulders. I haven't seen her hair down since she was a teenager. She always wears it up, twisted into a knot and pinned in place behind her neck. She obviously hasn't fixed her hair for the day, which is probably why she's angry I didn't call first.

I walk past her. "I need to speak with Royce."

"Your manners are atrocious." She follows me and grabs my arm. "Royce is still dressing. He is not ready for visitors."

"It's almost ten in the morning." I yank my arm back. "The man should be dressed by now." I have difficulty being nice to Victoria because she still refuses to show any kindness toward Rachel, and I know she gossips about her to the other women.

"Royce has been on the road and didn't get home until midnight last night. He's resting and then he has to leave for New York. He has no time to meet with you."

"He told the guard to let me in, so obviously you are incorrect." I start down the hall but she steps in front of me.

"You are done being friends with him." She scowls at me. "My husband is on a path to greatness and cannot associate with people like you."

I glare at her. "And what is that supposed to mean?"

She waves her hand, haughtily, in the air between us. "You're a disgrace, Pearce! Marrying that piece of trash girl, then having a—"

"Stop!" I grab her wrist. "You will NOT speak of her that way. And if you don't stop gossiping about her, I will—"

"Pearce." Royce appears, dressed in a suit and tie.

I let go of Victoria. "Hello, Royce."

Victoria hurries over to him. "I was just telling Pearce that he must give us more notice before stopping by. I haven't even done my hair yet."

"It's fine, Victoria," he says, moving past her. "Run along and do your hair."

She glowers at me, then storms off.

Royce adjusts his tie. "So, Pearce, what was so urgent that you felt the need to race over here, unannounced?"

"Can we talk privately?"

"Certainly. Let's go to the study." He turns and walks past the foyer to the other side of the house, stopping when we reach the study. It's a dark room with no windows. It has a fireplace, some brown leather chairs, and the walls are lined with bookcases. He turns on a lamp and we sit in adjoining chairs, facing the fireplace.

"Did you do it?" I ask, getting right down to business.

"Do what?" he asks, tugging on the sleeves of his dress shirt and adjusting his cuff links. He's obsessed with his appearance. His clothes always have to look perfect or he becomes agitated.

I lower my voice. "The woman you had an affair with. Did you...harm her?"

He chuckles. "You're still thinking about that? What's wrong with you, Pearce? Don't you have your own problems to deal with? Or is your life so mundane that you feel the need to spice it up by interfering in the lives of others?"

"Just tell me. Did you do it or not?"

"No." He tilts his head to one side, and then the other. "My neck is killing me from sitting on that plane. I need to schedule a massage."

"Did she have the baby?"

"Yes." He rubs his neck. "A girl. Another damn girl."

"What about the mother?"

"I took care of her," he says casually.

My body stiffens. "What does that mean?"

"It means I took care of her. I gave her enough money to keep quiet."

I relax again. "So she asked you for money?"

"No. I simply gave it to her." He slowly grins. "I can sometimes be compassionate, Pearce. The girl had to drop out of college and she has no job. I didn't want my child growing up in poverty. The two of them now have plenty of money to live a comfortable life."

I nod. "Good. I'm glad you finally came to your senses and acted responsibly."

"I know how to clean up my messes. She won't be bothering me again." That grin is still on his face, which concerns me. Is he lying to me? Hiding something behind that grin?

"Is that the only reason you came over here?" he asks. "Because I must tell you, Pearce, our friendship won't last if you continue to lecture me on my behavior. You're not exactly a saint. In fact, didn't you arrange for a murder to take place today?"

I move to the edge of my chair. "How do you know that?"

He chuckles. "Because it was *my* assignment. I was supposed to complete it weeks ago but I was traveling and just didn't get around to it. The deadline to complete it was today. I told them I didn't have time."

"And they accepted that?"

"It pays to have power." He smooths his slicked back hair in place.

It's just like Jack said. Royce can do no wrong. The organization needs him, so they'll let him get away with things the rest of us wouldn't be allowed to.

"I suggested they give the assignment to you," he says.

I burst up from my seat. "Why the fuck would you do that?"

"Because you needed it. You need to toughen up, Pearce. You're too emotional, probably because of that woman you're with. This is why one should never fall in love. It makes you too emotional, and you can't have emotions in the business we're in. If you do, you'll let your guard down and be killed. I'm just looking out for you, Pearce."

I stare down at him, seething with anger. "I do NOT need you to look out for me, nor do I need you concerning yourself with my emotional state. It's none of your damn business. And if you EVER tell them to give me an assignment like this again, you will be the one getting killed."

He smiles. "See? I've already toughened you up." He rises from his chair. "I need to go. I have to be at an event in the city at noon and I'm meeting with an associate at eleven to help me relax. I've been feeling a bit tense."

When he says 'associate' I immediately think of Shelby.

"Are you meeting with Sophia?" I ask.

"No." He pats me on the back. "I wouldn't take your girl, Pearce. I know how special she is to you." He walks to the door.

"So you haven't been with her recently?"

"If I had been, do you really think I'd tell you?" He smirks. "See yourself out." He leaves, and I'm left alone in the study.

I don't know what to do with him. He's always been wild and out of control, but now it's even worse. Being chosen as our future president has given him more power than he can handle. He's going to get himself in trouble, and yet no one seems to care. Nobody is keeping tabs on him or punishing his bad behavior.

I'm done dealing with him. I can't control him. And now he's interfering with my life, using his influence to dictate my assignments. I need to stay away from him. From here on out, I will see him at meetings and parties, but that's it. I'm going to keep my distance from Royce.

As I'm driving back to work, my Dunamis cell phone rings. What now? I sigh as I answer it. I punch in my member number and listen.

"Freelancer 579 needs to contact you," the voice says. "Will you accept the call?"

Freelancer 579 is the one I hired. Freelancers aren't allowed to call us directly. They have to call into a main number and then the calls are diverted to us. There must be a problem or he wouldn't be calling. Or maybe he has a question.

"I'll accept the call," I say.

I hear a clicking noise and then, "Is this Pearce Kensington?"

The freelancers aren't supposed to know our names. They know us by numbers, not names. And this doesn't sound like the man I hired.

"Who is this?"

"It's the man you tried to kill, you fucking bastard! I do your dirty work and this is how you repay me?"

I pull the car over to the side of the road. "Tell me who you are. I know you're not freelancer 579."

He lets out a short laugh. "Freelancer 579 is dead. I killed him five minutes ago. This is freelancer 486. The one you screwed over."

"I don't know what you're talking about. I've never hired you before."

"Liar!" he screams. "You told me to deliver a package. I did exactly what you told me to do. It's not my fucking fault that you gave me the wrong address! And now you're trying to kill me for your own fucking mistake!"

As he talks, I'm putting this together. This is Royce's mistake. Royce's original assignment wasn't to kill this man. It was to deliver some type of package to someone. Probably a package that contained confidential information that was not to be seen by anyone but the person it was intended to go to. But Royce gave the freelancer the wrong address, and now he's covering his tracks and blaming the freelancer for the error, thus causing the need for him to be killed. I got the kill assignment, and somehow this man found out my name and thinks I'm the one who gave him the wrong address. He obviously doesn't know about Royce. He knew Royce as a number, not a name. So how did this man get my name?

"It wasn't me," I tell the man. "I didn't give you that assignment."

"Stop lying!" He breathes in and out, loudly, into the phone. "If I'm being killed, I ain't going alone. I'm taking your wife with me. How do you like that, you fucking asshole?"

I grip the phone and get back onto the road. "What are you talking about? Where are you? What did you do?"

I hit the gas and speed off, heading toward home.

"She's a beauty. But then again, I suppose rich guys like you can buy whatever woman you want."

"Where are you? Tell me where the fuck you are!"

"I'm watching her," he says in a slow deranged voice. "Tight jeans. White sweater. Long dark hair."

"If you get anywhere near her, I'll kill you myself."

"Go ahead. I know I'll be killed eventually. But I'm not going alone. I want you to suffer. I'm sick of you bastards making us do your shit, risking everything, while you sit back and count your millions."

My tires screech as I round a corner. "We'll work this out. I'll pay you whatever you want. Just tell me where you are!"

I listen, but there's no sound. He hung up. Fuck!

I speed down the street. I'm almost home. When I get there, I pop the trunk and quickly unlock the hidden compartment that contains my guns. I grab the loaded handgun, attach the silencer, then race into the house. It's quiet and nothing looks out of place.

"Rachel?" I call out. I run up the stairs, checking every room. They're all empty. I check out the back window. She's not there either. Shit!

I get my phone out and call her, but hear ringing here in the bedroom. I follow the ringing and see her phone sitting on the dresser. Dammit! I hurry back down the stairs. Where would she go? If he saw her, she must be out in public. She never goes anywhere but the store and the park. The park. That's gotta be it. The park she goes to is surrounded by trees and bushes, the perfect place for him to hide.

My heart's thundering in my chest as I run back out to the car and peel out of the driveway. The park is only a couple miles from the house. I get there and see Rachel sitting on a bench, holding Garret. There are some children behind her, kicking a ball around. Thank God they're there or I'm sure that man would've shot her by now.

I scan the perimeter of the park, looking for any movement in the bushes or trees. My eyes dart to the right when I see a flash of red. I look again and see another flash of red through the bushes. That's him. I get out of the car, my gun hidden in my coat, and walk quickly down the sidewalk. Rachel and the other mothers are off in the distance. I parked by the tennis courts, which are several hundred feet from the playground.

I take my gun out as I approach the area where I saw him, but now I can't find him. I scan left and right, and when I look forward again, I see him. He's right in front of me, wearing a red jacket, crouched down behind the bushes and facing the playground. There's a rifle in his hand. If he shot it from here, he likely wouldn't hit Rachel. He's too far away, unless he has perfect aim. But he could easily hit one of the other mothers, who are standing closer to us.

I lift up my gun, aiming it at the center of his back. I secure my other hand around the base of the gun, and without hesitation, I depress the trigger. The silencer hides the noise. He collapses forward. I shoot him again. And then once more.

He's dead. And I feel nothing. No remorse. Not even anger. Either I'm too shocked to feel anything, or my dark side has taken over and I'm someone else right now.

My eyes are fixed on the now lifeless body lying on the ground. That man tried to kill Rachel. All because of a mix-up. Because Royce fucked up his assignment. But how did this man get my name? How did he know where I live?

I go back to the car and press nine on my Dunamis phone and wait. Nine is the autodial for clean-ups. A man answers and I give him the address.

Within minutes, people will be here to take the body and get rid of any evidence, including the man's car. I don't know who the clean-up people are, but they're very good at their job. They almost never leave evidence behind. And in the rare cases when they do leave evidence behind, we get rid of it before the police can do anything with it.

I take out my personal phone and call Royce. He's on his way to New York so he's probably in the back of a limo right now.

"What the fuck did you do?" I ask him when he answers.

He softly laughs. "I haven't the slightest idea what you're talking about."

"You gave him my name. You told him I was you."

"It's for your own good. You were getting too complacent. Letting your guard down."

"Are you insane? If I'd arrived here a minute later, he would've killed her!"

"Killed who? What are you talking about?"

"He came after Rachel! He almost killed her and Garret."

"Oh." He pauses. "I thought he'd come after you. Not her."

"You wanted him to kill me?"

"No. Of course not. I wanted *you* to kill *him*, which I knew you would. You have the best aim out of anyone. Remember when we used to go to the shooting range and—"

"Royce! Listen to me. Despite what you think, today was not a game or a test or an assessment of my shooting skills. This is real life, and my wife and child were almost killed."

"That was not my intention. I didn't know he'd come after her. I told you, I thought he'd come after *you*."

"And we're supposed to be friends?" I let out a harsh laugh.

"It's a thin line between friends and enemies." His tone becomes darker and his voice deepens. "And as for the little incident today, it was a warning. You stay the fuck out of my business, or I promise you, I will get in yours. Keep your mouth shut about Sophia. And if you tell anyone about my bastard child, I will kill her mother. Do we have an agreement?"

"Yes," I say, gritting my teeth.

"Good."

"I don't know what's going on with you, Royce, but you've changed, and we can no longer be friends. I need you to stay away from me and stay away from my family."

He chuckles. "Pearce, don't be so overdramatic. You and I will always be friends, just like our fathers are friends. The Kensingtons and Sinclairs have been friends forever. That will never change."

"Goodbye, Royce." I end the call, then get out of the car and go around to the trunk. I hide my gun back in its compartment. Out of the corner of my eye, I see a white work van driving by. It's the clean-up crew, coming to take the body.

I shut the trunk and walk past the tennis courts, across the grassy field to the bench where Rachel is sitting, holding Garret.

"Pearce." She smiles and gets up as I approach. "What are you doing here?"

"I thought I'd take you and Garret out for an early lunch. I checked at home and you weren't there, so I assumed you were here." I smile as if nothing happened. I didn't just shoot a man. That was someone else. The other Pearce. Now I'm back to being the real me. A husband. A father. The man with the normal life.

"We'd love to have lunch with you." She hands me the baby.

I hold him tightly with one arm and pull Rachel against me with the other. He almost killed her. He could've killed Garret. He could've killed my whole family.

"I love you," I whisper to her.

She smiles at me, completely unaware of what almost happened. "I love you too."

"Let's go." I walk her to her car and put Garret in his car seat and tell her to meet me at home. Then we go out for lunch and I take her back to the house.

Before I return to work, I say to Rachel, "Don't go to that park again."

"Why not? I love that park."

"The news reported that there have been several assaults there. It's too dangerous. I don't want you going there."

"I haven't heard about any assaults. Our neighbors take their kids there. They wouldn't do that if it were dangerous."

"Rachel, please. Just don't go there. We have a large back yard. You don't need to go to the park. If you'd like, I'll put up a swing set for Garret or a sandbox. Whatever you want."

"Pearce, I think you're overreacting. I only go there during the day when other moms are around.

"I'm not arguing about this. You're not going there until I know it's safe." I kiss her. "I'll see you tonight. I love you."

When I'm back at work, I go straight to Jack's office and tell him what happened.

"I told you Royce was fucked in the head," Jack says. "And this is the guy they pick for our future president."

"Do you think he'll do it again?"

He shakes his head. "No. As long as you keep his secrets, he'll shut up. Just the fact that he did this to you shows that he fears you. He's worried you'll tell his secrets, so he tried to scare you into keeping quiet. And it sounds like it worked."

"I have no desire to tell his secrets. Or to be friends with him. I'm going to stay away from him." I see the image in my head of that man with the gun pointed at Rachel and I finally feel some emotion. Rage. Pure rage. At that man, and at Royce. "Jack, I hate to leave again, but I don't think I can stay here after what happened. I can't focus on work."

"I understand. Go ahead. I'll see you tomorrow."

I leave, but when I get home, I can't relax. How could I? My family was within seconds of being killed.

Just when I think my life is on the verge of being normal, it veers back to the hell that is my reality.

CHAPTER EIGHT

RACHEL

This whole last week, Pearce has been tense and stressed. I think it's because his father is coming to our house tonight. He's probably worried that Holton will criticize the house and where we live, and then the two of them will start fighting.

Last Sunday when we were at Holton and Eleanor's house for dinner, Pearce was okay at first, but by the end of the night he seemed on edge. I'm assuming his father said something when I wasn't around that upset him.

Pearce has also been tense because he's suddenly extremely worried about the crime in our town, which I don't think even exists. I've asked the neighbors and nobody has heard news of any assaults or break-ins in the area. Pearce is always very protective of Garret and me, but this past week he's been almost overprotective. He doesn't want me even leaving the house unless he's with me. He acted this way back when we were dating, but that's only because I lived in a dangerous neighborhood. Now we live in a small town that is very safe, so he has no reason to worry.

The phone rings as I'm frosting my cake. I made a carrot cake for dessert tonight. For dinner I'm making a roast, mashed potatoes, and glazed carrots. I'm sure Holton will hate it, but it's impossible to please that man so I just made something Pearce and I like that wasn't too much work.

"Hello?"

"Rachel, it's Shelby. Are you busy?" She sounds out of breath.

"Kind of. I'm getting ready for dinner. Pearce's parents are coming over. Is something wrong?"

"Yeah. I need a ride."

"Did your car break down?"

"No. I um…I was out with this guy and we weren't getting along so he stopped his car and left me on the sidewalk with no way to get home."

"Are you serious? That's horrible." I wipe my hands on a dish towel.

"And now it's getting dark and I don't know what to do. There's nothing around here but houses. I was lucky to find a gas station so I could call you." Shelby doesn't have a cell phone so she must be calling from a pay phone.

"I'll come get you. Where are you?"

"Stamford. It's a long drive for you. Are you sure you don't mind?"

"Of course not. Just give me the address."

I write it down as she tells me, then I hang up and call Pearce.

"Rachel, are you okay?" He's asked me this every time I've called him this week. I don't know why he's so worried about me.

"Yes, I'm fine. Shelby just called and I have to go pick her up. If you get home before me, just leave the roast in the oven. I'll finish making dinner when I get back."

"Why are you picking up Shelby?"

"She was on a date and got in an argument with the guy and he left her on the side of the street. Can you believe that?"

"Since when is she dating?"

"I didn't ask. I'll ask when I see her."

"Where is she?"

"In Stamford."

"Where in Stamford?"

I tell Pearce the address.

"Let me get her," he says abruptly.

"You're at work. It's only four. I have time to get her."

"Rachel, just let me do it. I can leave right now."

"Pearce, you're acting strange again. What's going on with you this week?"

"Nothing. It's just a long ways for you to drive and you'll have to take Garret and pack up all his things."

"It's not that far, and Garret and I could use a road trip. We've been cooped up in the house all week. I'll be home soon. Love you! Bye."

It takes about forty minutes to get to the address Shelby gave me for the gas station. The way Pearce reacted when I told him the address, I thought it might be in a bad part of town, but instead it's in a very exclusive area surrounded by gated mansions. The gas station is just outside the neighborhood, and right behind it I can see tall iron gates covered in greenery.

The gas station looks brand new, and as I drive up, Shelby comes out. She's really dressed up, in a black wool coat, black skirt, beige blouse, and black high heels. I've never seen her wear clothes like that. I didn't even know she owned clothes that nice. Her date must've been planning to take her to a fancy restaurant.

She gets in the front seat. "Thanks. I owe you one. I'll babysit whenever you want." She looks back at Garret and smiles. "He gets cuter every time I see him."

I pull out of the gas station and head to New Haven. "So what happened?" I glance over at her. Her coat is open and I notice two buttons missing from her blouse. "Oh my God, did he force himself on you?"

She looks down at her blouse. "No. I just lost one on the way here and the other one must've already been missing."

She didn't notice a button missing from her blouse? It's right in front of her bra. You'd think she'd notice that before going on her date.

"Did you just buy that coat? I've never seen you wear it before."

"It's my mom's. She let me borrow it for my date."

It looks like a very expensive coat. I didn't think her mom had money for expensive clothes, but maybe she's had it for a while.

"Who was the guy you were with?" I ask. "Where did you meet him?"

She directs her attention out the side window. "I met him at a bar last night. He seemed like a decent guy, so when he asked me out I said yes. But he turned out to be a jerk."

"Who did you go to the bar with?"

She picks at the polish on her thumbnail. "I don't want to talk about it. I just want to forget about the date and spend the rest of my night on the couch, eating junk food and watching TV."

"What's Logan doing tonight?"

She shrugs. "I don't know. I haven't talked to him in weeks."

"He hasn't called you?"

"He has, but I'm not answering his calls." She gazes out the side window again.

"Did you have a fight?"

"No. In fact the last time I saw him, he made me dinner and gave me a necklace that he knew I really wanted."

"That sounds like a date," I say kiddingly.

But she's not smiling. "It wasn't a date," she says softly. I notice her lip quivering.

"Shelby, what's wrong?"

She faces forward and closes her eyes. I notice a tear going down her cheek. "I just miss him."

"Then go be with with him."

"I can't."

"Why not? You love him, so why do you keep pushing him away?"

She wipes her cheek. "It's complicated."

"All relationships are complicated. Look at Pearce and me. We come from completely different worlds, and yet we made it work."

"It's not the same." She sniffles and takes a tissue from her purse.

"I know it's not the same. I'm just saying that you two can make this work."

"No," she says bluntly. "We can't. So just stop talking about it."

"Shelby, tell me—"

"Rachel, I mean it." There's anger in her voice and her body is tense. "You don't know the whole story, so just stay out of it."

I keep quiet for the rest of the drive. I don't know why she won't tell me her reason for not dating Logan. I know she still loves him, so why does she refuse to be with him?

When we're almost at her apartment, she says, "I'm sorry for yelling at you."

"I just wish you'd tell me what's going on."

"Nothing's going on. Just forget it." She gets her keys from her purse.

I park in front of her building. "Call me tomorrow, okay?"

She nods, then waves toward the back seat. "Bye, Garret."

I check the rearview mirror and see him in his car seat, looking content. He loves riding in the car.

We arrive back at the house just after six. Pearce is in the kitchen, going through the mail. I kiss him quick, then hand him Garret. "You watch him while I finish dinner."

"How was your day, Garret?" Pearce asks in a serious tone. "Did you get much work done?"

I laugh. "If you count lying around and eating all day, work, then yes, he got a lot done."

"Good boy." He kisses his cheek. "So what did Shelby say?"

I take the carrots and potatoes out, which I already prepped. "She wouldn't tell me much about the guy she was with, but I asked her about Logan and she started crying. She said she hasn't talked to him in weeks."

"He stopped calling her?"

"No. She just won't answer the phone. But she said she wants to be with him, so I don't get it. She said it's complicated, whatever that means." I open the oven door to check the roast. "You should talk to Logan. Have lunch with him next week."

"We already have a lunch scheduled for Monday, but I'm not asking him about Shelby. The two of them need to work this out themselves."

I check the clock. "I have to hurry. Can you go up and change Garret?"

"Of course." Pearce comes over and kisses me. "Thank you for making dinner. I'm sure my parents won't appreciate it, but I do."

I kiss him back. "I just hope they like it."

The rest of the hour I race around, trying to get everything ready, including myself, and right at six fifty-nine, the doorbell rings.

Pearce greets them at the door as I'm hurrying down the stairs.

"Hi." I give Eleanor a distant shoulder hug, which is all she'll tolerate. I simply smile at Holton since I know he wouldn't tolerate any type of hug. "Welcome."

They smile and nod. They both look very serious, even more so than normal. Maybe they were arguing on the way over.

"How is our grandson?" Eleanor asks Pearce, who's holding Garret.

Pearce hands him to her. "You can ask him yourself. We've been working on his conversation skills."

"Pearce has long conversations with Garret," I explain. "He tells him all the business news."

"Good," Holton says. "He'll be running the company someday so he needs to be educated in business at any early age."

I bite the inside of my cheek so I don't say what I want to say, which is that my son will pick whatever career he'd like. He's not going to be forced to run Kensington Chemical. I'm so glad Pearce isn't working there anymore. Even if his father wasn't his boss, Pearce still wouldn't like working there. He has no interest in chemical manufacturing.

"Would you like a tour of the house?" I ask Holton since he's never been here.

"No. I don't need one." He coughs and then keeps coughing.

"Would you like some water?" I ask him.

"Scotch and water."

"I'll get it," Pearce says. "Mother, would you like the same?"

"Yes. Thank you."

I'm not used to this drinks-before-dinner ritual, but Pearce's family does it every night. And then they always have wine with dinner. If I drank that much, I'd be drunk.

While they have their drinks in the living room, I put Garret to bed. We have dinner at seven-thirty. Both Holton and Eleanor are quiet during dinner and I'm worried they don't like the food.

"How is everything?" I ask.

"It's delicious," Pearce answers, even though I wasn't really asking him.

His parents say nothing, but they're eating their meal so it can't be that bad.

When they're done, I say, "Would everyone like dessert? I made carrot cake."

Eleanor dabs her napkin over her lips. "Before we have dessert, we have some news to share."

Holton sits back and folds his arms over his chest. He's sitting next to Eleanor and across from Pearce. His eyes are on Pearce.

I'm getting a bad feeling about this.

"What is it, Mother?" Pearce asks.

"Would you like to tell them?" she asks Holton. "Or should I?"

"I don't want to tell them at all. You're the one insisting on sharing our personal lives with them."

"Pearce is our son. This is something he should know."

Holton says nothing. He seems annoyed.

Eleanor continues. "Your father saw his physician earlier this week and some tests were run."

"What kind of tests?" Pearce asks her.

"Tests on his lungs. He's had issues with coughing recently and was coughing up blood."

"Eleanor!" Holton says. "Not at the dinner table."

"I am only trying to explain what led you to go to the doctor."

"I have cancer," he blurts out.

The room goes silent. Pearce and I are staring at Holton. He looks so healthy and fit on the outside. I can't believe he has cancer.

Pearce sits up straighter. "Father, I'm very sorry to hear that. What kind of cancer?"

"Lung cancer. And that's all you need to know."

Eleanor looks at Pearce. "Your father will be starting treatments next week. He will be taking a leave of absence from work, which means that we need you to take over at the office while he's gone."

Pearce's shoulders slump in disappointment. I feel the same way. But I know Pearce will agree to it. Holton is awful to him, but Pearce is a good son.

"Of course," Pearce says. "I'll tell Jack first thing tomorrow."

"How long is the treatment?" I ask.

"Ten weeks," Eleanor says. "After that, they'll run more tests and go from there."

"Stop giving them details," Holton says. "It's none of their business."

"Well." Eleanor smiles at me. "Perhaps it's time for dessert."

"Um, yes, okay." I get up and start clearing the plates. I guess the discussion is over.

Pearce helps me clear the table, and as he follows me into the kitchen, I hear his father say, "She has him doing kitchen work? A Kensington should NOT be touching dirty dishes. Why don't they have a maid?"

"Rachel, come on." Pearce goes past me and I realize I stopped walking when I heard Holton's remarks.

"I'm sorry about your father," I tell Pearce as we set the dishes in the sink.

He nods. "Yes, that was very surprising."

"I hope he'll be okay."

"He'll be fine. He has excellent doctors."

"How do you feel about going back to the company?" I whisper, so his parents won't hear.

Pearce sighs. "It won't be temporary. If I go back, I'll be going back for good."

"You can't go back and work for Jack?"

"No, my father won't allow it. I've worked for Jack long enough. It looks bad for a Kensington to be working for someone else instead of the family business."

"So you knew you'd go back there someday? Why didn't you tell me that?"

"I assumed you knew. I'm their only son. They have no one to take over when my father retires." He picks up two of the dessert plates I have sitting on the counter. I plated the cake before dinner. "Let's go or they'll wonder what's taking us so long."

During dessert, Holton talks to Pearce about work, and it becomes just like last week's dinner, where Eleanor and I just sit there and listen. Afterward, I invite them to stay and talk in the living room, but they decide to leave. Holton probably isn't feeling well. Even though I don't like him, I do feel bad for him.

I also feel bad for Pearce. Going back to Kensington Chemical. The stress. The long hours. The weekends. I was getting used to seeing him all the time. But I guess that's over now.

CHAPTER NINE

PEARCE

My father has cancer. I was so shocked when my mother told us the news that I wasn't sure how to respond. I kept imagining Shelby's father; all bones and barely able to speak. Then I remembered that my father will be treated at the Clinic so will be getting the very best medical care. I wanted to ask my mother more about my father's treatments, but I couldn't with Rachel there. She can't know about the Clinic.

So the next day, when Rachel's upstairs with Garret, I call my mother.

"Pearce, I was just heading out. What do you need?"

"I wanted to know more about Father's treatments. Which clinic is he going to?"

"His treatments will be done at the hospital, not the Clinic."

"Why? The Clinic is far superior than any hospital."

"Not when it comes to cancer. The Clinic's treatments thus far have been unsuccessful, so your father will be going to the hospital, but his doctor from the Clinic will remain involved in his care." I hear a door open. "I need to go. Goodbye, Pearce. Oh, and tell your wife that the dinner she prepared was very good. I don't believe I told her that."

"I'll tell her. Goodbye, Mother."

My mother is making a real effort to accept Rachel. I never thought she would. But when Garret was born, she realized she wouldn't see her grandson if she continued to treat his mother poorly.

I'm at home, sitting in my office. I need to call Jack. I dread telling him the news. He knew eventually I'd have to quit, but both of us were hoping it wouldn't be for a while.

"Jack, it's Pearce," I say when he answers.

"I already heard," he says. "Holton has cancer and you're going back to the company."

"Where did you hear that?"

"Through the Dunamis grapevine. Word travels fast."

"He wants me to start back there on Monday."

"I assumed he would. So back to a hundred-hour work week? Rachel's not going to like that."

"I'm not going back to that schedule. If my father disagrees, he can fire me again."

"Pearce, it's not just your father making you go back. This came from the top. The higher level members are concerned your father won't make it, and they need you ready to step in and take his place."

"Why would they think my father won't make it?"

"Lung cancer has a low survival rate. Didn't you discuss this with him?"

"He wouldn't tell us anything. But my mother told me the Clinic couldn't help."

"They could, but their treatments are no better than what he'd get at a hospital. I'm sure your father will be fine. He's a tough bastard."

"I don't know if he's tough enough to beat cancer." I hear someone yelling for Jack, probably his wife. "I'll let you go. Tell Martha I said hello."

"I will. And don't worry about cleaning out your office. I'll have everything packed up and sent to you."

"Thank you, Jack. I'll miss working with you."

"Damn straight, you will." He laughs. "Goodbye, Pearce."

On Monday morning, I return to my old office at Kensington Chemical. It sat there empty while I was gone, waiting for my return. I didn't want to get up this morning, knowing I had to come here. I'm trying to be positive, but it's difficult because I have such bad memories of this place.

"Welcome back, Mr. Kensington!" a man says as he passes by my office door. I have no idea who he is. I've never seen him before.

"Good morning, Mr. Kensington." A young blond woman walks into my office. "I'm Candace. Your new secretary."

I didn't have my own secretary before, but apparently I do now.

"Would you like some coffee?" she asks.

"Yes. Thank you."

She takes off and another person comes into my office. A man who is probably in his forties. "Mr. Kensington. I'm Lou Armin. Your new head of marketing. I just wanted to introduce myself."

I shake his hand. "Nice to meet you."

Everyone is being overly friendly today. But I won't get any work done if they keep stopping by. I go to close my door and notice a nameplate on the wall next to it that reads, *Pearce Kensington, Interim CEO.*

So that's why everyone's being so nice. They're sucking up to the boss. Last time I was here, I wasn't even allowed to make a decision and now I'm the CEO.

People continue to come by my office all morning and I get nothing done. At eleven, I go to meet Logan for lunch. He's already at the restaurant when I arrive.

We greet each other and give our order to the waiter. I don't have much time and neither does Logan.

"So how's the baby?" he asks.

"Getting bigger every day." I take a sip of water. "How's work going?"

"Good. I went to a conference last week. Some of the doctors I trained with in Europe were there."

"What was the conference about?

"New innovations in cancer treatment. I won't bore you with the science, but basically, the newest treatments are going to focus on turning off the genes that cause cancer so they won't continue to multiply."

"When will this treatment be available?"

"Probably in twenty years." He shakes his head. "It's ridiculous how long it takes for these treatments to be approved, at least here in the States. There are so many regulatory hoops to go through. Research. Clinical trials. But human trials are already being done in Europe, and so far, the results looks very promising."

"I was asking because I just learned that my father has lung cancer."

"Oh. I'm sorry to hear that."

"He begins treatment next week. He's taking a leave of absence from work so I'm now the interim CEO at Kensington Chemical. I don't know when he'll be back at the office. It depends on how his treatment goes. I've heard lung cancer doesn't have a high survival rate. Is that true?"

"It depends on when it's detected. If you'd like, I could contact your father's physician and look over his treatment plan, just as a second opinion. I could also suggest some clinical trials your father could be part of that would give him access to the latest treatments."

"Are there any that offer this new treatment involving genetics?"

"Not here in the States. He'd have to go to Europe."

"What if he was willing to try the treatment without being part of a clinical trial?"

"It's not allowed. If the physician dispensing the treatment got caught, he or she could go to jail and would likely never practice medicine again."

"That seems rather extreme. If the patient is willing to try it, he should be able to."

Logan sighs. "Don't get me started, Pearce. You know how I feel about the constraints on health care in this country. I could go on all day."

I smile. "Yes. I know it frustrates you."

"Well, anyway, if you need any assistance with your father's care, just let me know. I wish I could've done more for Shelby's father, but he was too far gone by the time I met him." He pauses. "Has Rachel talked to Shelby recently?"

"Yes. Rachel had to pick her up last—" I stop because I didn't mean to say that. Now he'll ask me about it and I'll have to make something up. Shelby said she was on date, but I know she wasn't. I knew as soon as Rachel told me the address. That gas station is next to a very exclusive neighborhood where one of the members lives. I'm guessing his wife came home when he wasn't expecting her and he had to kick Shelby out.

"Did Shelby's car break down?" Logan looks concerned. He still cares about Shelby, even though she's made it clear they can't be together.

"No. She just…she had a date that didn't end well." I decide to tell him Shelby's made-up story. If he thinks she's dating again, maybe he'll stop pursuing her.

"What do you mean it didn't end well?" Now he sounds angry.

"I don't know all the details. They argued and he left her on the sidewalk and took off."

He sighs and looks down at the table. "She should have called me. She knows I would have picked her up."

"I thought you two are no longer speaking."

"That's just Shelby being Shelby. She does this all the time. She talks to me and then she doesn't. The woman drives me insane."

"Logan, I think it's time to let her go. She is obviously not ready for a serious relationship. Maybe you should start dating other people."

"I would if I wasn't still in love with her. I can't go on a date with another woman while I'm still in love with Shelby. It wouldn't be right. I'd be thinking about Shelby the entire time. So has she been dating much?"

"I'm not sure." I should lie and say she is, just so he'll move on.

"I still have the engagement ring," he says, taking a piece of bread from the basket. "I keep hoping she'll change her mind."

Our lunch arrives and I steer the conversation back to his job to get his mind off Shelby. Logan has nothing else in his life right now except work, and it reminds me of how I used to be before meeting Rachel. I was miserable. At least Logan likes his job, but I know his life would be better if he were able to be with Shelby.

As we're waiting for the check, an idea pops in my head. I don't know why I didn't think of it before. Probably because it wouldn't work. But maybe it would, now that my father is sick and needs better medical treatment than the Clinic physicians or a hospital can currently offer. And this could benefit all the members, not just my father.

"Logan, if you could treat your patients using whatever method you thought was best, even if those treatments were not yet approved, and not face jail time for doing so, would you do it?"

He laughs. "Well, obviously, yes. That would be my dream job. Unfortunately, this is real life. Why do you ask?"

"I was just wondering." The check arrives and I set some cash out. "It's on me today."

"Thank you, Pearce."

"Would you like to meet again next week?"

"I need to check my schedule, but let's plan on it for now."

"Very well. I need to get back to the office. I'll see you next week." I leave and drive to my parents' house. I'm not sure if my father will be home. My mother didn't specify what day his treatments start.

I'm greeted at the door by the maid.

"Is my father home?" I ask her.

"Yes. But he's resting. He's in his room."

My father never rests. He barely even sleeps. So if he's resting, it means he's really not feeling well. I don't like the way my father treats me, but I don't want him to suffer, or die. He's still my father and I do care about him.

"Father." I enter his room. He's lying in bed in his pajamas and robe, but he's awake.

"Pearce." He quickly sits up, then starts coughing. "What are you doing here?"

"I wanted to talk to you about something."

"I told you to call before coming over," he scolds.

"I didn't have time. This can't wait."

I sit in the chair by his bed and tell him about the new cancer treatment Logan told me about.

"So what do you think?" I ask. "Is this something you'd like to try?"

"I need to see the research before I decide. And I would like to talk to Logan's colleagues in Europe who have actually tried this treatment on their patients. I would hope his colleagues are older than him. I'm not taking medical advice from some 30-year-old kid."

"Logan is young, but very intelligent. But yes, I'm sure he could put you in touch with the physicians involved in the research. But he'd be the one administering the treatments."

"He could go to jail for that. And lose his medical license. Why would he take the risk?"

"He wouldn't, unless he had the organization's protection from the law."

I tell my father the idea I had when I was at the restaurant, which is that I want to invite Logan to work for the Clinic. The physicians who work there are not members, but they are given limited knowledge of Dunamis. They have to sign a contract before they receive that knowledge. The contract basically says they'll be harmed if they ever tell our secrets, and yet we still find plenty of people to take these jobs, and not one physician has ever attempted to tell our secrets.

Being a doctor for us has many rewards. Large sums of money. Not having to deal with the hassle of insurance. And the freedom to treat your patients using whatever means necessary to keep them alive and well, even if those treatments aren't approved. Our doctors can even work with the lab at Sinclair

Pharmaceuticals, the company owned by Royce's family, to develop their own drugs.

"Logan would be an excellent addition to the Clinic," I say. "He has many innovative ideas and treatments that would benefit the other members."

"And what are you getting out of this?"

"I'm helping you."

He huffs. "You have no interest in helping me. You hate me."

"That's not true, Father. I care about you and I want you to get better."

"It's more than that. What is it?"

"Logan is my friend. I'm helping him out."

"And?"

My father knows me too well. He knows I'm hiding something. So I tell him.

"If I recruit Logan to work for the Clinic, I want the organization to release one of our associates from her contract."

"What does an associate have to do with this?"

"Logan has been dating Sophia on and off for over a year. He wants to marry her, but she can't agree to it because of her job with Dunamis. Logan, of course, isn't aware that she works for us."

He chuckles. "Sophia. Yes. I know her well."

I cringe, not wanting to think about how many times he's been with her.

He coughs. "Why the hell do you care so much about this man's love life?"

"He will be more committed to his job if he's not pining over this woman. And it works out well because she already knows about us. She'll know not to ask him questions."

"He won't marry her if he knows what she did for us."

"He won't know. None of our physicians are told about the associates."

"If he thinks she's unaware we exist, he'll have to lie to his wife. He may not be willing to do that." He smirks. "Although you seem to have no problem lying to *your* wife."

I ignore his comment. "Logan can tell her he's working for a private clinic, which is what he already does. It's just a different clinic. It's not that big of a lie. And he won't be told all our secrets so there won't be much to lie about. The only thing he'll be told is that we're a private, very exclusive organization that is able to protect him from any repercussions that could come his way by performing these unapproved treatments."

"Many of our physicians know far more about us than that."

"Only because they've worked for us for years. Logan doesn't need to know details."

"You're putting yourself at risk by doing this," he says.

"What's the risk? I'm simply offering them something in exchange for something else."

"I'm not backing you up on this. This is all you."

And yet it benefits him. I should've known he wouldn't support me. But I'm doing it anyway. My father will get access to this new treatment, Logan will find the job at the Clinic fulfilling, and Shelby will be free from her contract, and free to marry Logan.

"I'm going to present this at the meeting on Friday. This needs to be decided quickly so you can start the treatments."

"I haven't even agreed to them yet." He coughs again, this time into a tissue.

"Father, do you need something? Some water? Anything?"

"Stop treating me like a child." He crumples up the tissue and I see a spatter of blood on it. "You should be at the office. Get out of here." He shoos me away.

I leave and go back down the stairs.

"Pearce, what are you doing here?" My mother approaches me from the hall.

"I was telling Father about a new cancer treatment. He can tell you more about it." I lower my voice. "He doesn't look well."

She pats my back. "He'll be fine, dear. Get back to the office."

My parents live in a state of denial when it comes to illness and death. They express zero emotion and just continue on as if nothing's wrong. My grandfather on my mother's side died of stomach cancer, but when he was diagnosed, my mother acted as though he had a cold and would get over it in a week or two. When he died, she didn't shed a tear. I've never seen her, or my father, cry. I don't think they'd cry even if *I* died.

I go back to the office and find a pile of work on my desk. My father probably called his secretary as soon as I left his house and had her gather up all his work and leave it on my desk.

That night, I don't get home until after ten. Rachel is watching TV in the family room.

"I'm sorry I'm late," I say, leaning down to kiss her.

"You missed dinner," she says. "And you didn't even see Garret today."

I sigh. "I know. I'm sorry."

"Pearce, is this how it's going to be now? Are you going to be working every night and on the weekends, like you did before?"

"I hope not, but with my father gone, I *will* have to put in some extra hours."

Her shoulders slump and she nods.

"Rachel." I sit next to her. "You know I don't want to do this. I'm only doing this to help my father."

"I know." She leans her head on my shoulder. "I just don't want it to be at the expense of our son. I don't want him to grow up with his dad never around."

I kiss her head. "That won't happen. I'll always be here for both of you."

But as the week continues, I begin to doubt that statement. I'm swamped with work and I can't keep up. I get home at ten every night. Rachel doesn't say anything, but I know she's upset.

On Friday, I go to the Dunamis meeting which is scheduled from ten to one. It's an update meeting, but they reserve an hour at the end for members to bring up topics to be discussed. It's noon, and they just asked if anyone would like to speak

"I would," I say, getting up from my chair.

"What is the topic?" Martin, the man leading the meeting, asks.

"I would like to recruit someone to the Clinic. A man who attended Harvard when I was there. Dr. Logan Cunningham."

"Proceed to the microphone," Martin says.

I walk to the front of the room. My father is there, sitting in the first row. Leland Seymour is a few seats down from him. He's giving me a smug grin, like he knows something he shouldn't.

I glance away from Leland and direct my attention to the other members. "We have been saying for months that we need to add more physicians at the Clinic." I continue, explaining Logan's background and the research he did when he was in Europe. I mention the cancer treatment, but don't specifically mention it benefitting my father because I know he'd be angry if I brought up the topic of his health in a meeting.

But then someone else brings it up. It's Edward Milcrest, who is known for questioning everything. "Who else would benefit from this, besides Holton?"

"We would all benefit. As I said earlier, Logan has connections with top physicians and researchers all across Europe. He has access to treatments we can't get through the normal channels here in the US."

"Do you think he would agree to this?" another member asks.

"I'm confident I could convince Dr. Cunningham to work for us, but I would like to request something in return." I'm nervous to bring this up, but I have to. This is my one and only chance to save Shelby. "I request that you release one of our associates from her contract. Dr. Cunningham has been seeing her for over a year and would like to marry her. But she has declined his proposal because of her obligation to us. Despite that, he continues to pursue her. It is my personal opinion that he would be much more committed to his work if he were in a stable and permanent relationship with her."

There's silence, followed by chattering from the crowd.

Leland stands up and faces the members. "Quiet!" When he has their attention, he turns to me and says, "Which associate?"

"Sophia," I say.

His grin appears again as he turns back to the other members. "Does everyone know Sophia? The feisty blonde?"

The men nod, some whispering to each other.

"Her real name is Shelby," Leland says. "At least that's what Pearce's wife said when she introduced me to Shelby."

Shit. I forgot he saw them together.

Leland looks back at me and smiles. "Perhaps Pearce is only suggesting this because he's embarrassed that his wife's best friend is a whore. Or perhaps it's because he wants Shelby all for himself. I do believe you took her reservation card at one of our banquets. Isn't that right, Pearce?"

I take a deep breath, trying to remain calm. "This is not a personal matter. This is for the greater good of the organization. I am offering to recruit someone who is highly intelligent and extremely talented who will bring new and innovative treatments to the Clinic. Will doing so benefit my father? Yes. In the short term. But in the long term it will benefit all of you." I pause and wait for someone to respond. There's silence, so I say, "I take that to mean you are not interested. Thank you for your time."

As I walk back to my seat, I hear my father's voice on the microphone. "I have investigated the treatments Pearce was referring to and found them to be quite intriguing. I am not solely referring to the cancer treatments, but other treatments as well. I think the research should be presented before we come to a decision."

Martin appears beside him. "Let's take an informal vote. Raise your hand if you're interested in considering Dr. Cunningham for a position at the Clinic."

More than three quarters of the room raises their hands. It's only because of my father. They wouldn't listen to me, but they'll listen to him. I'm shocked that he stood up there defending me, but then realize it's not about me. He's trying to save himself. He thinks he's dying and he's grasping for a lifeline. And I offered him one. Now he just needs to convince the others to go along with it.

"Pearce," a man behind me says.

"Yes?" I turn and see Spencer Turnbaum addressing me from the back row. He's a banker and a brilliant businessman. He's a few years older than my father.

"You said that Dr. Cunningham already works at a private clinic?" he asks.

"That's correct."

Spencer directs his attention to the room. "I propose we buy the clinic he works at, but only Dr. Cunningham will know about us."

"Why would we buy it?" someone asks.

"We need more locations," Spencer says. "And this would protect the identity of our members. If someone were to discover that we all go to just a handful of medical clinics, they could put the pieces together and see that we're all connected. That would then lead to an investigation about us, as well as the Clinic itself and the treatments offered. It would be far less risky for us to own private clinics that cater to the wealthy, rather than just us specifically."

"That is an excellent idea that warrants further discussion," Martin says. "I suggest we continue with this topic for the time left remaining. Any objections?"

I watch to see if Leland will raise his hand to object, but he doesn't. I don't know why Leland is always against me. I know I was rather harsh with Katherine the last time I saw her, but I had to be. She almost spilled our secrets to Rachel. And I needed to put an end to Katherine's delusions that she and I could someday be together.

For the rest of the hour, the members discuss the pros and cons of buying the clinic Logan currently works at. Dunamis wouldn't be the one actually buying it. Instead, it would be bought by one of our members who is in the healthcare business and already owns several medical facilities. Dunamis would fund the purchase, but not be linked back to it.

Following that discussion, my father spends a few minutes explaining the research he referred to earlier. By the time the meeting ends, the members decide to make an offer to Logan. Actually, I will be the one making the offer.

"If he accepts our offer," Martin says to me, "you will be his handler."

A handler is someone who keeps watch on the people who work for us. Usually, the older members act as handlers, but since I suggested Logan, it makes sense that I would be his handler, which means that if he screws up, he and I will both be punished.

"That's fine," I say, agreeing to it.

"What about the whore?" someone in the back of the room asks.

Martin nods. "Yes, what do people think about Pearce's request to release the associate?"

I use my body language training to hide all emotion; keeping my face blank, my body relaxed. If the members think this is going to benefit me in any way, they won't allow it. I'm still a "problem" and I will be given no favors.

"I vote no." I hear the voice and know it's Royce without even looking. "As a member, it's Pearce's duty to recruit this man without asking for anything in return. In addition, his request is something we have never done. Before we can even entertain the idea, we need to bring it to the higher level members."

I'm not surprised Royce is going against me. He's angry with me because I've been avoiding him ever since he forced that assignment on me. He thinks we should remain friends, even though his little stunt almost killed my family.

"What do the rest of you think?" Martin asks.

I hear Jack's voice behind me. "If Dr. Cunningham is as enamored with the girl as Pearce says he is, then I say we release her. We all know how a woman can get in your head and disrupt your focus on work. We've agreed that we want to hire this man and I don't want some stupid associate standing in the way of that, or interfering with this man's performance on the job."

Jack said 'stupid associate' to convince the members that he doesn't care about Shelby. But I know he does. He has all along. Every time I told him how she was being abused by Royce, I could tell Jack wanted to help, but couldn't. But now he is.

"I agree," Martin says. "We'll bring this matter to the higher level members, but for now, who agrees with the decision to release the girl?"

More than half the room raises their hands.

"Then it's settled," Martin says. "I'll inform the higher level members and they will make the final decision. This concludes today's meeting. We will meet again next month."

My father finds me as we're leaving the room. "You need to hurry up and get this done." He holds onto my arm, looking like he might pass out. He doesn't look good. He's pale and his breathing is labored.

"Father, why don't I take you home? I don't think you should be driving."

He lets go of my arm. "I can drive just fine! Now take care of this and tell me when it's done."

I go back to the office and call Logan. "Could you meet me for dinner tonight?"

"I suppose I could. Why?"

"I have an opportunity you might be interested in."

We meet, and he accepts the offer. He doesn't know everything yet, but I told him that we're a secret group and he didn't find it odd. He said the physicians he worked with in Europe have associations with similar groups. I knew such groups existed, but I had no idea Logan knew about them. I guess it really is a small world.

CHAPTER TEN
One Year Later

RACHEL

"I don't know when I'll be home," Pearce says. "Go ahead and eat without me."

I close my eyes and inhale a breath, trying to remain calm. "This is the sixth night in a row you've missed dinner."

"I know. But we'll have dinner together tomorrow. I promise. Sweetheart, I need to go. I have a meeting starting in a couple minutes."

He hangs up and I set the phone on the kitchen counter.

"Mama." I look down and see Garret holding onto my leg, looking up at me.

I pick him up and hug him. "Daddy's going to be late again. It's just you and me for dinner."

He lays his head on my shoulder like he's sad about the news. I know he's not. He's too young to understand, but in a year or so he will, and he'll wonder why his daddy is never around.

This was my biggest fear when Pearce went back to work for Kensington Chemical. He stayed late on his first day back and has continued to work late ever since. He's there on the weekends too. It's just like when we were dating, but at least then he'd get home in time to have a late dinner or snuggle with me on the couch and watch some TV before bed. Now he doesn't even do that. The past few months, he's been getting home at eleven or midnight and then he's gone by six the next morning.

His father is partly to blame. Holton recovered from cancer and went back to work four months ago, but only part-time. A couple months later he resumed his regular hours and took over as CEO again, and since then he's been making Pearce work nonstop.

Pearce could refuse to work all those hours but he hasn't, and I think it's because he actually likes what he's doing now. During his father's absence, Pearce was able to make decisions and make things happen. He liked the feeling of accomplishment and wanted to keep it going. He's a very competitive, goal-oriented person, which I love about him, but he's taken it to the extreme. His life has no balance. It's all work and nothing else.

This can't continue. It's bad for our marriage, but it's also bad for Garret. He needs his father. And Pearce is missing all of Garret's milestones. He missed seeing Garret take his first steps and wasn't around when he said his first word.

"Bah!" Garret points to the family room where his mini basketball is sitting on the floor.

Pearce bought that ball for Garret when he was just an infant. When I saw it, I imagined Pearce playing with Garret, showing him how to roll the ball and toss it and bounce it. But instead, I'm the one who's done that because Pearce isn't here.

I bring Garret to the family room and set him on the floor. He's in his little jeans and white t-shirt. He's so adorable I could kiss and hug him all day, so I do. He gets lots of hugs and kisses.

I roll the ball to Garret and it hits his leg. He laughs and bats at the ball, rolling it toward me.

"Good job!" I roll it back to him as the phone rings. "I'll be right back." I run to the kitchen and grab the phone, taking it back to the family room. "Hello?" I roll the ball to Garret again.

"Rachel, it's Shelby. Guess what I'm craving now?"

Shelby is four months pregnant. She and Logan got married last spring. They started dating again last November and by December they were engaged. I was shocked when she accepted his proposal. She was so adamant about staying single forever, and then all of a sudden, she agreed to marry him. I'm glad she did. Logan is so good to her. And he's so excited about the baby. They both are.

I laugh. "I don't know. I'm going to guess pickles mixed with mac and cheese?"

"No, but close. Pickles spread with peanut butter."

"Shelby, that's disgusting."

"I know, right? I mean, it sounds disgusting but I tried it and it was sooo good."

"What does Logan think of this? Maybe he should be running tests on you. Maybe you have some kind of nutritional deficiency."

"He said it's normal to crave weird combinations of foods, although he was grossed out by the pickles and peanut butter."

Garret crawls over to me, annoyed that I haven't pushed the ball back to him. "Mama!"

"Yes, honey, just a minute."

"Is that Garret?"

"Yes. He wants me to play ball with him." I'm sitting on the floor and he climbs on me and hugs me.

"He is so cute," Shelby says. "I love how he gives everyone hugs."

"I know. He's a hugger, just like his mom."

He lets me go and crawls over to get his ball, then bats it toward me, making noises as he does.

"I can't believe how much he looks like Pearce," Shelby says.

"Yeah, he looks more and more like him every day."

"Is Pearce there? Logan wanted to ask him something."

"No. He's still at work."

"What time will he be home? Or should I just have Logan call him at the office?"

"Tell him to call the office. Pearce won't be home until…" My voice trails off as I watch Garret rolling his basketball back and forth as he says 'dada' over and over. He misses his dad.

Tears fall down my cheeks as I'm suddenly hit with an overwhelming sadness.

"Rachel, are you still there?"

I nod. "Yes."

She hears my shaky breaths. "Rachel, what's wrong?"

"Everything," I say, sniffling.

"What do you mean?"

"I don't know...I just...I feel like I'm losing Pearce. And I don't know what to do about it." I wipe my tears, but more keep falling. "He works constantly. I never see him. He never sees Garret. This has been going on for months. I can't keep doing this, Shelby."

"I didn't know it was that bad. Have you talked to him?"

"Yes, and he keeps saying he'll be home more, but then nothing changes. He's always at work."

"I'm sorry, Rachel. I don't know what to tell you." I hear someone talking in the background. "Logan just got home. He brought dinner. Can I call you back later?"

"Let's just talk tomorrow. I have to feed Garret and get him to bed."

"Okay. I'm really sorry, Rachel. Maybe you should try talking to him again."

"I will. Bye."

We hang up and I set the phone aside. I shut my eyes, tears pouring down my cheeks.

I feel tiny legs crawling on me as tiny arms go around my waist. "Mama."

I open my eyes and see Garret hugging me, his eyes sad, a frown on his face. He doesn't like seeing me cry. And seeing him showing so much compassion at such a young age makes me cry even more. He's so small, yet he has such a big heart.

"I love you, sweetie." I pick him up and hug him and kiss his head. I wipe my face, trying to pull myself together. Then I stand up, still holding him. "Mommy's going to make us some dinner, okay?"

For dinner we have grilled cheese sandwiches and fruit. I cut Garret's sandwich into mini dinosaur shapes and tell him about dinosaurs as we eat. He may not understand, but I tell him anyway. We have milk and cookies for dessert and then I read him some stories. At eight, I put him to bed.

Then I watch TV, by myself, like I do every night. Pearce will get home after I'm asleep, and he'll be gone when I wake up. It'll be like he wasn't even here.

I fall asleep on the couch with the TV still on.

"Rachel." I wake up and see Pearce sitting next to me. The room is dark, but from the glow of the TV, I can see him there in his suit. His tie hangs loose around his neck and the top two buttons of his shirt are undone. His head looks heavy and tired.

"Sweetheart, let's go to bed." He rubs my arm, which is the most he's touched me all week.

"What time is it?"

"It's one-thirty. I got caught up in some things at the office and ended up being there later than I'd planned."

That's always his excuse. He's always getting 'caught up' in things at the office. I don't even know what the hell that means.

"Just go." I turn my back to him and pull the blanket over me. It's the cashmere blanket Pearce bought me in Italy. That trip seems so long ago and yet it's only been a few years. "I'll sleep here."

"You're not sleeping here. Come on." He tugs on me but I resist.

"Pearce, just go to bed."

"I want you there with me."

"You'll only be in bed a few hours. What difference does it make if I'm there or not?"

He reaches for the remote and shuts the TV off, then turns on the lamp on the end table. "Rachel, what's going on?"

I don't know how to answer that. I don't even know where to start. Why does he need me to explain this to him? He should already know the answer.

"Are you going to say something?" He sounds angry. How dare he sound angry. He has no right to be mad. He's the one who's never here. "Rachel, I need to get to sleep. I'm exhausted. So if you have something to say, just say it."

I turn back to face him. "You really don't know?"

"Know what?"

I close my eyes, a lump in my throat. "Just forget it."

He sighs. "I'm sorry I'm late. I know I missed dinner but it couldn't be helped. There were issues with one of our clients and I had to schedule an emergency meeting and—"

"Stop." I sit up. "Just stop making excuses. I'm tired of hearing about meetings and clients and all the other people and things that come first in your life. What about your son? Where does he fit in all of this? Are your clients more important than him? You've already missed almost the entire first year of his life, spending it at the office instead of here with your family. And for what? We don't need the money. So why are you doing this?"

"I'm helping out my father. You know that. We've talked about this."

"Yes, but your father is better now. You don't have to keep working all these hours. Jack runs a company that's larger than yours and he works a normal day."

"Jack is in a different industry than us. It's not comparable."

"What are you saying, Pearce? That nothing's going to change?"

He doesn't answer. He just rubs his forehead and then his eyes.

"Pearce, I can't be in a marriage like this. I can't—"

"Rachel, you're tired and so am I. Let's talk about this tomorrow. I promise I'll be home for dinner."

"No." I drop my head, shaking it side to side. "You won't be home for dinner. Something will come up. Then you'll call me and say you'll be late and we'll repeat this scene again tomorrow. I can't keep doing this, Pearce. If this is really how you want to live your life, then go ahead. But you're going to do it alone." My voice cracks as I say it. "I'm not going to watch Garret stand at the door every night, waiting for you to get home, only to be disappointed when you never show up. I'm not going to have you promise to play catch with him and then never do it. Or promise to show up at his baseball games and then not be there. If that's how it's going to be, I'd rather have you not be in his life at all." Tears are now streaming down my face.

Pearce just watches me, not saying anything. Then he slowly stands up and goes upstairs. No discussion. No goodnight. No kiss. No hug. Nothing. I don't know what that means. Is he saying this is over?

I break down, my tears now a full-out sob. I don't know why I said that just now. I don't want a divorce. I don't want to break up our family. I didn't think Pearce did either. I thought when I said those things, he would make a commitment to change. To stop working so much and to spend time with Garret and me. But that didn't happen. I know he loves us, so why is he doing this? Why is he pushing us away?

I cry myself to sleep and wake up to the sounds coming from the baby monitor. Garret is babbling in his crib, which he always does when he wakes up. He hardly ever cries. He wakes up happy and content.

I go upstairs to his room. When he sees me, he smiles and holds his arms out for me. Coming in here every morning is the absolute best way to start my day.

"Good morning." I pick him up and hug him. "How's my big boy today?"

The clock in his room says it's just before seven. I wonder if Pearce already left for work. I didn't hear him go so maybe he's still home. I walk down to our bedroom. He's not there. The bed is made like he didn't even sleep in it. Maybe he slept on top of it instead of under the covers. Or maybe he didn't sleep at all and went back to work after I fell asleep.

"Mama." Garret kisses my cheek.

"Thank you, sweetie." I kiss him back. "Are you hungry? You ready for breakfast?"

We go back to his room and I change his diaper, then we go downstairs for breakfast. And so begins another day as a single parent.

At five-thirty I wait for the call that I know is coming. Every night, between five-thirty and six, Pearce calls to tell me he'll be late. That he won't be here for dinner and isn't sure when he'll be home. I don't even want to answer the phone. Maybe I won't. Maybe I'll just let it ring.

"What should we have for dinner tonight?" I ask Garret. I'm holding him on my hip, standing in the kitchen, looking in the cupboards.

"Would you like spaghetti?" I open the fridge and move stuff around to see what's in there. I spot half a jar of marinara sauce. I have partial containers of everything because I'm always eating alone and can never finish the whole thing. "How about chicken?"

"Dada," I hear Garret say.

"Daddy's not having dinner with us. Daddy's at work." I open the meat drawer. "If we want chicken, we'll have to go to the store."

"Dada," he says again.

I bounce him a little. "I know, sweetie. You want Daddy, but he's not home." I take the marinara sauce out. "Let's just have spaghetti."

"Rachel."

When I hear his voice, I close the fridge door and slowly turn around. Pearce is standing behind me, holding a bouquet of yellow tulips, which is what he used to always bring me when we were dating.

I set the jar of sauce on the counter. "What are you doing here?"

He smiles. "I live here."

"I know, but...why aren't you at work?"

"It's five-thirty. I'm done for the day." He sets the flowers down. "I want to be with my family."

"Dada!" Garret reaches for him.

Pearce takes him from me. "Daddy's right here." He kisses his cheek and Garret lays his head on his shoulder. I almost cry seeing them together. I don't even remember the last time Pearce held him.

"Is this just for tonight?" I ask, not wanting to get my hopes up.

"No," he says, his face very serious. "I, um…I'm sorry, Rachel. I don't know what's been going on with me. I really don't. But it's not going to continue. I miss you." He glances at Garret's head on his shoulder. "And I miss him."

"We miss you too."

Pearce leans down and kisses me. "I love you. And I am very sorry for how I've been treating you. And Garret. I'd like us to talk about it later, after he goes to bed."

I nod.

"For now, let's have some dinner. Would you like to go out?"

"I'd kind of like to stay in." I want Pearce here. At home. I want the three of us together as a family.

"Then we'll order something. Whatever you'd like."

"I'll order it. You play with Garret. He wants to play ball with you."

"Bah!" He points to the mini basketball that's in the family room.

"Daddy's going to change clothes quick." He sets him down and Garret starts crying.

"He thinks you won't come back," I say.

Pearce scoops him up and over his shoulder. "Then I guess you're coming with me."

Garret's crying quickly turns to laughter as his dad takes him up the stairs. When they come back down, Pearce gets on the floor with Garret and tosses the mini basketball around. He plays with Garret differently than I do, in more of a rough-and-tumble way, chasing him and tackling him. And Garret loves it. He needed his dad. I just wish it hadn't taken Pearce this long to figure that out.

CHAPTER ELEVEN

PEARCE

The past few months I've been consumed with work, at the expense of spending time with Rachel and Garret. It started when I took over as interim CEO. I was finally able to take charge and make decisions, and within a month, I was seeing results. We were operating more efficiently, reducing costs, increasing profits, and I'd managed to land a new client. I became addicted to the success and wanted more. I wanted to prove to my father that I could run this company without him and do a better job. But in the process of doing that, I neglected my family.

"He went right to sleep," I say as I come down the stairs. Rachel is sitting on the leather couch in the living room. I just put Garret to bed, which I haven't done in months.

"I think you wore him out," Rachel says.

"He wore *me* out." I sit next to her. "He never stops moving. You must be exhausted after spending the day with him."

"It's my workout." Rachel smiles. "Between all the chasing and the lifting and picking up his toys, I've never been in better shape."

I turn her toward me, my hand on her arm. "I should've been here, taking care of him, giving you a break at night."

She nods. "Yeah, you should have. Not because I need a break, but because he needs you."

"I know he does."

"Then why haven't you been here for him? And why haven't you been here for *me*? For *us*? I need to understand, Pearce, because if I don't, I'll keep thinking this is only temporary."

"It's not temporary." I look her in the eye. "Last night when you said Garret might be better off without me, it was like being punched in the gut. It killed me to hear you say that. But I needed to hear it. It woke me up and made me realize I could lose you. Both of you. It's what I fear the most, and yet it was happening right in front of me and I didn't even notice. I was letting it happen. I was the cause of it, and yet I did nothing to fix it."

I look down at her hand, picking it up and holding it in mine. "I wanted to prove to my father that I could do it. That I could run the company better than he could. That I am not the failure he keeps saying I am. And I did it. I achieved my goal. I did more for that company in six months than he's done in six years. And he knows it, yet he won't acknowledge it." I gaze down at the couch. "He still thinks I'm a failure. He called me that just this morning."

"He's wrong, Pearce. Don't listen to him." She lifts my face up to look at her. "Why would he even say that?"

"One of our biggest clients didn't get a delivery on time. It wasn't my fault. I had nothing to do with it. But since the order was placed when I was interim CEO, my father blames me, saying we should've allowed more time for the delivery. He knows this is not a task for the CEO. Someone at a much lower level handles the orders, but he still called me into his office to reprimand me because he couldn't find anything else to yell at me about. It just proved to me that my father will never be satisfied. I could triple profits every quarter and he still wouldn't be satisfied. He'd still say I could do better."

"So you've spent the past year trying to prove yourself to your father?"

"Yes. And in doing so, I realized that he's not the only reason I spend so much time at work. I realized that if someone isn't there to stop me, I'll keep working to succeed. If I see I'm making progress, I want to keep going. I'm driven by results. I find it addictive. So when my father was absent because of his illness and I was seeing results from my efforts at the company, I couldn't stop. I had to keep going. And when he came back, it became even worse because I was so damn determined to prove myself to him. To show him what I'd done and that I could do even more." I pause. "That's not how I want to live. I don't want to spend the rest of my life trying to get his approval. And I don't want to let my addiction to success take over and consume me. I need you to stop me, Rachel, like you did last night. If you ever see me get this way again, I need you to tell me."

"I tried to, but you wouldn't listen."

"You made a few comments, but that's it. You were too nice about it. These past few months, you've let me get away with too much. You need to be tougher with me. I can handle it. I need you to be direct and tell me when things are getting out of control." I place my hand along the side of her face. "And please, don't ever let it get to the point where you consider leaving me."

"Pearce, when I said that I didn't mean I want a divorce. I love you and I don't want to break up our family. I was just so frustrated with you and I didn't know what to do or say to get your attention."

"Well, that definitely got my attention. And you were right. I have not been a good father to him these past few months. And I have not been a good husband to you. I am very sorry for that. You deserve much better." I lean in and press my lips to her forehead. "I promise you, I will be the man you deserve. I love you more than anything, Rachel. And although my behavior this past year may have made you doubt that, I am telling you right now, that you and Garret are more important to me than anything else in this world. I will prove that to you going forward."

She nods. "Okay."

I smile at her. "You're being too easy on me again. You should be telling me how much I screwed up, and making me beg for your forgiveness."

"I don't need to. I think you finally realize that things need to change."

"What are you doing tomorrow?" I ask.

"I was going to take Garret to the pumpkin patch and let him pick out a pumpkin. That was always one of my favorite things to do as a kid in the fall."

"Can I go with you?"

"But tomorrow's Thursday. What about work?"

"I'm taking the day off, unless you don't want me around. It sounds like you have a busy day."

She smiles. "I want you around. Would you go to the pumpkin patch with us?"

"I would love to. I've never been to one before. And you'll need me there to carry the pumpkins. I'm sure they're quite heavy."

She hugs me. "Thank you."

"Don't thank me. This is what I *should* be doing. Spending time with my family. I should've been doing it all along." I hold her face with both my hands. "I love you," I whisper over her lips, and then I kiss her, softly and gently.

For months, our kisses have have been rushed, quick pecks on my way out the door. But now I'm going slow, savoring the feel of her soft lips, her warm breath. Her body relaxes as I take the kiss deeper. I recline her back on the couch and lay over her, letting our bodies mold into each other. We haven't been this close, this intimate, for so long that I can't even remember how long it's been. I don't know how I let things get to this point, but I can't let it happen again.

I break from the kiss and my lips trail down the side of her neck. She breathes out, and when I cup my hand around her breast, she softly moans. I've missed that sound. I've missed the feel of her beneath me. I've missed her scent and the feel of her skin.

She pushes her hips into me and I press back into her, letting her feel me and what she does to me. I whisper in her ear, "I need you."

"I need you too," she whispers back, her breathing ragged.

I lift her up off the couch. She goes up the stairs and I follow her to the bedroom. We quickly undress each other, then I shove the covers back and we get into bed. I look at her lying there and, again, I wonder how I let my absence go on for so long. She's my wife and she's beautiful and I love her with everything I am, so why have I not been here with her? In our home? In our bed? Together like this?

I kiss her stomach, her breasts, her neck, as my hands wander over her body, feeling her soft smooth skin. When my hand slides up her inner thigh, her breath catches, and her fingers rake through my hair.

"Pearce," she whispers, her hips grinding into my hand. I want to keep pleasuring her, not worry about myself, but I can tell she wants more.

I lie over her and put myself inside her. We both exhale at the feel of being united like this again. My hips move in a slow rhythm as I kiss her. She matches my movements, gradually guiding me to go faster. I do, but I'm finding it hard to hold back. She feels too good and it's been too long. She's moaning and pushing into me, and I can't stop it. I release, but when I do, I feel her coming as well.

She holds onto me, trembling beneath me. As her body relaxes, she rests her head back on the pillow. "I really needed that."

I brush her hair off her face and kiss her. "We're going to be doing that a lot more from now on."

She smiles. "I'd like that."

I look into her eyes. "What can I do for you, Rachel?"

"What do you mean?" She threads her hand through my hair.

"Can I run you a bath, or get you something to drink, or give you a massage? Just tell me and I'll do it."

"I just want this. Us. Together. I feel like you've been gone for months and I've missed having you in my life. I want my husband back. I want you back, Pearce. For good. That's all I want."

I kiss her. "I'm back, sweetheart. For good."

I roll onto my back and she nestles against me. I pull the covers over us and she falls asleep in my arms.

The next day, the three of us have breakfast together, then go to the pumpkin patch. One of the neighbors told Rachel where to go, which is good because I wouldn't begin to know where to find one.

It's a warm day for October, bright and sunny and perfect for picking pumpkins.

"Dada." Garret points to a mini pumpkin. Rachel and I are standing behind him. We're at a large farm and there are several acres of pumpkins all around us.

Rachel crouches down next to him. "Do you want that one?"

He tries to pick it up but it's too heavy and he ends up falling down and scraping his hands on the prickly vines. He starts crying.

"Garret!" Rachel races to pick him up. She holds him against her and he cries even harder. "We better go home." She sounds panicked.

"Rachel, he's fine." I pick up his hand and look at it. "There's no blood. It's just a scrape."

"Yes, but it could get infected. I need to get him home." She's overreacting. Garret is fine. But her reaction is scaring him and making him cry even more.

"Let me take him," I say to her.

She reluctantly gives him to me.

I hold him in one arm and face him toward the pumpkin patch. "Look at all those pumpkins, Garret." He stops crying and gazes out at the field. "Do you want to go look at the really big ones?"

He looks at me and smiles. I wipe the tears off his face. "Let's go see the big pumpkins." I start walking off.

114

I hear Rachel behind me, talking quietly. "Pearce, we need to get him home."

"He's fine," I say quietly back. We reach a patch of giant pumpkins and I set him down next to one. "That's as big as you are, Garret."

He laughs and hits the pumpkin with his palms.

"Let's get that one." I remove it from the vine, hoist it up in one hand and pick Garret up with the other.

Rachel is watching me, but keeps looking at Garret with worry and concern. I've been at work so much that I haven't seen her with him other than a few minutes a day. I didn't realize she was so overprotective of him.

"Why don't we get a few of these smaller pumpkins that are more Garret's size?" I say to Rachel as we come to that part of the field again.

"Um, okay." She bends down and points to one. "Do you want this one, Garret?"

He claps his hands together.

I laugh. "I guess he likes it. Get that one and a few more that size."

As we walk to the entrance to pay, Garret grips my shirt and lays his head on my shoulder. It warms my chest and makes me smile. I love him so much. I can't believe I've missed so much of his first year. So many moments, just like this one, I've missed because I spent all my time at work.

My son needs me and I haven't been here for him. Ever since I got home last night, he's followed me around, and when I hold him, he clings to me, like he thinks I'll leave and never come back. It hurts me to see him act that way, knowing I'm the cause of it.

We get home and have lunch and then I put Garret down for a nap. I go back down to the kitchen where Rachel is cleaning up.

"Hey." I go up to her, taking the dish towel from her and setting it aside. "What was going on today?"

"What do you mean?"

"Why did you get so upset when Garret fell down?"

"He was hurt. I was worried about him."

"Do you always react that way when he falls down?"

"If he's hurt, then yes." She sounds angry, defensive.

"Rachel, he's just learning to walk. He's going to fall down. You can't react that way every time he does. It scares him."

She backs away. "Don't tell me how to react. You've been with him one day. That's it! I take care of him all day, every day. I think I know how to take care of him."

"I never said you didn't. I'm just saying that you can't react that way every time he falls down."

She folds her arms over her chest. "So I'm just supposed to let him fall and not do anything?"

"If he's not hurt, then yes. He'll get back up. That's how he learns. He falls and then gets back up."

"That may be how your parents treated you, but that's not how I'm raising our son. If he falls, I'm picking him up and holding him."

I nod. "Okay."

I walk into the family room. I don't want to fight about this. We can talk about it later when she's calmed down, because right now, she's very angry.

"What are you trying to say, Pearce?"

I turn and see her standing behind me.

"Just forget it. I don't want to argue. It's a nice day. Why don't we go sit out on the patio?"

"He was hurt," she says, holding my arm. "He scraped his hand and it could've become infected."

She's not letting this go. Maybe we should just have this conversation now. She acted this way with Garret when he was an infant. She took him to the doctor for every little thing. I thought she was just being extra cautious because it was her first time being a mother. I didn't know she was still this way with him.

"Garret wasn't hurt," I say. "He was fine. Children his age are always falling down and getting cuts and scrapes. And he'll get even more as he gets older. I'm only saying that you can't react that way every time this happens."

"You mean OVERreact." Her voice cracks and I suddenly understand why she's getting so upset. It's not about me. It's about her.

"I didn't say that, Rachel. But you *did* scare him when you reacted that way today. He was crying even harder when he saw how upset you were. When I re-directed his attention, he was fine." I put my hands on her shoulders. "I'm not saying I'm an expert on how to raise a child. In fact, I'm the last person to ask for advice. I'm just describing what I observed today. And I'm only saying it because I don't want our son to be afraid to run and jump and play outside. But he *will* be afraid to do those things if he thinks his mother is going to cry or panic if he gets the tiniest scrape."

"Oh God." She walks over to the couch and sits down. She buries her face in her hands, her shoulders shaking.

I go over and sit next to her, putting my arm around her. "Rachel, what's wrong?"

"I'm acting just like my mom used to," she says, her breath shaky. "She never let me do anything. She was worried I'd get hurt. If I had a bruise or a small cut, she'd race me to the doctor. And I hated it. I felt guilty. Like I'd done something wrong. I was so afraid to get hurt because I knew it would worry my mom. I didn't want to worry her or make her sad." She sniffles. "And now I'm acting just like her. I'm doing the same thing to Garret."

I hug her into my side. "You worry about him because you love him."

"Yes, but I don't want to smother him. I don't want to keep him from being a little boy and doing the things little boys do, like run around and kick balls and climb trees." She sits back and wipes her face. "He's our only child, and I'm so worried about something happening to him. Because if it does, we can't have another. It's just like when my sister died. My parents only had one child left and that's why mom acted so overprotective of me. And now I'm doing the exact same thing."

I keep quiet and leave her with her thoughts. What she said is exactly what I suspected was happening, but I didn't want to say it. It's better if she realizes this herself. It's like me realizing that I need to stop working so much. Rachel made that comment the other night that triggered me to come to that realization, and now I've done the same for her. That wasn't my intention when I brought up what happened today, but that's where it led.

"I need you to stop me, Pearce, just like you did today." She turns and looks at me. "You were so good with him and I was a nervous wreck."

I hold her hand. "Why don't we agree to help each other? I'll keep you from overreacting with Garret and you keep me from working too much."

She nods, then hugs my chest. "I like having you home."

"I like *being* home." I kiss her head and we remain there on the couch.

I think it will take a while for her stop being so protective of Garret, just like it will take time for me to adjust to being away from the office. But at least this is a start.

"Should we go sit outside?" I ask.

She pulls back, her lips turning up. "Or we could do something else. Garret usually sleeps for a half hour."

I check the clock. "Plenty of time. Get upstairs."

She jumps up and races up the stairs. We meet in the bedroom and I make love to my wife for the second time today. We also did it when we woke up this morning. We're making up for lost time, all those months when we should have been together and weren't. I'm furious at myself for losing all that precious time, both with Rachel and with Garret. They're my family, my life, and I cannot let work come between us ever again.

The next day I return to work, prepared for my father to yell at me for taking yesterday off. As I'm walking down the hall, I hear him behind me.

"Pearce! In my office. Now!"

I sigh and turn around and follow him to his office.

"Where the hell were you yesterday?" he asks as he sits behind his desk.

I close the door and remain standing. "I took the day off. I told your secretary I wouldn't be here."

"What was so important that you couldn't be here?"

"My family," I say, being honest. I could've lied, but why? I should be allowed to take a day off to be with my family. "I needed to spend time with Rachel and Garret."

"That's what weekends are for."

"I'm always *here* on the weekends. I'm here seven days a week."

"That's called having a job."

"I have both a job *and* a family, and the past year I've devoted all my time to my job and neglected my family."

"How much damn time do you need with them?"

"More than I'm currently spending with them. So starting today, I'm cutting back on my hours. Rachel has been raising our son alone and it's time I stepped in and helped."

"Get a nanny, like everyone else."

"We don't want our son being raised by someone else."

"He's a baby. He doesn't know if you're there or not."

"He *does* know, and he needs his father."

He taps his pen on his desk as he looks at me. "I'm not allowing you to cut back on your hours. I'm your boss and I will not allow it."

"You're my father, and this is your grandson we're talking about. You should want me to spend time with him."

"He's a damn child. He'll never remember whether or not his father was around. I was never around when you were a child and you survived."

He doesn't get it. I don't know why I thought he would. He's never been a father to me. He doesn't know how to be one. Growing up, he was a dictator. A disciplinarian. But never a father.

"We obviously disagree on this," I say, "but despite your objections, I will be cutting back on my hours and will no longer be working weekends unless absolutely necessary."

He goes to say something, then stops.

"You can't fire me, Father. The organization forbids it. They expect me to take over as CEO someday."

"I am well aware of that." He scowls at me as he continues to tap the pen on his desk.

"I have to go. I have a meeting." I turn to leave but hear him talking.

"This is all HER doing, isn't it?"

I turn back to him. "If you're referring to Rachel, then no. This was not her decision. This is *my* decision."

"You're lying. I've seen you the past few months. You've actually liked working here. You were seeing results from your efforts. You could see how all those hours of work were paying off. But then that woman told you to stop working so much so you could stay home and change diapers while she sits around watching TV."

"That is not what happened. And Rachel does not sit around watching TV. She raises our son and takes care of the house. It's a full time job."

"Then she doesn't need you to do it. Let her do her job, and you do yours."

"I'm not arguing about this, Father. I am cutting back my hours whether you like it or not."

"That woman is your downfall, Pearce. You're just too blind to see it."

I walk out of his office. Staying there would just lead to us fighting. He doesn't accept my decision and he never will. He doesn't understand the importance of family. I thought after nearly dying from cancer, he'd realize that family is what's important in life, but he didn't come to that realization. He's back to his old self. He'll never change.

CHAPTER TWELVE

RACHEL

Last night I woke up thinking about what Pearce said about my reaction to Garret falling down. My mother used to react the same way when I used to fall down as a child. She'd pick me up, completely panicked over something as simple as a bruise or a scrape. I can't be that way with Garret. I promised myself I wouldn't be. But that's exactly what I've done. The fact that Pearce recognized it after spending just one day with Garret and me proves how much I overreacted yesterday.

I'm sure I'll continue to do so, which is why I need Pearce around. He needs to tell me when I'm being that way with Garret, because right now, I don't even recognize when I'm doing it. I really hope Pearce meant it when he said he'd stop working so much. I want to believe him, but I won't until I actually see him at the dinner table every night and at home on the weekends.

"Mama." Garret kicks his little legs, splashing water everywhere.

I took him to the pool today at the gym that's in the next town over. We have a family membership but Pearce has only been here one time. He prefers to work out at the gym by his office.

Garret and I have been coming here almost every day since the end of September when the weather became too cool to use our outdoor pool at home.

"Good job," I tell him, as I hold him in the water. My hands are around his tummy so that his arms and legs are free to move back and forth like I taught him.

I let go of him for just a second and am shocked to see that he's able to stay afloat all by himself. I fight the urge to grab him, and just let him keep going.

"Garret, you're swimming!" I can't believe it. He's actually swimming on his own! I wonder if he's been able to do this for weeks and I just didn't know because I wouldn't let him try. I was too afraid he'd drown, even though I'm always right next to him. But today, I let him go and he did it. He actually kept his head above the water.

I pick him up and hug him. "Sweetie, you were swimming all by yourself!" I kiss his wet cheek. He kicks his legs, hitting my stomach. "You want to try again?"

It's clear he does. He keeps trying to push away from me and he can't take his eyes off the water. I lower him back into the pool and let him go and he paddles right past me.

"How did you teach him that?" I hear a voice and pick up Garret before directing my attention to the woman standing next to the pool. She's holding a little girl who's probably around two.

"I've had him in the pool since he was just a few months old," I say, trying to hold him as he squirms in my arms, wanting to get back in the water. "But this is the first time he's swam on his own like that."

She smiles. "You might have a future Olympian there."

I laugh. "We're not quite at that point yet."

"I'm Janelle." She leans over to shake my hand. "And this is Abby." She points to her daughter, who turns away and clings to her mom.

"Hi. I'm Rachel." Garret's still squirming, desperate to get back in the water. "And this is Garret."

"I've seen you here before. You come here a lot." She smiles. "And you're always in the pool."

I smile back. "I was on the swim team in high school and college, so the pool is like my second home."

"Have you ever thought of giving lessons?"

"Swim lessons?"

"Yeah. The gym is looking for an instructor. They had a college kid giving lessons here in the summer. He did okay, but as a mom, I'd much rather have an adult teaching my child. And you're so good with your son, I bet you'd do great with other kids."

"I don't know. I've never taught anyone but Garret."

"You should think about it. Talk to the guy at the front desk. He can tell you more about it." Her daughter starts fussing. "I need to get her home for her nap, but it was nice meeting you."

"Yeah, bye."

She leaves and I let Garret swim some more. He loves it. He's so excited that he's able to do this on his own. And he never would've done it if I hadn't let him. If I hadn't overcome my worries and let him at least try.

On our way out, I stop at the front desk and ask the manager about the swim instructor job. He tells me about it and gives me an application to fill out. I think I might do it. Since Garret was born, I haven't done much other than take care of him. I haven't done any volunteer work or even left the house much. But now that Garret is older, I feel like it's time to go out in the world again and do something. And teaching kids to swim would be a good start. It's just a few hours a week and I can bring Garret with me.

The manager told me I could put Garret in the gym's day care free of charge while I teach. When he said it, a wave of panic went through me because I've never left Garret with anyone but Pearce. I don't like the idea of Garret being cared for by strangers. But he can't be with me when I'm teaching, and like Pearce said, I need to stop being so overprotective of Garret. The day care is staffed by older women who look like grandmothers. I'm sure he'd be okay being there for an hour or two.

As I'm driving home, I decide I want to do this. I want to teach swimming lessons. It sounds fun and will get me out of the house.

"What do you think, Garret? Should I teach other children how to swim?" I glance at him in the rearview mirror. He's too busy playing with his plastic car to hear what I said.

We're sitting at a stoplight and I glance in the mirror again and notice a black car behind me. That same car was behind me when I left the gym. I've now driven ten miles and made multiple turns down several roads and that car is still behind me. The driver is wearing a black suit and has a black hat on, like one of those hats that chauffeurs wear.

Is he following me? Why would a chauffeured car be following me? He's probably not. I'm probably imagining things.

The light turns green and I continue down the road. It winds to the left and then the right. There are several places to turn off, but the car remains behind me. I'm almost at the town square, just a few miles from home. I'm not sure what to do. Should I go home? But what if he follows me home?

"Grrrrrrr." I hear Garret making his race car sounds. I check the mirror and see him holding his toy car up in the air, then notice the black car is still right behind me.

I slow down as I approach the town square. Instead of veering to the right, heading down the road that goes to the house, I drive around the town square. The car follows me. Shit. Why is he following me?

I've now made an entire loop around the square. I notice a car parking in front of the diner and I pull into the spot right next to it as the black car drives away.

I turn my car off and take some deep breaths. Why was I being followed? And who was that man who was following me? What if he knows where I live? What if he's heading there right now? Waiting for me to get home?

I get out of the car and open the door to the back seat. "Garret, we're going inside to have a snack, okay?"

He reaches his arms out to me as I unhook him from the car seat.

"Morning, Mrs. Kensington."

I turn back and see Mr. Thomas standing on the sidewalk. He works at the grocery store and sometimes I see him at the park with his grandchildren. He's an older man with white hair. He's very friendly and always hands out lollipops to the kids in town.

"Hi, Mr. Thomas." I take Garret and meet up with Mr. Thomas on the sidewalk.

"Hi, little man," he says, smiling at Garret. "Look what I've got for you." He hands him a red lollipop. I don't let Garret have lollipops yet. He's too young and could choke, but I always let Mr. Thomas give him one anyway.

"Thank you," I tell him.

"Having an early lunch?" he asks.

"Um, no. Just a little snack."

We walk to the diner and Mr. Thomas holds the door open for me. He goes to the counter and asks the waitress for coffee. I take Garret to a booth, still shaken up from what happened.

Maybe that man wasn't really following me. Maybe he was just lost. But it really felt like he was following me.

I decide to call Pearce, but when I do, he doesn't answer. So I order Garret some chocolate milk and we sit there for a half hour.

Garret's tired and needs a nap. We need to get home. I call Pearce again but he doesn't pick up. He's probably in meetings.

When I get to the house, I don't see that black car anywhere on the street. My next door neighbor is weeding her flower garden and my neighbor on the other side is sweeping off her porch. So at least I'm not alone. I relax and take Garret into the house and put him down for a nap.

As I'm coming back downstairs, I jump when I hear a loud knock at the door. Maybe it's one of my neighbors, although my neighbors don't usually knock that loud. The knocking continues and I cautiously open the door.

126

Holton is standing there in his black suit and gray tie. I tense up and my pulse quickens. I don't know why he makes me so nervous. He's my father-in-law. He shouldn't make me nervous. But he does. He has since the first day I met him.

Pearce's parents have been back in our lives for over a year now and we haven't had any problems with them. They're still not friendly to me, but we get along okay, and Eleanor is much nicer to me now than she was before I had Garret. But Holton still makes me very uncomfortable.

I see the serious look on his face and start to worry. Did something happen to Pearce? Is that why he wouldn't answer his phone? Is his father here to tell me something bad happened?

"Holton. Is something wrong?"

He steps past me into the house. "I need to speak with you about my son."

Now I'm panicking. I close the door and turn to him. "What happened? Is he hurt?"

"Hurt?" Holton gives me a strange look. "He's fine. He's at the office." He points to the couch. "Sit down."

I don't like him ordering me around, but I sit anyway. He sits in the chair.

"Pearce is entering a very critical phase of his career," he says. "As the future—"

"Wait. Could you please explain why you're here? I wasn't expecting you and I just got home and—"

"Do NOT interrupt me," he says, even though he just did so to me. "I'm here because my son apparently is unable to say no to you."

"I don't understand what you mean."

"This morning my son informed me that he will be cutting back his hours at the office."

"Yes, but that was—"

"Let me finish!" He raises his voice.

By now, I should be used to this man and his rude behavior, but I'm not. I don't understand why he's always so angry and hostile. He had cancer and almost died. You'd think that would make him turn a new leaf. Be happy to be alive. Be thankful for his family and our support during his treatment. But it didn't have that effect on him.

He continues. "My son is being groomed to take over the company someday. He's the future CEO of Kensington Chemical."

Why is he telling me this? I already know all this. But I sit quietly and let him talk.

"As I was saying, Pearce is in a critical phase of his career. He's making connections with clients, learning the business, acquiring the skills he'll need to be CEO. He cannot be sidetracked by a needy wife, demanding he be home at a certain hour."

I want to yell at him for making such a rude and sexist comment, but that wouldn't do any good. I've learned that getting angry only makes him continue the behavior. He likes getting a rise out of people. It makes him feel powerful. It's better if I don't react at all. He finds it irritating. And he hates it even more if I'm nice.

I smile at him and calmly ask, "May I speak now? Or do you have more to say? I'm in no rush, so feel free to continue."

As predicted, he's annoyed by my reaction, as evidenced by the sneer on his face. "I need you to convince my son to return to his regular hours. As the wife of an executive, it is your job to take over the household chores and childrearing, so that Pearce's sole focus can be his career. If you are unable to handle those duties, there are plenty of suitable companies that can handle them for you. Eleanor can give you the names of such services."

I nod, like I'm agreeing to it, even though I'm not.

He leans back and crosses his legs. "Now that we have that settled, let's talk about Garret."

"What about him?"

"I have researched the private schools in this area and picked the one that would be most appropriate for my grandson. There's a waiting list, so I added his name to the list."

Now I'm really angry and finding it hard to hide. It was bad enough he's trying to control Pearce, but now he's trying to control Garret as well?

I straighten up and look him in the eye. "Garret is only fourteen months old. Pearce and I have not yet discussed his education, but when we do, *we* will be the ones deciding which school he will attend. I appreciate your concern about Garret's future, but it is not your place to put him on a list for a school I know nothing about. I don't even know if we're sending him to private school."

"Of COURSE he's going to private school," Holton says, raising his voice again. He uncrosses his legs and sits up taller. "My grandson is not going to be educated in a public school filled with inferior teachers who graduated from state colleges and are nothing more than babysitters. And his classmates will not be low-class delinquents with degenerate parents. He will not be associating with those people. It's bad enough you force him to live in this trashy neighborhood." He huffs out an angry breath. "If my son were able to say no to you, he would never live in a place like this. This tiny run-down house is a disgrace! It sickens me to know that this is where my grandson is being raised!"

I sit there, waiting for his rant to end. It reminds me of the time Holton came to the loft, trying to convince me to divorce Pearce. When Holton gets like this, it's best to just let him get it out of his system.

I notice the silence and say, "Are we done here?"

He stands up and removes something from his suit jacket. It looks like a brochure. He hands it to me as I get up from the couch. "This is where my grandson will be attending school. You will be receiving paperwork from them in the next day or so. You and Pearce will sign the paperwork so that Garret is on the official wait list. My signature only allowed him to be on the temporary list."

"I need to discuss this with Pearce before we make a decision."

129

"That is where he is going. There is no need to discuss it."

"As I said earlier, where Garret goes to school is not your decision."

Holton steps closer to me, his eyes like daggers, glaring back at me. "Do not challenge me. I will always win."

An icy chill runs through me and I feel myself shaking a little from his words and the dark, eerie tone he used when he said them.

He turns and walks to the door.

"Did you have me followed?" I blurt out.

He pivots back to me and smirks. "Why would I have you followed?"

"I…I don't know. I just…I just wanted to ask." I shouldn't stammer. I don't want him knowing how he intimidates me.

"So you feel as though you're being followed?"

"I'm not sure. There was this car and I felt like…I felt like it was following me." I shouldn't be telling him this. I should tell Pearce, not his father.

"And you didn't feel safe?" The sides of his lips turn up just slightly.

I quickly shake my head. "I'm sure it was nothing. Just forget it."

"You should be more careful."

"Why do you say that?"

"You're married to my son." Holton opens the door, and as he walks out, I hear him say, "You're always in danger."

I shut the door and lock it. Was he threatening me just now? Or just trying to scare me into doing whatever he says? Whatever he was doing, I didn't like it.

I look at the brochure he gave me. It's for a prep school and has photos of children wearing navy and white uniforms. How dare Holton just sign Garret up without even asking Pearce and me. It's not Holton's decision and he needs to stay out of it.

I pick up the phone to call Pearce, but then decide to wait until he gets home. We need to discuss his father's visit in person.

At five-thirty, Pearce walks through the door. I'm relieved. Part of me was sure he was going to call and say he'd be late.

"Dada!" Garret toddles over to him, going so fast he almost falls.

Pearce picks him up and kisses his cheek. "Were you waiting for Daddy to get home?"

I go up and give Pearce a kiss. "He's been looking at the door all afternoon. He keeps coming over here to check if you're home."

Pearce talks to him. "I'm right here. And I'll be here all weekend." He tosses him in the air and Garret laughs.

"Pearce, could we talk for a minute?"

"Yes, but let's go to the bedroom so I can change."

The three of us go upstairs. I take Garret from him and go sit on the bed.

"Your father stopped by," I say, as Pearce takes his suit jacket off.

"Why was my father here?" He puts his jacket on the hanger.

"To tell me to convince you to go back to working all the time."

"He should not have done that. I'll have a talk with him on Monday." He hangs his pants up and puts some jeans on.

"He was really angry. He blamed me for why you're cutting back on your hours."

"Just ignore him." Pearce undoes his tie and takes his dress shirt off. "He expects me to be just like him, ignoring my family and spending all my time at work. When I told him I don't want that, he didn't believe me, which is why he blames you. I made it clear to him that it was my decision. He just chooses not to accept that." He takes a polo shirt from the closet and puts it on.

Garret wriggles in my arms, wanting to get down. I set him on the floor and he toddles over to Pearce. He's lost all interest in me now that his dad's home.

"Holton also told me that he signed Garret up for private school."

Pearce picks Garret up. "Which one?"

131

"*Which one?* That's all you have to say? Aren't you mad about this? He didn't even talk to us about it."

"Yes, I agree he should have talked to us first. But we do need to get Garret on a waiting list. It takes years to get into those schools. We should've signed him up months ago."

"So we're sending him to private school? That school is almost a half hour away. There's a public school here in town."

"Rachel, we have more than enough money to send him to a private school."

"It's not about the money. Maybe I don't want him being around snobby rich kids who go around flaunting their wealth."

"Garret will get a far better education at a private school. And I'm sure not every child there is snobby or flaunting his or her wealth. Why don't we just go look at the school and then we'll decide?"

I sigh. "Fine."

I'm sure we'll end up sending him there. I read the brochure and it sounds like an excellent school. I want Garret to have the best education possible. I just didn't want Holton thinking he'd won. But I can't let my feelings for him be a detriment to my son's education.

"Let's play some football before dinner," Pearce says to Garret as he hoists him over his shoulder and walks out of the room.

I follow him down the stairs. "I thought I'd order a pizza for dinner."

"Sounds good." On the way to the kitchen, he stops and pulls me in for a kiss. "I didn't get a proper hello."

I smile. He's in a much better mood now than he was just a few days ago. He's more relaxed, more like the Pearce I knew before his father got sick.

"I love you," he says, kissing me again.

I smile. "I love you too."

"I've been thinking about you all day."

"What about?"

He leans down and talks in my ear. "About what I'm going to do to you later tonight after we put our son to bed."

I close my eyes as he kisses my neck. "I can't wait."

"Dada." Garret points to the football that's on the floor. Pearce is still holding him and Garret is squirming to get down to get his ball.

"Yes. We're going to play." He picks up the ball and takes off with Garret.

I call the pizza order in, and when I'm done, I go in the family room and smile as I watch my two guys playing with the mini football. Garret tries to throw it, but it just lands right in front of him.

"Oh, Pearce, I forgot to tell you. Garret was swimming all by himself today. I let him go, and he paddled all the way to the edge of the pool."

"That's great," Pearce says as Garret tries to tackle him. Pearce pretends to fall on his back. "Did you like swimming, Garret?"

Garret climbs on Pearce's chest and collapses on top of him. It's too cute watching him with his dad.

"I think I'm going to start giving swimming lessons at the gym," I tell him. "I met a woman at the pool and she suggested it. Then I talked to the manager and got an application. It would just be a few hours a week and Garret could stay in the gym's day care center while I'm teaching."

Pearce sits up, setting Garret on his lap. "I don't want him there."

"Where?"

"At the day care center. We don't know those people. I don't want him there without you."

"It's staffed by older women, and it seems very clean and organized."

"I don't care. It's not safe."

"Pearce, you just scolded me for being too overprotective. And now *you're* the one being overprotective."

"I didn't scold you for protecting him. I just didn't want you overreacting to him getting a cut or falling down. That's different. When it comes to his safety, we can't be too cautious. And since we don't know anything about this place or the people who work there, I don't want him left there alone. Even for an hour."

Garret crawls off him to get his ball and Pearce joins me on the couch. "Can you teach classes on the weekends? That way I could watch him while you're gone."

"What's going on, Pearce? Is there something you're not telling me?"

"Rachel, this isn't anything new. We've talked about this before. We have a lot of money and people know who we are. That means we always have to be careful, especially when it comes to our son."

We watch him, babbling to himself as he pushes the ball around the floor.

"I have something else to tell you," I say quietly. "Maybe I'm imagining it, but I think someone was following me today."

Pearce abruptly turns and faces me. "When? Who was it? Could you see who was driving?"

"It happened when Garret and I were coming back from the gym. It was a black car. Some kind of sedan. Four doors. The driver had a suit on and a chauffeur cap."

"Are you sure he was following you?"

"He was behind me all the way from the gym to the town square. I circled the square and he followed me until I pulled into a spot in front of the diner."

He rubs his jaw. "Too obvious," he mumbles.

"What?"

"If this person was following you, he wouldn't be so obvious about it."

"That's true. So maybe he was just lost."

"Why didn't you call and tell me about this?"

"I did, but you weren't in your office."

"Then call my cell phone. That's why I bought it. So you'd always have a way to reach me."

"I didn't want to bother you if you were in a meeting."

"I don't care if I'm in a meeting. If you need me, you call me."

"Okay." I pause. "I should probably tell you something else."

"What?"

"When your father was here, I kind of, um…I asked him if he was having me followed."

"Why would you ask my father that?" Pearce sounds angry.

"I don't know. I was still shaken up from the whole thing and then your father threatened me and—"

"My father WHAT?" He raises his voice and Garret looks over at us. I nudge Pearce and he lowers his voice. "My father threatened you?"

"Maybe it wasn't a threat. It just felt like one. He said I was never to challenge him. That he'll always win. And then he told me to be careful because I'm in danger just being your wife."

Pearce faces forward, his body tense, his jaw clenched. "I'll have a talk with him."

"No. Don't say anything. He already hates me. I don't want to make it worse."

"He's the one making it worse. He can't speak to you that way. I won't allow it. And he is not to be here when I'm not around. If he comes to the door, don't answer it."

Garret crawls over to Pearce, pulling on the leg of his jeans. "Dada! Bah!"

He smiles at me. "Guess halftime is over." He gets back on the floor and grabs the football. Garret watches him, his eyes wide and a big smile on his face as he waits for Pearce to throw it. He tosses it so that it lands right in front of Garret, who pounces on the ball and laughs.

It makes me so happy to see them together like this. I could watch them for hours.

The pizza arrives and we have dinner. As we're eating, I keep thinking about that car. Something doesn't feel right. I swear that car was following me. But why?

And why did Holton say I needed to be careful? Was he warning me about something? Or was he just talking in general? He's said things like that to me in the past and I've just ignored him. Maybe I should do that again. Just ignore him and not let his words have power over me.

I really don't like that man. I don't think I ever will.

CHAPTER THIRTEEN

PEARCE

Monday morning, I storm into my father's office and slam the door.

"Good morning, Pearce," my father says, sipping his coffee from behind his desk.

"You will NOT threaten her! Do you understand me?"

"I will do whatever I have to do to protect this company. And if putting a scare in the girl is the only way to get her to convince you to come back to work, then so be it."

"I have already told you that it was MY idea to stop working so much. Not hers. And even after cutting back my hours, I am still working more than a forty hour week." I slam my palms down on his desk and lean toward him. "I do not want you at my house again, unless you are invited and I am home. You are not to speak with Rachel unless I am present."

"I will do as I please. And if you truly believe that she is part of this family, then there should be no restrictions on when I see her or talk to her." He smirks. "That's not how families act, now is it?"

"We are not a normal family. And that is all thanks to you. Mother is trying to make an effort to make this family work, but you keep going behind her back, trying to tear this family apart again."

"I have done no such thing. If you want to blame someone for tearing this family apart, blame your wife. Ever since she came into our lives, there has been nothing but conflict and chaos."

I take my hands off his desk and stand up straight. "Did you have her followed?"

"Perhaps," he says, unable to hide his grin.

"Why the hell would you do that?"

"I wanted to know what she did all day. Where she went. What it is she's doing that makes her unable to care for your son."

"I never said she was unable to care for Garret."

"You said she needs you to be home with him, taking care of him."

"I WANT to be home with him! He's my son. My only child. I don't want to miss his childhood, sitting here in this office."

My father pounds his fist on the desk and shoves himself up from his chair, nearly knocking it over. "How the hell do you expect to run this company someday if you are ill-prepared to do so?"

"I AM prepared. I proved it when you were out sick. I ran this company without you for months, and I did a better job than you."

He lets out a single harsh laugh. "If you really think that, Pearce, then you are delusional and think far too highly of yourself. Fucking up orders? Missing deliveries? You call that running a company?"

"It was one order. One delivery. And it is not the CEO's job to monitor orders." I take a breath. "I am not going to waste time going over all that I accomplished while you were gone, because you already know. The fact that you refuse to admit it just shows that you're threatened by my success. You don't want your peers in the business world seeing what I've done and comparing us, because you know that I would come out ahead."

"Get out of my office!" he yells. "Now!"

"Tell me you will not threaten her again. Or have her followed."

"I will do as I please. Now get out of my office."

I remain where I am. "If you harm her in any way, I promise you I will do all I can to destroy this company. It is the one and only thing you love, and I will take it down, piece by piece, until there is nothing left."

"And if you did, the organization would punish you. This is as much their company as ours, and if you destroy it, they will destroy *you*."

I go to the door, swinging it open so hard it hits the wall, then I storm down the hall to my office.

"Mr. Kensington?" My secretary is standing at my door.

"Not now, Candace." I shoo her away and slam the door shut. I return to my desk and call Rachel. "It was my father," I say when she answers.

"What?"

"My father was the one having you followed."

"Why would he do that?"

"Because he's crazy, that's why. He said he wanted to know where you go during the day."

"Why would he care where I go?"

"He doesn't. He was only doing it to get back at me for cutting my hours. He wanted to scare you because he knew how much it would anger me."

"You're right. That's crazy. What is wrong with him?"

"He's like a child. He lashes out when he doesn't get his way. I'll talk to my mother and see if she can manage him." Someone knocks on my door. "I have to go. I just wanted to let you know not to worry."

I hang up as Candace opens the door. "Mr. Kensington, the man from Henderson Plastics is here and he's been waiting for five minutes."

"Yes. Tell him I'll be right there."

She nods and goes back out in the hall. I get up to leave and my phone goes off. My Dunamis phone. Shit. I do not have time for this. I answer, hoping it's just a meeting notice. I type in my member number, but instead of getting a recording, I get a live voice.

"You have been given an emergency assignment to be completed today. Details will be sent to your office within the hour."

"I wasn't given notice this was coming. Are you sure you have the right person?"

"Yes. This is a reassignment."

A reassignment is when another member was unable to complete a job for a personal reason, like an illness or a sudden family emergency. Or maybe this was Royce's doing. He has way too much power if they're letting him continue to pick who gets his assignments. It's supposed to be random.

"Who was the original assignment for?" I ask.

"Your father. Due to his recent illness, he feels he's unable to do the work that's required."

I forgot about the family rule. Reassignments go to family members first, and if a family member can't do it, then it goes to one of the other Dunamis members.

"I just spoke with my father. He's fine. He can call a freelancer and have this done. It's just a simple phone call."

"No. This is a hands-on assignment. There's no time to bring in a freelancer."

My father did this on purpose, knowing I would get his assignment. He probably called the organization as soon as I left his office and told them to give the assignment to me.

"I assume this is a termination?" I ask.

"Yes. Details are forthcoming. Take action as soon as you receive the folder. This ends the call." The phone clicks off and I shove it back in my pocket.

My father is perfectly capable of shooting someone. His health is fine, thanks to me saving him. He never even thanked me for that. If it weren't for Logan's treatments, my father would be dead. I saved his life. And how does he repay me? By scaring my wife and giving me his kill assignment.

I go down to the conference room where the client is waiting. I secured this client while my father was on medical leave. It was a huge win. It's a large multi-year contract worth millions of dollars.

"Pearce." Mr. Henderson stands up to shake my hand, and as he does, I see my father sitting there. What the hell is he doing in my meeting? "Holton said you've been called away on emergency business. He said he'll be taking your place today."

"Is that so?" I glare at my father.

"Go ahead, Pearce," he says. "Take care of your emergency. I'll take care of Mr. Henderson."

I want to strangle him. Pummel him. Anything to release this uncontrolled rage I'm feeling toward him. This is my punishment for speaking out to him earlier. He threatened my wife. Had her followed. And yet I'm the one being punished.

I return to my desk, too furious to work, but now I have to sit here and wait for the folder to arrive. Fifteen minutes later it does.

"This just came for you," Candace says. She hands me a white envelope.

After she leaves, I rip open the envelope and take out the folder. The assignment is to kill a 25-year-old man. Caucasian. Five foot eleven. A hundred and sixty pounds. Bald. Dragon tattoo along his right arm. Released from prison a week ago.

As usual, it doesn't say what he did. He's not a freelancer. He's an innocent. He must've seen or overheard something that's confidential. But he's a criminal, which makes him somewhat easier to kill. It's concerning that I'm justifying it that way. As if his life isn't worth as much as someone else's so it's okay to kill him. I need to stop thinking that way.

The rest of the folder has information about where I can find this man. Since this is a last minute assignment, the instructions detail exactly how and where this should happen. I review the notes, memorizing the address and what this man looks like, and then I shred the contents of the folder, which is what we always do. We read it, memorize it, then destroy it.

The day continues and I somehow manage to make it through without screaming at my father. He did this to anger me, but I'm not going to let him see my anger. I refuse to give him the satisfaction. So I go about my day, acting as if nothing has happened. When I see him at an afternoon meeting, I smile and act cordial, which I can tell irritates him.

At five, I leave to go home. I'd rather just wait at the office until it's time to do the assignment, but I promised Rachel I'd be home for dinner.

"Hello, sweetheart," I say, faking a smile as she greets me at the door.

"Hi." She kisses me and I feel Garret grabbing my leg. I look down and see his arms raised toward me.

"Hello, Garret." I pick him up and he hugs me.

It's a double life. A double life. I can do this. It's not me. It's someone else. I say the words in my head as my wife and son look at me as though I'm a good man, when the truth is, I'm not. I'm a horrible man. I'm going to kill someone in a few hours, because if I don't, they'll come after me. The organization will punish me. Or worse, they'll do something to my family.

"We're having roasted pork loin and scalloped potatoes," Rachel says. "And apple cobbler for dessert."

"It smells delicious." I set Garret down. "I'll go up and change." I go to the bedroom and put on jeans and a black t-shirt. I need to blend in tonight, and the black will hide any blood. But just in case, I'll bring another shirt.

When I go back downstairs, the food is plated and on the kitchen table. We usually eat in the kitchen instead of the dining room. It's easier since Garret tends to make a mess. He's not the most coordinated eater yet. He's in his high chair, highly focused on trying to pick up pieces of potato with his fingers and get them to his mouth.

"Dinner looks wonderful, Rachel." I kiss her and hold her chair out for her.

"I hope you like it. The pork was a new recipe."

As we're eating dinner, I say, "I have to go back to the office tonight."

"You do?" Rachel reaches over and catches Garret's cup before he dumps it on the floor. "Why?"

"I have a meeting first thing tomorrow morning and I wasn't able to get all the materials ready before I left tonight."

"You should've just stayed. We could've pushed dinner back a few hours."

"Yes, but then it would've been past Garret's bedtime. I wanted to see him before he goes to bed."

She smiles. "So how long do you think you'll be gone?"

"Probably a few hours."

She doesn't question me any further. We continue our dinner and have dessert. Then we put Garret to bed and I head out.

The assignment is taking place at a bar in New Haven so it's a bit of a drive. On the way there, I pretend I'm someone else and not the man who just had a nice dinner with his wife and child. I don't know who I am right now. A hit man? A mobster? I really don't know. There's no term for it. Jack would say it's my dark side, so I guess that's what I'll call it. But I don't want a dark side. I hate that side of me.

I drive to an area of town that isn't far from the homeless shelter where Rachel used to work. I'm relieved she's not working there anymore. She keeps saying she's going to go back there some Saturday for a visit, but so far she hasn't.

When I reach the bar, I pull around the back and park behind a dumpster. They need to give us different cars if they're going to make us do this. I don't exactly fit in driving a Mercedes. But I have to drive the approved vehicle. It's a rule, mainly for our safety because the car has bulletproof glass and a stash of weapons in the trunk, hidden in a locked compartment.

I open the trunk and unlock the compartment and take out my gun and attach the silencer. Then I take out another handgun and lay both guns on the floor of the trunk. I slip my wedding ring into my pocket and scrunch the fabric of my shirt to wrinkle it, then head inside.

The bar is crowded because it's a Monday night and football is on. It's loud, with men yelling at the TV and each other, and beer bottles clinking together as the waitresses dole them out. There's a fist fight going on near the pool table but nobody seems to care.

I take a seat at the bar and order a whiskey. I down it and order another.

"Rough day?" the bartender asks. She has short, jet black hair with red streaks in it and piercings in her nose and eyebrow.

"Yeah," I say, dropping a twenty on the table. "Give me two more."

She smiles and winks, then turns her back to me and leans over to reach for the whiskey bottle. She purposely aims her ass in my direction, bending over enough that I can see her red thong underneath her very short black skirt. I look away.

The guy next to me nudges my arm. "What's wrong? You don't like a hot ass?"

I don't look at the guy. I focus on the TV above us. "She's not my type."

"An ass like that is everyone's type."

She comes back with the two glasses of whiskey, then leans over the counter, putting her breasts on display in front of me. "Haven't seen you here before."

"I'm new in town," I say, swigging my whiskey.

"Where are you from?"

I nod toward the TV. "I'm trying to watch the game."

She slowly retreats back behind the bar and waits on someone else.

"What the fuck, man?" the guy next to me says. "That chick would've gone home with you. Did you see how she looked at you?"

"I told you. She's not my type."

"You got a girlfriend? A wife?"

I'm not here to talk, so this man is really getting on my nerves. I finally turn and look at him. "No. She's just—" I stop when I realize that this is him. He looks just like the photo. Bald head. Dragon tattoo on his right arm. This is the man I'm supposed to kill. He wasn't supposed to be here for a half hour.

144

"Why isn't she your type?" he asks.

"I don't like piercings," I blurt out.

"You don't know what you're missing. Piercings are fucking awesome. I was once with this girl who had—fuck!" He whips around to see who just hit him in the shoulder. The man is about six foot two and three hundred pounds of pure muscle. He walks off, not even realizing he bumped into someone. The guy next to me turns back and drinks his beer, then says, "I would've beat the shit out of that guy if I hadn't just got out of prison. My parole officer would send my ass right back there if I got in a fight."

If he's that afraid of going back to prison, he may not take me up on my offer. But I have to at least try.

"If you want to take down a guy that big," I say, "you need more than your fist."

"Yeah, no shit. But the cops took my gun when they raided my place."

"So get another one." I drink the last of my whiskey. It warms me, but I don't feel the least bit drunk.

"You know someone?" He doesn't look at me as he asks. We're both facing forward, our eyes on the TV.

"In the back parking lot," I say. "Cash only."

"How much?"

"Five hundred."

"What kind?"

"Nine millimeter. Brand new."

"Two hundred. That's all I got. I can pay you the rest in powder."

I assume he means cocaine.

"Meet me out there in five." I step off the barstool and go back outside. And then I wait. I'm not even nervous. Why am I not nervous? I feel like this isn't me. Like I'm just watching this happen, like a scene in a movie.

Five minutes later he comes out the back door. He sees me and makes his way over to my car.

"A Mercedes?" he says. "What the fuck kind of business you in?"

"You got the money or not?"

"Yeah." He starts taking wads of cash out of his pockets. "My ex is going to kill me. This money's supposed to be for fucking child support."

"How many kids?" I shouldn't have asked. It only makes this harder.

"One. A girl." He counts the money and hands it to me.

Fuck. I'm taking a father from his daughter.

I can do this. I can do this. He's not a good father. He was in prison. He committed a crime. But so have I, and I'm about to do it again. Am I really that different from the man standing before me?

"You gonna give me the gun, or what?"

I wake from my thoughts and see him staring at me. "I think you promised me something else."

"Yeah. Got it." He reaches down and pulls a small plastic bag from inside his sock.

I have to do this. I don't have a choice. It's not me. It's someone else. It's not me.

He hands me the plastic bag and I stuff it in my pocket. I thought he'd ask to see the gun before he paid me for it, but he didn't so I don't show it to him. I open the trunk and reach in and pull out my gun with the silencer attached. I aim it at him.

"Hey, what the—"

He crumples to the ground. It's done. I shot him in the chest. Right in the heart.

I toss the gun back in the trunk and get in the car and drive off. I take out my Dunamis phone and dial nine for the clean-up crew. Someone answers and I leave the address.

"Hurry up," I tell whoever I'm talking to. "People keep coming out of the bar. Someone might find him. He's behind the dumpster." I hang up and shove my phone in my pocket.

After I've been driving for a half hour, I pull over at a gas station and go into the restroom, taking the cocaine with me. I flush it down the toilet, then stuff the plastic bag in the trash. When I come back out, a police officer holds the door for me as I exit.

I smile at him. "Thank you, officer."

He nods and goes inside.

I get back on the road, and a half hour later I'm home. I park the car in the garage and pop open the trunk and store the guns back in their compartment along with the wad of cash. Then I go inside, straight to the bathroom to wash my hands. My shirt reeks of smoke and beer so I take it off and stuff it in the washing machine, but I'm worried Rachel will take it out and notice the smell. She has a pile of Garret's clothes sitting there, so I add them to the washer, add some soap, and start the machine. Tomorrow I'll tell her I spilled something on my shirt and had to wash it.

It's after ten and Rachel must've gone to sleep because the house is quiet and only the light above the stove is on. I go upstairs and hear Garret in his room, babbling to himself. I go to check on him and see that he kicked his blanket off. I go to cover him up, but he sees me and reaches out to me. "Dada!"

I take him from his crib and hold him against my chest. And suddenly, the emotion I'd shoved deep down inside me breaks to the surface, washing over me like a tidal wave, drowning me in guilt. I shot a man. I killed him. It wasn't self defense. It wasn't because he had a gun pointed at my wife or my child. I just killed him. I know I had to. Dunamis didn't give me a choice. But still, I took a life. A man is dead because of me.

I look down at Garret, who's falling back to sleep on my shoulder.

"I won't let them take you," I whisper. "I won't let you become me."

"Pearce?" Rachel walks in wearing her robe. "Is everything okay?" she whispers.

"Yes. He woke up, but he's asleep now." I lay him back in his crib.

Rachel and I go into the hall and down to our room.

"Did you just get home?" she asks.

"Yes."

"Why aren't you wearing a shirt?"

"I spilled soda on it. I put it in the wash."

"You don't drink soda."

She's right. Why did I say that? I try to explain. "For some reason, I had a craving for soda so I stopped and got one. But it spilled and got all over me. I think I'll take a quick shower."

"Okay." She gets back into bed as I go in the bathroom.

After I shower, I slip into bed, trying not to wake her.

"Goodnight," she whispers, her back to me. "I love you."

"I love you too." I put my arm around her waist and pull her closer, holding her against me.

It wasn't me. It wasn't me. I keep repeating the words in my head.

I'm not the man who did that. I'm not a murderer. That wasn't me. It was someone else. I have to believe that. Otherwise, I can't live with myself.

CHAPTER FOURTEEN
Five Years Later

RACHEL

"Mom, did you see me?" Garret asks, out of breath and wiping the water from his eyes.

"Yes. You were super fast," I say, taking a towel from the stack. "We need to get going, so can you help me clean up?"

"Okay." He climbs out of the pool.

I teach swim lessons on Tuesday afternoons and every other Saturday. Garret always comes with me. He loves swimming. He could stay in the pool for hours. He's a really good swimmer and I'm not just saying that because he's my son. He really is good.

I wrap the towel around him and kiss his head. "Great job, today."

He looks up at me. "Can we come back tomorrow? I don't want to wait until Saturday."

"I don't know if we'll have time. You have a busy week. You have football practice tomorrow."

Garret loves sports and wants to play all of them. Right now, he's on a little kids' football team. He's only six but he takes it very seriously. He even draws out plays in a notebook and then practices them with his dad in the back yard. Garret also plays soccer, basketball, and baseball, and when he's not doing those things, he swims. I don't know where he gets all his energy.

"Honey, could you pick up the other towels?" I ask Garret as he tosses his towel in the bin. I just taught a bunch of five-year-olds and they're not always good at picking up after themselves.

I put the equipment away as Garret gathers the towels and adds them to the bin. He's so helpful. He helps out at home too. I couldn't ask for a better kid.

"Bye, Mrs. Kensington!" Alyssa waves at me as she walks out of the locker room.

She's one of the little girls in my swim class. She's only in kindergarten but acts older than that. She loves fashion and tells me she's going to be a designer someday. She wears these crazy outfits that she puts together herself. Today it's a denim skirt with pink-and-white striped tights, a pink shirt with hearts all over it, a white sequined headband in her hair, and furry white boots on her feet.

"Bye, Alyssa." I wave back at her. "I'll see you next week."

I notice her eyeing Garret as he picks up the towels. Then suddenly she slips on some water around the pool and falls.

"Alyssa, are you okay?" I hurry to get to her but Garret gets there first.

"I got it, Mom," he says, helping her up.

I stand back and watch the two of them.

"Thank you, Garret," Alyssa says, tilting her head and smiling at him.

"You shouldn't wear those boots." He points to them. "That's why you fell. You should wear sneakers."

"The boots go with my outfit." She sticks her hip out to the side and poses for him. "Don't you like it?"

He shrugs. "It's okay, I guess. But it's too much pink."

I cover my mouth as I laugh. This is too funny.

"What is she up to?" I turn and see Leah, Alyssa's mom standing next to me, holding Alyssa's pink coat.

"I think she's flirting with my son," I say.

Leah laughs. "Sorry about that. She has a huge crush on him. She talks about him all the time."

"That's funny. I guess I never noticed how much she liked him."

We stand there watching them.

"He's a very cute little boy," Leah says. "I can see why she likes him."

"He looks just like his dad. And he's probably going to be just as tall as him. He's already the tallest boy in his class."

Alyssa is still talking to Garret and he's starting to look bored.

"Why not?" Alyssa yells, sounding both angry and offended. She puts her hands on her hips.

"Because I don't want a girlfriend," he says, walking away from her.

Alyssa is now pouting as she watches Garret pick up the last two towels.

Leah nudges me and smiles. "I'll have a talk with her. I'll see you on Saturday."

"Yeah. Bye."

Leah leads her away, and as they go, I hear Alyssa mumbling, "Boys are stupid."

Now that they're gone, I laugh.

"I'm done," Garret says, meeting me by the locker room doors.

"Thanks for your help, honey. Go change and I'll meet you out front."

I always worry about him being in the men's locker room alone. He's not really alone. There are other kids and adults in there, but he's only six so I worry. But he kept insisting he could change in there by himself so I let him try it a couple weeks ago, and so far, there haven't been any problems.

He's mature for his age and looks older than he is because he's tall. It kind of makes me sad because I don't want him to grow up. I want him to be six forever. I said the same thing at five, and four, and three. Time goes way too fast.

I go in the women's locker room and quickly change, and when I get to the front entrance of the gym where I always meet up with Garret, he's already there, in his jeans and a white polo shirt, looking just like his dad. It's really amazing how similar they look. He's a miniature version of Pearce.

151

Garret's talking to Brady, the guy who works at the front desk. He's a college student and loves sports so Garret always talks to him.

"My dad took me to a Yankees game last summer," Garret tells Brady. "And he might take me to a Patriots game. My dad played football in high school. I'm going to play too. I'm going to be quarterback."

"What about your swimming?" Brady asks.

Garret shrugs. "I can do both. I have to get better at swimming. I'm not as good as my mom. She's really good. She's so good she was on a swim team. I want to be on one too, someday. My dad can swim but he's not good like my mom."

Hearing him talk about Pearce and me makes me smile. He's still at the age where he thinks his parents are cool, especially his dad. I'm sure in a few years he'll think we're not.

"Ready to go?" I come up behind Garret and put my arm around him.

"Yeah." He looks at Brady. "See ya later."

"Bye, Garret." He smiles at me. "Bye, Mrs. Kensington."

"Bye. Tell your mom I said hi."

His mom and I were on a committee I chaired for an auction held last month to raise money for lung cancer research. I learned all about lung cancer when Holton had it, so when this opportunity came up to help with the auction, I volunteered.

I started volunteering a lot more once Garret began kindergarten. I'm now on several committees for different organizations. I also give talks on American history to school groups. It's not the same as working at a museum and giving tours, but it at least lets me use my history degree and knowledge.

"Which store do you want to go to?" I ask Garret. We're on the hunt for a Halloween costume. It's Tuesday, and Halloween is on Thursday, but Garret couldn't decide on a costume so we didn't get one yet.

"Jared got his at the mall. He's gonna be a fireman."

"What do you want to be? Have you decided yet?" I turn onto the road that takes us to the mall. We don't have a mall in our small town but there's one that's not far from the gym we just left.

"Maybe a football player," he says. "Or a baseball player."

He's so obsessed with sports. It's all he talks about. In order to have conversations with him, I had to have Pearce give me lessons in every sport. My dad taught me about football but that's it. I didn't know anything about soccer or baseball or basketball.

"You could be a superhero," I say.

"I guess." He doesn't sound too excited about that. "What was dad when he was a kid?"

"Your dad didn't dress up for Halloween. Your grandparents didn't celebrate it."

"Why not?"

"They're not really into holidays."

"I love holidays. Halloween, Thanksgiving, Christmas, Easter. Except I don't like Valentine's Day. It's for girls."

"It's not just for girls. It's for everyone. Someday you'll like a girl and you'll want to give her a valentine."

"No way." I glance at him in the rearview mirror and see him making a face. "I'll never like a girl enough to give her a valentine."

"Not now, but you will someday." It makes me wonder what his future wife will be like and when he'll meet her. Will he meet her in college? Or maybe he'll meet her at work, when he's older.

"I do NOT like Alyssa," he proclaims. "You need to have a talk with that girl, Mom." He's so serious I almost laugh.

"What's wrong with Alyssa?"

"She wants to be my girlfriend. I told her no but she didn't listen. She told me she's gonna tell her whole class I'm her boyfriend."

"It's okay, honey. You don't go to her school. Nobody will know who she's talking about."

"I don't care. I still don't like her. She wears too much pink and she smells funny."

"Garret, that's her perfume." I'm trying really hard not to laugh.

"Well, it stinks."

I pull into the mall and park by the Halloween store. It's only here for October and then it turns into a Christmas store. We go inside and Garret looks around a little, but ends up picking out a football player costume.

While we're at the mall, I stop in one of the department stores to check out the dresses. Pearce and I have a party to go to this weekend and I'm not sure what to wear. The party is at Royce's house. I don't like Royce or Victoria, and neither does Pearce, but we're still expected to make an appearance. It's one of those rules of high society. You attend parties hosted by people you don't like and pretend that everyone gets along. It's something I've come to accept over the years although I still find it completely ridiculous.

"Rachel." I look behind me and see Grace Sinclair, Royce's mother. She and I are on a committee for the leukemia society.

"Hello, Grace." I look at the little girl standing next to her. "Hi, Sadie."

She ignores me and focuses on the contents of the tiny pink purse that's hanging off her shoulder. Sadie's not friendly to me because her mother doesn't like me. I'm convinced Victoria told her daughters to never speak to me. Whenever I see them at parties, Victoria and her daughters always avoid me, and if Garret is there, they ignore him too. Royce still speaks to me, but only long enough to say a polite hello and then he hurries off to talk to someone else.

"Sadie, say hello," Grace says.

"Hi," she mumbles, not looking at me.

Grace sighs at Sadie's response, then turns to Garret and smiles. "Hello, Garret. How is school going?"

"Good," he says. "I'm on a football team."

"Football is stupid," Sadie says, zipping up her purse.

"Sadie, that's not nice," Grace says to her. "Just because you don't like something doesn't mean it's stupid."

"So what are you doing way out here?" I ask, because Grace's house is forty minutes away. Her Connecticut house. She and Arlin own several homes.

"This mall has a store that Sadie likes. It's a candy store that has a large assortment of specialty candy you can't find elsewhere. We're headed down there now. You could come with us if you'd like."

I smile. "Thank you, but I think Garret will get plenty of candy on Halloween. So is just Sadie with you?"

"Yes. Victoria has Emily and the baby. Sadie doesn't have school tomorrow so she's staying with grandma and grandpa for the night."

I like Grace. She always seems genuine, not fake, like the other rich people I know. She's extremely wealthy but very down to earth. She's always been nice to me. Her husband, Arlin, is also really nice. I don't know what happened to Royce. He didn't turn out like either one of them. He's even more obnoxious now than when I first met him. And he still talks down to women, even though he now has three daughters.

"Are you going to Royce's party this weekend?" Grace asks.

"Yes. We'll be there." I try to sound enthusiastic even though I'm dreading this party.

"Then I'll see you this weekend." She smiles and holds Sadie's hand. "We need to get our candy and head home."

"Goodbye, Grace," I tell her. "Bye, Sadie."

As they leave, Sadie turns back and sticks her tongue out at Garret.

He rolls his eyes. "See? That's why I'll never like a girl."

"You just need to meet the right one." I put my arm around him and lead him out of the store. "Let's go home. We need to get our movie night set up."

"Yes!" He punches the air. "Movie night!"

We started movie night a few years ago. Pearce doesn't like going to the theater because of the sticky floors and the people who talk during movies. So I started movie night at home, complete with a concession stand. I put up a folding table and set out popcorn, candy, and drinks. I even make a concession stand sign with drawings of the dancing popcorn and soda people that always appear before the movie starts.

We usually have movie night only on Fridays, but since it's Halloween week, we're having it every night this week and watching scary movies. For Garret's sake, 'scary' is limited to Halloween-themed cartoons, mostly Scooby-Doo.

"Can I make the sign?" Garret asks as we're driving home.

"You have to. That's your job." Lately, Garret's been making the concession stand sign. We could've just used one of my old ones but he likes to make a new one every time.

When we get to the house, Garret races inside with his costume. I go to the kitchen to get dinner started. Pearce walks in a few minutes later.

"You're early." I give him a quick kiss. "It's only five."

"It's movie night. I couldn't be late." He pulls me closer and gives me a longer kiss.

"Look at my costume," Garret says from behind us.

We break apart and look at him.

"Do you like it?" I ask him.

"Yeah, it's like a real uniform." He goes up to Pearce and hugs him. "Hey, Dad."

He hugs him back. "Would you like to go throw the ball around before dinner?"

"Yeah! I'll be right back." He turns and runs out of the kitchen and back up the stairs.

Pearce takes me in his arms again. "Did you get a costume too?"

I laugh. "No. I think my trick-or-treat days are over."

He leans down by my ear. "I was thinking more along the lines of a sexy nurse costume or maybe a French maid."

"Hmm. I like that idea." I smile. "I might have to go back to the store."

We kiss again just as Garret runs into the kitchen. "Why are you guys always kissing? It's gross."

Pearce laughs. "You'll understand when you're older. I need to go change."

While he's upstairs, Garret starts taking the licorice and other candy from the pantry.

"Honey, we're having dinner first," I tell him.

"I know. I'm just getting it ready."

He likes to help me set up the concession stand.

"Then let me get the table out." I go in the laundry room and get the foldout table and set it up in the family room. "Okay, it's all set."

He already has the licorice arranged in a glass and the M&M's in a bowl. He does it just the way I do.

"I'll make the sign when I get back." He yanks open the sliding door to the back yard. "Tell Dad I'm outside."

"Okay, honey. I'll tell him." I smile as I watch him leave. He's such a good kid.

And Pearce is such a great dad. Before we had Garret, Pearce was so worried he'd be a bad father. Holton never did anything with Pearce when he was a child so Pearce had no example of how to be a father. But he figured it out, and now he's a great dad. And he loves being a dad. I think, in a way, having Garret allowed Pearce to relive his own childhood, which he never really had.

"You're wanted outside," I say as Pearce comes back in the kitchen, wearing jeans and a t-shirt.

"Then I better get out there." He kisses me. "I love you."

I smile. "I love you too."

We have dinner, followed by movie night, which is like a party to Garret since it's on a school night instead of Friday night. Then Garret goes to bed and Pearce and I have our own private party in our bedroom.

The next morning, I take Garret to school, then go to a meeting for a holiday fundraiser I'm planning with some other women in town. We're raising money to help restore the historic church that's just outside the town square. It's a beautiful church and none of us want it to be torn down, which is what will happen if it's not restored.

In the afternoon, I go to pick up Garret. He attends the private school Holton signed him up for years ago. I don't like that Holton did that without consulting Pearce and me, but it turned out to be a really good school.

As I'm driving there, Shelby calls. I haven't talked to her forever.

"Shelby, are you pregnant again?" I'm teasing her, because it seems like she only calls me when she's pregnant. She and Logan now have three kids, a boy and twin girls. They live in New York. They moved there four years ago.

She laughs. "I'm not pregnant, but I know what you're saying. I promise to call you more."

"It's okay. I'm just kidding. So how have you been?"

"Exhausted. But I love it. I guess you were right. I guess I'm the mom type after all."

"I knew you were." I smile. "How's Logan?"

"He's been working a lot. But we're going on vacation next week. Leaving the kids with my mom."

"I wish I could get Pearce to go on vacation. He's always so busy with work that we never go anywhere. Maybe I could get him to go somewhere between Christmas and New Year's when Garret's out of school."

She's quiet and I check my phone. "Shelby, are you there?"

"Yeah. I um…I was just thinking, doesn't Pearce always have some kind of conference for his company that week?"

"Yes, but maybe he could skip it this year. I don't know. I have to talk to him about it."

"How have his parents been?"

"They've been okay. They go in phases. Sometimes good, sometimes bad. But the past few months have been mostly good. I've continued to be overly nice to Holton and it drives him crazy. He doesn't know what to do. I even made him a cake for his birthday. He wouldn't eat it, but I don't care. I'm still going to make him one every year. "

She laughs. "Kill him with kindness."

"You need to come visit us sometime. I haven't seen the kids for almost a year."

"Yeah, I know. I'll talk to Logan and we'll figure out a time when we can come there." I hear crying in the background. "I have to go. I'll call you when I get back from vacation. Bye, Rachel."

"Bye, Shelby." I hang up just as I'm pulling into Garret's school. Other parents are already lined up, waiting for their kids. At three-thirty the kids start filing out. Usually Garret is one of the first ones to leave because his classroom is by the door. But I don't see him. Maybe he stayed behind to talk to the teacher. He's probably telling him about his Halloween costume.

Garret's a talker. He talks to everyone. He's not at all shy. He's very confident, like his dad, and outgoing, like me. Growing up, I always made friends easily, and so does Garret. He's the most popular kid in his class.

At three-forty, most of the kids and parents have left. I get out of the car and go inside to his classroom. He's not there, but his teacher is there, grading papers at his desk.

"Mr. Elton," I say, getting his attention.

He looks up and smiles. "Hello, Mrs. Kensington."

"Do you know where Garret is?"

He seems puzzled by my question. "Garret left around two-thirty."

"What do you mean he left? Where did he go?"

"He was called down to the office. The secretary said someone was here to pick him up. I assumed it was you or your husband."

"No." Unless Pearce picked him up. But why would he do that and not tell me? And why would he pick him up an hour early? "Would you excuse me?"

"Of course." Mr. Elton goes back to grading papers.

I go out in the hall and call Pearce. When he picks up, I ask, "Do you have Garret with you?"

"No. I'm at the office. Why do you ask?"

Panic hits me like a lightning bolt, striking my chest and coursing through my limbs.

"Someone took Garret!" I frantically glance around the hall, hoping he'll suddenly appear, but the halls are empty.

"Rachel, what are you talking about?"

"He's gone! Someone took him! Someone took Garret!"

"Where are you right now?"

"At his school. I came to pick him up, like I always do, but he's not here."

"Did you ask someone at the school if they'd seen him?"

"Yes. I talked to his teacher and he said someone picked up Garret over an hour ago."

"But he doesn't know who?"

"No. He assumed it was you or me."

"Shit!" Now Pearce is panicked. "This doesn't make sense. They can't release a child to someone who isn't a parent. It's against their policy. Did you talk to the principal?"

"No. I'll go down there right now."

"Call me back after you talk to her."

"I will." I run down the hall to the principal's office. The light's off and the door is closed. How could she have left already? School just ended.

"Can I help you?" a woman asks. I've seen her before. I think she's a teaching assistant for one of the other grades.

"Yes. I'm looking for the principal."

"She left for the day. She had an appointment to get to."

"What about the secretary?"

"She went home sick over an hour ago. Is there something I can help you with?"

"No. I have to go." I race out of the building and call Pearce. I'm so panicked, I feel like I'm hyperventilating. "She's not there," I tell Pearce. "The principal left and the secretary is gone.

Someone has Garret! We don't know where he is! We don't know who has him! Oh my God!"

"Rachel, just calm down. I'll figure this out." I hear noise; a door opening and then people talking. Pearce must be walking down the hall at the office.

"Who would take him?" I'm crying now as I hurry to my car. "Why would someone take our son?"

"Sweetheart, just take some breaths and try to calm down. I will find him. I promise you." I hear a loud noise, like a door slamming against a wall. "Are you sure he didn't go home with one of his friends?"

"He knows better than to do that without telling me." I get in the car.

"He's only six. He doesn't always think before doing things. Maybe one of his friends asked him to come over to his house and Garret just forgot to call and tell you."

"Maybe." I take some breaths and calm down a little, considering that could be a possibility. But if that were the case, he wouldn't have left early. "No. Pearce, that's not it. His teacher said he left an hour ago and that he was called to the office. Someone was waiting for him. They purposely went there to get him."

"Rachel, I need to hang up and make some calls. I'll find him. Just give me some time."

"Who are you calling? The police?"

"No. I can't talk right now. The longer we wait, the more— never mind. I have to go."

"I'm calling the police."

"No!" Pearce almost yells it. "Don't call the police. It's too soon. He hasn't been gone that long."

"Pearce, he's a child! And he's missing! We have to tell the police!"

"Not yet. Just give me a minute to make some calls. Are you okay to drive?"

"Yes. But where should I go? What should I do?"

"Just go home. I'll meet you there."

He hangs up and I start the car and pull out of the school parking lot. I manage to make it home but I'm not sure how. I don't even remember driving here.

I race inside. "Garret!" I yell it as I search the house. "Garret, are you here?" I go upstairs but he's not in any of the rooms. I check out the back yard and then the front. He's not there either. He's gone.

I collapse on the couch in the family room, sobbing into my hands.

He's not here. My son is missing. Someone has him. Someone took my son.

CHAPTER FIFTEEN

PEARCE

"Where is he?" I ask my father's secretary. He's not in his office and he's the only person I can think of who might have Garret.

"He's in a meeting," she says.

"Here in the building?"

"No. It was somewhere else. I don't know where. He didn't tell me."

"Did he say what the meeting was for or who it was with?"

"No, he didn't say."

"When did he leave?"

"Around noon. Mr. Kensington, is something wrong?"

I don't answer her. I turn and go back down the hall toward the parking garage. I call my father's cell phone. He doesn't pick up.

Is he really in a meeting, or does he have Garret? But why would he have Garret? Why would he pick him up at school in the middle of the afternoon? It's not like he'd take him out for ice cream or to the movies. My father doesn't do things like that. He doesn't do anything with his grandson, other than lecture him on the importance of a good education and discourage him from playing sports. My father thinks sports are a waste of time so he hates that Garret is involved in them. I believe in letting Garret do the things he likes to do, so if he has an interest in sports, I encourage it, as long as he gets his school work done.

I'm on the phone again, calling one of our freelancers. He's not a criminal. He's a private investigator. He's the one who makes the folders we get containing the information about the targets of our assignments. He's very good at what he does. He can get information about most anyone and he does so quickly.

"Mr. Kensington?" he answers.

"Yes. It's Pearce. My son, Garret, is missing. Someone picked him up at school and we don't know who."

"What time did he go missing?"

"Around two-thirty. I'll pay you triple your normal fee if you drop whatever you're doing and see what you can find out. I need a lead. Anything."

"Are you sure a family member didn't pick him up? Or maybe he went home with a friend."

"Those are both possibilities, but until I know for sure, I need you to start looking for him. I don't want to waste any time."

"I understand. I'll get right on it. I'll call you back if I find out anything."

He hangs up and I speed down the road, heading home. I'm sure Rachel's a nervous wreck. She could barely talk when we spoke on the phone. She was crying and sounded completely panicked. I'm panicking too, but I can't let her know that. I need to be strong for her.

When I get home, I find her on the couch, sobbing and surrounded by wadded up tissues. I race over to her and take her in my arms.

"Pearce." Her body crumples into my chest, her shoulders shaking as she cries. "He's gone."

"He's not gone." I hold her tightly against me and rub her back. "We'll find him."

She pushes me back. "Did you call the police yet?"

"No. It's too soon for them to consider him missing." I'm not sure if that's true, but I'm not ready to call the police. I have a strong feeling this involves the organization so I can't get the police involved.

This could very well be my punishment for marrying Rachel. The punishment I've been waiting to receive for almost eight years now. I keep waiting and wondering when it will happen.

Every time something bad happens, I think that's my punishment. When Rachel's parents died, I found their accident suspicious and thought maybe the organization did something to their car to make it go off the road. They knew I loved her parents so it wasn't that far-fetched of an idea to think they were responsible. But then later, Jack told me that he heard my punishment still hadn't been done, so I've continued to wait, wondering what it will be and when it will happen.

They could've taken Garret just to scare me. They wouldn't kill him. He's one of their own. A future member of the organization, although I'm still hoping to get him out of it. But they could take him temporarily just to torture me. Because that's what this is. Pure torture. Having your child go missing? Not knowing who has him? Thinking something bad will happen to him? It's agonizing. I'm barely keeping myself together. I want to break down like Rachel is doing right now, but I can't. If I do, she'll lose all hope.

She shoves me away. "Pearce, I can't do this. I can't sit here and not do anything. We have to call the police. Someone has to start looking for him."

"The police won't do anything. He's only been missing for a couple hours. Did you call any of his friends' parents?"

"Yes. Before you got home, I called everyone I could think of. Nobody has seen him."

"Did you try calling the principal at home?"

"Yes, but her son said she's at the oral surgeon and will be knocked out for hours." Rachel runs to the kitchen. "I'm calling the police. I have to at least report this."

As she picks up the phone, the doorbell rings. She drops the phone and races to the door. I follow behind her.

She opens the door and Garret's standing there. With my father. Shit. I knew it. I knew he was behind this.

"Garret!" Rachel pulls him inside and into her arms. She kneels down and looks at him. "Sweetie, are you okay?"

"Yeah." He smiles. "Grandfather got me an ice cream cone."

My father steps inside the house, his eyes on Garret. "Yes. Garret and I had a lovely afternoon."

Rachel bolts up and glares at my father. "How DARE you!"

I come up behind her. "Rachel. Take Garret upstairs."

"Dad, what are you doing home?" Garret asks.

"I decided to come home early." I set my eyes on my father.

"Will you play ball with me?" Garret asks.

"Yes." I glance down at him. "But not right now. I need to speak with your grandfather."

Rachel takes his hand. "Come on, honey. Let's go up to your room."

"Mom, I missed football practice," he says as they walk up the stairs.

Once they're upstairs, I wait until I hear the door to Garret's room close.

Then I go up to my father. "What the fuck were you thinking? Taking my child and not telling Rachel or me?"

"I'm his grandfather. I have every right to do something with my grandson now and then."

"Yes, with his parents' permission. You don't just take him out of school and not tell anyone."

"Both the principal and the secretary were aware that I had him. Perhaps you should've spoken to them before overreacting like this."

"Neither of them were there when Rachel went to pick him up, which you probably knew, and which is probably why you picked today to do this!"

He lets out a laugh. "I don't keep track of the schedules of the staff at your child's school. I have better things to do with my time."

"Why didn't you call us? Is it that hard to pick up a phone? And why didn't you tell me you were doing this before you left? We work in the same damn office!"

"It was a last minute decision. I was driving near Garret's school and thought it would be nice to take him out for ice cream."

I lower my voice, just in case Rachel is trying to listen from upstairs. "That's a lie. You've never once taken him out for ice cream. You never do anything with him. You were up to something. And you didn't just get ice cream. It doesn't take two hours to get fucking ice cream. Where did you go? Where did you take him?"

He slowly grins. "I took him to meet some people. Or rather, for them to meet him."

He means the members. He took Garret to meet some of the members of the organization.

I lower my voice even more. "Why the fuck would you do that?"

"They were interested in meeting him."

"He's a child. Why the hell would they want to meet a child?"

"He's our future, Pearce. They've been going around meeting all the members' children. I knew you'd never take him to meet them, so I did."

"Why are they so interested in the members' children?"

"They're assessing them. Seeing what their talents are. Seeing what future role they could play within the organization."

"Garret is not playing ANY role! He's not—" I stop before I say it. If my father knew I was trying to get Garret out of his obligation to be a member, he would make sure it never happened. I have to do it behind his back.

My father's brows rise. "He's not what? What were you saying?"

"That he is not to be around those people unless I am present. If they want to see him, I will be the one to bring him to them. Not you!"

"All the better," he says calmly. "I will inform them that you will be playing a more active role in your son's future. But I will still be involved. I don't trust you to do the right thing, Pearce."

167

"Which is what?" I ask through gritted teeth.

"To give the boy the opportunities he deserves. There are many roles to play within the organization, and as a Kensington, Garret needs to be at the top. He needs to be a leader. A decision maker."

"I'm not going to force Garret into a certain role. Unlike you, I want my son to be happy. I will never force him to do something he doesn't want to do. You had your chance, Father. With me. Now you need to step back and let me raise my son. You need to stop interfering."

"I will do what needs to be done. If you neglect to promote the boy's future within the organization, I will do it for you."

"You will do no such thing!" I raised my voice, so I lower it again. "Stay out of his life. He is not your responsibility. He is MY son. NOT yours."

"He has my name. He's a Kensington. And I will not allow you to disgrace that name again. You did it once, by marrying her, but you will not do it again. I will make sure of that."

I point to the door. "Get out of my house."

He stands there, not moving. "They said Garret has great potential. He's intelligent. Good looking. Personable. Confident. And very articulate for someone his age. He has many qualities that would be advantageous to us. He has a great future ahead of him."

I force myself to keep quiet. I can't fight with my father about this. If I do, he'll take it as a challenge and be even more determined to control Garret's life. When my father knows I don't like something, he does it all the more. And I've made it clear that I hate having him interfere with my son's life. But I shouldn't have told him that. I shouldn't have expressed my anger. I did exactly what he wanted me to do. I let his actions affect me and I let him know it.

I go around him to the door and open it. "Goodbye, Father."

He meets me there, a smug grin on his face. "I'll see you on Saturday. I'm looking forward to it. Royce always has such interesting parties." His grin widens. "Katherine Seymour will be there. She graduated from college last spring."

He mentioned Katherine because he knows how much she annoys me. Her presence is just another reason why I don't want to attend Royce's party, but I don't have a choice. It's a party for the members and attendance is mandatory.

"Father, you should get back to the office."

"So should you. But I suppose you'll use the excuse of your earlier hysterics as the reason why you're unable to do so." His eyes fix on mine. "Weakness of the mind can get you killed, Pearce. You should learn to be stronger."

As he walks to his car, Rachel comes down the stairs. "Where is he?"

"He left." I shut the door.

"What? But I wanted to talk to him! Yell at him! He almost gave me a heart attack! Does he have any idea what he put us through?"

I pull her into my arms. "Yes. He said he told the principal to tell us he had Garret, but I know that's not good enough. He should've told us directly."

"He is never allowed back here! Or back in our lives."

"We can't do that, Rachel. I work for him. And cutting him out of our lives would mean Garret would never see his grandmother."

"Then quit your job. And if Garret wants to see Eleanor, she can come here without Holton."

I step back and hold her shoulders and look at her. "I know you're upset. I am too. I'm furious. But Rachel, I need you to understand that my father does not back down from a challenge. If we try to cut him out of our lives, or keep Garret away from him, he'll take that as a challenge and he will fight us until he gets his way. And what he did today? That's nothing. He's capable of far worse."

She folds her arms over her chest. "Your father is crazy. There's something seriously wrong with him. He should not act this way."

"I know, but that's just how he is."

"So you want me to just forget about this? Pretend it didn't happen? Just let him get away with it?"

"If we don't want a repeat of what happened today, then yes. He likes to play mind games, like he did today, and he's an expert at them. You don't want to get on his bad side, because if you do, he will make your life hell."

"Your father is a bully, Pearce, and I'm sick of him controlling us like this! I'm sick of walking on eggshells around him. It's ridiculous! It's not normal!"

"I know, and I'm sorry. But please, just listen to me. If you want to get back at him, if you want to get revenge, then just keep treating him the way you've treated him the past few years. He can't handle the way you're so nice to him. It confuses him and annoys him. He keeps trying to provoke you and it never works. That gives you power, Rachel. Yelling and screaming at him would give *him* the power, which is just what he wants."

She nods. "Yes. I've already figured that out."

I pull her into my arms again. "I'm sorry, sweetheart. I'm sorry that he acts this way. I wish he didn't, but I can't change him. He is who he is."

She sighs. "I know."

"What did Garret say about today?"

"He said his grandfather took him to meet some of Holton's friends and then he took him for ice cream. So who were these friends? Did you ask him?"

"They were some business colleagues of his. My father wanted to show off Garret to them. He's very proud of Garret. He just needs to learn to express it a different way. And I told him that. I told him he is never to take our son out of school again without telling us. And I said if he wants his friends to meet Garret, I will be accompanying him."

"Did he agree to that?"

"Yes."

"Dad, are you ready?" Garret comes bounding down the stairs. "We have to play ball before it gets dark."

I let Rachel go. "I'll go change out of my suit and meet you in the back yard."

"And then we get to have movie night!" I hear Garret say to Rachel when I get upstairs.

"Should we get it set up?" she asks him.

She tries to sound happy, but I know she's still upset. I am too. I'm completely enraged with my father, even more so now that I know he took Garret to meet with members of the organization.

I would love to cut my father out of my life, like Rachel suggested, but it's too risky. If I did that, he'd do something far worse to get back at me.

Keep your enemies close. When it comes to my father, that saying couldn't be more true.

CHAPTER SIXTEEN

RACHEL

It's a day later and I'm still shaken up from what Holton did. When I dropped Garret off at school this morning, I told the office they are never to let him leave with anyone but Pearce or me. The principal apologized for not calling and telling us, but added that she assumed it was okay for Garret to leave with his grandfather. I made it clear that it was not. She gave me a funny look when I said it, but she doesn't know Holton. He is not a normal grandfather.

"I want to do it," Garret says as I open the container of black Halloween makeup I bought to go under his eyes.

"Okay, but don't use too much." I hold it out for him.

He dips his finger in the container and makes a black line under each eye. He looks in the mirror. "Cool! I look just like a real football player."

He's in his costume and looks adorable. I hope he doesn't actually play football for real someday. It's too dangerous. I'd much rather have him on the swim team.

"Let me get your picture." I hold my camera up.

"Not in the bathroom, Mom." He runs out into the hall before I can snap the photo. "We have to go outside and I have to get my football."

The doorbell rings. It's probably Eleanor. She's here to see Garret in his costume before he goes trick-or-treating. Jack and Martha are also coming over, but they're coming later, for dinner. I invited Eleanor to join us but she declined. She seems uncomfortable around Martha and she acts strange around Jack. I've asked Pearce if there's some kind of history there I don't know about, but he didn't say there was, so maybe they just don't get along.

"Grandmother!" Garret says when he answers the door.

Eleanor and Holton don't like the 'grandma' and 'grandpa' labels. It's too informal. So Garret has to call them 'grandmother' and 'grandfather,' which were nearly impossible for him to say when he was a toddler, but they still corrected him if he didn't call them that.

"Look at you," she says, smiling at him. "Already in your costume."

He hugs her. Garret doesn't know that Eleanor isn't a hugger, but even if he did, he'd still hug her. Like me, he hugs everyone.

"I'm going to be quarterback someday," he tells her

I walk up behind him. "Hi, Eleanor."

"Hello, Rachel." Eleanor comes inside. "I brought Garret something. I hope that's okay."

"Of course." I like that she brings him things. It reminds me of when my own grandmother would come to visit. She'd always bring me something, like a pack of gum or some candy. And I like that Eleanor doesn't spend a lot on whatever she buys Garret. It's usually something small and not too expensive.

"Garret, I brought you a gift." She sets a large shopping bag on the floor. Inside is a wrapped box.

"Can I open it?" he asks me, sounding excited.

"Yes. Go ahead."

He takes the box out and rips it open. It's a set of wooden blocks of different shapes and sizes that can be used to build things. The photo on the box shows a boy building a skyscraper.

Garret points to the photo. "Mom, look what I can build!"

"Yes, that looks like fun." I smile at Eleanor. "Thank you. That was very nice of you."

Garret hugs her again. "Thank you, Grandmother."

"You're welcome. I also brought you this." She reaches in her purse and pulls out some chocolate candies shaped like pumpkins and wrapped in a small see-through bag.

He takes them from her. "Thank you."

"Honey, why don't you go put your gifts in your room," I tell him.

He takes them and runs upstairs.

Eleanor smiles as she watches him. "He's so excited. I suppose this is a big night for him."

"Yes. He's been looking forward to trick-or-treating for weeks."

"We never took Pearce. Holton wouldn't allow it." She looks down at her skirt and smooths the fabric with her hand. "It was probably for the best. You can't trust what people hand out to your child."

"We're only taking Garret to houses where we know the people. It should be fine." I hesitate, thinking I shouldn't bring this up, but then I do. "Did Holton say anything to you about yesterday?"

She looks up. "I don't know what you're referring to."

He didn't tell her? I guess that makes sense. The two of them don't talk much. Or maybe he was purposely hiding this from her. I'm telling her anyway.

"Yesterday, Holton took Garret out of school without telling Pearce or me. We didn't know where he was or who had him. We were worried sick. Then just as I was about to call the police, Holton showed up here with Garret."

"Oh." She furrows her brows. "I was not aware of that. I can see why you were concerned. Holton should not have done that. He doesn't always think through the consequences of his actions."

"I think he knew it would upset us. I think that's why he did it." I shouldn't have said that. Eleanor is very loyal to Holton and doesn't like people saying anything bad about him. She already admitted what he did was wrong, which was her apology. I should've accepted it and moved on.

"Where did he take Garret?" she asks.

"Apparently they went to see some of Holton's friends. I don't know who, and I don't know where he took him."

She thinks for a moment, her brows still furrowed, her gaze on the floor.

"Eleanor, is something wrong?"

Her head jerks up and she fakes a smile. "No." She stands up. "I'm sure Holton will not do such things in the future. I should be going."

"You don't have to leave. You just got here."

"I have an appointment to go to." She walks to the door. "Goodbye, Rachel. Tell Garret to enjoy his Halloween."

"Okay. Bye."

She leaves, and I'm left wondering what she knows that she's not telling me. The way she reacted when I told her what Holton did makes me think she knew something that she didn't want me to know. Maybe she knows who these friends are that Holton took Garret to see. Maybe she doesn't like them.

Garret runs downs the stairs. "Mom, where'd Grandmother go?"

"She had to leave."

"I built a tower with those blocks. You should see how high I made it!"

"That's good, honey. I'm glad you like them." I lead him over to the couch and we sit down. "Garret, where exactly did you go yesterday with your grandfather?"

"I already told you. We got ice cream." Garret's bouncing up and down on the couch. He can't sit still. He's too excited about Halloween.

"But before you got ice cream, where did you go?"

"To a big house. Like a hotel." He picks up his toy car from the coffee table and starts driving it over the couch.

"So it was a hotel?"

"No, but it was big like a hotel. Even bigger than Grandfather's house." He moves to the floor, driving his car over the rug. "It had lots of rooms. And we went in this one

175

room with a long table and we sat there and they asked me questions."

"Who asked you questions?"

He shrugs. "Other grandfathers. I don't know their names."

"How do you know they were grandfathers?"

"Because they were old and they dressed like Grandfather and talked like him." He continues to drive his car around the floor.

"Did you know any of these men?"

He shakes his head. "No. Grandfather said they're his friends."

"What did they ask you?"

"About school and stuff."

"What stuff? What else did they ask you?"

"Who my friends are. Stuff like that." He looks up at me. "Can I go outside now?"

"Sure."

He jumps up and runs to the back door to go outside. I don't understand this. Why would Holton's friends want to talk to Garret? Holton could've just told them about Garret. They didn't need to meet him. And if these men were all dressed like Holton, that means they were all in suits, which means they likely all have jobs. So why would they want to meet Garret in the middle of a workday?

When Pearce gets home, I tell him what Garret said about Holton's friends.

"Do you know who these men are?" I ask him. "Did your father tell you?"

"No. But my father's friends frequently meet socially during the day. They're at the office well into the evening so they like a midday break. That's not unusual." He kisses me. "Now where's my little football player?"

"In the back yard. He's waiting for you." I hug Pearce. "Thanks for coming home early. Garret's really excited about you taking him trick-or-treating."

"Are you sure you don't want to come with us?"

"I have to stay here and hand out candy."

He takes a piece of chocolate from the giant bowl of candy I have sitting on the counter. "This is a very odd tradition. Handing out candy to children."

I laugh. "It's not odd. You're the odd one for never going trick-or-treating."

"Dad!" Garret comes running in, then stops suddenly, pointing at Pearce who's unwrapping a chocolate bar. "Hey! Mom said no candy before dinner."

I smile and take it from him. "That's right. You have to have dinner first."

"Told you," Garret says, shaking his head. "You have to follow the rules, Dad."

I try not to laugh. Pearce goes over and musses up Garret's hair. "Where's your helmet?"

"Upstairs in my room."

"Go get it. We'll do a few plays before your Uncle Jack gets here."

The doorbell rings.

"I think they're early," I say.

"I'll get it!" Garret runs to the door.

"Who's this big guy with the shoulder pads?" I hear Jack say.

Pearce and I walk into the living room. Jack's holding Garret and giving him a hug. He loves Garret and so does Martha.

"Uncle Jack, do you want to play football?" Garret asks.

Jack sets him down. "Maybe later. I want to talk to your mom and dad first."

"Okay. Hi, Aunt Martha." He hugs her.

"Hi, honey. Look what I brought you." She hands him a box. It looks like a science kit, but with a Halloween theme. It has images of monsters around a volcano of green goo. I'm guessing the creation of the green goo is the science experiment.

Garret takes it. "Cool!"

Jack looks at me. "I told Martha you'll spend hours cleaning that sh—" He stops before he swears in front of Garret. "That green stuff. But she insisted on getting it for him."

"Boys love things like that," Martha says. "The messier the better."

I smile at her. "I'm not worried about the mess. Thank you for giving that to him. I'm sure he'll have fun with it."

Garret hugs her again. "Thank you, Aunt Martha." He hugs Jack. "Thank you, Uncle Jack." He takes the box and runs up to his room.

"How'd you get the kid to be so polite?" he asks Pearce.

"He's such a sweet boy," Martha says before Pearce can answer. "I love how he gives everyone hugs."

"Have a seat," Pearce says, motioning them to the couch. Pearce and I take the two chairs at the end.

"You just get home?" Jack asks Pearce, who is still in his suit.

"Yes. I came home early tonight."

"Early?" Jack says. "If you still worked for me I would've sent you home at noon. It's Halloween. You gotta spend time with the kid."

"He's not done with school until three-thirty," Pearce says.

"Except for yesterday," I mumble.

Jack heard me and asks, "What happened yesterday?"

"Holton took Garret out of school without telling us," I say. "I went to pick him up, but he wasn't there and nobody knew where he was. It nearly gave me a heart attack."

Martha shakes her head. "What is wrong with that man? He should know better than to take Garret like that without telling you."

"It all worked out," Pearce says, as though he's trying to change the subject.

Jack's looking at Pearce like he knows something. Was Jack one of the men who was there? But he's not friends with Holton. And Garret would've told me if Jack was there.

"So Martha and I have some news," Jack announces.

"What is it?" I ask.

"We're moving to Virginia."

"Oh, no," I say, disappointment in my voice. "Really?"

Martha sighs. "I know. I'm not happy about it, but a lot of Jack's clients are in the DC area and he wanted to be closer to them."

"So you're going to live near DC?" Pearce asks Jack.

He nods. "Land of the thieves and the liars." He laughs. "I should fit right in."

Jack's looking at Pearce, and again, it's like he's communicating something with his expression, but then he quickly looks back at Martha and me.

"We're going to miss you both so much," Martha says. "And my little Garret. I don't know what I'm going to do, not being able to see him."

"We'll come and visit you," I say. "I'm just so sad you have to leave. When are you moving?"

"In a few weeks," Jack answers. "We've already got the house on the market."

"You're selling the house?" Pearce asks. "So I guess you're not coming back."

"No." Jack gives Pearce another one of those telling looks. I don't know what it means. "We plan to be there for years. At least until I retire."

"I see," Pearce says. "Well, that's too bad."

Pearce sounds sad when he says it. This is a big loss for him. He considers Jack to be like a second father. In fact, he spends more time with Jack than Holton. Pearce and Jack have lunch, go golfing, go out for drinks. And Martha is like a mother to me. We see each other all the time. I'm really going to miss her.

"Is it time to eat?" Garret runs down the stairs.

"Not yet," I tell him.

"Come see your Aunt Martha." She holds her arms out to him and he climbs on her lap. She hugs him. "I'm going to miss you."

"Why? Where are you going?"

"Your Uncle Jack and I are moving. We won't get to see you as much."

Garret frowns. "Do you have to move?"

"Yes. But we'll try to visit you. Or you can come visit us."

He hugs her. "I don't want you to move."

"I know, honey."

This is too sad. I need to lighten the mood. "Garret, can you help me set the table? We need to eat because it's almost time for trick-or-treat."

"Okay." He climbs off Martha's lap and we go in the kitchen.

I give Garret simple chores to do around the house, and setting the table is one of them. He doesn't mind doing it. In fact, he likes having little jobs to do. It makes him feel like he's contributing.

After dinner, Jack and Martha leave and Pearce takes Garret trick-or-treating. They stay out for an hour and then we have our movie night. As Garret watches his cartoon and goes through his candy, Pearce and I sit on the couch and talk about Jack and Martha leaving. We're both sad about it. It won't be the same without them here.

On Saturday night, we drive to Royce's house for the party he's hosting. Garret came with us. Victoria hired nannies to watch the children during the party. Royce and Victoria live in a huge mansion and she designated one of the rooms in the house as a playroom for the children. There will be games and movies playing to keep them occupied.

I'm actually the one who suggested we bring children to these parties. A few years ago, I was talking to some of the other mothers and they were saying how difficult it is to find a sitter that will stay late into the evening. Not everyone has a live-in nanny. Some just have nannies that work during the day. And Pearce and I don't have a nanny at all and never have.

Victoria would never listen to one of my suggestions, but when one of the other mothers mentioned the idea to her, she agreed to try it. She had a dinner party and hired three nannies to watch all the children. It worked out so well that the practice has continued, not just with Victoria, but with the other moms too. So now, when Pearce and I go to parties, we're usually able to take Garret with us, which is good because we don't like leaving him with a sitter. I feel much better having him just down the hall.

"How long do we have to stay here?" Garret asks as Pearce drives down the long entrance road to the house.

"A few hours," Pearce answers. "And you need to stay in the playroom. Don't come out to the party." He says it in a harsh, almost angry tone.

"Pearce." I give him a look, questioning why he's being so strict with Garret. He's never had a problem before with Garret joining us at the party. He never stays long. He usually only leaves the playroom if he wants to tell us something or ask us a question. Or sometimes he'll come out to see his grandparents or Jack and Martha.

"Royce doesn't want children there," Pearce says quietly.

"Then he shouldn't have invited them," I say quietly back.

"That was Victoria's doing," he says, seeming annoyed.

"I thought you wanted—"

"Ma'am?" I turn and see my door is now open and a man wearing a black suit and white gloves has his hand extended to me.

I take his hand and get out of the car. There are at least ten valets here, waiting to park cars. It's all too much. The amount of money spent on these parties almost makes me ill. That money would be better spent on so many other things. Homeless shelters. Women's shelters. Children's charities.

Garret comes around the car and I hold his hand and walk to the door, with Pearce right behind us. Several maids are waiting inside to take our coats.

"I'll take the child," one of the maids says as she approaches him.

"That's okay," I tell her. "I'll take him. I know where to go."

She backs away, looking offended. I didn't mean to offend her. I just like to see for myself that Garret is in the right room, and I'd like to meet the nannies.

"I'll take him back there," I say to Pearce. "I'll meet you by the bar."

He nods as he scans the room. He's probably looking for his father so we can avoid him.

I take Garret to the side of the house where the playroom is located. When we get there, Victoria is walking out.

"Hello, Victoria." I smile at her. "Thank you for inviting the children. It's much more convenient than finding a sitter."

She looks me up and down, then walks off, not saying anything. She is so strange. I don't know why she hates me. She has no reason to. I'm always nice to her, even when she's rude to me or ignores me, like she did just now.

"Come on, honey." I lead Garret into the room.

"It's all girls," he says, his shoulders drooping in disappointment.

"I'm sure some boys will be here soon. You want to color?" I steer him toward a long table that has pads of paper and crayons and markers on it.

"Coloring's boring. I want to do *that*." He points to a game that's on the floor in the corner. It's the one where you toss bean bags on a tic tac toe board.

I take him over there, and on our way, we pass Sadie, who's having her nails painted by one of the nannies. She glares at Garret as he walks by. She must be one of those little girls who hates boys. Or maybe she just hates Garret. Probably because her mother hates me.

A little girl walks up to Garret. "You want to play?"

She offers him a mini bean bag. He takes it, his eyes on the girl. He's staring at her like she's the prettiest girl he's ever seen. She's about eight years old with dark brown hair and bright green eyes and freckles on her nose. She's cute.

"Yeah, I'll play," he says, still staring at her. His not-liking-girls stage sure didn't last long. He definitely likes this little girl.

"I'll see you later, honey." I kiss his cheek.

He backs away. "Yeah, see ya."

I think I embarrassed him with the kiss. But he's too young to be embarrassed by that. He can't be interested in girls at his age. He's not old enough. He's still my baby boy.

I reluctantly walk away, and go up to the nanny to introduce myself. I meet the other nannies as well, and when I leave, I turn back and see Garret and the girl playing the game. They seem to be having fun, but I hope some other boys show up.

When I get back to the party, I don't see Pearce by the bar. I don't see him anywhere, but the room is very crowded so it's hard to find people.

"Hello, Rachel." I look beside me and see Katherine standing there. Katherine Seymour, the girl who had a crush on Pearce for most of her teen years. She's older now. I'm guessing early twenties. I've seen her at some other parties the past few years but we haven't spoken. The last time I talked to her was before Pearce and I had our fake wedding. Katherine was trying to convince me not to marry him.

"Hello, Katherine." I turn to face her. She's wearing a tight black dress but she has almost no curves so there's nothing to show off. She's very thin. "How have you been?"

"Well. Thank you." She talks like her mother now. Very formal and stiff. When she was younger, she had more of a whiny, spoiled kid tone to her voice. "And you?"

"I'm also doing well." I have nothing to say to this girl. I feel like anything I tell her will be used against me later. I've found her mother to be quite conniving, not with me personally, but with other women I know, who she claims are her friends.

"I hear that you have a child," Katherine says.

"Yes. A son. He's six."

"Are you planning to have more?"

"We haven't decided yet." I'm not telling her the truth. That's a personal question and none of her business. I need to put the focus back on her. "So are you still in college?"

"I graduated. Last spring." She moves her long blond hair to one side and smooths it with her hand.

"Where did you go to school?" I already know the answer because Leland told us at a party a couple years ago, but I ask her anyway.

"I went to Moorhurst. It's in Connecticut."

"Yes. I know where it is. What was your major?"

"English."

"Why did you choose English?"

"I had to pick *something*. It's not like it matters what I picked. I'll never use the degree. I'll never have a job."

"You could still use your degree."

"You don't use *yours*." She smirks. "You're just a housewife. You didn't need a degree for that."

Up until now, I thought Katherine might be maturing. She was being almost pleasant until her rude comment.

"I'm still glad that I have the degree," I say. "And someday I might use it."

"You won't. Pearce doesn't want his wife working."

Another rude comment. And she says it as if she knows him well enough for the comment to be true, which it's not.

"Katherine, I should go find Pearce."

"Are you going anywhere for the holidays?"

Damn. I was hoping to get away from her. "No. We don't have any plans."

"*We* do. Father is taking the family to Grand Cayman for Thanksgiving. And Paris for Christmas."

"That sounds nice. I'm sure you'll have fun." I turn to leave but she keeps talking.

"We're taking the private jet. Have you ever been on a private jet?"

"Yes, I—" I stop myself before I say it. I almost told her I was on the Sinclair jet, but that's a secret. Pearce and I took Royce's jet to Las Vegas when we eloped, but Katherine can't know that. "Actually, no, I haven't been on a private jet."

"Why not? Pearce's family has a jet. Why wouldn't you use it?"

"I'm not comfortable on small planes. I think they're dangerous."

"My father's company makes airplane engines, and he said private jets are safer than big planes."

"Well, I'd still rather be on a regular plane. I need to find Pearce. It was nice seeing you, Katherine." It's such a lie. I didn't like seeing her. Or talking to her. There's something not right with that girl. She's strange, almost eerie. I think it's the expressions she makes. She always has this half-smile on her face like she knows a secret and is reveling in the fact that other people aren't aware of that secret.

I walk away, searching the room for Pearce. I don't see him anywhere. He always does this at parties. He disappears and I can't find him. I wish he wouldn't do that. I already feel out of place at these parties and it's even worse when I'm surrounded by people I know don't like me. It's always the same people at these parties, and even after all these years, some of them still don't approve of me.

"Rachel!" It's Martha, waving at me from across the room.

I smile and head over there. I don't want her to move away. I'm really going to miss her.

CHAPTER SEVENTEEN

PEARCE

"What's the real reason you're moving?" I ask Jack. We went into a room down the hall so we could talk privately.

"Royce," he says as he shuts the door. "I have to go down there and babysit him."

"Royce is moving?"

"To an estate in Virginia."

"When is he moving?"

"I don't know. Within the year, I suppose. They haven't decided."

"This is because of the presidency?"

"Yes. He has to live among his fellow politicians. Be seen with them. Go to their parties. Interact with them."

"So what are *you* supposed to do?"

"Keep him in line. As I've said many times, Royce is a fuck-up. You leave him alone for two seconds and he gets himself in trouble. Drugs. Women. Gambling. He's a menace to both himself and the organization. And yet they still want him as president. Although I admit he is damn good on camera. He looks good. He sounds good. And when it comes down to it, you need someone who can perform well on TV. Someone who can act the part. So as much as I hate to admit it, Royce is perfect for the role. Problem is, he knows it, which is why he thinks he can do whatever he wants and get away with it."

I feel like I should tell Jack about Royce's affair and the child that resulted from it. If Jack is going to be looking after Royce, he should know this information. But I promised Royce I wouldn't say anything. He said if I did, he'd go after the child's mother, and I can't risk endangering her or the child. So I decide to keep quiet.

"I also have to keep watch on our other politicians," Jack says. "The ones who are already in office. Senator Wingate in particular."

We placed Wingate in office a couple years ago to act as an insider to help us accomplish our goals. He's not a member. He simply works for us in return for keeping his political position. Thus far, he's proved to be a valuable asset, but he can sometimes be challenging to work with. I'm sure Jack will set him straight.

"Who else are you watching?"

"Who the hell knows?" Jack takes a cigar from the humidor sitting on the table on the far side of the room. "They'll tell me when I get there."

"Why did they choose *you*?"

He lights the cigar. "I'm supposed to use my surveillance equipment to spy on them. Plant cameras and microphones in their offices and homes." He walks over to me, the cigar in his hand. "But truthfully, I think your father is the reason I was chosen."

"My father? What does *he* have to do with it?"

"Holton hates the fact that you and I are like family. He thinks I've taken his place as your father, and I suppose in a way that I have. But that's his own fault for not doing the job himself. He also hates that Martha and I are so involved with your son, but again, if he'd act like a damn grandfather to the kid, Garret wouldn't be so attached to us."

"You really think my father had you sent away?"

"I can't say for sure, but I wouldn't put it past him. It sounds like he's trying to get more involved with Garret's life. I assume he took him to meet the members? Is that why he took him out of school?"

"Yes. I was extremely angry. I still am. Is it true that the members are assessing all the children?"

"Not all of them. Only the ones who show promise." He puffs on his cigar.

"Why would they think Garret does?"

"I don't think they did until Holton brought him to their attention. At Garret's age, parents have to ask for their children to be assessed. It's not something that just happens. Assessment is usually not done until a kid's in high school, and even then, it's usually done secretly. They observe the kid from afar. The assessment of younger children is all new. Some of the members want their kids to excel at the organization, so they pushed the organization to get this process started at an earlier age."

"That's the absolute last thing I want for Garret. I don't want the members even remembering Garret exists. I want him in the background, hidden where no one can see him."

"Well, he's front and center now, thanks to your father."

"We have to stop this, Jack." I lower my voice. "You said we could get him out of this. We need to start working on that now, not later."

"It's going to be a lot harder now, Pearce. With this move to Virginia, I'll no longer be your mentor."

"That doesn't mean we can't talk anymore."

"Actually, it does. That's what I wanted to speak to you about." He points to the two chairs that are next to us. "Let's have a seat." We both sit down and then he says, "I've been told to keep my distance from you."

"By who?"

"I don't know who made the order. I was just told this yesterday. It was part of my instructions regarding the move. But again, I think Holton had a say in it. I could be wrong, but I have a gut feeling that I'm right."

"So I'm not supposed to talk to you?" I huff out a breath and shake my head. "This is completely uncalled for. We should still be allowed to talk."

"We can talk, but only at Dunamis meetings or events. And Martha and I won't be able to visit you. We're not supposed to see your family again. Martha will need to end her friendship with Rachel. I haven't told her this yet. She's going to be heartbroken."

"How do I explain this to Rachel?" I stand up and walk to the side of the room, angry and frustrated and needing to move. "You and Martha are like family to us. And now suddenly you won't talk to us? Rachel won't understand, and neither will Garret."

"You'll have to find an excuse they'll believe." He sets his cigar on the ashtray and comes over to me. "Listen, Pearce. I love you like a son. You know that. But we can't put ourselves at risk. We can't put our families at risk. We have to do what they tell us even though it's not what we want."

"What do I do about Garret? I was counting on you to help me get him out of his obligation."

"I'll keep working behind the scenes to get the rules changed, not just for him, but for all our young men. You'll need to do the same." He pauses. "But if we don't succeed, at least now they're not making us do the kills. That's a big change, Pearce. A change for the good. Your son will never have to do the things that you and I did."

He's referring to the fact that members are no longer allowed to do kill assignments themselves. Now only freelancers are allowed to do them. The change happened because one of our members was almost caught after shooting someone. The organization punished the man for being careless, but the other members rallied together, saying that this was an example of why we shouldn't be doing the kills ourselves. It's too risky. We don't want our crimes being traced back to us. They could still be traced back to us when using a freelancer, but it's much riskier if we commit the crime ourselves.

"That change is not going to last," I say. "They only stopped us from doing it because of that one incident. A few years from now they'll have forgotten about it and we'll be back to doing the kills ourselves again."

"Maybe. Maybe not. But even if things go back to how they used to be, freelancers will still be the first option. Members will only be assigned to do it in emergencies."

"And yet, I had to do it multiple times in a five year period."

"Well, you're the exception to the rule." He motions to the door. "We need to get back to the party or people will start looking for us. It's best if we're not seen together, so I'll go first."

I stand there in a state of disbelief. "I can't believe they're doing this. There's no need to. You're a fellow member. I should be allowed to talk to you."

"I don't make the rules, Pearce."

I nod. "Yes. I know."

"This might be our goodbye so…" He gives me a hug. "I love ya, kid. I wish you the best." He steps back, his hand on my shoulder as he looks me in the eye. "Don't let those bastards intimidate you, especially your father. And don't ever forget what I told you. You are not defined by what they make you do. You're a good man, Pearce. Always remember that." He smiles slightly but it's strained. "Goodbye, Pearce." He walks around me and out of the room.

I remain there, feeling like someone just punched the life out of me. I lost Jack. For good. I can't talk to him. I can't see him. I feel like I'm mourning his death. I *need* Jack. He's the one person I can talk to about Dunamis. He's the only member I trust. And now he's gone and I have no one.

I'm sure my father is behind this. He takes away everything I want. Everything I need. Everything that makes me happy. He's even trying to take Garret from me. But I won't let him. I'm getting Garret out of this. I don't know how, but I'm going to do it.

I wish Garret wasn't here tonight. I don't want him around these people. I tried to talk Rachel into letting Garret stay with one of our neighbors, but she wanted to take him with us in case we're out late. But it makes me nervous having him here.

"Pearce." Royce walks in with a blond woman on his arm. "What are you doing in here?"

"I wasn't feeling well. I wanted to sit down for a moment."

He lets go of the woman. "Go wait in the room down the hall. I'll be there shortly."

She leaves and Royce closes the door.

"You're cheating on Victoria in your own house?" I ask.

He shrugs. "She knows I cheat. It isn't a secret."

"Yes, but your daughters could catch you."

"They're off playing in the children's room. They'll never find me." He walks over to where I'm standing. "Speaking of the children, did you talk to Sadie?"

"No. I haven't seen her."

"I've been teaching her how to give speeches." He smiles proudly. "She's becoming quite the eloquent speaker. She might end up being a politician someday. Just like her father."

Royce has come to enjoy having daughters, which is good because he now has three of them. He's more involved in his children's lives than I ever thought he would be. He takes them on trips and out on his sailboat. Those three little girls really softened him up. Unfortunately, when they're not around, he's back to his usual self.

Whenever I see his daughters, I think of the one he pretends doesn't exist. I've always wondered if he lied to me when he said he gave her mother money for her care. He won't tell me anything about this woman, so I've been unable to check to see if what he told me was true.

"What about your other daughter?" I ask, but then wish I hadn't. This topic always angers him so I usually avoid it.

His expression turns grim, his eyes narrowed. "I told you to never speak of her again."

"It was simply a question. I assume the girl is well taken care of? You gave her mother a generous amount, I presume."

"The woman has more money than she knows what to do with. And if she ever comes back asking for more, I'll send one of our freelancers after her."

"Royce, don't say that. Don't even joke about it. The child needs her mother."

"She looks like me," he mutters, gazing behind me as if he's imagining her. "The damn kid looks like me."

"You've seen her?"

"Photos of her. She has dark hair, the same color as mine, and her mouth...her smile...she looks like me when she smiles." As he says it, he has that softness about him, like when he talks about his other daughters. "I have to admit, she's a cute kid."

It's good to hear him talk about her this way. It tells me she'll be safe. If he has a soft spot for her, he'll leave her and her mother alone.

His gaze returns to me. "What can I say?" He chuckles. "I make good-looking children. Problem is, I only seem to be able to make girls."

"There's nothing wrong with girls," I say, trying to keep the mood light. His mood can change in an instant and I don't want it turning dark, like it was just seconds ago when I asked about the girl's mother.

He walks over to the bottle of bourbon that's sitting next to the humidor. "Victoria and I are planning to try for a boy."

"With all those children, you're going to need a bigger house." I'm kidding but I know he'll agree with the statement.

"We already bought one." He pours himself a drink. "Did you hear that we're moving?"

"No, I hadn't heard that," I say, not sure if what Jack told me was confidential.

"We're moving to Virginia." He takes a swig of his drink, pauses, then finishes the rest of it and sets the glass down. "I'm not sure when the move will happen. They haven't let me know yet."

"Royce, I should get back to the party." I head to the door.

"I heard Garret is being assessed."

192

I turn back and find Royce standing in front of me

"Yes." I nod. "My father set it up. I didn't ask for that to be done."

"Why wouldn't you want it to be done?" He fixes his cuff link, which likely came undone while he was doing whatever he was doing with the blond woman. "Don't you want your son to be a leader?"

"Of course I do." I need to play along. Royce has a big mouth, and if he senses I don't want this for Garret, he'll tell the other members. "It's just that he's still very young. I'd like him to remain a child a little longer."

"I had them assess Sadie. I'm trying to get them to consider her to be first lady someday." He laughs. "Wouldn't that be great? I'll be the president, and twenty years later, my daughter will be the first lady."

"That's very impressive. I'm sure you're quite proud of her." I fake a smile. "I really need to go. I'll see you later, Royce."

He follows me out and goes down the hall to whatever room that woman went into.

I go back to the party and search for Rachel. As I'm scanning the crowd, Katherine comes up to me.

"Hello, Pearce." She smiles. "How have you been?"

"Fine. But I can't talk now. I need to find my wife."

Katherine blocks my path. "What's the rush?"

"There is no rush. I would just like to find her."

"Could we talk for a moment?"

I sigh. "What would you like to talk about?"

Her hands are at her sides, rather than all over me, so that's an improvement. When she was a teenager, she was always touching me. She must be 22 or 23 now. She looks older. She's still very thin and lacking much of a womanly shape, but her face looks older.

"I just wanted to apologize for my earlier behavior," she says. "It was my youth causing me to act out of character. But I'm older now and realize that I behaved like a foolish child around you. I hope you forgive me."

"Yes. It's all forgotten." I didn't expect her to apologize. Maybe she's finally maturing.

"I spoke with your wife earlier," Katherine says. "She has on a lovely dress tonight."

Her compliment doesn't sound sincere, although I think she thought it did. She's trying her best to put on a fake nice act, but I see right through it. I continue to search the room for Rachel.

"I asked her if you'll be having more children."

I look back at Katherine. From her sly grin, I can tell she's testing me. Waiting to see my reaction. I'm sure Rachel told her nothing, so now she's trying to get an answer from me.

"You shouldn't ask such personal questions," I say. "Your etiquette classes should've taught you that."

"Your son is such a darling little boy. I'm sure after having him, you're wanting to have another." She smirks. "Unless Rachel is unable to."

How the hell did she know that about Rachel? Or again, is Katherine only saying it to see my reaction?

"Gossiping about people is not an attractive quality in a woman," I tell her. "If you're looking to find a boyfriend, I would suggest you stop talking about others and focus on yourself."

"I don't concern myself with finding a boyfriend. My father is in charge of that. He's the one choosing my husband."

"And you're okay with that?"

"Why wouldn't I be? Father knows what I like in a man."

"Does he have someone in mind?"

"Yes." She glances around the room. "In fact, he's here tonight."

"Who is it?"

"I'm not allowed to say."

"When are you being set up with this man? Has your father told you?"

"He said it may not be for a while. But I'm not in any hurry."

"Why would he wait? If he's picked someone, you should go ahead and marry him."

"It's complicated," she says, twirling her hair around her finger.

"Why don't you go talk to this future husband of yours? I need to find my wife. Enjoy your evening, Katherine."

I walk away and see Rachel coming toward me. She's wearing a deep purple dress tonight. The color looks good against her skin and her dark hair. She has on the diamond earrings and matching necklace I gave her when we got married. I've bought her several other pieces of jewelry since then, but these items are her favorite because they're the first ones I ever bought her.

"There you are." She smiles as she approaches me. I see that smile every day, and yet every time I see it, it still does something to me. Brings me happiness. Joy. Contentment.

I draw her into me and talk in her ear. "You look stunning this evening."

"Thank you." She pulls back, her smile even wider.

There isn't a single woman in here who even comes close to being as gorgeous as Rachel. It's not just her outside appearance. It's the positive energy she gives off. I notice it even more when I'm around these people. They all seem so unhappy with their lives. So desperate to tear people down. Just being around them is stressful. But then Rachel appears and I relax.

"Where have you been?" she asks.

"I was talking to Jack and then I ran into Royce. He's moving the family to Virginia."

"Just like Jack. Why is everyone moving to Virginia?"

"Royce wants to get more involved in politics. Working on campaigns the past few years has made him want to run for office."

"For Congress?"

"Maybe. I'm not sure. I didn't ask." I see my parents behind her. "My parents are coming over to talk to us."

She turns around and I put my arm around her.

Rachel greets them. "Hello, Eleanor. Hello, Holton."

My mother says hello. My father says nothing.

"That's a nice suit, Holton," Rachel says. "Is it new?"

He stares at her, not answering. I'm sure he thought she'd yell at him for taking Garret the other day. But instead, she's nice to him, and now he's confused, unsure how to respond.

"Holton, she asked you a question," my mother says.

"The suit is a year old," he says to Rachel.

"Oh. Well, it looks brand new." She smiles at him. He looks away.

"Where's Garret?" my mother asks Rachel.

"He's playing with the other children. I should probably go check on him. Would you like to come with me?"

She agrees to it, and the two of them go down the hall, leaving my father and me alone.

"Pearce," he says.

"Father."

We stand there in silence. It's sad how we never have anything to talk about. I could talk to Jack all night.

"So Jack told me he's moving," I say.

My father's mouth moves up into a slight grin. "Yes. I heard that as well."

"It's rumored that you were the one who suggested the move."

"Is that so? I'm pleased to know people think I have that kind of power."

"Yes. I thought you would be, which is why I told you."

He definitely did it. I don't know how, but he was somehow able to convince them to send Jack away. To get him out of my life.

"Your wife seems to be in a good mood this evening." My father never uses her name and it drives me crazy. He calls her 'that girl' or 'that woman' or 'your wife,' but never Rachel.

"Rachel is always in a good mood."

"That must become quite tedious after a while."

"Not at all. It's one of the qualities that attracted me to her."

He scans the room. "Are we done here?"

"I would say we've been seen together for an adequate length of time. Feel free to move along to someone you find more interesting."

He walks away without even saying goodbye. After the almost two-year period in which my parents weren't speaking to me, they made the decision to talk to me at social events regardless of what's going on with us behind closed doors. My mother doesn't want other people knowing about our family problems, so she made a rule that we must talk and smile and pretend to like each other for at least a few minutes at a party or other social gathering. That's why they came over to talk to Rachel and me. I know my father didn't want to. He has nothing to say to us.

"There are some other boys in there now," Rachel says. She's back beside me and my mother has returned to my father, who is talking to one of the members.

"What do you mean?" I ask Rachel.

"When we first got here, Garret was upset because the room was full of girls." She laughs. "Although I think he has a little crush on one of the girls. When I was in there just now, he was sitting next to her and drawing her a picture." She nudges me. "You never drew ME a picture."

I kiss her cheek. "I'll be sure to do that for our anniversary." I point to the side of the room. "There's Grace and Arlin. Do you want to go talk to them?"

"Yes. Let's go over there. They're such a nice couple."

We spend the next half hour talking to them. Then they leave to get a drink and talk to some other people.

I check my watch. "We've been here a couple hours. Let's go home."

This is a Dunamis party and members are expected to stay for at least an hour, so I've done my duty.

"Okay," Rachel says. "Let's go get Garret."

We go to the children's room and find Garret playing a ring-toss game with some of the other boys.

I call out to him. "Garret, let's go. We're going home."

"I'm almost done." He tosses a blue ring and it lands on the target. "Yes! I won!" He runs over to us and the other boys yell, "Bye, Garret!" all at the same time. Garret makes friends wherever he goes. He has a lot of friends at school too. I was never that popular as a child.

We start to leave but he pulls on my suit jacket. "Wait. I have to tell Lexi goodbye." He runs over to a little girl with dark brown hair, wearing a blue dress. She's the only girl in the room not wearing pink or purple.

"That's his crush," Rachel whispers. "An older woman. I think she's eight."

Garret says something to her, then gives her a quick hug and runs off. I catch Sadie watching him out of the corner of her eye. She's already nosy like her mother.

"Okay, we can go." He waits until we're out of the room and then he takes my hand, like he always does. When we're in a public place, I like to always know where he is, so he's been taught to either hold my hand or Rachel's hand. And although he doesn't need to do so here at the party, he does because it's all he knows.

"Dad, can we watch a movie when we get home?"

"I think it'll be too late for that."

"But it's not a school night." He looks up at me with those big blue eyes. I find it hard to say no to him. He's so cute, wearing his dress pants and shirt and tie. All the children are required to dress up for these parties, even if they're going to spend the evening in the play area.

"Haven't you had enough movies this week?" I ask him.

"Nope. I like movies. And I like watching them with you and Mom, even though you kiss sometimes. But I try not to look."

Rachel smiles at me.

"Okay," I say. "One movie, but it has to be a short one."

"Are you leaving already?" Cecil Roth steps in front of me, blocking my path.

"Yes. We need to get home."

I smile and act friendly, even though I'm not fond of Mr. Roth. He's someone who believes in creating even stricter rules for our members. And he always votes for the harshest punishment for members who act out. So I try to stay on his good side, but he doesn't like me because I married Rachel.

Right before I married her, Roth introduced my father to his business colleagues in Europe. That trip landed us two new clients in England and one in Germany, making our company international. Then I married Rachel, and Roth stopped helping us get new business. It's just another reason why my father hates me.

"I remember you," Garret says to Roth. "You were one of the grandfathers."

Grandfathers? I'm not sure what Garret means.

Roth smiles. "I'm not a grandfather."

"Oh." Garret stares at him. "You look like a grandfather. You have gray hair and wrinkles."

Rachel covers her mouth to hide her laughter. But I'm not laughing.

"Garret, when did you meet Mr. Roth?" I ask.

"When Grandfather took me for ice cream."

So Roth was one of the men assessing Garret. I wonder if Roth assessed all the children, or just Garret.

"How are you doing, Garret?" Roth asks him, leaning down so he's at Garret's level.

"I'm good." Garret steps closer to me. I think Roth scared him by getting in his face like that.

"We really need to go." I put my arm around Garret's shoulder and usher him away. "Goodbye, Cecil."

"Pearce, who was that?" Rachel asks, coming up beside me.

"Cecil Roth. He's a business associate. A friend of my father's."

"Is he one of the men who met Garret the other day?"

"Yes. I wasn't aware that he was there that day, but according to Garret, he was."

We're at the door now and I give the maid the ticket for our coats, and the valet the ticket for our car.

"Wait here," I tell Rachel. "I'll be right back."

"Where are you going?"

"Martha wanted to say goodbye to Garret." It's not true. It's just an excuse so I can get Garret alone. "I see Martha going down the hall. We'll be right back."

I take Garret back to the room where the party is going on.

"I don't see Aunt Martha," he says.

"She must've left." I pick up Garret so he can see the people in the crowd. "Garret, I need you to tell me if you see any of the men you and your grandfather met with last week."

He scans the room. "I see Mr. Roth."

"Besides him, anyone else?"

"I see Grandfather."

"Yes, but do you see any of those other men?"

He shakes his head. "Nope. Can we go home now?"

"Yes." I set him down and take his hand and we meet up with Rachel.

"Did you find her?" she asks.

"No. She disappeared into the crowd. Is the car ready?"

"Yes. Here's your coat." She hands it to me, then helps Garret with his.

We go home and Garret watches his movie while Rachel snuggles with me on the couch. I'm trying to relax, but I feel on edge after being at that party. I don't like the fact that Roth met Garret last week. And I really don't like that Jack is no longer allowed to communicate with me outside of Dunamis meetings. I feel like I'm being punished, but for what? Surely that's not THE punishment. The one I'm still waiting for.

No. My punishment for marrying Rachel will be much bigger than that. So what is it going to be? And when will it happen?

I can't take it. I can't take another moment of waiting and wondering. Another hour. Another day. Another week. Another year. I just want it to be over. Right now.

What are they waiting for? Why haven't they done it? The longer they wait, the more worried I get. They wouldn't wait this long unless it was something really big. So what the hell is it?

CHAPTER EIGHTEEN
Four Years Later

PEARCE

"If you can get me those reports by Monday, we'll be good on our deadline," I say, ending the meeting. "I'll see you next week."

I leave the weekly marketing meeting and head down to my office. My father stops me in the hall.

"Pearce, we need to meet this afternoon about that new client in Ohio."

"Yes, I know. I'm meeting someone for lunch. I'll come to your office as soon as I get back."

"Who are you meeting for lunch?"

"Logan. I mean, Dr. Cunningham."

My father smiles. "Give him my best."

"Yes. I'll do so." I hurry past him and continue to my office. I'm already five minutes late meeting him and the restaurant is ten minutes away. I call Logan quick to tell him I'll be late.

On the way there I get stuck in traffic and end up arriving even later.

"I'm sorry I'm so late," I say, taking the seat across from him. "You came all this way to see me, and then I show up late. I apologize. I should've kept a closer eye on the clock."

"It's fine." Logan looks tired. Or maybe it's stress. Logan has been working at the Clinic now for almost ten years and he's slowly learning more about the organization. It's a hazard of the job. The longer you work there, the more you find out.

"How is work?" I ask him.

Before he can answer, the waiter stops by our table. "Would you like a drink?" he asks me.

I notice Logan already has a drink. That's odd. He rarely drinks, and when he does, it's never at lunch.

"I'll have a bourbon, neat," I say to the waiter. He takes off.

I don't usually drink at lunch, but if Logan's imbibing, I might as well join him.

"How have things been with your father?" Logan asks.

"Better than usual. The past year or so, he's been almost tolerable. He still tells me I'm doing everything wrong and need to work harder, but he doesn't do it nearly as much as he used to. Just once or twice a day instead of his usual five or six times."

Logan smiles. "I don't know how you put up with it."

"You learn to tune it out after a while."

"Do you ever see Jack?"

"No. I haven't seen him in years."

Logan knows about my friendship with Jack. He knows Jack was like a father to me. When Jack moved, I told Logan that Jack was so busy with work that he didn't have time for me anymore.

I told Rachel the same thing. Rachel talked to Martha a few times after they moved, but then Martha stopped returning Rachel's calls. Rachel couldn't understand why and the only explanation I could give her is that Jack and Martha didn't have time for us anymore. She was deeply hurt and upset, not just for herself, but for Garret. He missed his Uncle Jack and Aunt Martha.

Eventually, we all moved on. We don't talk about them much anymore. I see Jack at the end-of-the-year Dunamis meetings, but that's it. He no longer attends the Dunamis events here in Connecticut. Instead, he goes to the meetings in DC. There's a Dunamis chapter there because so many of our members live in the DC area.

"That's too bad," Logan says. "I know you two were close."

"People move on. That's just how it goes."

Actually, I still talk to Jack. I just can't tell Logan that. Or Rachel. A couple months after Jack moved, I received a box in the mail. I opened it up and inside was a very small cell phone. When I turned it on, there was a number already programmed in it. Instead of a name attached to the number, there was simply the word 'rare.' I immediately thought of Jack because that's how he likes his steak. I hit the send button and he picked up on the third ring.

"You didn't think I'd never talk to you again, did you?" he said when he answered.

I smiled. I was thrilled to hear his voice again. "How are you able to do this? They can track a cell phone. They can hack into it and listen to our conversation."

"With an ordinary cell phone, yes. But not this one. I rigged it so it can't be tampered with. I've already tested it out, and trust me, we're safe. Those fuckers will never find out. But keep it hidden away in a safe place. I don't want them finding it."

"Jack, thank you for doing this. I've had no one to talk to and—well, I just really needed to talk to you again."

"How's Rachel doing?"

"She's very hurt that Martha won't return her calls."

"I'm sorry about that. Martha feels horrible about it. Every time Rachel calls or leaves a message, Martha turns into a blubbering mess, wanting to call her back. Rachel was like a daughter to her and she misses her terribly. And don't even get me started on Garret. Martha loves that boy. She feels like she lost her grandson."

Jack and I talked for an hour that day, and ever since then, we've talked once a week, sometimes more. I seek out his advice, or he just listens when I'm struggling with the Dunamis side of my life. He's more than a mentor. He's like family to me. I'm closer to him than I am my own father.

The waiter brings my drink, waking me from my thoughts. Logan and I give him our order.

"How's Shelby?" I ask once the waiter is gone. "Rachel said Shelby wants another baby."

"Yes. We've talked about it." He doesn't sound very enthusiastic.

"You'd rather stop at three?"

He swirls the liquor around in his glass. "I wouldn't mind having a fourth. Shelby's a great mother. She loves the kids more than anything. When the twins started kindergarten a few months ago, Shelby could barely let them go. Now all three of her babies are in school. I think that's why she wants another one."

"And yet I'm getting the feeling you don't want that."

"It's not that. It has to do with something else. That's why I drove here to talk to you."

"What is this about?"

"Shelby." He looks down at the table. "And her past."

Shit. He knows. He knows about Shelby.

"I'm not sure what you mean," I say.

"I've become aware of some things over the years. Things I wish you had told me, Pearce."

We can't talk about those things. Not here. Not now. Logan should know that, but since I'm not sure if he does, I feel the need to tell him.

"We could talk about this after lunch. Someplace more private."

He glances left and right. "I'll keep it vague."

"Then go ahead." I drink my bourbon. I may need a couple more to get through this conversation.

"I know about the associates. One of my patients came in last week and—well, it doesn't matter how I found out. But I did, and ever since then I've been putting some things together."

"What are you referring to?"

"The way Shelby behaved when we were dating. I could never figure out where she went at night. She'd disappear. She wasn't at her apartment. I couldn't reach her on the phone. And when I asked her about it, she'd get very defensive and tell me to stop spying on her." He picks up his glass and finishes his drink. "I always wondered how she was supporting both herself and her parents. When I was treating her father, her mother told me how proud she was of Shelby for working two jobs to help pay for her father's medical bills. But I knew Shelby only had one job and I knew it was only part time. Again, I asked her about it, but she wouldn't give me an answer. I started to think that maybe she was selling drugs. She always had that pager with her wherever she went. But there were no signs that she was selling drugs. I couldn't find any at her apartment and she didn't have buyers coming to her door."

"What are you saying, Logan?"

His glass is now empty but he takes a drink anyway, the ice clanking around. He sets the glass down on the table and looks at me. "I think Shelby was an associate."

I keep quiet and wait for him to continue.

"I know that's horrible to say, but when I think about it, it makes sense. The money. The pager. Being gone almost every night." He shuts his eyes and squeezes the bridge of his nose. "I just don't want to believe it."

I give him a moment, then ask, "Do you love her?"

He opens his eyes and looks at me. "Of course I love her. She's my wife. The mother of my children."

"Then why are you obsessing about her past?"

"Because I need to know. I need you to tell me, Pearce. I know you know the truth. So tell me. Was she an associate?"

Our meals arrive and the waiter asks, "Can I get you both another drink?"

"Yes," we say at the same time. The waiter goes to get them.

"Pearce, tell me. I need to know."

I set my napkin on my lap. "You don't need to know. You and Shelby have a beautiful family. A happy marriage. Why would you want to ruin that?"

He sighs. "So she *was* an associate. Tell me how long."

"I'm not comfortable talking about this. I'm sorry, Logan, but I can't."

"How did she get out? I heard they're in for life. So how did she get out?"

I ignore his questions and begin eating my meal. If I'd known this is what we were going to discuss, I wouldn't have shown up. I was hoping he'd never find out about Shelby, and now that he knows, I don't know why he's asking me about this. Why would he want to know this about his wife? It's over. It doesn't matter now.

If Shelby found out that Logan knew the truth about her past, she'd be devastated. And ashamed. She'd think Logan would forevermore see her as a whore and not the woman he loves.

I'm angry at him for asking about this. More angry than I should be. Then I realize it's because my situation is so similar to Shelby's. Living this secret life. Feeling ashamed. Not wanting the person I love to know the truth.

Years ago, I wanted Rachel to know the truth about me, but I don't anymore. I'm not that man. The one who does bad things. The one who arranges murders. Covers them up. So I don't want her knowing. I don't want her thinking that's me when it's not. Being with Rachel the past twelve years, I've become a new man. A loving husband. A caring father. Rachel helped create that man, and that's the only man I want her to know.

The same is true for Shelby. She doesn't want Logan to know her for what she's done in the past. Things they forced her to do.

Don't define yourself by what they make you do. Those were Jack's words and I live by them. They help me get through the bad days. The days when I feel like the bad side is taking over. The days when I feel horrendous guilt for what I've done and for the lies I've told my wife. When I have those days, I repeat Jack's words in my head. Then I go home and hug Rachel and Garret, and I'm back to being the other me. The good father and the good husband, who doesn't do bad things.

I don't want Logan defining Shelby by the things she's done. I don't want him seeing her as an associate. She only did it because she was desperate to help her father. She shouldn't be punished for that.

"Are you going to divorce her?" I ask bluntly.

Logan's eyes shoot up to mine. "No! Of course not."

"Then stop asking questions. Surely, you've been taught the rules by now. Rule number one?"

"Don't ask questions. Yes, I know the rule."

"Then follow it. Stop asking questions. If you love Shelby and you love your family, then you'll forget you ever knew this. Shelby is not that girl anymore. She never was. She was just trying to help her family and didn't realize what she was getting herself caught up in."

"I just wondered why she—"

"Logan, stop it. I mean it. You have to forget about this. You have to wipe it from your brain and pretend you never knew about this. If you don't, you'll look at Shelby differently and she'll know that you know. And I guarantee that will hurt her more than if you stabbed her with a knife. She'll never get over it. She loves you, and she doesn't want you thinking about her that way. She won't be able to live with the fact that you know. She'll never be happy again. Is that what you want?"

"No. Absolutely not."

"Then let it go. Find a way to put it out of your mind for good. She is not that girl. She is your wife and the mother of your children. That's it."

He nods, his eyes on the table. "I feel sick that she had to suffer through that." He shakes his head. "If I'd known, I would've done anything to get her out of it. I would've given her the money for her father. I would've—"

"There was nothing you could've done. She was part of it before you even knew her."

"But she couldn't tell me," he says quietly to himself. "They're not allowed to tell."

"Yes. So don't be mad at her. If she'd told you, her punishment would've been severe. And they would have come after you as well. She had no choice but to hide this from you."

He looks up at me. "So how did she get out? I don't understand. They don't let these girls leave. They own them. They own them for life." He pauses, his expression darkening. "Unless...unless she made some kind of deal with them." His eyes dart around in sheer panic. "Oh, God, what did she do? What kind of deal could she possibly have—"

"Logan." I interrupt him before his panic takes over. I didn't want to tell him this but I don't have a choice. "It was you."

"What?" His brows draw together. "What are you talking about?"

"You were the reason they let Shelby go."

"But how did she—"

"She wasn't involved. It was me. I made the deal. I offered to recruit you to work at the Clinic in exchange for them letting Shelby go."

He takes a moment to think, then says, "You put yourself at risk by doing that."

I nod. "Yes. But it wasn't completely selfless. In return, you helped my father."

"That was still a selfless action. Given the way your father treats you I'm surprised you—"

"We all received benefit in some way," I say, cutting him off.

It's a topic I don't care to discuss. I wonder if Logan truly believes I shouldn't have tried to save my father. I've wondered that myself sometimes, when he's been hateful to me or my family. But I did what I thought was right at the time. And I'm sure Logan would do the same if it were his father who needed help.

"Let's just put this behind us," I say, picking up my knife and fork.

"Pearce, no," he says. "I can't let this debt go unpaid."

"There is no debt." I keep my eyes on my plate as I cut my steak. "It was my decision to make. Neither you, nor Shelby, asked me to do it. You don't owe me anything."

"If it weren't for you, I wouldn't have Shelby and our three beautiful children. I owe you, Pearce. Whatever you need…I'll do it."

I look at him. "The only thing I want you to do is to not tell Shelby that you know about her past. She suffered during those years, but you brought her happiness. So don't take that away from her. She loves you, and the children, and her life. She's happy now. Just let her be happy."

He nods, then rubs his forehead. He needs time to process this and get it out of his head.

Our lunch continues and he doesn't mention another word about Shelby. I hope he listens to me and doesn't confront her about this. I don't think he will. He loves Shelby. He'd never want to hurt her. And he has his own secrets to keep. He's not exactly a saint. Not anymore. The longer you work at the Clinic, the more darkness you're exposed to. Shelby knows this, and soon Logan will realize that she does. But she doesn't know all that he does for the Clinic. And he'll never tell her. He can't. Because if he did, she'd look at him differently. She'd see a different man.

This is why we must keep that part of our lives separate from the other part. Our Dunamis life is not our real life. *Don't define yourself by what they make you do.*

That simple phrase has changed my life and allowed me to hide this from Rachel. It's been twelve years and she still doesn't know about that side of my life. And she never will.

On Saturday morning, I take Rachel and Garret out for breakfast at Al's Pancake House. It's in a different town than where we live. It's an old greasy spoon diner, but Rachel and Garret love it. I tolerate it for their sake, but I'd never choose to come here myself. I don't like pancakes, and almost the entire menu is pancakes. Every kind imaginable.

We've been coming here for years. It's become a tradition on Saturday mornings. Rachel likes traditions. She thinks it's good for children to have routines that they can look forward to, and

Garret definitely looks forward to our Saturday morning trips to Al's Pancake House.

"I'm getting blueberry this time," he says, closing his menu.

"You always have blueberry," I tell him.

He shrugs. "It's what I like."

I put my arm around Rachel, who's sitting next to me in the booth. "What are you getting, sweetheart?"

"I think I'll try the pumpkin-walnut. It won't be on the menu after Thanksgiving." She gives me a kiss. "How about you?"

"The usual. Eggs and bacon." I kiss her as I take her menu.

"Gross!" Garret covers his eyes. "Do you have to kiss at breakfast? It's embarrassing. People are watching."

Rachel laughs. "Nobody's watching, honey. And even if they are, I don't care. I love your dad. I can't help but kiss him."

I squeeze her shoulder and kiss her forehead. "I love you too, sweetheart."

Garret rolls his eyes. "I'll never be that mushy with a girl."

"You will," Rachel says. "Someday you'll meet a special girl and you'll say all kinds of mushy things."

"Nope." He shakes his head and folds his arms over his chest. "Never. I don't even like any girls."

Rachel smiles at him. "You like Cassie."

"Only because she gives me her chocolate chip cookies at lunch."

"Oh, speaking of cookies." Rachel turns to me. "Charles is coming over at eleven to make cookies for the bake sale. We need to run home after breakfast and let him in the house before Garret's game."

Charles is a chef that Rachel got to know a couple years ago. He's catered several of the charity events she's worked on. He also works at a restaurant. He's an excellent chef. He's in his forties. He never married or had kids, but he's good with children. He catered Garret's birthday party last August and the kids ended up wanting to spend half the time just watching him cook. He put on a show to make it entertaining for them.

"Charles wants to come to one of my games," Garret says.

211

Garret is on a basketball team. He also plays football, but the season just ended. And he swims. We hired a swim coach for him because Rachel thought it would be better for someone else to teach him rather than her. As his mother, she finds it hard to correct him when his form is off.

"You should invite Charles to the game next Saturday," Rachel says.

"There's no game next week," Garret says, twirling his spoon around on the table. "Everyone will be gone for Thanksgiving."

"That's right. I keep forgetting that. Well, he can go to the one the following week."

The waitress arrives at our table. She reeks of smoke. She must've just got off her break. "What can I get you?"

I motion to Rachel. "She'll have the pumpkin-walnut pancakes and I'll have the scrambled eggs and bacon." I look at Garret to order.

"I'll have the blueberry pancakes. And a large orange juice."

She leaves and Garret says, "Why do you always order for Mom?"

"Because I like to," I say.

"It's what men used to do in the old days," Rachel says. "You were considered a gentleman if you ordered for a lady. And your father is a gentleman." She kisses my cheek.

Garret covers his eyes. "No more kissing!"

Rachel just laughs. "Pearce, we need to stop at the grocery store later. I need to get some things for Thanksgiving. I don't want to go to the store when we get back. It'll be too crowded."

"Do you guys have to leave tonight?" Garret asks.

Rachel and I are attending a political fundraiser in DC tomorrow. The fundraiser is for Senator Wingate, who is up for re-election. Wingate is a challenge to work with, but the organization keeps him in office because he's on a key committee in Congress. To make his senate win look real, we need big name supporters surrounding his campaign. I'm one of those big name supporters. I've been making a name for myself in the business world the past few years, giving speeches, appearing on financial news programs, and doing interviews for business magazines. Wingate needs more support in the financial community so the organization has assigned me to show support for him, hoping it'll convince other financial leaders to do the same.

"We'll only be gone a couple days," I say to Garret, sipping my coffee. "We'll be back Monday night. And while we're gone you get to spend time with your grandmother. "

He frowns and draws circles on his placemat with his spoon. "I don't want you to go."

Rachel reaches over and holds his hand. "We'll be back before you know it. And on Tuesday, since you'll be on school break, maybe we'll have a movie night."

He smiles. "Really?"

"Yes, and you get to pick the movie. And on Wednesday I think we'll go to the pool in the morning. Your dad's coming home at noon, so you two can go out and play football in the afternoon while I start prepping for Thanksgiving."

"And on Friday we'll do the tree?" he asks.

She smiles. "We have to. It's tradition. We always do the tree the day after Thanksgiving."

"I already bought your ornament," I say to her. I still buy Rachel an ornament every year. "I'll give it to you when we get back."

"Mom, when can we get *my* ornament?"

"How about next Saturday? That way the tree will already be up."

"I'm getting a race car one this year."

Rachel always takes Garret shopping to pick out an ornament. It's another tradition. We have a lot of traditions at the holidays. It's good for Garret, but I enjoy it as well. I feel like it makes us closer as a family because these traditions are unique to just us.

The waitress brings our food, and Garret and Rachel do what they always do, in their continued attempt to get me to order pancakes. It never works.

"These are soooo good," Rachel says, her face right next to mine, slowly chewing her pancakes with her eyes closed.

"Sooo good." Garret mimics her, complete with the slow chewing and his eyes closed.

"Nice try," I say. "I'm still not ordering them."

The two of them laugh and go back to eating their breakfast.

I don't like this diner, but I love coming here with Rachel and Garret. I love seeing them so happy. I love spending time with them. It's a family tradition, with the two people I love most in the world.

CHAPTER NINETEEN

RACHEL

"Do you need anything else, Charles?" I have the flour, sugar, and other ingredients all lined up for him.

"No. I think I'm all set." He smiles.

He's such a nice man. I met him years ago at an event he was catering. The food was so good that I got his card and started hiring him for some of the charity events I was involved in. He's also catered some dinner parties I've hosted here at the house, Garret's last birthday party, and three summer cookouts with the neighbors. He's been over here so much the past year, he's almost become like a member of the family. Garret loves him because Charles likes talking about sports.

"Charles!" Garret runs in the kitchen and gives Charles a hug.

"Hello, Garret." Charles laughs as Garret practically knocks him over. "You ready for your game?"

"Yeah. Watch this." He steps back, then jumps up and pretends to dunk the ball. "Did you see how high I jumped?"

Charles smiles. "That was good. Keep practicing and you'll be just like the pros."

"Do you want to come to my game after Thanksgiving? I don't know when it is, but Mom does."

"I'll have to check my schedule but if I don't have to work, then yes. I'll plan to be there."

"I'll give you the details later," I tell him.

He nods at me, then looks back at Garret. "I brought you something." Charles hands him a paper box. "They're for after your game today."

Garret opens the box and inside are a dozen sugar cookies decorated to look like basketballs.

"Mom, look!" Garret holds one up.

"Thank you, Charles," I say. "That was sweet of you."

"I was making sugar cookies for an event and I had some extra dough. I thought Garret might like those."

"I think I'll like them too," I say. "I love sugar cookies." I take the box from Garret. "Honey, go upstairs and get your gym bag. We need to leave."

Charles watches Garret run off. "He's such a good kid."

I smile. "Yeah, he is. So what are you doing for Thanksgiving?"

"I usually go to my brother's house in Vermont, but he's going to his in-laws' house this year so I'll be staying here."

"You should come over and have Thanksgiving with us."

"Oh, no. I don't want to intrude on your holiday."

"You wouldn't be intruding. We'd love to have you. I always make more than enough food. It'll just be Pearce, Garret, and me, and Pearce's parents. What do you say?"

He pauses to consider it. "I suppose I could. But you have to let me help with dinner."

"Gladly. Would you like to make the stuffing? I'm not very good at stuffing."

"That's my specialty, so yes."

Pearce walks in. "We need to get going, Rachel, or we're going to be late."

"Yeah, I'm just waiting for Garret. He's upstairs getting his gym bag." I go stand next to Pearce. "Charles is going to join us for Thanksgiving."

Pearce smiles at Charles. "Good. We're happy to have you." He looks at me. "You did warn him about my parents, right?"

"No." I bite my lip.

Pearce laughs and looks at Charles. "If you met my parents, you might change your mind, especially if you knew my father."

Charles nods. "I'm sure I'll be fine."

Garret races up to us, holding his gym bag. "I'm ready."

We go to his basketball game, and when we get back home, Eleanor is there. Charles is finishing up in the kitchen, the cookies all boxed and ready to be picked up by the woman who's coordinating the bake sale. I tell Charles goodbye and pay him for his work.

Then I go over some things with Eleanor. She's never babysat Garret at our house before. The few times Pearce and I went on an overnight trip without Garret, he stayed at Eleanor's house, but he wanted to stay home this time so she agreed to come over.

"I think that's it," I say once I've gone over everything. "Just call if you have any questions. I'll keep my phone on."

"We'll do fine, won't we Garret?"

"Yep," he says, standing beside me.

She smiles. "I'll let you say goodbye. I need to go upstairs and unpack my suitcase."

When she's gone, Garret hugs me. "Don't go."

He sounds so sad, and he won't let go of me. Usually he's the one who ends our hugs first, but this time he doesn't, so I keep hold of him. "Don't you want to spend time with your grandmother?"

"Yes, but I don't want you to go."

I gently back away so I can see his face. He's frowning and his eyes are wet. I crouch down to his level and hold his hands. "Honey, what's wrong? Why are you so upset about this?"

"I don't know." He sniffles and a tear runs down his cheek. He wipes his face with the back of his hand. "I just don't want you to go."

"It's just for a couple days." I'm trying not to cry, but seeing him this sad is making me tear up.

"Why can't Dad go without you?"

I can't tell Garret the reason why. The truth is that Pearce *could* go alone, but I'm going with him because this trip is a little getaway for our anniversary. The real one, not the fake one in March. Garret only knows about the fake one. Pearce and I never told him we eloped. We will when he's older, but right now, he's too young to understand.

"Your dad is going to a big party for the senator and he didn't want to go to the party all by himself." I wipe a tear off Garret's cheek. "If he did, who would he dance with?"

Garret shrugs. "He doesn't have to dance. He could just drink coffee and talk to people."

I smile at his comment. I'm sure there won't be coffee at this party. There will be nothing but liquor. There's always a lot of drinking at these political fundraisers.

"Honey, I already told him I would go."

"You could change your mind." He sounds hopeful just saying it.

"I could, but your dad really wants me there. And I promise you, the time will go so fast that before you know it, we'll be home. Then we'll have Thanksgiving, and on Friday, we'll spend all day decorating for Christmas, like we do every year." I smile. "And Saturday, the three of us will go out for pancakes and then I'll take you to the store to pick out your ornament. Maybe we'll go to the pool in the afternoon. We'll even make your dad go."

Garret's not smiling back. He's just watching me, tears falling down his face. "Don't go, Mom. Please."

My own tears start falling, so I hug him so he won't see them. "Honey, you're making this very hard. It's just a couple days."

"Rachel, are you ready?" Pearce appears with our suitcase.

I let go of Garret and stand up. Pearce sees the tears on my face, and then on Garret's.

"What's going on?" he asks in a concerned tone.

"Garret doesn't want us to go," I tell him.

Pearce leans down to Garret. "Why don't you want us to go?"

He sniffles. "I just don't."

"We've gone away before and you've been okay."

He shakes his head. "I haven't been okay. I didn't like it. I don't like it when you go."

Pearce hugs him. "And we don't like leaving you. But this event is just for adults. You'd be bored. You'll have much more fun here at home with your grandmother." Pearce pulls back and looks at Garret. "We'll call you as soon as we get there. And we'll call you tomorrow. Several times. And on Monday."

Pearce's words don't help. Garret gazes down at the floor.

When Pearce stands up, I whisper in his ear, "Maybe I should just stay here."

He whispers back. "We have plans. Anniversary plans."

I look at Garret again. "Honey, your dad and I need to get to the airport."

He nods, his eyes still on the floor.

I hug him. "I love you, sweetie."

"I love you too," he says quietly, his voice shaky.

Eleanor comes back downstairs. We tell her goodbye, then Pearce and I head out to the car.

"I don't know why he's so upset," I say to Pearce, wiping my eyes with a tissue. I've been crying the entire way to the airport.

"He just isn't used to not having you around. You're always with him, and when you're not, he misses you." Pearce smiles and takes my hand. "I miss you too when you're not around."

I sniffle. "I hope he'll be okay."

"He'll be fine. I told my mother to watch a movie with him tonight. You know how he loves movies. That'll keep his mind off of us."

"Yeah. I guess." I take some breaths and end my crying as we approach the airport.

I'm still thinking about Garret when we're on the plane. It's a short flight to DC, and as soon as we land I call him. He says Eleanor took him for ice cream and now he's watching a cartoon. He sounds better, not as sad.

The next day, Pearce and I spend the morning in bed, enjoying some alone time.

"Happy Anniversary," Pearce says, kissing me.

"Happy Anniversary." I smile and stretch out over the luxuriously soft sheets. My body is still in a blissful state of warmth and pleasure from what Pearce and I just did.

He captures me in his arms and nuzzles my neck. "I love you even more than I did twelve years ago."

I smile and run my finger down his chest. "Did you ever think this wouldn't work out since we only dated a few months before getting married?"

"Never. I knew right away you were the one."

"I felt the same way about you." I sigh. "And now I'm happier than I've ever been."

His lips touch my ear and I hear his deep voice, "I bet I could make you even happier."

He does. And then we order room service. Pearce booked us a suite at the best hotel in DC. Both the room and the food are incredible.

After a leisurely breakfast, we spend the afternoon touring the Smithsonian. Pearce knows how much I love museums, so he doesn't rush me. He lets me take my time, wandering through the exhibits, but I can't take too long because the fundraiser is at seven. It's a dinner and dance at a hotel in DC, a different hotel than the one we're staying at.

It's a black tie event, so Pearce is wearing a tuxedo and I'm wearing a royal blue evening gown. We arrive in a limo. Everyone else arrives in one too. I haven't been to an event this exclusive before. The guest list includes a lot of well-known people. When we walk in the ballroom, I see several celebrities and some politicians I've seen on the news.

Senator Paul Wingate, the guest of honor, approaches us as soon as he sees us.

"Pearce. Welcome." Wingate shakes his hand.

"Rachel." He lifts my hand up and kisses it. "You look gorgeous, as always."

"Thank you." I smile and take my hand back.

Wingate reminds me of Royce Sinclair. Always putting on a phony act. Smiling for the cameras. Then as soon as the cameras shut off, his true self comes out. His temper flares. He yells at his staff. Complains about everything.

Yet for some reason, Pearce insists on supporting Wingate's campaign. He says Wingate has bold ideas and is taking the country in the right direction. I'm not sure I agree with that, but Pearce does, so he donates a lot of money to Wingate's campaign. Enough money that we received an invitation to this very exclusive event.

"You'll be attending my speech tomorrow afternoon, correct?" Wingate asks Pearce.

"Of course. I'm looking forward to it."

"After my speech, I'm hoping you'll say a few words on my behalf. I've asked several of my top donors to do so."

"Certainly. I'd be happy to."

He flashes his wide politician smile at us. "Excellent. Well, enjoy your evening." He waves at someone across the room, then hurries over there.

"I was hoping we could skip that event tomorrow." I say to Pearce. "And maybe go home early."

"Sweetheart, Garret is fine. Stop worrying about him. He sounded happy when we talked to him."

"I know, but he was so sad when we left. I'd just feel better if we were home with him."

"We'll be home tomorrow night."

"But he'll be asleep when we get there."

"You can go in his room, kiss him goodnight, and then he'll wake up and see you first thing Tuesday morning." Pearce leans down and lowers his voice. "Until then, you're all mine. And I plan to take advantage of every moment I have alone with you." His hand moves to my back. The dress I'm wearing is backless and the feel of his warm hand on my skin sends a tingle through me.

"How long do we have to stay here?" I quietly ask.

"Two hours, max," he says under his breath.

A waiter walks by with a tray of champagne. Pearce grabs two glasses and gives me one.

He holds up his glass. "To my beautiful bride."

"To my handsome husband." We clink glasses and take a sip of champagne.

"We should probably mingle with our fellow donors." He ushers me past a group of older men, moving us farther into the ballroom.

"Do you know anyone here?" I ask him.

"A few people." He nods to the area behind me. "Let's go over there. I'll introduce you to Kiefer Douglas."

"The director?" I whisper, shocked that Pearce knows him. "How do you know Kiefer Douglas?"

"I met him a year ago. I was thinking of having him do some promotional videos for the company."

"You never told me that."

"I just didn't think about it."

Pearce places his hand on my back and leads me over to Kiefer. He's thin, with wavy blond hair and a dark tan. He looks like a California surfer, but he's actually an up-and-coming Hollywood director. He's worked on some of my favorite romantic comedies.

"Kiefer." Pearce shakes his hand. "Good to see you again."

Kiefer smiles. He has very white teeth. Almost too white. "Pearce. I didn't know you'd be here tonight."

"I've been supporting Wingate for quite some time." Pearce glances at me. "This is my wife, Rachel. Rachel, this is Kiefer Douglas."

"It's nice to meet you." I shake his hand, feeling nervous. "I'm a big fan of your movies."

"Thank you. I have two coming out this summer. A romantic comedy and an action film."

"I can't wait to see them." I motion to Pearce. "Although I can't get Pearce to go to the theater, so we'll have to wait until they're out on video."

"You don't like going to the movies?" Kiefer asks him.

"I can't take the crowds and the sticky floors. I'd rather watch at home. So where is your wife this evening?"

"Kelly stayed home with the girls. I'm out here for several days and she doesn't like leaving them for that long."

"How many children do you have?" I ask him.

"Three. All girls. Caitlyn is 14, Kylie is 12, and Harper is 10."

"Our son, Garret, is 10. It's a fun age."

He laughs. "Maybe for boys, but with girls, it's a bit of a nightmare. Constant drama over boys and what to wear to school and nonstop hair emergencies. I try to stay out of the way and let Kelly handle all that."

I laugh. "I can see how girls could be a challenge at times, especially during the teen years."

An older man comes up behind Kiefer and taps him on the shoulder. "Kiefer I wanted to introduce you to someone."

"Certainly." He smiles at us. "It was good seeing you, Pearce. Nice meeting you, Rachel. Enjoy your evening."

"He seems very down-to-earth for someone so famous," I say when he's gone. "I didn't expect him to be like that."

"Yes. He's very laid back. Easy to talk to."

"Do you see anyone else you know?"

"Not right now."

I scan the crowd, seeing if I recognize anyone. I doubt that I would, but you never know. With all the volunteer work I do, I meet a lot of people.

As I'm looking to my right, I spot a man standing near the entrance to the ballroom who kind of looks like Jack. He sees me too, and we hold gazes for a moment. I look back at Pearce.

"Pearce, I think Jack is here."

"Probably. I'm sure he's become more involved in politics since living here. And he's always been a supporter of Senator Wingate."

"Let's go talk to him." I pull on Pearce's arm but he doesn't move.

"Rachel, I don't want to talk to him."

223

"Why? Maybe he can explain why he stopped talking to us."

"I'm not going to ask him that. He obviously wants nothing to do with us. And that's fine. We've moved on."

"I haven't. I still miss Martha."

"I know you do. But we need to move past this. Jack and Martha have moved on with their lives. We need to accept that."

My eyes search for Jack again, but now I don't see him. He's gone. I don't see him anywhere in the crowd. But I spot someone else I know, at least I think it's him. I can only see the side of him but he kind of looks like Leland Seymour. He's talking to someone at the bar.

"Pearce, I think—"

"Pearce." A man interrupts me before I can finish. He's an older man. Short and fat with white hair. I met him last year at a client event for Kensington Chemical. Pearce said he's a difficult client who's always complaining and needs constant attention. I'm sure Pearce isn't happy to see him.

"Gerald." Pearce shakes his hand and puts on a fake smile. He can fake a smile as good as anyone in this room. He says it comes from years of having to pretend to like people you really don't like. "I didn't know you were attending this event."

"I wasn't sure if I'd have time, but then my schedule opened up."

Pearce motions to me. "I think you've met my wife, Rachel."

He nods. "Yes. Hello." He focuses on Pearce again. "So I was talking to your sales guy the other day and I'm not happy with the delivery schedule he gave us."

I hear Pearce groaning under his breath.

The two of them will talk business for at least ten minutes, so I figure now is a good time to use the restroom.

"If you'll excuse me," I say, "I'm going to go freshen up in the ladies' room."

Pearce leans down to me and whispers, "I'll try to get rid of him."

I smile at Gerald. "Nice seeing you again."

He ignores me and continues talking to Pearce. I walk off and exit the ballroom and go down the hall to the restroom. When I walk in there, I enter into a room with fancy chairs and small couches and a chandelier hanging from the ceiling. Beyond that is the actual restroom. I use the facilities, then go to the mirror to refresh my lipstick. A woman who works there keeps trying to give me a towel to dry my hands, so I take it, then leave her a tip.

My phone rings and I stop in the room that's just off the restroom to answer it. I thought it might be Garret calling, but it's Shelby.

"Hi, Shelby." I sit down on one of the upholstered chairs.

"Hi. Are you busy?"

"I'm at a fundraiser in DC. It's at a hotel. I was just leaving the restroom."

"Oh. Sorry. I didn't know you were out of town. We can talk later."

"Let's just talk now. I'm trying to kill some time. Pearce is talking to someone about work and I didn't want to stand there and listen. So what's going on?"

"Logan and I decided we're going to try for another baby." Her voice rises in excitement.

"Shelby, that's great! When did you decide?"

"Yesterday. Logan has been super sweet to me the past few days, even sweeter than normal. Buying me flowers. Bringing home dinner so I wouldn't have to cook. I couldn't figure out what was going on with him. Then he hired a sitter yesterday and took me to a nice hotel for the night and told me how much he loves me and how he wants to try for another baby."

I smile. "I'm so happy for you, Shelby. I know how much you wanted this. I just can't believe you'll soon have four kids. That's a lot for someone who used to say she didn't want kids."

She laughs. "I know. It's crazy, but I love it. I love being a mom. Speaking of kids, did you bring Garret with you?"

"No, he's at home. Eleanor's staying at the house with him. He was so upset when we left."

"Because he didn't want you to leave?"

"Yes. He begged me to stay home. His little face looked so sad and he had tears in his eyes. I almost couldn't go."

"That's sweet how much he misses you guys."

"Yeah. I miss him too. I don't like leaving him, but at least we won't be gone long. Pearce and I are flying back tomorrow night." I check my watch. "I'd love to talk some more, but I should probably get back to the party."

"Yeah. I'll talk to you later. I just had to call and tell you the news. Hey, if I don't talk to you this week, have a nice Thanksgiving."

"You too. Bye, Shelby."

I hang up and go find Pearce. Gerald is gone and Pearce is standing there alone.

I come up behind him. "Excuse me, but are you single?"

He turns around. "I'm afraid not. I'm married to the most beautiful woman in the world."

"In the world?" I smile. "Really? Can you verify that?"

"I can." He cups my cheek and presses his lips to mine for a kiss. "Definitely the most beautiful. And I love her more than words can say."

"I love you too."

Pearce takes a step back and holds his hand out. "Would you like to dance?"

"I would love to." I take his hand and we make our way to the dance floor. There's an orchestra playing and the sound fills the room. Mostly older romantic songs meant for slow dancing.

We dance to several of them, Pearce leading me across the floor. It's nice to be out with him like this. All dressed up. Dancing. Having champagne. It feels like a true anniversary celebration.

The ballroom has an almost magical feel. The ceiling is dark blue with gold swirls painted on it and there are lights embedded in it that look like stars. There are more sparkling white lights around the perimeter of the room.

After some more champagne and more dancing, I'm ready to go. I'm in a romantic mood, ready to go back to our lavish suite and be alone with Pearce.

"Are you ready to get out of here?" he asks, as if he read my mind.

"Yes. Let's go."

The limo brings us back to the hotel. As soon as we're in the room, Pearce takes off his tux jacket and tie, then walks up to me, his eyes on mine. His gaze holds purpose and intent, and I feel the heat rising in the room. He holds my face with his hands and kisses me with those slow sensual kisses that sparked fireworks inside me when we first met. They still set off fireworks in me. I love his kisses. They're bold. Assertive. Determined. They convey what he wants, and fill me with anticipation of what's to come.

He reaches behind me and unzips my dress. Then his hands move slowly up my spine, to my shoulders, and he slips the dress off. I step out of it, wearing just my black lace lingerie and heels.

His eyes rake over me as he unbuttons his shirt. "I've been imagining you like this all night. My imagination didn't do you justice. You look gorgeous."

His shirt drops to the floor, followed by his pants and boxers. My heart picks up its pace at the sight of him. His muscular body. His smooth skin. His arousal. Even though I've been with him for years, he still makes my heart race. He still stirs up those intense feelings of desire. Just seeing him in his tux got me going, and now, my body is longing to be with him.

He steps up to me and kisses me as he unhooks my bra. I slip it off, then pull away from him and walk backwards to the bed. I kick my heels off and lie down, Pearce's eyes on me the entire time. He stalks toward me, and my pulse spikes, wanting him, craving what he's about to do to me. His strong hands grip my hips and he leans down and gently kisses my stomach. My breath catches at the feel of his light, airy kisses. He stops just long enough to slide my panties off, then his hands caress every part of me as he slowly kisses his way up my body, up the inside of my thigh, my hip, along my stomach, and up my chest. The feel of his lips grazing over my skin sends a shiver through me, followed by a flood of fiery hot sensations deep within my core. Sensations that keep building in intensity as his hand settles between my legs while his mouth teases my breast.

I grip his hair as the sensations overtake me, the tension releasing, pleasure coursing through my body. He positions himself over me and enters me with one forceful thrust. I inhale sharply, then breathe out as he begins a rhythm of deep powerful thrusts that recoil the tension in my core. It escalates as his pace quickens. Then I feel it once again. The relief. The overwhelming pleasure that has me calling out his name.

After one more powerful thrust, his body shudders from his own release, then stills as he hovers over me, out of breath. He lays a kiss on my forehead and then my lips. "I love you," he whispers, then his eyes meet up with mine. "I love you beyond what I can even express. I never thought I could love someone this way until I met you. And each day I spend with you, I love you even more."

"Pearce." I smile at him and lift my hand to his cheek. "I love you too. So much. With all my heart."

He moves off me to the side. I turn toward him, lying under his arm and hugging his chest.

I feel him kiss my head. "Happy Anniversary, sweetheart."

I lift my head up and kiss his lips. "Happy Anniversary."

CHAPTER TWENTY

PEARCE

I wake up and check the clock. It's seven, which is too early to get up. But I don't want to go back to sleep. I have other things in mind. Last night with Rachel was amazing and I'd like a repeat performance.

I brush her hair aside and kiss the nape of her neck. She stirs a little and a smile appears. "Pearce."

"Good morning, sweetheart." I leave kisses along her shoulder.

"That feels really good," she says.

"My kisses?"

She smiles wider. "Not just your kisses. All of you."

My naked body is pressed up against her and she can feel how hard I am. She reaches back and strokes me with her hand. I love how she touches me. How she feels. Her scent. She continues to touch me as I kiss her soft skin, my hand roaming over her body.

After a while, she turns around and kisses me, gently pushing me onto my back and straddling me. She lines herself up then slowly sinks down on me, her hands sliding up my chest, landing on my shoulders. I love it when she's on top. I like gazing at her gorgeous body as she moves over me.

"You're beautiful," I say as my hands skim over her curves.

She leans down and puts her lips on mine, her soft hair falling over my chest. I grasp the back of her neck, keeping her at my lips and kissing her deeper. She moans, her hips grinding into me.

When I know she's close, I flip her over onto her back. She smiles and grabs hold of me and I thrust hard and fast inside her until we're both reveling in that deep satisfying afterglow, like we had last night.

"Let's just stay here until we have to leave," she says, catching her breath.

"That's a very good idea." I kiss her cheek, then down her neck, and along her collarbone.

She laughs. "Pearce, we should probably take a break before we do it again."

"I don't need a break." I continue to kiss her. "I already want you again. I can't get enough of you."

The phone rings. I glance up and see that it's my cell phone. My regular one, not the Dunamis one.

"Just let it ring," I say, going back to kissing her.

The phone stops ringing, but then starts up again.

"Pearce, you better get it. Maybe it's Garret."

"He always calls *your* phone, not mine."

"Just see who it is."

I sigh and reach for my phone and flip it over. "It's my father. It's probably something about work. It can wait." I set the phone down and pull her body into mine and resume kissing her.

The phone rings again.

"Shit," I mumble. I reach over to check the phone. "It's my father again. What the hell does he want?"

"You better answer it. It must be important if he keeps calling."

I sigh again as I sit up and lean back against the headboard. I pick up the phone. "Yes, Father. What do you need?"

"I need you to get back here." He sounds tired, his voice weaker than normal. "I came down with the flu last night. I'm very sick. I can't go to the office."

"So stay in bed."

"I will, but I have that meeting at two today with those men from London. They flew all the way here for the meeting. I can't be there. I'm too ill. I need you to do it, Pearce."

"I can't. I have to go to Wingate's speech."

My attendance at his speech isn't optional. Dunamis is making me go there and say a few words about why I'm supporting Wingate. There will be photographers and reporters present, and Dunamis wants me there so the public sees me supporting Wingate's campaign. My father knows this, so I don't know why he's asking me to take his place at the meeting.

"I called and told them," he says. "I explained how much I needed you at this meeting and they agreed to let you fly back early."

Rachel gets out of bed and goes into the bathroom.

I lower my voice. "Father, you know I can't miss this speech. I'm expected to show my support publicly, by speaking to the press."

"They want your wife to do it. She just needs to repeat whatever you were going to say. The press knows she's your wife so we'll still receive the benefit of the public seeing that a Kensington is endorsing Wingate."

"She's not going to agree to that. She doesn't even want to go to this event. She'll want to fly home with me. She misses Garret."

"She can still come home tonight. She can leave after the event."

"I know, but she—"

"Pearce, this isn't a choice. This has already been decided." He coughs. "Goddammit, I'm going to be sick again. I can't talk. Just take care of this for me." I hear him stumbling into what I'm guessing is the bathroom. The phone drops against something and I hear a door shut. I end the call, not wanting to hear the sounds of him getting sick in the bathroom.

"What did he say?" Rachel asks as she comes out of the bathroom, wrapped in one of the white hotel robes.

231

"He has the flu and can't go to work. He needs me to go to a meeting at two. I told him I would, because this is a very important meeting with a potential new client."

"So we're leaving?"

"Come sit down." I move over on the bed. When she's seated, I say, "Would you be willing to stay here and attend Wingate's speech and say a few words about why we're supporting him?"

"You want *me* to do to? I wouldn't know what to say. I haven't even been following his campaign. This is your thing, Pearce, not mine."

"I know, but there are going to be reporters there and I want them to quote us in the papers. It will show our support for Wingate's campaign."

"But they want to hear from *you*, not me."

"As my wife, you represent me. I'll tell you exactly what to say. I'll write it out. It'll be short. Just a paragraph or two saying why I'm supporting him."

"Can I fly home right after I do this? I don't want to stay here if you're not here."

"Yes. I'll see if I can get you on an earlier flight."

Originally, Rachel and I had planned to go out for dinner after Wingate's speech. It was going to be our anniversary dinner since we weren't able to go out for a special dinner last night. I made reservations at a five star restaurant that's supposed to be the best in town. In order to have time for dinner, we booked a flight that leaves at nine tonight.

"So you'll do this?" I ask her.

She sighs. "If you really want me to, then yes."

I hug her into my side and kiss her. "Thank you. I promise I'll make it up to you. I'll plan another weekend trip. Just the two of us."

"You don't have to. But I'd take a nice dinner, since we're missing tonight's anniversary dinner."

"Deal." I kiss her again. "Why don't you go shower while I get the flights changed?"

"What time are you leaving?" She stands up and adjusts her robe.

"I'll try to get a flight out at ten or eleven. It's only an hour flight so I'll have plenty of time to get to the meeting."

"Will you leave when it's over? I want you to go home and be with Garret."

"Yes. The meeting will be a couple hours, but I'll go home when it's done. I'll send my mother back to her house. She needs to check on my father. He didn't sound good."

"That's too bad. I hope he's better by Thanksgiving." She returns to the bathroom to get ready.

I check the flights and find one that leaves at ten-fifteen this morning, but the evening flights are all booked.

"I'm booked on the ten-fifteen," I tell her when she comes back out from her shower. "But I couldn't get you an earlier flight. People must be flying out early for Thanksgiving. Or maybe it's business people trying to get home before the holiday."

"So I'm stuck on the nine o'clock." She dries her hair with the towel. "Well, at least you'll be home with Garret."

"I'm sorry, sweetheart. I know you don't want to be here alone."

"It's okay. I'll go back to the Smithsonian. There's so much I wasn't able to see yesterday."

"That's a good idea." I kiss her on my way to the bathroom. "I'll go get ready."

I'm annoyed by the change in plans. I don't like leaving Rachel here alone. I'd like to call up Jack and have him keep an eye on her, but I can't. Someone from the organization might see him watching her and become suspicious. They might find out I've been secretly talking to him and that would get us both in serious trouble.

At least Rachel won't be here long. She'll only have a few hours on her own, and the Smithsonian is a safe area, full of tourists. She'll be fine.

At nine o'clock, we're standing by the door to our room. The valet has already come to pick up my bag, which is waiting for me in the car that will take me to the airport.

"I need to go," I tell Rachel.

"Good luck with your meeting." She hugs me, then gives me a kiss. "Give Garret a hug for me."

"I will. We'll pick you up at the airport tonight. I know it'll be late but he doesn't have school tomorrow and I know he'll want to see you before he goes to bed." I cup her face with my hand, my thumb brushing over her cheek. "Goodbye, sweetheart." I kiss her, then slowly pull away. "I love you."

She smiles. "I love you too. Have a safe trip."

I get to the airport, and as I'm waiting to board the plane, I realize that I forgot to call Wingate to tell him I wouldn't be at his speech. I wonder if someone from the organization already told him. I call him to find out.

"Hello, Pearce," he says as though he expected my call. "I heard you can't make it today."

"Yes. I'm sorry about that. But Rachel will be there. I wrote out what I was going to say, so she'll just read off the card."

"Sounds good. When is she flying home?"

"Not until nine tonight. I tried to get her an earlier flight but there was nothing available."

"She's welcome to fly up with me. I have an event in Hartford tomorrow morning so I'm going there right after today's speech. You'd have to drive to Hartford to get her, but she'd arrive home a lot sooner than she would taking that other flight."

"Are you taking the jet?"

"Yes. A few of my campaign workers are coming with me, but I have a couple open seats if your wife would like one."

"Let me call and ask her. What time does the plane land in Hartford?"

"Around six. Maybe a few minutes after."

"I'll call her right now and let you know." I hang up and call Rachel's cell phone.

"Do you miss me already?" she asks, laughing a little. "It's only been a half hour."

"I *do* miss you, but that's not why I'm calling." I tell her Wingate's offer. "This would get you home a few hours earlier. What do you think?"

"Maybe I should just take the other flight. You know how I don't like small planes." She pauses. "What do you think I should do?"

"It's up to you."

"Do you think it's safe?"

"I've flown on private planes my whole life and never had a problem."

She sighs. "Then I guess I'll do it. I really want to get home."

"I'll call him back and let him know. Garret and I will drive up to Hartford to pick you up. We'll stop somewhere for dinner on the way home."

"We should go to that cute little diner Garret likes so much. The one that's in a train car that we take him to on his birthday. He's been so sad with us gone the past couple days. This would cheer him up."

I smile. "Having us home will cheer him up, but yes, we can take him there." An announcement blares above me, telling me it's time to board. "I have to go. The plane is boarding. I'll see you soon. I love you."

"I love you too."

We hang up and I board the plane. During the flight, I prepare for my meeting. When we land, I get in my car and drive straight to the office. I call my mother quick to tell her I'll be home early and that she can go home when I get there.

The meeting goes well. I convince the men from London to sign a multiyear contract with us. It puts me in a good mood that gets even better when I get home and see Garret greeting me at the door. I've missed him. I know I wasn't gone long, but I still missed him.

"Dad!" He hugs me, a big smile on his face.

"Did you have a good day?"

"Yes." He pulls me inside the house. "And now I don't have school for almost a whole week!"

"Hello, Pearce." My mother comes down the stairs with her suitcase.

"Hello, Mother." I give her a shoulder hug. "Thank you again for staying with Garret."

"We had a good time." She smiles at him. "Goodbye, Garret."

"Bye, Grandmother." He gives her a hug. She's still not comfortable with hugs, but she doesn't mind them when they're from her grandson. She hugs him back, then lets him go and he comes back over to stand next to me.

"How's Father doing?" I ask her.

"I talked to him an hour ago. It sounds like he's starting to feel better, but I need to get home to check on him."

I open the door for her. "We'll see you on Thursday."

"Yes. See you then."

She leaves and I shut the door and turn back to Garret. "I have a surprise for you." I take him over to the couch.

"What?" he asks excitedly.

"Your mother's taking an earlier flight home. She'll be here at six, but she's landing in Hartford so we have to drive up there and get her. And on the way home, we're taking you to that train car diner you like so much. We're going to have dinner there."

"Yes!" He jumps up and pumps his fist in the air. "Can I get a boxcar sundae?"

That's his favorite item on the menu. It's also his mother's favorite. It's a huge sundae that has crushed cookies layered with ice cream. It's so big that it takes the three of us to eat it all.

I smile. "Yes. We'll be sure to order the sundae. We'll split one, like we always do."

"When are we leaving?"

I check my watch. "Not just yet. A little after five."

The doorbell rings. I get up to answer it. I open the door and see the little boy from down the street. He's nine.

"Hi, Mr. Kensington," he says, looking up at me. He has curly brown hair and his face is full of freckles. "Can Garret come out and play?"

Garret appears next to me. "Hey, Sam."

"Hey. Do you want to play football?"

"Garret and I have to leave soon," I tell him. "But you could toss the ball around in the back yard for a few minutes."

"Come on, Sam." Garret motions him to come inside and they run to the kitchen and out the sliding door to the back yard.

I take my suitcase upstairs and unpack everything. I toss the clothes in the hamper, then zip up the suitcase and set it by the door to take downstairs. I change out of my suit, putting on jeans and button-up shirt. I go in the bathroom and wash my face and put on some cologne. I consider shaving, but then decide to leave the stubble on my face because Rachel likes it.

I was just with her this morning, but I already miss her. The house just isn't the same when she's not here. Now I understand why Garret was so upset when we left. It doesn't feel right when we're not all together as a family.

I look out the window and check on the boys. They're tossing the football to each other, running around the back yard. Garret's smile is back, now that I'm home and now that he knows his mother will be home shortly.

He was so excited when I told him we'd go to the diner. It's in a small college town. We usually only go there for his birthday, but he likes it so much we should take him there more often.

I check the clock. It's almost five. Rachel should be on the plane by now. They probably took off ten or fifteen minutes ago.

I bring my suitcase downstairs and store it back in the closet. Then I go in the kitchen and get a glass of water and sit at the kitchen table. The boys are yelling and laughing out back.

The phone rings and I get up to answer it.

"Hello?"

"Is this Pearce Kensington?" It's a man's voice.

"Yes. Who is this?"

"It's Officer Lander from the Virginia State Patrol."

I freeze, my heart beating faster, my stomach clenching as I take short, shallow breaths.

"What is it, officer?" I can barely get the words out, my heart now thundering in my chest because this is all too familiar to the phone call I received years ago regarding Rachel's parents. An officer called. And he sounded very serious. Just like the man I'm talking to now.

It's not the same, I tell myself. *It can't be. It's not.*

"I'm very sorry to have to tell you this…"

No! Stop! I want him to stop. Please stop. I don't want to hear anymore.

But he can't hear my begging. My internal pleas.

He continues, but I only hear certain words. Certain phrases.

"…there was an accident.…plane went down…soon after takeoff…"

Stop. Please stop.

"…went up in flames…no survivors…"

Oh, God. No. Please, no. Please. It isn't real. This isn't real.

"…investigating the cause…will let you know…anyone you'd like us to call…"

I try to breathe, but I can't. I'm gasping for breath, my lungs constricted from the agony of his words. I can't think. I don't know if I'm awake or if this is some horrible nightmare.

"Mr. Kensington? Are you still there?"

"Yes." I hold the phone to my ear. "I…I just…how did this happen?"

"We won't know until the investigators have had time to go through the wreckage."

I cringe at the word 'wreckage,' imagining a mangled plane and dead bodies everywhere. "You're sure there are no survivors?"

"It went up in flames after impact," he says solemnly. "I'm sorry."

No. God, no. Please, no.

"Do you need me to call anyone? Other family members?"

"No," I manage to say.

"We'll get back to you as soon as we learn more about the crash. Let me give you my number in case you have any questions. Do you have a pen?"

"Not now. I can't. I'm sorry."

"I understand. I'm very sorry for your loss. Goodbye, Mr. Kensington."

CHAPTER TWENTY-ONE

PEARCE

I drop the phone, my whole body trembling as I sob into my hands. How could this happen? There must be a mistake. She was fine. Everything was fine. It was more than fine. It was good. Perfect. Everything was perfect. She'd get home early. We'd have dinner with our son. Then we'd go to bed and I'd kiss her goodnight and she'd fall asleep in my arms, like she always does.

This can't be true. It can't be. She'll be home. We'll go pick her up. And then she'll come home.

The officer was incorrect. He had his facts wrong. He was confused. It was someone else. Not her.

I race to the family room and grab the remote. I find a news channel and see fire and smoke coming from the middle of an open field. I see the edge of something. A wing. The wing of a small private plane.

"Oh God. No." I back up and sit on the couch, my eyes not leaving the screen. On the bottom it reads, 'Private plane goes down in Virginia field. Senator Paul Wingate killed.'

I turn up the volume and the newswoman says, "…no survivors. Given the severity of the crash, it's believed the people on board died on impact. Senator Wingate was heading to Hartford for an event tomorrow and was accompanied by his press secretary and two speech writers. Also on the plane was Rachel Kensington, wife of billionaire Pearce Kensington."

I drop the remote, my arms collapsing at my sides as the woman keeps speaking.

"Our sources say Mrs. Kensington had just attended a speech given by Senator Wingate. Apparently he had offered her a seat on his plane so she could get home to her family in Connecticut. Kensington was originally scheduled on a commercial flight leaving later this evening."

"No!" I squeeze my eyes shut and rub my hands over my face. "She's not dead!"

I hear a man's voice on the TV. "Early reports say the plane appeared to be experiencing problems soon after take-off. Eyewitnesses report seeing it nosedive into this open field, then burst into flames. Investigators are now…"

"She's not dead!" I scream at the TV. "You're wrong! She's not…she's not dead!" I grab the remote from the floor and fumble to find the off button. I finally do, then I throw the remote at the TV, shattering the screen.

The phone rings and I race over to get it. Maybe it's the officer, telling me he was wrong. That she wasn't on the plane. She changed her mind. She decided to wait. To take the commercial flight.

"Hello?" I answer.

"Pearce, it's your mother," she says softly. "I'm so very sorry."

I feel the wetness on my face and realize I'm still crying.

"I just saw the news," she says. "I'll be right over."

"No! Don't come over! It's not true. The news reports were wrong. It's not true!"

"Pearce. I'm coming over."

"You are NOT coming over! Nothing happened! Do you hear me? She's fine. She's on her way home. Garret and I are—"

Garret.

Oh, God. Garret. I have to tell Garret.

"How is he?" she asks.

I glance out the kitchen window and see him running with the football, a huge smile on his face. "I…I haven't told him."

"You need to tell him, Pearce. You don't want him to see it on TV before you tell him."

"Stop talking! Stop telling me what to do!"

"I need to come over. This isn't the time to—"

"You are NOT coming over! I will deal with this." I see Garret outside playing and feel a heaviness in my chest. A throbbing pain just over my heart. "Don't come over. I will tell Garret." I say it softly. "Goodbye, Mother."

I hang up and stand there a moment, watching Garret play. He's so happy. I want him to be happy just a little longer. Because soon, it'll all be over. His happiness will end. Just like mine has ended.

I will never be happy again. Never. My wife. My soulmate. The love of my life…is gone. Forever. And I will never be happy again.

After a few minutes, I clean up my face then open the sliding glass door that leads to the back yard. "Garret, come inside. Sam, you need to go home."

"Dad, can we have a few more minutes? I was showing Sam this new play I came up with."

"No. Get inside. Right now." I take some deep breaths to regain my composure. I can't break down when I tell him this. It'll be hard enough on him. He needs me to be strong. To give him hope that we'll somehow get through this, even though I don't think that we will. I don't know how it's possible.

The boys run up to the house and come inside. I close the door behind them. They go to the sink, filling up glasses of water.

"Sam!" I stand next to him. "You need to go home. Right now!"

Both boys hear the anger in my voice and slowly set their glasses down.

"I guess I'll see ya later," Garret says to Sam, his eyes on me.

"Yeah, bye." Sam runs out of the kitchen, through the living room, and out the front door. I wait until I hear it shut, then go up to Garret.

"Let's sit down." I put my hand on his shoulder and lead him to the couch.

"Am I in trouble?" he asks.

I shake my head. "No. You're not in trouble."

"Then what's wrong? Why did you yell at Sam?"

"I didn't mean to. I just needed him to leave."

"Are we going to pick up Mom now?"

I swallow past the giant lump in my throat. "No."

"But you said we'd leave after five. It's after five."

"We're not going." I look down at his small hands and hold them in mine.

He glances down at our joined hands. "Why aren't we going?"

"Because something happened." I'm not looking at him, but I hear his breath quicken. He knows it's bad. He can sense it.

"What happened?"

"There was an accident."

"What kind of accident?"

Fuck. I can't do this. I can't tell him this.

"Dad, what kind of accident?"

I take a deep breath and swallow. I look up and see him watching me. I don't want to tell him. But I need to. I have to tell him.

"The plane your mother was on went down in a field in Virginia."

He yanks his hands from mine, his chest rising and falling as he takes shallow breaths. "It crashed?"

I nod. "Yes."

His eyes move all around my face, like he's trying to read me. Trying to figure out what this means.

"Is she okay?" he cautiously asks.

I slowly shake my head. "No. She's not okay." I pause, my eyes on his. "She's gone, Garret."

He inhales sharply and quickly stands up. "No. She's not gone. She's not." His lip quivers and tears stream down his cheeks.

"Garret." I reach for him but he backs away.

"I…I made her a card to…to welcome her back." His voice is shaky, his breath uneven hiccups. "It's upstairs. I'll…I'll go get it. We'll bring it…to the airport."

My eyes are tearing up again and the lump in my throat now burns like I just swallowed acid.

"We're not going to the airport, Garret."

"She's not gone!" He screams it as tears pour from his eyes. "She's not! She's not gone!"

I bolt from the couch and pick him up and hold him against me. "I'm so sorry, Garret."

"Put me down!" He starts kicking at me.

I bring him back to the couch and hold him, hugging him tightly against my chest. "I'm so sorry."

"She's not dead!" He's sobbing now. I can't bear to see him hurting this way. My own pain was bad enough, but now I feel his as well and it's excruciating.

I tried to be strong for him, but I can't. My body's shaking, tears pouring down my face.

He looks up at me. He's never seen me cry. Not once.

"Dad?" he says through his tears.

I place my hand on his head and press it back down on my shoulder. I don't want him to see me breaking down. He can hear my sobs and feel my trembling body, but I don't want him to see my face.

I kiss his head and close my eyes and just hold him.

Minutes pass. I don't know how many. And then suddenly, Garret shoves away from me, yelling at me, "You did this!"

I tighten my arms around him, keeping him on my lap. "Garret, stop."

"You did this!" He's punching my chest, screaming. "You made her go! I told her not to. She said she had to! That you were making her go!"

"Garret, no. She wanted to go."

"No, she didn't! She said she wanted to stay! She wanted to stay here with me. If she had, she wouldn't be gone!"

He uses all his strength to fight me, but I won't let him go. I force him into my arms, against my chest.

"It was an accident, Garret," I say. "A horrible accident."

"No!" He's crying so hard he can barely catch his breath.

I can't deal with this pain. I can't take seeing him hurt this much and also feel my own pain. It's too much. The pain is unbearable. But I'm his father. I'm all he has left. So I will try to absorb his pain, and do whatever I can to help him get through this.

I squeeze my arms around him. "I'm so sorry, Garret. I'm so sorry."

We remain there on the couch. The phone keeps ringing, but I don't answer it. I don't care who's calling or what they have to say. The only thing that matters right now is my son.

An hour goes by and Garret's crying slows. My shirt is soaked with his tears. His little body is crumpled within my arms, his head resting on my chest, his hands clinging to me.

All we have is each other now. He only has me. But I don't think I'm enough. I know I'm not. He was so close to his mother. The two of them did everything together. I know Garret loves me and looks up to me and thinks I'm a good father. But that's only because his mother made me that way. Now she's gone, so what will become of me? Will I turn back to the man I was before I met her? I don't want to, but what if I do? What if I can't help it?

Another hour passes and Garret falls asleep in my arms. He's exhausted from crying so much. I kiss his forehead, then rest my head on his.

I think back to when we had him. Rachel almost died during the delivery. I was so scared I would lose her. I begged God not to take her. And now he has. He took her from me. But why? Am I being punished for all the bad things I've done? If so, it's not fair. It's not fair to my son. He did nothing wrong. He's just a little boy. He needs his mother.

I hold him closer and lightly rock him, like I did when he was just a baby. He falls into a deeper sleep and I carry him upstairs to his room. I put him in his bed and pull the covers over him and kiss his head.

It's still early, and I couldn't sleep even if I tried, so I go back downstairs. I sit at the kitchen table. I remember when we bought this table. It was right before Rachel and I had our fake wedding. I worried the wedding would never happen. I thought for sure they'd stop it. Even though the organization agreed to it, and even planned it, I still didn't trust that they'd let it happen. I thought that would be my punishment for my secret marriage to Rachel that had happened months earlier. I thought they'd let me think I could have her, but then they'd take her away. They'd stop the wedding and force me to divorce her.

But that never happened. And I still don't know my punishment for marrying her.

I burst up from my chair. Is this it? Is this my punishment? Did they do this to Rachel? But they didn't know she'd be on the plane. It was a last minute decision and nobody knew except Wingate and me.

And Dunamis wouldn't kill Wingate. He's too valuable, which is why they were going to make sure he was re-elected. So if they wanted to kill Rachel, they'd find a different way. They have many ways to kill people. Easier ways. Less public ways.

It wasn't them. It was an accident. A horrible tragic accident.

The phone rings again and I'm tempted to disconnect it from the wall. I don't want to talk to anyone and I don't want the loud ringing to wake up Garret.

It keeps ringing and I pick it up just to make it stop.

"Who is it?" I bark into the phone.

"It's Jack." I hear heavy breathing, like he's out of breath.

"Jack, why are you calling me at home? We can't—"

"They already know. Or at least one of them does. Someone found my phone. The one I've been using to call you. It's missing, and I don't know who has it."

Shit. That's bad. For both of us.

"I can't deal with this now. Rachel—"

"Yes, I know," he says. "I need you to meet me. Right now."

246

"What? What are you talking about?"

"This is urgent. Meet me at 225."

That's the number we assigned to the location we said we'd met at if we ever needed to talk in person without them finding out. We gave the location a number so if they were listening in, they wouldn't know where Jack and I were meeting. We have several locations, each with a different number. Location 225 is five miles from here. It's a scenic turnoff. A place tourists can stop and take photos of the leaves in the fall.

So Jack's here in Connecticut. But he was just in DC. He was at Wingate's fundraiser and I know he attended Wingate's speech. How did he get here so fast? He must've taken his jet.

"Pearce! Meet me at 225. Leave right now."

"I can't! I can't leave Garret here alone. And I can't take him with me. He's asleep. I can't wake him up. He's been crying for hours. He needs to sleep."

"I need to talk to you. It can't wait. Just leave Garret there and come meet me."

"What is this about?"

"I'll tell you when you get here."

"I can't do this right now. I can't even think straight. We'll have to meet later."

"Pearce! Listen to me! This is a goddamn emergency! I'm not joking around here. Get in your fucking car right now and meet me at 225!" His voice is frantic. I've never heard him sound this way.

I hesitate. "Fine. But I can't be gone long." The phone is silent. "Jack?" He hung up.

This better be a matter of life or death or I am going to kill Jack. My wife just died and he wants to meet? Now? What the hell is wrong with him?

I go upstairs and check that Garret is asleep. He is, so I go back downstairs and out to my car. I speed down the road, turning down the side road that takes me to the location where I'm meeting Jack. It's very dark and hard to see but I spot the large sign, alerting tourists that a scenic overlook is just up ahead.

Jack's car is waiting just past the sign, but it's hidden behind the bushes so I almost didn't see it. I park and turn off the engine. I storm over to Jack's car, furious that he's making me meet with him at a time like this.

His window is down and he says, "Get in."

He puts his window back up as I go around to the other side of the car. I get in the front seat, slamming the door shut.

"What the hell is this about? My wife just died! And you think *now* is a good time to meet?"

He turns to me. "Just listen to me." He still sounds out of breath. Panicked. "I have to tell you something. Something that changes everything. Earlier today, I was with—"

He falls forward, his head hitting the steering wheel.

"Jack?" I push him back against the seat.

It's so dark I can't see anything, so I turn on the overhead light in the car. I notice the hole in the glass.

A bullet hole.

In the side window.

Right next to Jack's head.

I turn him toward me and see blood running down his face.

"Shit!" I quickly shut off the overhead light and duck down, assuming more shots are coming. The shooter had to have seen me. Just moments ago, I got out of my car. He had to have seen me walk over here and get in Jack's car.

I don't have my gun with me. I'm sure Jack has weapons in the trunk, but I can't go out and get them. Not now. Not with someone lurking in the bushes, waiting to kill me.

It could be anyone. A freelancer. An enemy of Jack's. A fellow Dunamis member who found out that Jack and I had been secretly communicating. Jack said someone found his phone. If that person told Dunamis, they'd know Jack didn't follow the rules. But they wouldn't kill him because of that, would they? They need him. He's extremely valuable because of his knowledge of surveillance equipment and his company's development of it. They wouldn't kill him just for talking on the phone to me.

It's possible Jack did something else to anger them. He could've betrayed them some other way. But how? What could he have done that would make them want to kill him? Tonight? At this very moment?

Maybe he didn't do anything. Maybe this is my punishment. Maybe it's finally happened. They know how much I love Jack, so they took him from me. The one person I could confide in. The one person who knew both sides of me and still believed I was good. The one person who gave me hope that I could get out of Dunamis someday, and keep my son out of it.

Jack's body is limp, slumped back against the seat.

"Jack?" I shake him a little, hoping by some miracle he's alive, but I know he's not.

He's dead. Jack's dead.

I move his suit jacket aside and find what I was looking for. There's a gun in a holster attached to his belt.

I take it, and check to make sure it's loaded. Then I listen for noises. Rustling of the trees or the bushes. But it's a windy night and it's hard to discern rustling from the wind from the rustling of a person's movements.

My mind suddenly switches to Garret. I can't leave him alone at the house. What if he wakes up and sees I'm not there? He'll panic. He'll think I'm gone, just like his mother.

I have to get out of here. I have to go home. I slowly open the door, my gun aimed and ready. Again, I listen for any noises, but I only hear the howling wind. I decide to make a run for it. There's a good chance the shooter won't hit me if I'm running.

I bolt to my car, then shove my keys in the ignition and start the engine. I back up onto the road and speed off. I check that no one's behind me, following me. There's nobody there. Not a single car.

When I reach the house, I park in the garage and close the door. I go inside and make sure every door and window is locked. Then I race up to Garret's room. He's still asleep. Sound asleep. I don't want him in here alone, so I carefully pull back his blankets and pick him up and take him down to my room. I set him on the bed and lie next to him, putting my arm protectively around him.

"It's okay," I whisper. He's still asleep so I'm saying it more to myself than to him.

But it's a lie. It's not okay. Nothing is okay.

Rachel is dead.

And now Jack is dead.

What the fuck just happened? Why was Jack killed? And why did he want to meet with me? What was he going to tell me?

CHAPTER TWENTY-TWO
Earlier That Day

RACHEL

It's four o'clock and I just finished making my remarks about Senator Wingate. Actually, they were Pearce's remarks. I just read them off a card. It took less than two minutes to read. I'm annoyed I had to stick around all day just to do that. But Pearce really likes this guy and wants him to win so I agreed to do it.

At least I'll get home at a decent hour thanks to Wingate offering me a seat on his plane. I don't like private planes, but luckily it's a short flight, just over an hour.

"I'm not sure when we're leaving," Wingate says quietly to me. We're surrounded by people wanting to talk to him. Reporters. Donors. Lobbyists. "If you want to go without us, we'll meet you there. The airport has a nice waiting area with some televisions and reading material."

"Okay. I'll head over there."

He pulls out a business card and a pen and writes down the name of the private airport. "Just tell your driver to take you there."

"Thank you." I smile as he walks off.

Three members of his staff are going with us on the plane. I met them earlier and see them now scattered around the room, engaged in conversation. At this rate, we won't fly out on time. The plane is supposed to take off at four forty-five but it's already after four and there are people lined up waiting to talk to Wingate.

We're in the same hotel we were at for the party last night, but we're in a large conference room instead of the ballroom. My phone rings and I go out in the hall to answer it. I thought it might be Pearce calling, but it's someone else. I don't recognize the number.

"Hello?"

There's silence, but then I hear a voice. "Rachel Kensington?" It's a man's voice, but it's distorted, like when someone's trying to hide their identity.

"Who is this?" I ask, suddenly feeling nervous. Why would someone distort their voice?

"Listen very carefully. You need to follow my instructions exactly as given. If you don't, you will die."

I gasp and an icy chill courses through me. "Who is this? Tell me!"

"Go in the women's restroom, the same one you were in last night, just outside the ballroom. Go in the first stall and—"

"Who is this?" I'm gripping the phone, shaking. "Is this a joke? Because it is not funny. I'm hanging up!"

"You'll die," the voice says in its distorted tone.

"Why do you keep saying that?" My words are breathy and almost incoherent because I'm shaking so much. "Who is this? Please. Tell me."

"This is not a joke. If you want to live, if you want to see your family again, you will listen to me. You will follow my instructions."

I swallow hard and nod. "Okay. Go ahead."

"As soon as we hang up, you will go in the women's restroom. You will go in the first stall, closest to the door. In the stall, you will find a backpack. Inside it are clothes, shoes, and a black wig. You will put these items on, then stuff the clothes and shoes you're wearing into the backpack and leave it in the stall where you found it. Do NOT call anyone. Leave your cell phone in the backpack. Then walk to the hotel entrance. Do not act frightened or rushed. You must act normal. Walk at a normal pace. Do not draw attention to yourself. Do not talk to anyone, other than the valet. He'll ask if you need a car. Tell him you've already called for one. Then look for a black limo with a driver wearing a chauffeur's hat, a black suit, and a red bow tie. Do not get into any other limo. Those are your instructions. You must leave right now."

"I'm not doing this! I don't even know who you are!"

"Do you want to live?"

"Yes! Of course!"

"Then do as I say. And hurry. We're running out of time."

"No. I can't do this. I don't believe what you're telling me. Why would I listen to you? You could be planning to kill me yourself. Or kidnap me." I'm shaking even more now. I see people leaving the conference room and wonder if I should go up to them and tell them what's happening, or go find a security guard and ask him for help.

"You need to trust me, Rachel."

"How can I trust someone I don't even know?"

"You know me. And I know you."

"Then tell me who you are."

"If I tell you, you must agree to follow my instructions."

"Okay. I will." It's a lie, but what's he going to do? He can't force me to follow his orders. I'm in a public place. I'll just go find security as soon as he hangs up, or I'll call the police.

I hear his voice again. "How do you like your steak?"

My breath catches and the phone slips from my hand.

It's Jack. Jack's the man on the phone.

I quickly pick up the phone and put it back to my ear.

"Don't say anything," he says. "Just do as I told you. And hurry. The limo is waiting out front."

I walk down the hall to the women's restroom. I go inside, past the small room with the couches and chairs, and head to the stalls. I stop at the first one and go in and shut and lock the door. Hanging on the hook on the back of the stall door is a black backpack. I unzip it and find a long-sleeve black dress, a black and brown patterned scarf, black heels, and a short black wig.

The dress I'm wearing is an emerald green sleeveless dress with a jacket. There's gold stitching around the sleeves of the jacket and the neckline of the dress. My shoes match the dress; heels in the same emerald green.

I quickly change into the other clothes, tying the scarf loosely around my neck. My hair is already up, so I slip the wig over my head, adjusting it and tucking in the stray strands of my hair, hiding them. I stuff my dress, shoes, and cell phone in the backpack, then walk out of the stall. I take a deep breath as I look at myself in the mirror. It doesn't even look like me with the jet black hair that frames my face, curling around my chin, bangs straight across my forehead.

Why is Jack doing this? Why did he say I would die if I didn't do what he said? Is Jack not the man I thought he was? Can I trust him? What if I can't?

I consider not meeting him out front, but my gut tells me to do it. Jack was like a father to Pearce. He was like a grandfather to Garret. He wouldn't do anything to hurt me, would he? I hope not. Then again, he hasn't spoken to us since he moved here. Why wouldn't he talk to us? What has he been up to the past few years? Did he get himself in trouble? Get involved with the wrong people? But what does that have to do with me?

There's noise in the hallway. I need to get out of here. Am I really doing this? I could just change back to my original clothes and go back to the conference room and wait for Wingate and his staff to finish up, then ride to the airport with them.

What should I do? Part of me feels like I should trust Jack, but the other part of me doesn't.

I'll call Pearce. Why didn't I think to do that earlier? What is wrong with me? I go back in the stall and take my phone from the backpack. But the screen says 'service disconnected.' Shit! He canceled my cell phone service? How did he do that so fast?

I return the phone to the backpack and leave the stall and walk out of the restroom. People are coming and going from the conference room, while others are strolling up and down the hall, talking on their phones. Should I stop someone and ask for help? But Jack said not to talk to anyone. He told me to go straight to the hotel entrance.

Dammit! I don't know what to do. This is crazy! It doesn't make sense. Why would someone be trying to kill me?

A woman goes around me on her way to the restroom. I step out of the way and move down the hall a little. I need to make a decision. And fast.

I take a deep breath and replay Jack's words in my head. *This is not a joke. If you want to live, if you want to see your family again, you will listen to me. You will follow my instructions.*

I start heading to the front of the hotel. I'm doing this. I'm putting all my faith in Jack, trusting that he wouldn't do this unless he had to. Unless he really thought my life was in danger.

When I get to the hotel entrance, I spot a woman wearing a green dress out of the corner of my eye. I glance over and gasp when I see that she looks just like me. Like I used to look until I put on this disguise. She's my height, my size, and has the same color hair, and it's pulled up just like I was wearing it earlier. And she has on the exact same emerald green dress I had on, and the same shoes.

I watch as she hurries out the door and gets in a black Mercedes that has a driver. The car drives off, and behind it I see a black limo with a driver wearing a red bow tie. I go outside.

The valet approaches me. "Do you need me to call you a car?"

I smile at him. "No. I already have one. Thank you."

The driver in the limo nods toward the back seat, signaling me to get in. I walk over and open the door and step inside. Once I'm in, I hear the doors lock and we drive away.

"Jack?" I lean forward toward the partition that separates us.

"Don't talk until we get there." The voice comes out of a speaker in the back. It kind of sounds like Jack, but I'm not sure if it's him. I couldn't see much of the driver's face because he had his head down and a chauffeur's hat pulled low over his forehead.

We drive for almost an hour. Wingate's flight already left and soon Pearce and Garret will be waiting for me at the airport. I need to call Pearce and let him know I won't be there.

The limo slows down as it approaches a building that looks like a warehouse. A large door, like a garage door, lifts up and we drive inside the building and down a ramp, parking in front of an elevator. It looks like we're in a parking garage, but there are no other cars here. No people. Nothing.

The driver gets out and opens my door. "Come on."

I step out of the car and look at him. "Jack?"

He removes his hat. "Yes." He takes my hand. "Come with me. I'll explain everything."

We go in the elevator and he stares at a panel on the elevator wall and the light on it goes from red to green. Then the elevator begins moving down, and keeps going for what seems like forever. It finally stops and we exit the elevator and Jack leads me down a narrow hall lined in concrete.

"Go ahead," he says, motioning me into a room at the end of the hall. It's also lined in concrete.

I cautiously enter the room, with Jack right behind me.

"What is this place?" I ask, feeling a little claustrophobic. It's a small room and I know it's deep underground. I feel like we'll run out of air if we stay here too long.

He doesn't answer my question. Instead he goes over to a bottle of scotch that's sitting on the table. There's nothing in the room but a long metal table and eight metal chairs.

"Would you like a drink?" He holds up one of the two short glasses that were sitting by the scotch.

"No," I say, even though a drink would help calm my nerves. But I need to stay focused and alert.

He takes a seat at the end of the table, near the scotch. "Sit down."

I sit next to him and notice I'm shaking again. I don't like this. I don't like that he took me to this underground room. The Jack I know wouldn't do this. Why would he take me here? What is this place?

His hand covers mine. "Rachel. I'm sorry about this, but I didn't have a choice."

I pull my hand back. "What's going on here, Jack? Are you going to hurt me?"

"No. Just the opposite. I'm trying to save you." He reaches in his shirt pocket and takes out a folded piece of paper. He unfolds it and sets it in front of me. It doesn't say who it's from. There isn't much on it. Just a few short phrases. I read what it says.

Grievance against: Member 1479K.
Order: to remove obstacle created by Member 1479K
Obstacle: 35-year-old female, mother of member 1525K
Previous attempts to rectify this matter: several attempts, including private meetings and warning letters; all met with resistance and a refusal to cooperate
Remedy: flight from DC To Hartford

"What does this mean?" I ask Jack, holding up the sheet of paper. "Is this about me?"

"Yes. They were going to kill you on today's flight."

I suck in a breath, then swallow. "Who's 'they'?"

"I'll explain in a moment. But for now, you need to see this." Jack takes something out of his suit jacket. It looks like a cell phone with a very large screen. He sets it in front of me. "I can't get television reception down here, but this is what was airing on the news just now. I recorded this when we were in the car."

He taps the screen and a video begins playing. A reporter holding a microphone is standing in a grassy field. Off in the distance I see a fire burning, black smoke filling the air. Fire and rescue trucks are lined up next to it.

"According to witnesses," the reporter says, "the plane nosedived into the field soon after takeoff. It's believed everyone on board died on impact. Senator Wingate was accompanied by his press secretary and two speech writers. Also on board was

257

Rachel Kensington, wife of billionaire businessman, Pearce Kensington."

I cover my mouth with my hand. "Oh my God."

The reporter continues. "Mrs. Kensington had just attended Senator Wingate's speech. It's not yet clear why she was on the plane. Records show that she was already booked on a commercial flight leaving later tonight."

The video ends and I slide the phone back toward Jack. "All those people are dead? Wingate? His staff? The pilot?"

He nods. "Yes."

"And…me?" I grab Jack's arm. "People think I'm dead? Pearce? Garret?"

"Yes."

"Jack, we need to tell them! I can't let them think—"

"I'll tell them, but not right now. For now, this is how it has to be. Everyone has to think that you're dead. They planned this, and if they knew you were alive, they'd try to kill you again. And next time, they'd make sure they succeeded."

"You keep saying 'they.' Who's 'they'?"

"The people who made the order." He points to the sheet of paper.

I pick it up again. "I don't understand. What's Member 1479?"

"It's a membership number."

"Membership in what? What are you talking about?"

"The organization. It's a secret society. Every member has a number."

Secret society? I know secret societies exist. They have for hundreds of years. I learned about them in my history studies. But why would a secret society be trying to kill me?

My hands are shaking as I clutch the paper. "Who's 1479?"

He pauses, then says, "Pearce."

CHAPTER TWENTY-THREE

RACHEL

My eyes dart up to Jack's, my heart pounding. "What are you saying, Jack?"

"Pearce is a member of the organization. It's a secret society that has been around for hundreds of years. I am also a member."

I quickly shake my head. "No. That's not true."

"Rachel, I wouldn't lie about this. I have no reason to. This group exists and your husband is part of it."

My eyes return to the paper. "Who's 1525?"

He looks down, then back up at me. "Garret."

I slam the paper down on the table. "My son is not a member of anything! He's just a little boy!"

"Yes, but someday he'll be a member, like Pearce. Membership is passed to sons. Holton is also a member."

"No. This can't be right." I take a breath, but it hurts to breathe. My chest is tight, like I can't get any air in. "If Pearce was part of a secret society, I would know. He couldn't keep a secret like that from me."

"He can and he did. He has for years. He couldn't tell you. If he did, he'd be punished. And you'd be killed."

"Stop it!" I shove up from the chair, the metal legs scraping against the concrete floor. "Stop saying these things! This is absurd! Are you drunk? Or on some kind of drug?"

"It's the truth, Rachel." He leans back in his chair. "All these years, didn't you wonder why he sometimes suddenly left late at night?"

"He had to go to work."

"He didn't go to the office. He was doing an assignment."

"What assignment? What does that mean?"

"We're given assignments." He takes a drink of his scotch. "You might want to sit down for this."

I return to my seat and Jack tells me what these assignments are. When he's done, I feel like I might throw up. My stomach feels sick and my throat is burning as I fight back tears.

"Pearce would never hurt anyone."

"He isn't given a choice. None of us are. So to live with ourselves, we have to pretend it's not us. We have to separate ourselves from our actions. The Pearce you know is not the Pearce who does these things. It's someone else. Someone he would never let you see."

"What if he told them no?"

"They would punish him. Hurt him. Hurt *you*. Or kidnap your son."

"No! This isn't true. It can't be!"

"I'm sorry, Rachel, but it is."

"Why do they make Pearce do these things?"

Jack explains the purpose of the assignments. He tells me about how this secret group tries to control things. Politics. The economy. Major industries.

I'm listening, but finding it difficult to believe. This can't possibly be real. But Jack is very serious, so maybe this group really does exist.

"I'm sure from your history studies you learned about secret societies," he says.

"Yes. But generally, the purpose of such groups is to help their members get ahead in their careers. Network with the right people. Get access to top positions in politics and business."

"Our group does that as well. But we also do other things."

"Like manipulate the outcome of political elections."

He nods. "Yes."

"How do they not get caught?"

"We have people planted on the inside. People placed within the government, law enforcement, financial institutions, major corporations. Some of these people are members. Some aren't. Senator Wingate wasn't a member, but he *was* working for us on the inside."

"And if people find out about this group, they're hurt. Or…killed."

He nods again. "Yes."

"Pearce is NOT part of this! This group you're talking about is evil. Pearce is not evil. He doesn't hurt people. He's kind. And loving. A good father. A good husband."

Tears break free from my eyes as my emotions overwhelm me. Anger. Sadness. Disappointment. They all hit me at once, and I know the reason I'm feeling this way is because part of me believes everything Jack is telling me. It would explain why Pearce acted the way he did. Why he'd sometimes have to leave suddenly, saying he forgot to do something at work. He'd come home later and be quiet and withdrawn, completely different than when he left. Or sometimes he'd get a call on his work phone and I'd see his expression change. He'd look worried, almost panicked. Then he'd hug Garret or me really tight, tighter than normal. And sometimes he'd look really sad for no particular reason. I thought it was just his personality. He had a horrible childhood, so I thought maybe those memories haunted him sometimes, filling him with sadness.

For years I found ways to explain his behavior, all reasons that made sense to me. Never in a million years would I have thought Pearce was part of some secret society. Why would I? It's crazy! The thought hadn't even entered my head.

"You saved him, Rachel," Jack says. "Before you met him, Pearce had nothing to live for. His father treated him like shit. He worked nonstop. And he was forced to be part of this group. He hates being part of it. He would do anything to get out, but he can't."

"What about our son? What about Garret?"

"Pearce and I have been trying to find a way to get him out of his obligation. We've both been talking to the other members, seeing who else wants to get their sons out before it's too late."

"When is it too late?"

"Once they're initiated as members, they can't get out. Initiation usually happens when a man is 20 or 21."

"Garret is 10. Twenty isn't that far away."

"Let Pearce and I worry about that. For now, we need to worry about you. If everything worked as planned, the organization now assumes that you're dead."

"Why do they want me dead?"

"Because Pearce married you. A member's wife is supposed to be chosen for him and the woman's father is usually a member. So when he broke tradition and secretly married you, the organization was furious."

I think back to when Pearce and I were dating. He kept trying to hide our relationship. And his parents were so angry when they met me, as if he shouldn't be with me. And our elopement. It was so sudden. Pearce was so insistent that we had to get married that weekend. I found it odd that he was in such a hurry, but he said if we didn't, his parents would try to interfere. Now I know why. It's all piecing together and finally making sense.

"When they found out what he had done," Jack says, "Pearce thought for sure they'd force him to divorce you, but they didn't. Instead, they told Pearce he would be punished, but he wasn't told what the punishment would be or when it would happen. The plane crash today was his punishment."

"That note you showed me said there were meetings and warning letters. Is that true?"

"No. They only put that in there to justify their actions. There was one meeting that occurred right after your wedding in Vegas. During that meeting, they told Pearce he would be punished, but they never told him he had to divorce you. In fact, they were the ones who planned the March wedding."

This is all too much to take in. The lies. The secrets. I don't know if I believe Jack. Or trust him.

"How do I know you're telling me the truth?" I ask. "You could've just made up those words on that piece of paper. Maybe YOU'RE the one who doesn't want me to be with Pearce. Maybe you're just trying to get rid of me."

He huffs in anger. "I would NEVER do that! I know how much Pearce loves you. I know how happy you've made him. I'm doing this so that you two can be together again If I'd let you get on that plane, you'd be dead. You saw the news footage. I saved your life, Rachel."

I nod, realizing he's right. I keep telling myself that video wasn't real. But it was. I saw it with my own eyes.

Jack slides the cell phone back over to me. "I didn't want to show you this, but since you don't seem to believe me, you should probably see it. I recorded this last night. Leland Seymour was at Wingate's party. I asked him if we could talk privately so we went up to his hotel suite and had some drinks."

Jack presses the screen and another video appears. It shows Leland and Jack talking. They're standing by a tall table that looks like a bar, with liquor bottles and glasses. They both have drinks in their hands.

"Why are you here?" Jack asks him. "You're not supposed to be at this event."

"You know I've always been a fan of Senator Wingate. I like his obstinate attitude. It's refreshing." Leland takes a swig of his drink.

"And yet it's going to get him killed," Jack says. "I assume that's why you're here."

"You can only fight them for so long. You know that, Jack. As his handler, you should've warned him."

"As his handler, someone should've told me the goddamn plan!"

"We couldn't." Leland takes another drink. "You're too close to the target."

"I'm not close to Wingate. I rarely even talk to him. I watch him from afar."

"I'm not referring to Wingate." Leland sets his glass down on the bar. "I'm referring to the other target."

Jack pauses, then says, "Does this have to do with Pearce?"

Leland laughs. "Pearce. He's completely naive. An ignorant optimist. Thinking he could marry that woman and get away with it."

Jack is quiet, his expression blank. Then he says, "You're right. Pearce never should've married her. I tried to tell him that many times, but he wouldn't listen to me. He's a goddamn fool. And now he'll lose his life over it."

"Not *him*. His wife." Leland pulls a sheet of paper from his suit jacket and hands it to Jack. It looks like the piece of paper Jack showed me.

Jack puts his glass down and reads what's written on the paper. "So this is Pearce's punishment? It's about damn time they did something. How long have they been planning this?"

"Since right after his fake wedding."

"That was years ago. Why the hell did they wait so long?"

Leland picks up his drink. "That, my friend, is confidential. I've already told you more than I should. I trust you won't use this information to betray us, Jack." Leland stares at him, a slight grin on his face.

Jack walks to the door, the piece of paper still in his hand. "Goodnight, Leland."

The video ends and Jack takes his phone back. "When I was questioning him, I had no idea about the plan they had for you. I recorded Leland just in case he told me something he shouldn't, and surprisingly he did. But I thought he'd tell me about Wingate, not you."

"They wanted to kill me this whole time?" I feel breathless as I say the words. I feel like my lungs keep constricting, leaving me struggling for air. "How was all this going on and I didn't know about it?"

"They're good at hiding their secrets, even among their own members. They hid it from me. They hid it from Pearce. I'm sure only a very small number of people knew this. Usually, an assignment like this would involve a committee of members because it's much more complicated than a traditional assignment. And obviously, Leland Seymour was on that committee."

"Why Leland? Why is he involved?"

"Leland is a member. He owns MDX Aerodynamics. They make airplane engines and parts. If the organization wants to rig a plane to go down, Leland is the one they talk to. He's taken down planes in the past and I'm sure he took this one down as well."

"How could Leland do this to me? I know him. I've been to his house many times. I've met his wife and his daughters. How could he do that to me? Even if he doesn't like me, I'm still Pearce's wife. And Leland is friends with Pearce."

"We have no friends. We trust no one. Friends. Enemies. They're one in the same."

"How did you know something might be going on? Or did you just find out by accident?"

"Leland wasn't supposed to be at Wingate's party, so when he was, I became suspicious. I knew something was being planned for Wingate, which made me even more suspicious. Because if Wingate was being killed, I should've been told. I've been assigned to keep an eye on him so he doesn't step out of line, so if he was being killed, I should've been the first to know. But I wasn't."

"So that's why you went up to Leland's room to talk to him?"

"Yes, but I wasn't expecting to find out you were part of the plan. When Leland gave me that piece of paper, and confirmed you were being killed, I panicked. But I couldn't let him see that. I had to go along with the plan and act like I was fine with it. I left his hotel suite and went back to the ballroom. I knew you were scheduled on a commercial flight, so that piece of paper

265

didn't make sense. You and Wingate would be on separate flights. I went up to Wingate and casually asked him who was going to be on his plane to Hartford. He didn't mention your name, but I knew they'd find a way to get you on that plane. Taking down a private plane is much easier than taking down a commercial jet. And sure enough, the next day I talked to Wingate's press secretary before his speech, and she mentioned that you were flying to Hartford with them. Luckily, I already had a plan in place to make sure you didn't get on that flight. And that's how we ended up here."

I think back to earlier today, after he called me. "There was a woman at the hotel. She looked just like me."

"Yes. I hired her so that they'd think it was you that got in that Mercedes. They tapped into the hotel cameras and were watching you, except it wasn't you. It was a different woman. And while they were distracted, watching her car drive away, I was able to pick you up in the limo, hopefully without being noticed."

"What about the plane? I wasn't on it."

"The Mercedes arrived at the airport, as planned, and they saw the fake you go inside. And you were listed on the flight records, so they assumed you were on the plane when it went down."

"But why would Wingate leave without me?"

"Once everyone else was on the plane, I called Wingate, pretending to be Pearce, and told him you'd changed your mind and were taking the later commercial flight. So Wingate and his staff took off without you."

"If they investigate, they'll know I wasn't on it."

"When the plane crashed, it went up in flames. The fire destroyed everything. There won't be much, if any, remains."

My stomach knots. "So they killed all those innocent people just to get rid of me?"

"And Wingate. He's always been difficult to deal with and the organization had had enough. Wingate knew too much to stay alive, so they arranged for his plane to go down."

"Why didn't you save Wingate? And all those other people?"

"The plane had to go down. In order to save you, I had to make it look like their plan worked." He sighs. "I wish I could've saved those people, but I had to make a choice. It was you or them. And I chose you. You're like a daughter to me, Rachel, and Pearce is like a son."

"Then why did you stop talking to us?"

"Because they ordered me to. I was Pearce's mentor for years, but they thought I was getting too close to him. Too emotionally involved. So they forced me to move to DC and told me to keep my distance from Pearce. But I haven't done so. I've been calling him every week on a phone that can't be traced."

"You have?" I stare down at the table. "He never told me. He hasn't told me any of this. I feel like our whole marriage has been a lie."

"It hasn't been a lie. Look at me, Rachel." He waits until I do. "Don't you ever doubt how much Pearce loves you. If he could have, he would've told you everything. He wanted to, many, many times. But doing so would've put you at risk. People who find out our secrets get killed. So I'm telling you now, everything I've told you today must remain confidential. You can never tell anyone what you know. Do you understand?"

"Yes." My head is pounding, my thoughts racing so fast I can't keep up. I don't want to believe any of this, but for some reason I do. Maybe because deep-down, part of me always knew Pearce was hiding something from me. I just didn't know what.

"Why didn't you tell Pearce?" I ask. "When you found out about the plan they had for me, why didn't you tell him?"

"Because Pearce can't think straight when it comes to you. If he knew of their plan, he would've gone on a rampage, trying to kill every damn one of them, and in doing so, he would've got himself killed."

I take a breath, trying to calm down enough to stay focused on what he's saying. "So what happens now? What do I do?"

"You're leaving. Tonight. You're taking an overnight flight and you're leaving the country. You are no longer Rachel Kensington. You have a new identity. A new passport. A new history. You didn't grow up in Indiana. You grew up in Maryland. Your father worked on a fishing boat." He reaches under the table and slides out a drawer. Inside is a folder. He takes it out, sets it on the table, and slides it over to me. "You need to memorize the contents of that folder. That's the new you. You will assume the identity I've created for you."

"So I'm dead now?" Tears fall from my eyes. "I'll never see my son again? I'll never see Pearce?"

"You will. It'll just take time. I'm going to see Pearce tonight to tell him what happened. I'll tell him you're alive. Then it'll be up to him to find a way to get you back."

"You just said you didn't want to tell him because of how he'd react."

"Once he knows you weren't on that plane and that you're alive and safe, he'll be able to think this through and come up with a plan. Pearce knows how they work. He'll understand why I did this and why the crash had to happen. When I meet with him tonight, I'll tell him how I think he should handle this, but ultimately it'll be up to him. He has to be the one to do this. I can't do any more to help him. Or you. I've already put myself and my family at risk by doing this."

Jack must see the hopelessness on my face because he reaches over and holds my hand. "Pearce will get you back. I don't know how, but I know he'll find a way. As long as he knows you're alive, he will spend every waking moment trying to find a way to get you back. But it could take months, or even years, so you need to be patient. And you must never contact him. Or me. Or anyone else from your former life. If you do, you'll put us all in danger. You need to wait for Pearce to come get you."

"No!" I yank my hand back from his. "I can't do this. I can't leave my family behind. Just take me to Pearce. I'll hide out at home. Or somewhere near the house. I'll stay in hiding until Pearce can figure this out."

"It's too risky. We can't risk someone finding you. If they discovered you were alive, they would kill you, and they wouldn't bother with a plane crash. They'd kill you as soon as they saw you. And what if Garret was with you when they did it? What if you were shot at, but the bullet accidentally hit your son?"

"Oh, God." I cover my face with my hands. "Don't even say that!"

"This is why you can't go back. Not yet."

"Then I'll move somewhere else. I'll go to the West Coast, far away from anyone who knows me."

"You can't be here, Rachel. You can't be in the US. We have members all over the country and all of them know who you are. And the public knows you. If someone saw you, they'd report it. You're supposed to be dead."

"I can't leave the country. I can't be that far away from my family. There has to be a different way."

"There *is* no other way. The only way to keep you and your family safe is for you to go far away where nobody knows you."

I close my eyes, tears streaming down my face. "I don't think I can do it, Jack. Garret needs me. He's just a little boy. He needs his mother. I can't leave my son."

"You have to. You'd be putting yourself in danger if you stayed."

"Not if I stay hidden. Pearce will find me a safe place to hide where Garret could come see me."

"There's no safe place to hide you. Not here. Not in the US. If you remain here, they will find you. And when they do, you risk them harming more than just you. They could do something to Garret. Or Pearce."

I shudder at the thought. "Why? Why would they hurt them?"

"To punish you for their plan not working."

"That doesn't make sense."

"The organization has spent years planning this plane crash and they'd be livid if they found out it was all for nothing, especially the members on the planning committee. One of those members might take their anger out on Pearce or Garret." Jack gazes off to the side, rubbing his chin. "If Pearce doesn't do this exactly right…if anything goes wrong in his attempt to get you back…"

"What?" I ask, my eyes glued to him. "What is it, Jack? What would they do?"

He looks back at me. "They might decide to punish both of you."

"How? How would they punish us?"

"By taking Garret. Doing so would hurt both you and Pearce more than anything else."

"What do you mean they'd take him?" I'm shaking now, as more tears fall from my eyes.

"Rachel." His tone is soft yet still very serious. "This is just one of many possibilities. I'm not saying it would happen, but when people are out for revenge, all bets are off. These people..the members…they're ruthless bastards."

"Just tell me." I hiccup a breath. "Tell me what you meant when you said they'd take him."

He nods. "I meant they might…kill him."

"No!" I squeeze my eyes shut and more tears spill down my face.

"If they wanted to get back at you and Pearce—"

"What is WRONG with these people?" I scream. "They'd really do that? To an innocent little boy?"

"They tried to kill you. That's all the answer you need."

"But if they want Garret as a member why would they—"

"I didn't say the organization itself would do this. I said someone from the planning committee might. Someone who's angry that they wasted time on something that didn't work. Maybe that wouldn't happen, but it's a definite possibility. And as much as it hurts me to even bring that up, you need to know what could happen. You need to know what they're capable of."

I nod, and wipe my face.

"This is why you can't go back there. It's too dangerous. For you, but also for Pearce and Garret. You need to get far away from here and let Pearce figure this out."

"What if he can't?"

"He will. Just give him time."

I swallow past the burn in my throat and take as deep a breath as I can. "So where am I going?"

"That's up to you. I wanted you to be able to pick the location, but it needs to be someplace remote. A small town. A place they'd never look."

I pause to think. "I know where to go." I tell him the location and he says he'll tell Pearce.

"We need to hurry." He gets up from the table. "We're behind schedule. I'll give you ten minutes to look over that folder. After that, I need you to cut your hair and change your clothes. I'll bring you new clothes and a new wig and some glasses. You need to cut your hair short, so it doesn't show under the wig."

My vision's blurring and I feel lightheaded. I close my eyes and wait for the feeling to pass.

Jack touches my shoulder. "Are you okay?"

"Yes."

"Rachel, you need to be strong or you'll never survive this. You need to become someone new and live your life as if nothing has happened. If you act nervous or anxious, people will suspect something's up with you, and if that happens, you risk being found out."

"Yes. I understand."

He leaves the room and I'm left with the folder. Inside are sheets of paper outlining who I am. My likes, dislikes, where I grew up, what sports I played, what schools I went to. It's all very detailed and I'm sure I'll never remember it all. I see my passport and look inside at the photo. It's my face but the hair is so different that it doesn't look like me.

My name is one that's very common. I'm sure Jack did that on purpose so if anyone tried to find something out about me, it would be difficult. There must be thousands of people with this name. Probably more.

After I read through the folder, I shove it aside and sob, grieving the loss of my son and my husband. My former life. I imagine the pain that Garret and Pearce are feeling now, thinking I'm gone, and I sob even more.

When Jack returns with my change of clothes, he comes over and pulls me up from my chair and into his arms. "I'm sorry, Rachel. I'm sorry it's come to this. But Pearce will come for you. I promise you he will. Just be strong, and never lose hope."

I nod, then straighten up and wipe my tears. He leaves me alone in the room and I change into black pants, a white shirt, and a gray cardigan sweater. The clothes and the colors will make me blend in, not stand out.

I let down my hair, gather it together, take the scissors Jack left me, and cut straight across, watching my long brown hair fall to the ground. I cut it to chin-length, which is the shortest I ever remember having it. I make some more cuts to even it out, then I put on the new wig. It's light brown, much lighter than my normal color, and shoulder-length with long bangs. I put on the tortoise shell glasses and look at my reflection in the mirror Jack left in the room.

I take a deep breath as I see this strange person looking back at me. I can do this. It's just for a little while. Just until Pearce finds me. He'll find a way out of this. He'll find a way to get me back and keep me safe. I know he will.

Until then, I'll be someone else. I'm no longer Rachel Kensington. I'm Jill Smith from Maryland.

And today is the first day of my new life.

CHAPTER TWENTY-FOUR
Three Months Later

PEARCE

"Dad, did you hear me?" Garret asks.

We're eating dinner, sitting on the stools that line the kitchen island. Tonight's dinner is chicken, roasted potatoes, and a salad. Charles made it and I'm sure the food is very good, but I really don't know because I can't even taste it. I eat it, but I'm not aware of how it tastes. I'm not aware of anything right now. Not even my son.

"Dad?" I hear him again.

I look up from my plate and see Charles looking at me. He glances at Garret, signaling me to respond.

I turn to Garret. "I'm sorry, Garret. What were you saying?"

"That I don't have swim practice tomorrow. Coach is going out of town with his family."

"Okay." I look down at my plate again.

Out of the corner of my eye, I see Garret moving the food around his plate with his fork. His head is slanted sideways and resting on his fist, his elbow propped up on the counter. It's the classic bored kid look, but he's not bored. He's frustrated. With me.

Every night, we have dinner in silence. Or Garret says something, but I don't hear what he said because I'm not listening. I know I need to pay more attention to him, and I try. I really do. But then my mind wanders to Rachel and the life we used to have, and I get lost in the memories.

These past few months, I haven't been able to move on. I can't get past my grief. I find it hard to get through each day. I go through the motions; taking Garret to school, going to work, then coming home and having dinner. But I'm not really aware that I'm doing those things. The days just go by, one after another, and I never feel any better.

Some nights, I don't even show up for dinner. I work late or go in my room, but I know that's not fair to Garret, so tonight I'm having dinner with him. But whenever we have dinner together, it's always here at the kitchen island. I refuse to eat at the dining room table because it reminds me of Rachel. I tried sitting there once, but it was too hard. I kept imagining her there next to me, smiling and laughing as we ate our meal. She always led the conversation, asking Garret and me about our day, then telling us about hers. I loved our family dinners. I looked forward to them every night. And now? I hate dinner. If it weren't for Garret, I'd skip it altogether. I have no appetite. No desire to eat.

"I need to get to my other job," Charles says.

I glance up and see him wiping his hands on a dish towel. "Thank you, Charles. Dinner is delicious, as always."

Charles makes all our meals now. I hired him soon after Rachel died. He asked if there was anything he could do to help, so I asked him to work for me. He already had a job at a restaurant, and he did small catering jobs on the side, but he agreed to my offer. He had to change his work schedule at the restaurant from days to nights, but he did it because he felt so bad for Garret and me. So now Charles is here every afternoon to make dinner, then he leaves at six to go to his other job. He also does all the grocery shopping for us, but he makes sure he's always here when Garret gets home from school. I didn't like the idea of Garret being alone in the house every afternoon, so it's worked out well having Charles here. I've thanked him repeatedly for doing this for us and I pay him double what he'd make anywhere else.

"Garret, good luck with your science test tomorrow," Charles says.

"Yeah, bye," Garret mumbles.

Garret loves Charles, but tonight he's not being very friendly to him. I don't think it has anything to do with Charles. It's because of me. Garret is still upset that I didn't hear him when he told me there was no swim practice tomorrow. From his mood right now, I'm guessing he talked to me all through dinner and is just realizing now that I didn't hear a word he said.

I can't be this way. Garret needs me. He's still grieving the loss of his mother, just like I am. And I haven't been here for him. I'm too trapped in my own grief.

The room is silent, except for the sound of his fork lightly scraping against his plate as he pushes his potatoes around but doesn't eat them. I need to say something to him, but I have nothing to say. I never know what to say to him anymore.

"So you have a science test tomorrow?" I ask, remembering what Charles said.

Garret sets his fork down and says quietly, "I told you that ten minutes ago."

"Oh. I'm sorry. I didn't hear you."

"You never do," he says under his breath. He slides off the stool. "I'm going up to my room."

His plate looks like it hasn't been touched. He couldn't have eaten more than a couple bites.

"Don't you want to finish your dinner?" I ask as he walks away.

"I'm not hungry," he mumbles. I hear him go up the stairs and his bedroom door close.

I get up and take our plates to the sink. My plate is almost as full as Garret's. Neither one of us has been able to eat much since the plane crash. I scrape the food into the drain in the sink and run the garbage disposal. Then I put the plates in the dishwasher.

A memory flashes in my head of Rachel standing here at the sink. I'd always come up behind her and wrap my arms around her and kiss her neck. She'd tell me to stop distracting her while she's trying to clean up dinner, but then she'd turn around, a big smile on her face, and she'd kiss me and tell me she loves me.

God, I miss her. I miss her so much. I miss everything about her. Her smile. Her laugh. The way she danced whenever a song she liked came on the radio. The way she snuggled up next to me on movie night. The way she hugged me. The way she touched me. The way she looked at me.

The way she loved me.

I grip the edge of the sink with both hands, my body trembling as I sob. I haven't cried about her for weeks, but the memory of her here at this sink is so vivid, so real, that I'm suddenly overwhelmed with grief, unable to hold back the tears.

Why did this have to happen? Why? Why did I tell her to get on that plane? Why did I force her to stay behind? Why did I agree to go to that meeting? If I'd just said no, I would've been there with her. We would've had our anniversary dinner. We would've taken the later flight. She wouldn't have been on that plane. We'd be together right now.

"Dad?" I hear Garret's voice behind me, quiet and hesitant.

"Garret, go away." I'm still gripping the sink, my head hung over it, my face soaked with tears. I take a breath, but it's shaky and I know Garret hears it.

"Dad." I feel his small hand on my back. "Are you okay?"

"I said go away!" I scream it. "Get out of here! Go to your room!"

His hand drops from my back and I hear him slowly walk away. I turn around and see him leaving the kitchen, his shoulders slumped, his head dropped down.

I should be racing after him, holding him, listening to him, helping him get through this. But I can't. I can't even help myself, so how can I help *him*?

I hate myself right now, and the person I'm becoming. I feel like I'm reverting back to how I used to be and I can't seem to stop it. I'm not just becoming a bad father. I'm becoming a bad person.

Now that Jack's gone, I have nobody to talk to when I feel my dark side taking over. So when it does, I feel like I can't control it, so I let it take over and don't bother fighting it. I know I'm stronger than that. I know I can fight it, but part of me doesn't want to. Part of me wants to embrace that side of myself, and release some of the pent-up rage I'm feeling over all that I've lost.

And that's exactly what I did a few weeks ago. A kill assignment was given to me, and instead of hiring a freelancer, I did it myself. We aren't supposed to do that anymore. It's too risky. They don't want our members getting caught. But I did it anyway.

The target of my assignment was a lawyer who had worked for us in the past and was threatening to tell our secrets if we didn't pay him millions of dollars. He was a bad man. He abused his wife, nearly killing her one night. But we used our connections to cover up his sins in exchange for him helping us. It was wrong, but that's what we do.

When he made threats against us, I got the order to kill him. He lived in Manhattan so I drove there one night and found him in a bar having drinks with his mistress. When he left, I followed him.

It was late and dark and cold outside, so not many people were out. I snuck up behind him, shoved him into an alley and shot him. Not just once. But over and over again. And it felt good. It scared me that I was getting pleasure out of it, but at the time, I was so angry that it almost made sense that I felt that way. That's how I justified it. The next day, I felt no remorse. I just went on as if nothing had happened. But that anger is still there. I've heard that anger is a stage of grief, so maybe I'm stuck in that stage and can't move past it. I feel like I never will. I lost the woman I love and the man who was like a father to me, all in the same day. How do I get past that? How do I move on?

When I go upstairs later, Garret's door is closed. I walk up to it and don't hear anything. He must be asleep. I go down to my own room and change into pajamas and get into bed. As usual, I lie there unable to sleep. I can still smell her scent on the sheets. They've been washed many times, but they still smell like her. I thought of getting rid of them and buying new, but I haven't been able to bring myself to do it. Her scent is one of the last remaining pieces of her that remains in my life.

The other piece of her, the big piece that remains, is Garret. He's similar to her in so many ways. He looks exactly like me, but he acts just like Rachel. He has her personality. He's loving and caring. He's friendly and outgoing. He always tries to be optimistic. And he isn't afraid to show emotion. You know when he's happy or sad. He doesn't try to hide it.

Garret is so much like Rachel that sometimes it hurts to even be around him. It's like I'm seeing her through him. That should be a good thing. I should be comforted by the fact that part of her lives on through Garret. But instead of feeling that way, I feel anger toward him for reminding me of her. I shouldn't feel that way, but I do.

The next day, I go to the office and lose myself in my work. It's one of my coping mechanisms. I make sure every moment of my day is filled with constant activity so I don't have a chance to think about her. I work from the second I arrive to the second I leave. I take no breaks, not even for lunch.

"Pearce, do you have those reports?" My father is standing at my office door.

"Yes." I get up and bring him the folder.

"There's a conference call at five today. I need you to be there."

"Yes, fine," I say, returning to my desk. He walks away.

Since Rachel died, I haven't been fighting with my father. Then again, there's no reason to. We always fought about work or Rachel, but now Rachel is gone and I work at such a feverish pace that I get everything done on time and on schedule. My father has nothing to complain about.

I'm sure he'll be back to yelling at me in a month or so. I think the only reason he's kept quiet is because my mother forced him to. She knows how upset I am that Rachel is gone, so she won't allow my father to make my life even worse. Not yet. Not while I'm still such a mess.

My father hasn't even mentioned Rachel since she died, which is how he acts when anyone dies. He just continues on as if the person never existed. He acts the same way about Jack. The other members do too. After Jack died, everyone just went on as if nothing had happened.

I never found out who killed Jack. The story we were told is that one of his freelancers did it, but I'm not sure I believe that. A freelancer would only know Jack by his number, not his name, so someone had to have told the freelancer that information, but if that's the case, then who did it, and why? Why would someone want to kill Jack? It can't be because he was secretly calling me on that phone. Nobody even mentioned that to me or questioned me about it so I'm not sure if anyone actually knew that Jack and I had been talking. Maybe Jack just misplaced his phone and mistakenly thought someone took it.

I don't think I'll ever know what really happened to Jack. And I don't have time to worry about it. I have too many other things on my mind.

The work day goes by quickly and we have our call at five. It ends a half hour later and I head home. It's Friday night and I'm exhausted from the week. I usually leave at six, so it's not that my days are overly long, but I work so hard while I'm there that I'm exhausted when I get home. That could also be caused by the fact that I get almost no sleep at night.

When I arrive home, Charles is there, making dinner. Garret runs up to me, like he always does.

"Hi, Dad." He hugs me and I lean down and hug him back.

"Hello, Garret."

He should be mad at me for how I treated him last night, but he's not. That's another way he's like Rachel. He doesn't hold a grudge. The two of us can argue, and by the next day, he's over it.

"What are we having for dinner, Charles?" I take my coat off and set my keys on the counter.

"Pizza. It was Garret's request." Charles smiles at him. "He even helped me make it."

"I added the toppings," Garret says.

Charles checks the oven. "It should be done in a few minutes."

"I'll go up and change." I make my way up to the bedroom and change out of my suit.

When I come back down, Garret is waiting for me at the bottom of the stairs. He looks excited about something. He hasn't looked that way since before his mother died.

"I want to show you something." He takes my hand.

"What are you showing me?"

"Just wait." He drags me through the living room, past the kitchen, and into the family room.

"We're having movie night!" he says, his voice filled with excitement.

There's a stack of movies on the floor in front of the TV. And along the wall is the foldout table Rachel used to set up every Friday night for family movie night. We haven't had one since she died.

Garret takes me over to the table, which is topped with a big bowl of popcorn, cans of soda, licorice, and small boxes of candy. The licorice is sticking out of a glass jar, which is how Rachel used to always arrange it.

"I set everything up all by myself," Garret says. "Look! I even made the sign." He holds up a piece of paper that reads 'concession stand' and has dancing popcorn and soda people drawn on it. Rachel used to make a sign just like that, or sometimes she'd have Garret do it.

"That's why Garret requested pizza," Charles says, walking into the family room. "He said it's tradition for movie night."

"Yes," I say quietly. "It was."

My gaze wanders back to the concession stand and then the movies on the floor. It's all too much. It's too much of a reminder of her. Memories come rushing back as I look around the room. Memories of Rachel in my arms as we sat on the couch, with Garret on the floor in front of us, sitting in his beanbag chair. He even brought the chair out. I'd hidden it away, not wanting to see it because it reminds me of our movie nights.

"What do you think?" Garret asks.

I feel him looking at me, but I can't look back at him. I'm so angry at him right now. I don't want this. I hate it! It's just a reminder of how great our lives used to be. How much I want that life back. How much I miss her. How much I miss the three us together as a family.

"Go to your room!" I yell at him. "Right now!"

Garret backs away, startled. "Why? What did I do wrong?"

"Everything!" I scream as I storm over to the concession stand. "How dare you do this! This was HER idea! HER tradition!" I sweep my hand across the table, knocking the bowl of popcorn and the neatly arranged boxes of candy on the floor. "We will NOT disrespect her by doing this without her!" I take the sign and rip it in half and toss it on the floor. "Do you understand me?" I scream it at him.

Garret stands there, staring at me, his body rigid, like he's afraid to move. He's breathing fast, his lip quivering, but he manages to nod in response to my question.

"Go upstairs!" I yell at him. "Now!"

His eyes stay on my face for just a moment, then he turns and runs off and up to his room.

Charles remains in the family room as I assess the mess I made.

"I'll clean this up," I tell him. "You don't have to."

"I wasn't going to." He sounds angry and I look up and see the anger on his face.

"Why are you looking at me like that?" I ask.

"You don't know?" He sighs and shakes his head.

"What?" I ask.

"Did you not just see what happened here? Did you not see his face? What the hell were you thinking, yelling at him like that?"

"He knows better than to do something like this. Throwing his mother's memory in my face! Making this even harder on me! He knows how I'm suffering, and then he goes and does this!" I motion to the table.

"He was trying to help you," Charles says. "He said you were upset last night and he thought this would make you feel better."

"Well, he was wrong. He only made it worse."

"Garret didn't know that. He thought he was helping. He spent all afternoon setting this up. Making that sign. Helping me with the pizza. He thought you'd be happy. And then you yelled at him."

Guilt clouds over my anger as I think about what Charles said. He's right. Garret would never do this to hurt me. In his mind, he thought he was helping me. And the fact that he even wanted to help me, after the way I've acted toward him, just shows how caring he is, just like Rachel.

"He was trying, Pearce. Garret was trying desperately to get through to you. He's been trying for months. He's trying to get his father back."

"Don't lecture me about being a father." I feel my anger return. What Charles said is true. I know it is, but I don't want to hear it. I don't want to hear how I've failed my son. I don't need to be reminded of what a horrible father I am. "You don't have children, Charles. You don't know what it's like."

"No, I don't. But I'm not blind, and I can see what's going on here. You're still grieving the loss of your wife. I can't imagine how hard that must be for you, but it's also hard for your son to go on without his mother, and you're not there for him. He's struggling, Pearce. Just like you are. But you won't talk to him."

I pinch the bridge of my nose. "I can't. I'm not ready to."

"Then you need to get him into counseling. Give him someone to talk to. He's just a little boy. He doesn't understand what grief is or how to get past it. And you're not helping him."

"How the fuck am I supposed to help him when I'm drowning in my own grief?"

"You're his father. You're all he has. Stop being so goddamn selfish and think of your son. Stop ignoring him. Stop acting like you're the only one who's suffering here. Like his grief doesn't matter. Rachel would be furious if she knew you were treating Garret this way."

"Get out!" I yell at him. "Get out of my house!"

He looks surprised, which he shouldn't be. He said her name, and he knows I don't want anyone saying her name.

Charles slowly nods. "The pizza is on the counter. Your meals for the weekend are in the fridge. You just need to heat them up." He turns to leave but then stops. "Garret was invited to a birthday party tomorrow. He asked you multiple times last week if he could go and you never answered, but he really wants to go." He pauses. "And he needs some help with his math homework."

When I don't respond, he turns and goes back to the kitchen. Moments later, I hear the front door open and close as he leaves.

I sit on the couch and take a moment to calm down. I need to go apologize to Garret. It was wrong of me to yell at him like that. I almost sounded like my father.

Charles is right. Rachel would be furious if she knew I was treating Garret this way and not helping him get through this. And even though I know he needs help, I don't think I'm the one who can help him. I'm not ready to talk about her, or the plane crash. I can't answer his questions. I need to do as Charles suggested and get Garret into counseling. He needs to talk to someone. Someone better than me.

I go over and pick up the mess I made. I arrange the candy boxes back like Garret had them. There are all different kinds, in the small boxes like they sell at the theater. Charles must have taken Garret out earlier to buy them.

I get the small garbage can from the kitchen and throw out the licorice since it wasn't wrapped. Next I scoop handfuls of popcorn in the trash, then pick up the remaining pieces. I take the remnants of Garret's sign and hold it in my hand. It looks like he spent forever making it. He carefully drew the characters the same way Rachel used to draw them, and then he colored them with markers. I add the sign to the trash, then put the small garbage can back under the sink.

It's almost seven now and we haven't had dinner. The pizza is still sitting on the counter. I go up to Garret's room and knock on the door. He doesn't answer. I open the door and see him sitting on the floor, leaning against his bed.

"Garret."

He ignores me, which he should. I don't deserve his attention.

I sit on his bed. "Garret, come sit next to me."

He doesn't move, so I just say what I need to say.

"I'm sorry, Garret. It was wrong of me to react that way. I know you were only trying to help."

He's quiet, his eyes on the floor.

"I put the candy back like you had it. I threw out the popcorn, but we can make more. And the pizza is done. We just need to reheat it."

"I'm not hungry," he says quietly. I hear his uneven breaths and know that he's crying.

"Garret." I get up and go in front of him and hoist him up into my arms. His body is limp, his face wet from his tears. I sit back down on his bed and hold him across my lap. He puts his arms around me and rests his head on my shoulder. He should hate me right now, but instead he hugs me. He's so much better than me. He's such a better person. And it's Rachel who made him that way.

"I'm so sorry," I tell him, rubbing his back. "The past few months, I haven't been here for you, and I'm sorry. I know I haven't been a good father to you, Garret. I want to be, but I keep failing you. It's been so hard for me to go on without your mother. But that's not an excuse for me to ignore you and what you're going through. I can't promise you that things will go back to how they were, but I will try to do better. I will do the best that I can." I hug him tighter, and he does the same to me.

"I love you, Dad," he whispers.

I don't say it back. I don't know why. I think it, but I can't say it. Why can't I say it? What the fuck is wrong with me?

Garret pulls away and I bring my hand up to his cheek and wipe the wetness away. His blue eyes look so sad.

"Would you like to have movie night?" I ask him.

He rubs his eyes as he shakes his head. "No."

"Why not?"

"Because it makes you sad."

He's worried about me, and about how *I* feel. It should be the other way around. I should be worried about *him*. So why haven't I been? What is wrong with me?

"It's okay if it makes me sad," I tell him. "Sometimes memories can be sad, but that doesn't mean we can't still have movie night. So what do you think? Should we have some pizza? Watch a movie?"

He shrugs. "I guess."

"Would you rather do something else?"

He hugs me again, like that's his answer. Like he just wants me, his father, who has been absent for months now. Like he just wants me to spend time with him, be with him, listen to him. He wants his father back. The father he knew before his mother died.

I want that too. I just don't know how to get that person back.

CHAPTER TWENTY-FIVE

RACHEL

Every waking moment of every day I wonder if they're okay. I wonder what they're doing. I wonder if they're struggling as much as I am.

I miss them both so much that some days I can barely function. The first few weeks I was here, I stayed in bed. I couldn't get up. Celia, the landlady, kept coming up here to check on me. She thought I was sick. I told her I was, just so she'd leave me alone.

She wasn't trying to intrude. She's just a nice old lady who worries about people. She rents me the apartment that's just above her restaurant. It's a very tiny studio apartment with a twin bed, but it's all I need. It has a small patio, which is where I spend a lot of my time, just gazing out at the water. The apartment is built into the hillside and looks out at the Mediterranean Sea.

I live in the small village that Pearce and I went to on our honeymoon twelve years ago. I chose it because it reminds me of Pearce, and even though remembering him makes me sad, I still want to remember him, and the time we spent here. Those were happy times. Before I knew the truth about his secret life. Before I knew people wanted me dead.

"Rachel." Celia's voice startles me. I glance up and see her offering me coffee. "Sì?"

"Yes. Sì." I wait for her to pour it, then say, "Grazie." I'm still learning Italian. Celia gave me a translation book that a tourist left behind and I've been studying it every night, trying to learn the language. Living here and being immersed in it has helped me pick up words and phrases faster than learning it from a book, but I'm still not very good.

Most of the people here speak some English. They learn it in school but they don't use it much so sometimes I find it a struggle to communicate with them. Celia speaks fluent English which is good for me, but also for the English-speaking customers who come to her restaurant. This village doesn't get a lot of tourists, but there are some who stumble upon it, like Pearce and I did years ago.

Celia offered me a job at her restaurant about a month ago, so that's where I work. I don't think she really needed the help. I think she just wanted to get me out of my apartment. She knew I spent all day in there, alone and depressed. It's good she gave me the job. I only work five or six hours a day but it's something to do. Something to keep me busy.

Every day, I get up early and make bread. Then I come in later to help serve dinner. The job doesn't pay much, but it's all Celia can afford. Jack gave me some money, but not enough to live off of for more than a year. So in a few months, if I'm still here, I'll eventually need to get another job.

I'm on my break now and having coffee at one of the small tables by the window. I like sitting here and watching people stroll by, going to the little shops, getting what they need for the day. Life here moves at a much slower pace than in the US. People aren't in a hurry. They aren't constantly rushing everywhere.

The bells on the front door rattle and I quickly look up to see who's coming inside. It's the old man who owns the fish market down the street. He comes in every day to get coffee.

Every time those bells ring, I always look up, hoping I'll see Pearce come walking through the door. But he never does. I also look up because I worry that someone will show up here to kill me. I've even had nightmares about it. It's always the same dream. A man in a suit walks up to me, says nothing, and shoots me. I wake up sweating and out of breath.

When Jack told me people were plotting to kill me, I didn't believe it. Sometimes I still don't. But I saw the video. I saw the plane burning up in the field. I saw the order to kill me. So I know it's true. I'd be dead if Jack hadn't stopped me from getting on that plane.

I've spent a lot of time thinking about what Jack said. About how this secret organization exists. A group with so much power that they're able to control things. Big things. Like who will be president. I kept telling myself it wasn't true. That there was no way such a group could exist. But the more I thought about it, the more I believed it.

When we were first together, Pearce told me he felt like he was living a double life. I thought he was referring to how his life with me was so different than his life with his rich friends. Now I know that's not what he meant. When he said that, he was referring to his life in this secret group. He was trying to tell me the truth. He knew he couldn't, but he was trying to hint at it.

I believe Jack when he said Pearce wanted to tell me. I know he would have if he were able to. Maybe he wouldn't tell me everything, but he'd at least tell me this group exists and that he's involved in it. But I think he would've hidden what they do. He wouldn't want me knowing that he's hurt people. Had people killed.

I've been trying not to think about that, because when I do, it makes me feel like I never really knew Pearce. I was living with a murderer and I had no idea. But as soon as I think that, I tell myself that it wasn't him. Jack said Pearce was forced to do those assignments and that the Pearce I knew was not the man who did those horrible things. I want to believe that, and I'm trying to convince myself that it's true. The Pearce I know is kind and caring and gentle and loving. He doesn't want to hurt people, even people he doesn't know. The only way he'd do something like that is if they threatened him. Or threatened to hurt me. Or Garret.

I should be angry with Pearce for getting me involved in this, knowing what could happen. But instead of feeling anger, I feel sadness. For Pearce. He's had a horrible life. A horrible childhood. And then he was forced to join this group. He didn't know love until I came into his life. So when I did, he didn't want to let me go.

Some would say that was selfish. That he should've let me go, knowing he couldn't be with me. Part of me agrees with that, but the other part of me doesn't. Because I kind of understand where he's coming from. It's like me, wanting a child. I knew the risks. I knew if I got pregnant, something bad could happen to me, or the baby. And yet I still did it, because I wanted that baby so bad. Pearce wanted love even more than that. He wanted someone to love, and someone to love him back. Is that really so wrong? To want to be loved?

I've been trying to think of what I would've done if I were him. If I'd never been loved, and someone offered it to me, would I turn him away? Knowing I loved him back the same way? I don't know that I could.

And if someone threatened to hurt my family if I didn't do what they said, would I do it? Even if it meant harming someone else? I'd like to say I wouldn't, but the truth is, I probably would.

In my heart, I know Pearce is not a bad person. I know he doesn't want to do bad things. And I know he loves me more than anything and would do everything in his power to keep me safe.

So despite the bad things Pearce has done, and despite the fact that he kept that part of his life a secret, I still love him. I always will. Some might say that's wrong, but it's how I feel. Pearce is my best friend. My husband. The love of my life. My soulmate. And it kills me to know that he's forced to be part of this secret organization. That he can't get out. And that he couldn't tell me about it even though he wanted to.

I guess, if anything, I should be mad at Pearce for pursuing me all those years ago. If we'd never dated, I wouldn't have fallen in love with him and I wouldn't be in the situation I'm in now. But we can't go back and change the past. And truthfully, I wouldn't want to. I had a life with Pearce. One that I loved. Aside from the past three months, the past twelve years were the best years of my life. If I hadn't married Pearce, I wouldn't have the memories that I now cherish and use to get through each day. And if Pearce hadn't come into my life, I wouldn't have Garret, my little ray of sunshine. My sweet little boy who I love with everything I am.

I miss him so much. I miss them both so much. It's torture not seeing them. Not being able to hug them and kiss them and be with them.

I don't know how much longer I can do this. Jack didn't give me any kind of timeline. I thought Pearce would come find me after a couple weeks. But then those weeks turned into a month, and then another month, and another after that. I keep waiting, wondering when he'll show up.

The wait is agonizing. What is taking so long? Even if he hasn't found a way to be with me and keep me safe, he could at least come and see me. Nobody would have to know. This is a tiny village. Nobody here knows him. He'd be safe coming here. And I need to see him. I'm desperate to see him.

So where is he?

CHAPTER TWENTY-SIX
Three Years Later

PEARCE

"Welcome back," I say to Garret as he walks in the front door.

He lets out harsh laugh. "Yeah. No thanks to you. If you had *your* way, I'd still be over there."

"Your actions cost us a fortune!" Katherine says, appearing behind me. "You don't even care, do you?"

I wish she'd just let me handle this. Things are bad enough with Garret. I don't need Katherine making them worse.

"Don't fucking talk to me," he says as he passes her on his way to the stairs.

Katherine gasps. "Pearce! Don't let him use that foul language in the house."

"Katherine, please. He just got home. Let's not start fighting already."

"Good luck with that," Garret mumbles as he goes upstairs.

I follow him up there. "Garret, wait. I want to talk to you."

"There's nothing to say." He goes in his room and slams the door.

I open it before he can lock it. He's sitting on his bed.

"You didn't even say hello." I sit next to him.

"And you're mad about that? Seriously? You didn't even call to see if I was okay. You shipped me off to boarding school and forgot about me. And you're pissed I didn't say hello just now?" He huffs. "Just go."

"I didn't mean it that way. I was just—" I sigh. "I'm sorry we sent you there. We shouldn't have done that. It wasn't right."

"WE?" He turns to me. "There was no 'we' in that decision. It was all Katherine's idea. She hates me and she wanted to get rid of me."

"She doesn't hate you. She's just not used to being around children."

"I'm NOT a child."

"You're only 13. You're still a child."

"So you thought it was okay to send your CHILD all the way to London to go to school?" He rolls his eyes. "Great parenting there, Dad."

"I admit it was a mistake. You won't be going back to boarding school. You'll live here and go to Tolshire Academy."

"What?" He stands up. "You're saying I can't go back to my old school?"

"It's too far from where we live now. Tolshire is much closer and it's an excellent school. Even better than your old school."

"No. I'm not going there. I'm going back to my old school, where my friends are."

"That isn't an option, Garret. You're going to Tolshire. I've already enrolled you there. You start next Monday."

He points at the door. "Was this HER idea?"

"No. And you need to stop blaming her for everything. We can't all live under the same roof if you two are always fighting."

"She's the one who starts it!" he yells. "She purposely says things she knows will start a fight!"

"I don't care who's at fault. This fighting needs to end."

"Why are you sticking up for her? You know she lies. You know she manipulates you and everyone else. She's a bitch, Dad. Why the hell did you marry her?"

I stand up and face him. "You need to clean up your language. I mean it, Garret. You can't use that kind of language around the baby."

"You mean the baby you had to replace me?"

"Garret, that's not fair. You know that's not why we had her."

"Then why? Why did you do it?"

"Katherine and I are married. It's not surprising we would have a child together."

Garret throws his hands in the air. "You don't even like her! Why the hell would you have a kid with her?"

"Of course I like her. She's my wife."

"MOM was your wife! You loved MOM. You don't love Katherine. She's too young for you. You have nothing in common. You fight all the time. And she treats you like shit."

"You know nothing about our marriage. And you shouldn't, because it's none of your business."

"It is when she's trying to interfere with my life. Ship me off to boarding school."

"I told you that wouldn't happen again."

"Katherine wants me gone. She only wants you and Lilly living here. And since you always do what she says, you'll ship me off again."

"I don't always do what she says. You don't know what goes on between Katherine and me so stop acting like you do."

"You forgot my birthday last year," he says quietly "Because of her. Because she told you to."

I sigh. "I didn't forget. We just weren't able to have a party for you. It was a very busy time with the baby being born so close to your birthday." I pause, thinking back to the day I first held Garret in my arms. A day that now seems like a lifetime ago. "I will never forget your birthday. I still remember the day you were born."

Garret gazes at the floor. "If I'd known this would be my life, I wish you'd never even had me."

"Garret, don't say that."

"Just go away. Go be with your wife."

"I want to be with my son right now. You've been gone and I've missed you."

"Then why did you send me away?" He yells it. "And why didn't you call me?" His voice cracks.

I step up to him and force him into a hug. "You're right. I should've called. And I shouldn't have sent you away. I'm sorry."

"No, you're not!" He shoves me away and wipes the wetness from his eyes. "You always do this! You always say you're sorry, but then nothing ever changes. You apologize for not spending time with me, but then you work a hundred hours a week. You say you're sorry for missing my swim meet, but then you don't show up to the next one. You say you're sorry for never talking about Mom, but then I say her name and you yell at me. You're a fucking liar, Dad! Just stop trying to be a father and leave me alone! I'd do a better job raising myself than having you do it!"

He storms off to his bathroom and slams the door and locks it. He's sad and angry and frustrated, with both me and our situation. But I don't know what to do to make him feel better. This is our life now, and he's right. I'm a horrible father. He probably *would* be better off raising himself.

After the plane crash, our lives went to hell. Part of that was my fault. I couldn't get past my grief, so I buried myself in work. It was the only thing that distracted me enough to lessen the excruciating pain I felt from losing her.

But all those hours at the office meant that I never saw Garret. The first few months after Rachel died, I tried to be home every night for dinner. But then I started working later. Charles was with Garret every day after school, but when he left at six, Garret was alone. Most nights, he ate dinner without me and was asleep by the time I got home.

The parents of his friends took him to his swim practice and basketball games and football games. They offered to help because they felt bad about what happened to Rachel. But it wasn't their job to take care of Garret. It was mine, and I didn't do it.

Knowing I couldn't help him with his grief, I did as Charles suggested and sent Garret to see a child psychologist. He didn't want to go, but I made him, and it ended up being good for him.

After months of counseling, Garret was feeling better, and it gave me hope that I, too, could someday feel better and move on from this tragedy. And the first step in doing that was to be a father again. Rachel and Garret had always been the only light in my life. Rachel was gone, but Garret was still here and I needed him as much as he needed me.

But just as I'd committed to spending more time with Garret, my father retired and I became CEO of Kensington Chemical, which meant I couldn't cut back on my hours. So I still worked all the time, but I took breaks from the office to pick up Garret at swim practice or to have dinner with him. It wasn't ideal, but at least I was seeing him more.

Then something happened that took me away from him once again. The organization told me I had to marry Katherine. If I didn't, they threatened to do something to Garret. I knew they wouldn't kill him. He's one of us and they want him to be a member someday. But they could do something else to him, like scare him or injure him. Or they could kidnap him and make me think it's real so that I go out of my mind trying to get him back. They've done that to some of my fellow members who didn't cooperate with their demands. It's all fake, but the parents don't know that until they do whatever it was Dunamis asked them to do. It's just another way for them to control us.

I would never let them do anything to Garret, so I married Katherine, as I was ordered to do. Katherine insisted we live in a mansion and she didn't like any of the ones that were for sale, so we ended up building one. It's 18,000 square feet, which she said was too small but I refused to make it any bigger than that. And despite Katherine's objections, I built a wing onto the house that was just for Garret. It has an indoor pool, a basketball court, a small movie theater, and a room with a massive TV and arcade games. Garret was so upset when I married Katherine and made us leave our old neighborhood, that I wanted to do something to make it up to him. I wanted him to like living here. But he doesn't. He hates it. And he hates me.

He wants his old life back. He knows he can't get his mother back, but he wants to live the way we used to, in a normal house and a normal neighborhood, not in a mansion that's isolated on several acres of land and hidden behind an iron gate.

Now he has to go to a new school. It wasn't my decision. The organization is making him go there because it's where some of the other members send their children. It's also where important people who aren't part of organization send their children. People who could prove to be useful in the future, either in my business or personal life; lawyers, state politicians, and influential people in the community. I'll make connections with these people through Garret and his friendship with their children. I'm using him, I know, but my father and the organization have given me no choice.

This is how things are done in our world. Our friends are chosen for us and we don't associate with people who can't benefit us in some way. I tried to escape that world when I married Rachel, but now she's gone and I've been sucked back into it. Garret is getting older and I'm under constant pressure from my father and the organization to get Garret immersed in this life. The other members' children have already been living it. They grew up in mansions and have always had fake friends, but this is all new for Garret and he doesn't like it

"Sir, can I get you something?" the maid asks.

I just came downstairs and am standing in the living room deep in thought, worried about Garret.

"No. I'm fine," I tell her and she walks off.

That's another change Garret isn't happy about. Being waited on by the hired help who follow us around, constantly asking if we need something. I find it annoying as well. I shouldn't, because it's how I grew up, but now I'm used to doing things for myself.

Katherine has never done anything for herself, so she insisted we hire people. We have two maids, a team of gardeners, a driver, and a cook. I hired Charles as our cook. Katherine protested, but I wouldn't back down. Charles is like a brother to me and Iike an uncle to Garret, and he was a huge help after Rachel died. There was no way I was letting him go. I upped his salary and offered him a room in the house we built for the live-in help. He stays there during the week, then goes to his own house on the weekends.

"Pearce, we need to sit down and go over our social calendar," Katherine says as she walks up to me in the living room.

"Not right now," I say.

Katherine spends all her time planning our social life. She fills every spare moment of my time. If I'm not at work, I'm attending some high-society event with her. She knows I don't want to go to these things, but telling her no always turns into a fight so I've found it's just easier to go along with it.

"This weekend is the dinner party at my parents' house," she says. "My mother said Royce and Victoria will be there."

I'm dreading this dinner party. I can't stand her parents, especially Leland. I've always hated him. And I don't want to be around Royce. I try to avoid him whenever possible. In a few years, he's running for president, so he's even more obnoxious and pretentious than he used to be. But at least he's a decent father to his girls. He and Victoria now have four daughters. He's given up trying to have a son.

"Pearce, are you listening to me?" Katherine asks. "Next Monday we have to attend an auction for—"

"I can't discuss this right now." I glance upstairs. "I have to deal with Garret."

"You can't do anything about him, Pearce. He's a teenager. You know how children that age are. They're moody and obstinate. You need to stop coddling him and allow him to become a man."

"He's only 13. He's not even close to being a man. And he needs his father, whether he likes it or not."

She smooths my tie and looks up at me. "Our baby also needs a father, much more so than Garret does. He's practically grown up."

"He's not grown up. He's still a child. He acts out because I don't spend enough time with him. That needs to change. I can't be going to all these events with you. We're never home, and now that Garret is back, I need to spend time with him."

"You need to spend time with your wife!" She steps back and puts her hands on her narrow hips. She's still very thin, with almost no curves. The woman never eats.

"You're an adult. You don't need my constant attention. Garret is a child and he's struggling and he needs his father. I'm not going to abandon him just so I can attend charity events with you. We are cutting back on our social engagements and I am going to spend more time with Garret."

"I am NOT letting that out-of-control teenager take over our lives! I never should've agree to let him live here. He hasn't even been back an hour and he's already ruining everything! I'm completely stressed, and it's all because of him. He needs to leave. If you refuse to send him to boarding school, then have him go live with your parents."

"He is not living with my parents. He is living here. With us. And he is not out of control. He's just having a hard time adjusting to all the changes in his life. I'm not surprised that he's upset."

"So is that how it's going to be? He gets to act however he wants? Use foul language? Fight with me? Walk around yelling and screaming and slamming doors? And instead of being punished, you'll just make excuses for him?" She exhales forcefully. "No! I will NOT allow it. This is MY house and I will NOT allow Garret to control us or how we live!"

She storms off. I just let her go. I don't want to fight with her, especially about Garret. She doesn't like him and it's no use trying to change her mind. Even if Garret was a perfect child, she still wouldn't like him because he's not hers.

Katherine and I fight all the time, and not just about Garret. We fight about everything. I try to avoid it, but as Garret said, Katherine tends to instigate arguments. I think she actually likes creating problems. She likes the drama of it. The tension. It adds some excitement to her otherwise boring life.

When we first got married, Katherine and I tried not to fight. We didn't talk much so that helped. She didn't act like the immature teenager she used to be, but I still had no interest in her. But we slept in the same bed and she's somewhat attractive so we eventually had sex. I hadn't done it since being with Rachel, and after it was over I felt extreme guilt.

Katherine pushed me to do it again, saying it's what married people do. I reminded her that our marriage was fake, but she said that, to her, it was real. She even said that she loved me. I felt bad for her and felt like she actually wanted this to work, so I tried to be more receptive to her. I tried to make it more like a real marriage. I took her out to dinner, bought her flowers, kissed her hello and goodbye every day, and had sex with her at night. But I felt like it wasn't me doing those things. I felt like it was someone else. The me that existed before I met Rachel. The man who felt nothing. Who put on a fake act for appearance's sake. The man who did what he was told because he was too tired to fight. The man who really didn't care about anything because he felt nothing.

That's the man who married Katherine and it's the man I am today. A hollow shell. Uncaring. Unfeeling. Dead.

I think that's how Katherine convinced me to send Garret away to boarding school. I had no fight left in me, not even for my son. But even so, I was devastated when he left. It just confirmed that I'd failed him. I'd let Katherine, a woman he barely knew, send him away. I considered bringing him home, many times, but then I thought it might be better if he was far away from here. Away from me. Away from Katherine. But last week he set his room at the boarding school on fire and they sent him home.

Now he's back, and I need to try to be his father again. My past attempts have failed, but I'm not giving up. I love Garret with all my heart. I just can't seem to express it. It seemed so much easier when Rachel was in our lives. She exuded love. She gave it freely. And just being around her made it easier to express love myself. Now I feel unable to do so. Like I forgot how. I know that sounds ridiculous, but it's true.

I'm a failure as a father, and now I'm a father again. I have a new baby. A daughter. Lilly. I didn't want another child. I told Katherine that, and she said she didn't want one either. She said she was on the pill, and like an idiot, I believed her. But, of course, she lied, and last August we had the baby.

I should be happy, but I'm not. This isn't what I want. I'm back to hating my life. Hating who I am. Hating that I've lost all hope. That I've given up.

Maybe this was how it was supposed to be all along. Maybe I was meant to be miserable. Meant to hate my life. It's how my father raised me. He never wanted me to be happy.

So he got what he wanted. I'm not happy. I don't think I ever will be again.

RACHEL

"That's it for today," I say, closing the small yellow book. Marco and I are sitting at a table in the back of Celia's restaurant.

"Thank you, Miss Smith." Marco gets up and puts his little arms around me. It reminds me of Garret hugging me and I start to tear up.

"You're welcome," I say, smiling to hide my sadness. "I'll see you next week."

"Sì," he says, then quickly corrects himself. "Yes."

I nod. "That's correct. Goodbye, Marco."

I wave as he runs off to find his mother, who works in a shop down the street. Marco's parents hired me to tutor him in English. The children here are taught English in school, but that's not enough to make them fluent in it. Marco's parents want him to become fluent in English because they think it will help his future. Help him get into a good college and get a good job in a bigger city. This tiny village is beautiful and quaint, but it doesn't offer much for job opportunities.

A lot of the parents in this village feel the same way as Marco's parents. That's how I ended up being a tutor. Word got around that I'm from America and soon parents were asking me if I would teach English to their children. I've been doing this for two years now. The children are so eager to learn, and they're all very sweet. They bring me flowers they pick from the hillside or they draw me a picture or give me hugs.

The children remind me so much of Garret that I honestly don't know how I've been able to even do this. I keep telling myself I'm helping give these children a better life. A brighter future. But doing so is nearly killing me. Being around children makes me miss Garret even more. I think about him constantly. And when Marco gave me that hug, I almost broke down. I want those little arms around me to be Garret's. I want to hold him again and tell him how much I love him. I want to see his smile and those bright blue eyes. I want to hear his voice and hear his laughter.

I race to the bathroom and shut the door and fall to my knees, sobbing. I have to see my son. I can't keep waiting. He's growing up and I'm not there for him. Where does he think I am? Does he think I'm dead? Or did Pearce tell him the truth? If he knows I'm alive, does he know why I haven't come back? Does he know that I'm only staying away because I'm so terrified of what might happen to him if I showed up there?

As desperate as I am to go back, I can't risk it. I need Pearce to come get me.

Where is he? Why hasn't he come here? Why hasn't he at least sent me a message, telling me what's going on? What's taking so long?

These questions are on a continuous loop in my head. They drive me crazy because I don't have the answers. There's no explanation. I've heard nothing from anyone. Not Jack. Not Pearce. No one.

I know Pearce would do everything possible to get me back, so there must be some complication that's preventing him from doing so. Jack said I need to be patient, so that's what I need to do. I just need to be patient. Pearce will come for me. I know he will. He won't give up on me. It's been three years, but I know he's still trying to find a way to bring me home.

And until he does, I can't give up. I have to keep hoping. I have to have faith.

I have to believe that someday we will all be back together.

www.ingramcontent.com/pod-product-compliance
Lightning Source LLC
Chambersburg PA
CBHW021321250626
47155CB00002B/573